"OH, GOD, MAGGIE
WHAT YOU

Worth pulled her c
her head to look in
came down on hers,   ngry, not and
wet. Her lips parted, from desire or surprise. It
didn't matter. One taste of him and she was
lost.

Nothing had ever been this wonderful. He
tasted tangy and sweet all at the same time. Her
hand crept around his neck, and she reveled in
his strength as she moved her mouth against
his.

Worth responded with equal fervor. In one
motion, he twisted her sideways onto his lap.
She arched her back as he blazed a fiery trail of
kisses down her neck.

His mouth burned lower, to the very top of
her dress where the creamy swell of her breast
was just revealed. She felt his tongue and for a
moment she had the wildest thought—that her
dress should disappear entirely, and leave her
open to his caresses . . .

*

Hidden Fire

Phyllis Herrmann

POPULAR LIBRARY

An Imprint of Warner Books, Inc.

A Warner Communications Company

To our husbands
Ted and Joe
and
to our daughters
Jennifer, Mimi, and Alisa
who always knew we could.

One

*T*he shiny black carriage pulled away from the Back Bay brownstone into the main stream of traffic. It was midday and the sun shone with blinding clarity, glinting off the semicircular bays of the newly deserted house.

Mary Margaret Simpson turned her head to the side, unable to watch as the house grew smaller and more distant. How she had loved it there, surrounded by family and friends! Her loss weighed heavily on her heart.

Her gaze fell on the two solemn children who stared out the rear window of the coach. In only one week their faces had become pale and pinched, with purple smudges shadowing their eyes. Their loss was much greater than hers, but she could do little to comfort them other than hold them when they needed to cry.

"I don't want to go. It's our home, isn't it? Why do we have to leave it?" implored the older of the two, his ten years sitting heavily on his shoulders.

"Don't be ridiculous, Thomas Henry," chastened the full-bosomed matron seated next to Mary Margaret. Defying the heat of the balmy Indian summer day, she wore a stiff-necked travel coat, buttoned high and cut severely. No ruffles or flounces softened its austere lines. Her hat was similarly unadorned and did little to flatter her florid features. She was not aware of this lack. Her regal bearing and assumption of right added to her air of formidable authority.

"Now, turn around and sit in your seat like a proper gentleman," she ordered. "You couldn't possibly stay in that house now that your parents are gone," she added with crushing finality.

The boy flinched but stood his ground. "But, Grandmother Townsend—" he said, making one more valiant effort, unable to believe that he could not convince her. Mary Margaret knew his plea would fall on deaf ears, but it was not her place to interfere. Her only chance to help the children lay in insinuating herself into the Townsend household, and for now, that meant holding her tongue until their uncle arrived from out West to claim them.

"No 'buts' about it," Hester Townsend cut in with some asperity. "You heard what I said. Now, I expect you to obey me."

The firmness of her tone left no room for doubt. Thomas Henry Worthington's shoulders slumped as he took a last, lingering look down the block at the only home he had ever known. Mary Margaret leaned forward and placed her hand on his lower leg as he knelt on the rear seat. He craned his neck around and met her gaze. She gave his calf a reassuring squeeze, then lifted her hand to help him turn around. With her assistance, he righted himself on the seat and faced his grandmother.

"That's much better. Don't you think so?" the older woman asked.

"Yes, ma'am," he murmured as Mary Margaret released his hand. She could see the look of pained acceptance cross his features, the hint of desperation as he finally understood that for the time being, he had no other recourse but to obey Hester Townsend. His helplessness left a bitter taste in her mouth.

His younger sister, Rebecca, only four years old, took her cue from him and also turned around. Silently, he took her hand in his as they rode to meet their uncertain fate. Mary Margaret averted her gaze, knowing pride and an inbred sense of masculine dignity were the only forces keeping his tears at bay.

The carriage rounded another corner, continued past the Public Gardens, and skirted along the edge of the Common. Here, acres of green grass, sheltered by hundreds of elm trees, provided a peaceful refuge at the very center of the busy city. The tranquility of the scene reminded Mary Margaret of happier times when she and Claire had brought the children to play. How they had loved racing through the tree-lined malls in a wild game of tag, or standing outside the ten-foot-tall fence, admiring the graceful creatures in the deer park.

"A lovely day, don't you think so?" Hester Townsend asked conversationally, breaking into Mary Margaret's reminiscences. Mary Margaret assumed a listening pose but gave no answer to the vapid question. Nor did Hester Townsend seem to expect one, for she continued without pause, "If you would check with that Irish girl as soon as we get home and make sure things are in order for the children, I'll see to bringing them into the house."

"If you wish," Mary Margaret agreed, though she did not like it. Nor did she like Hester's attitude toward Kathleen, the children's nursemaid. "But I would be happy to help with the children, too."

"That won't be necessary. I'm sure I can handle everything. The sooner the children face up to what's happened, the better off they'll be."

"You'll be there with us, Aunt Mary, won't you?" Thomas asked worriedly. Addressing Hester, he added, "You told us she'd be staying with us. You gave your word."

"Really, Thomas Henry," Hester snapped. "This is a conversation for adults, not children. You mustn't intrude."

"My mama called me Tom," he said wistfully. His lower lip quivered at the mention of his mother, and Mary Margaret feared that he would be faced with the ultimate humiliation—losing control of himself in front of everyone. For there was no longer any doubt that a battle of wills was lurking, and not so far below the surface.

But Thomas managed to hold himself together, and

Mary Margaret breathed a silent sigh of relief. He had so little left, he deserved at least to keep his pride. She only hoped that Hester Townsend would have the good sense to leave it to him. Her hope died a swift death.

"Nonsense, child. Thomas Henry you were christened, and Thomas Henry you remain. I don't know what your mother was thinking of, even if she was my only daughter. The Townsends are a well-bred family. We do not resort to vulgar contractions. We would not want anyone to think you a common street urchin."

Under more normal circumstances, Hester's comment would have sparked a sharp retort from Mary Margaret. But today, circumstances were hardly normal. Her cousin and dearest friend, Claire Townsend Worthington, and Claire's husband, Henry Clay, had been killed in a road mishap. A hansom cab with a drunken driver had veered into their carriage at an unmarked corner nearly eight days ago. Within twenty-four hours, the children sitting across from her had been twice orphaned. Antagonizing Hester Townsend at this juncture would help no one, least of all the children, whom she had vowed to help in whatever way she could.

The horses turned again, their hooves beating a skittish tattoo on the cobblestoned road as they began the climb up Beacon Hill. The houses here were older, built in the first half of the century by the architect Bulfinch and his contemporaries. Down one street, the old Otis mansion stood in all its splendor. Not to be outdone, the Townsend house, scant blocks away, dominated its own grounds. Built in the Georgian style, though not of that era, the house had a gabled roof and massive chimneys.

Mary Margaret was the first to descend from the carriage. She hurried up the steps to the ornately decorated portico and pulled the bell. The immense double doors swung open, and the butler peered down at her from his mountainous height. Behind him, Mary Margaret noted with dismay, stood a row of servants, men and women, all at attention. How would the children feel, confronted by this sea of unfamiliar faces?

She quickened her pace, barely taking the time to nod

her greeting to the gathered crowd. If it weren't so improper, she would have taken the stairs two at a time, so anxious was she to get back.

All of the children's worldly possessions had been sent on ahead to their grandparents' house. Mary Margaret had seen to that, and had hidden their little treasures in the corners of the packing cases so no one would throw them out. Now she checked to make sure each cherished keepsake had been carefully unpacked and put in its proper place, ready to welcome them to their new home.

As soon as she was done, she hurried back downstairs. In the few minutes she'd been away, Hester Townsend had brought the children inside, removed their jackets, and was introducing them formally to the staff.

"Aunt Mary! Where were you? We didn't know where you had gone," Thomas cried out as soon as he saw her coming down the stairs. He grabbed his sister and ran down the hall, straight into Mary Margaret's arms.

Strictly speaking, Mary Margaret was not the children's aunt; she was a distant cousin of their recently deceased mother, but their relationship was close and loving. Without a second thought, she gathered both of them into her arms, heedless of the wrinkles they were pressing into her dark blue poplin dress.

"Really, these children are just as ill-mannered as I'd feared," Hester Townsend complained, if her detached, slightly disapproving tone could be called anything as unseemly as a complaint. "What have you been doing with them? I warned Claire that her permissiveness would lead to no good, and I see now that I was right. Why she couldn't get a real governess for them, I'll never know." This last was accompanied by a pointed look at Mary Margaret, followed by a perfunctory brush of each eye with a black lace handkerchief.

"Why don't I take them upstairs and show them their rooms?" Mary Margaret said, bypassing the older woman's unwarranted attack and sending her a quelling look. That look had served Mary Margaret well before and stood her in good stead once again. Whatever the venerable Mrs.

Townsend had been about to say was swallowed behind a discreet cough.

"Yes, do that," Mrs. Townsend commanded, recovering quickly. "The rest of you go about your business, too." Her gaze swept down the line, encompassing Mary Margaret as well as the servants. She made no secret of her attitude toward her less-well-to-do relation.

Mary Margaret stood, the pressure of her stays leaving her breathless for a moment. Then she leaned over and placed an arm around the children's shoulders. "Come along—let's go upstairs."

"Make sure you have them rest before evening tea," Hester called to Mary Margaret. "They might as well start getting used to their new schedule right away. Grandfather Townsend will be back then, and he will expect them to be on their best behavior. Hurry along now."

Mary Margaret did not waste a second in shepherding her charges up the stairs and out of their grandmother's reach. Anger churned inside her, but she would not let it erupt. The Townsends were the children's closest relatives in Boston, and were in full charge for the moment.

Thank goodness it is not to be a permanent arrangement, Mary Margaret thought to herself. She had been present at the reading of Henry Clay's will, much to the consternation of both Townsends, and knew what had been decreed.

Although the bequest to her had been small, based more on sentiment than need, she wondered if Claire and Henry had not acted on purpose, making sure that Mary Margaret was familiar with the provisions of their will. As Claire's closest friend, they would have expected her to see that every detail was properly executed. For, to everyone's surprise, guardianship of the children had not been left to Claire's parents, but to Henry Clay's brother, John.

John Adams Worthington. His name had such a presence to it, full of historical connotations, with its harkening back to the founding of the nation a century ago. Who would believe that John Adams Worthington was the black sheep of the family? If she had been writing one of her articles, Mary Margaret would have more accurately described

John's brother, Henry Clay, as the white sheep of the family, leaving it to her readers to draw the correct conclusion about the others. Henry Clay had been kindhearted and responsible, sober and loving, ethical to a fault—in short, everything John Worthington was reputed not to be.

And now this unknown scapegrace was the children's only hope of rescue from a house where they would be treated as mere possessions, instead of loved for themselves. Would he be better for them, or worse?

She knew from her own experience how difficult it was to grow up without love. Her fervent hope was to keep these dear children from having the same experience.

She sighed with frustration. There was so little she could do to change things. She was powerless in the Townsends' home, and even more so before the law. After all, how could an overeducated, unmarried woman of twenty-seven with no visible means of support except a small trust fund convince anyone, least of all a judge in Boston, that the children should be given into her care? All she could do right this minute was offer her love and hope that it would carry them through.

"This way, Rebecca." She nodded with her head toward a pair of doors at the far end of the long, carpeted hallway on the second floor. "You'll be right next door, Thomas."

The children followed her silently, not so much reluctant as passive, and she knew without their saying a word that all this was too much for them—too much upheaval, too much change, too much loss.

Inside the first room, the children stayed huddled by her side, their dulled gazes glued to the floor.

"You gonna leave us, too, Aunt Mary?"

The softly mumbled words barely creased the still air in the room. "Of course not, Rebecca." *At least, not for a while*, she amended silently, knowing the child was not ready for more elaborate explanations.

"But you're not staying here, near us, are you?" Thomas asked her, suddenly belligerent.

"I'm staying in the other part of the house, but I'll still be nearby. I thought we discussed this already," she offered calmly, unruffled by his sharp tone.

"*You* discussed it. You and . . . and her. *We* had no say in it—in anything." Thomas ended his tirade and took a deep breath, then reined in his temper with admirable skill, giving Mary Margaret a glimpse of the man he would soon become. He met her gaze and held it, his expression earnest and pleading. "Don't you see, we don't want to be here. We want to go home. Can't you take us home, Aunt Mary? Please."

Oh, the anguish of being found out—of losing a child's faith in your powerfulness as an adult, of wanting to accede to a child's dearest wish and being unable to do so. Mary Margaret felt all that and more as she whispered, "I can't, Thomas. I'm so sorry, but I can't."

In an instant, he had pulled away from her. "I hate you," he threw out in angry challenge, his arms stiff at his sides, fists balled. His neck looked scrawny and vulnerable where it stretched out of his shirt collar. His face flushed bright red. "I hate you all—you and them."

Without dropping his gaze, Mary Margaret reached behind her and pushed the door to the hallway shut, ensuring their continued privacy. "Please, Thomas, try to understand—"

"No! Why should I? No one tells us the truth anymore. You said the house was ours. You said we wouldn't have to come here . . ." Tears started running down his cheeks, and he swiped at them with his jacket sleeves. "You said Uncle John was coming for us."

Rebecca was whimpering now, too, frightened by the strange surroundings and her adored older brother's loss of control. In despair, Mary Margaret did the only thing she could think of. She gathered Rebecca into her arms, cornered Thomas before he could think of escaping, and bundled them both into her lap on the old, wooden-handled armchair that stood by the bedside.

For a long time, she just held them. Slowly, they relaxed against her, and even Thomas finally laid his head against her shoulder.

"What will happen to us, Aunt Mary?" he murmured, giving voice to his innermost fears. "Will our uncle come?

What if he doesn't want us? Then what? Where will we go? What will we do?"

The identical concerns had been running through her head since she had first learned of her cousin's tragic fate. Not for the first time, Mary Margaret damned John Worthington. What kind of man was he? A week had passed since the deaths of his brother and sister-in-law, and so far, he had only seen fit to send a telegram announcing that he could not leave the Wyoming Territory for a few more days but would travel east as soon as possible.

"I'm sure your Uncle John will be here soon," she promised rashly. "Only something extremely important could have kept him away this long, I'm certain." She wasn't certain at all, but it was the best she could offer at the moment. When that rogue finally saw fit to present himself, he'd better have a good excuse, or she would personally strangle him. "In the meantime, you know I'll take care of you."

"But why couldn't we have stayed home and waited for him?"

"Your grandparents think it's better for you to be here. They're your family, too, you know." She almost added that the Townsends loved them, but bit back the remark. Even she could not utter such a blatant exaggeration, especially to a sensitive, astute boy like Thomas. What little credibility she had would disappear in an instant.

"Some family," he snorted, lifting his head. "They never came to visit us except on holidays, and then they always complained about *everything* . . . and especially about Papa. They even said he killed her." His voice trailed off and his body tensed again.

"When did they tell you this?" Mary Margaret tried to keep the horror from her voice as she sat forward in the chair. Her movement jostled Rebecca, causing the half-asleep girl to grumble and shift into a more comfortable position.

"They didn't exactly tell me," he confessed, taken aback by her reaction. "I just heard them say it, that's all." He would not meet her eyes.

"I see. Eavesdropping again." It was not a question.

They'd been over this ground before, and Thomas knew it as well as she. "I'm sorry you had to hear that. It's not true, you know."

"No, I didn't think so," he answered, much comforted. He eased his head back onto her shoulder and sighed.

Damn them all, the lot of them, she thought furiously, though she would never say the words aloud. Did not one of them, outside of herself, care about these children?

A lesser woman would have been dismayed and retired behind her embroidery and crocheting with self-effacing grace, as became an aging spinster and genteel poor relation. But not so Mary Margaret Simpson.

She had been fighting for her rights all her life and was undaunted by insurmountable odds. At first, she had fought with her father over her education and independence, and later, more seriously, over her love for Reed Townsend, Claire's older brother.

She had never fully understood his objections to Reed, but then, she had never really understood her father's attitude toward her, or the distance he kept between them. He could be so warm and loving to his wife and students, but from her earliest childhood, she'd sensed a deep reserve in him where she was concerned. Maybe that was why she'd challenged him at every turn—to get his attention. She had won those battles more often than not, though in the end, she had lost what mattered most.

Reed Townsend, true to his high principles and sense of duty, had felt compelled to offer himself in the service of his nation and had died defending his country. Her parents had died shortly thereafter, leaving her bereft and alone. She'd had to conquer her despair and build a new life for herself. She knew too much of suffering to let the Townsends get away with inflicting more pain on Thomas and Rebecca.

They'd better take heed. She would take them all on—John Adams Worthington, too, if need be. Mary Margaret had seen the light of battle, and she would not rest until the war was won.

*   *   *

The telegram was burning a hole in Worth's vest pocket. Slowly he took it out, unfolded it, and read its somber message one more time: "Brother Henry Clay and wife killed in accident. John Worthington named executor, trustee of estate, and guardian to children. Await your arrival."

How could it be? How could death have struck down his vital, happy brother? Henry Clay had led a charmed life, or so it had always seemed to Worth. Everyone had liked him, at school and at work. He'd married the girl of his dreams, against tremendous odds, and made a life for himself among the elite upper class—and he a Worthington, no less! For as long as Worth could remember, pride and envy had warred inside him as he lived in Henry Clay's shadow.

And now, all of that was gone. Worth stretched to ease the cramped muscles in his back and put one hand to his nape to massage the tense muscles. God, he just couldn't believe it! He didn't want to believe it! Not yet, his mind implored, not so soon. Henry Clay was too young. There was so much left unsaid. . . .

Worth blinked rapidly to clear the sudden mist that obscured his vision. He folded the yellow sheet and stuffed it back in his pocket, next to the second telegram—the one from the Townsends.

At least the latter missive had brought no other painful revelations, and he was grateful for the small mercy. William Townsend and his wife had simply let him know they would care for their grandchildren as long as necessary. Under other circumstances, he might have found their insistence uncomfortable, or a challenge to his status. Now, he was merely thankful that he had one less calamity to deal with. He had his hands full as it was.

Marcus Robertson, who'd become like a brother to him here in Wyoming, was in a coma, hovering between life and death. Worth had spent long hours by Marcus's side, determined to do everything he could to keep his friend alive. Only this morning, in the still hours before dawn, had Marcus finally turned the corner. Though still pale, the older man's color was returning, and the silence in the room was due to the relaxed nature of natural sleep rather than the comatose slumber of a fevered brain.

Worth rubbed his hand over his face, trying to dispel some of his weariness. He'd been sitting in the same crouched position for days and probably looked as bad, or worse, than the patient. His body ached from the lack of movement, but he didn't begrudge his longtime friend one second of the time he'd spent with him—not after all that Marcus had done for him over the years.

Thank goodness Marcus had been in town when he had taken ill. Though the Robertson ranch was near Worth's, it was too far from Cheyenne to travel back and forth on a daily basis, and Marcus had needed the attention of the doctor every day. Though both ranches were fine for everyday living, neither had the facilities to care for someone so ill.

The three previous days had been a nightmare. Supervising Marcus's nursing care, overseeing the Robertson ranch along with his own, and taking care of the myriad details of his law practice, had drained him.

And always at the back of his mind were the words of the damnable telegram he had received last Friday—words he could not accept, even as they tore at the very fabric of his life. They had rearranged his priorities in an instant, and brought him face-to-face with his own mortality, as well as his brother's and Marcus's.

Now that Marcus's daughter Lucy was home, he was free to catch the next train east. Worth had wired her when her father had first fallen ill, and she had arrived just this morning. With Marcus's recent improvement, Worth felt comfortable letting her take over her father's care. All that remained was to notify his clients of his emergency in Boston and arrange for an associate to handle his cases while he was away.

The clatter of china caught Worth's attention. He glanced toward the source of the noise as Lucy Robertson entered the room, carrying a bowl of hot broth and a cup of tea.

"How is Daddy doing?" Lucy asked as she put the silver tray down on the dresser. She was obviously looking to him for reassurance. Her sweetly attractive face was pale with anxiety; a frown creased her delicate brow.

"He's resting quietly. You don't have to worry. His sleep is natural, and the doctor says he should be waking up any time." He smiled gently at her and was gratified to see her strained expression ease.

Worth watched Lucy cross the room to straighten the covers on her father's bed. He found it hard to believe that his friend could have a daughter who was so grown-up. Marcus was only a few years older than his own thirty-two, and here was Lucy, almost eighteen and on the threshold of leaving her girlhood behind.

"Worth, I can't thank you enough for all you did for Daddy . . . and me. I don't know how I could have borne it without knowing you were here to look after him. We'll always be grateful to you."

Tears gathered in the corners of her blue eyes and spilled over. Strangely moved, Worth reached into his pocket for his handkerchief and gently pressed the white cloth into her hand. For some reason he could not identify, he was hesitant to wipe away her tears himself, as he'd done when she was smaller.

"Don't cry, Lucy. The worst is over now. I'm just glad I could be of help. That's what neighbors are for."

"You're more than a neighbor, Worth—you're a friend, a true friend." Lucy's liquid blue eyes looked up into his, and Worth felt his breath quicken. Startled by his masculine response to his friend's daughter, Worth cleared his throat.

"Well," he said, "I better get on home and start packing." He backed away from her.

Lucy gently dabbed at her eyes and looked at him imploringly. "Oh, Worth, must you leave so soon? I'd feel ever so much better if I knew you were close by."

All at once, she was a vulnerable young girl again—a girl Worth had helped raise, living as close to the Robertson homestead as he did. He could not resist her appeal. He returned to her side and took her hands in his. They were so fine-boned and small.

"You know I would stay if I could, but I should be gone

already. If your father hadn't fallen ill, I'd be on a train bound for Boston this minute," he explained carefully. "My brother's children need me now. You heard the doctor this morning. He said your father was over the worst and on the mend."

Lucy squeezed his hands with her own. "How selfish I must sound to you, Worth. I understand, truly. And I really shouldn't expect you to stay here now that I'm home." She took a shuddering breath. "You must go and see to those poor children."

Relief coursed through him that she understood. She looked so fragile but seemed determined to be strong. He admired her courage, even though he knew she was trying to hold back her tears. She took her hands from his and walked to the window to regain her composure.

Sunlight streamed in through the lace curtains, making a halo of her long fall of blond hair. Her skin radiated a soft, ethereal glow. Her slender fingers toyed with the cameo brooch pinned at the throat of her dress. Silhouetted against the light, her blue muslin morning outfit hugged every curve of her lush figure. Worth heaved a labored sigh. He could no longer deny what his eyes and body had been telling him for several weeks—Lucy was no longer a child. She was a woman—a desirable woman.

"Worth, is that you?" The weak, male voice emanating from the bed startled him out of his musings. What would Marcus say if he knew of Worth's lustful thoughts about his only daughter? This was neither the time nor the place for such feelings, he told himself severely. Marcus expected more from him, and he expected more from himself. The events of the past few days must have rattled him more than he'd realized.

Lucy, on hearing her father speak, rushed over and knelt beside him. Worth joined her at the bedside.

"Daddy?"

"Marcus?" They spoke together, then Worth continued, "Lucy and I are right here. How do you feel?" Even though he had great trust in Doc Morgan, Worth was glad to finally hear his friend's voice.

"Like I've been drug through a knothole backwards,"

Marcus replied, and Worth laughed with relief. His old friend was feeling better. Marcus's joke lessened some of Worth's secret fears about his recovery.

"Oh, Daddy, I was so worried, and there I was, all the way in Kansas City, and . . ."

"Now, don't you go on so, Lucy," Marcus admonished. "I'm fine." He sniffed the air. "Is that soup I smell? My stomach feels like it's trying to eat my backbone. Why don't you ladle it up, sweetheart?"

When Lucy rose to do his bidding, Marcus tried to prop himself up against the headboard but was too exhausted from his illness. Worth, seeing his struggles, immediately leaned over and pulled him up against the pillows.

"You've been sick for a number of days, friend. Don't overdo. You need to rest and regain your strength."

"I'll be fine just as soon as I get something to eat."

Worth could see the illness had taken a lot out of Marcus. His face was gaunt and haggard; his skin seemed to hang on his large frame.

Lucy spread a linen napkin over the front of Marcus's nightshirt and spooned the soup into his mouth. "Cook made this especially for you, so you must eat it all," she warned him. "She'll have my hide if I bring any of it back to the kitchen."

While Lucy fed her father, Worth brought Marcus up-to-date on the happenings at his ranch, his brother's death, and his own impending trip to Boston. He left out the fact that Marcus's illness had delayed his departure by several days.

"I don't want you worrying about running your ranch, Marcus. You need to stay in town and recuperate. I've sent Jake over to help your foreman." With those last words, Worth saw some of the anxiety leave the other man's face. Jake had worked out at Worth's spread for close to four years and could be trusted to handle any problems at the ranch.

Lucy gathered up the luncheon dishes, and made sure her father was comfortable before she left the room. Worth couldn't resist watching her; his gaze was drawn despite his earlier warnings to himself.

Once she was out of earshot, Marcus began to question Worth.

"Are you ready to go back to Boston?"

Worth knew exactly what Marcus was asking. He and Marcus had become friends shortly after he had arrived in Cheyenne back in 1870. Over the ensuing six years, Marcus had gradually learned Worth's whole story.

"I don't have any choice. I have a responsibility to my niece and nephew, and to the memory of my brother, that far outweighs any of my old prejudices and concerns."

Despite his show of confidence, doubts assailed Worth. Could he put all his past experiences out of his mind and do the right thing for his brother's children? Was he capable of caring for two young orphans—seeing to their daily needs and planning their futures?

Those questions still haunted him as he took his leave of Marcus. Lucy waited at the bottom of the staircase, his felt slouch hat clutched in her hands, an awareness in her eyes he had never noticed before.

"You take care of yourself while you're away," Lucy said earnestly, handing him his hat.

"And you make sure your father doesn't go out to the ranch until Doc gives his okay. Your father can be a very hard-headed man," Worth teased to diffuse the growing tension between them.

Lucy laughed tremulously and agreed with Worth. "I'll keep him in bed if I have to bring half the ranch hands in to do it."

Worth smiled, and for a moment they stood, gazing into each other's eyes. Then, without warning, Lucy flung herself against his chest and wrapped her arms around his neck as she held him close.

He was so surprised that his arms moved in a reflex action to hold her. She was smaller and more fragile than he expected, but there was no longer any doubt in his mind that the child he had loved so innocently had blossomed into a young woman. She pressed a quick kiss on his cheek, her soft body clinging to his along his entire length.

How lovely she was. He wanted to pull her more tightly against him, to explore the rich delights she so sweetly offered. A shudder of regret passed through him as he came to his senses. Tenderly he pushed her away, softening his rejection with a light kiss to the top of her head.

She seemed to understand his reluctance and let her arms drop to her sides.

"Write me?" Lucy asked in a whisper, unwilling to let him go without a word.

For a moment, Worth could not answer her. He knew she was asking for more than just a letter, but he was not ready to make such a commitment. Not now, when so much in his life was uncertain. He needed more time, but he did not want to hurt her.

Taking a step back, he said, "I probably won't have a chance to write, the trip will be so short. You take care of yourself and your father. I'll be back before you know it." Shoving his hat on his head, he took one last look back, then left.

Worth glanced down at his watch. The train was pulling out of the rail station in New York City and the stationmaster had said they'd be in Boston by four.

He lifted the key from the end of his toggled chain, carefully fitted it into the slot on his watch, and slowly wound it. The last time he'd done this, his life had been completely different. Eight days ago, his brother and family had been alive and well in Boston, Marcus had been working out at the ranch, and Lucy had been enjoying a reunion with some finishing-school friends in Kansas City. Since then, everything had changed—everything and everyone but him.

The journey had left more time than he wanted for solitary contemplation—it seemed endless. The long days of dusty train travel, interspersed with half-hour stops for dining, had done nothing to relieve either his boredom or his anxiety for his niece and nephew.

The differing landscapes held no appeal. One town looked much like the next, one city the same as another. The sod houses of the plains had changed to the saltboxes of New England, but Worth noticed none of it.

He was no closer now to answering any of the questions

he'd asked himself in Marcus's room four days before, nor were his feelings in regard to Lucy any clearer than when he had started this trip. The only thing he did know was that Thomas and Rebecca were of the utmost importance, their well-being his main concern.

How would they feel about being adopted by an unknown uncle who lived in the wilds of the West? Would they want to move out to his home in Cheyenne? Was it fair to uproot them from the city of their birth?

The questions beat on his mind like the relentless clicking of the train wheels against the track, around and around without stopping, while he formulated his plan.

He remembered Mr. and Mrs. Townsend well from his days in Boston. They were not his idea of loving and giving parents. He seriously doubted that people like the Townsends ever changed, and if that was the case, the children would be far better off with him.

He knew that by his age most men were married and starting a family, but his background had always seemed to stand in his way. Although he had changed his life in many ways, setting up his law practice and working on his ranch, he had never thought himself worthy of the regard of a good woman. The shadows from Boston had followed him out West to the Wyoming Territory, bringing with them a legacy of doubt.

But over the last few months, he had found his life incomplete, and he longed for something more. The time had come for him to reevaluate himself, to take this tragic circumstance and use it well. He would forge a new beginning for himself, as well as his two charges, and place the life he had built in Cheyenne on a different track.

Worth looked out the dusty window. A glimpse of an abandoned building sent a shiver of recognition through him. It was the countryside of his youth. The train was almost in Boston. He eased himself back on the seat, took a long nine from his pocket, and rolled it between his fingers. He didn't smoke often, but. . . . Slowly, he lit the end of the cigar and let it quell some of the gripping tension building in his stomach. Gradually he relaxed and turned again to the sights outside the train window.

He watched the trees and country roads turn into more densely populated areas with larger buildings and more activity. *It might be interesting to see what changes have taken place over the last six years*, he thought as the passengers around him began to gather up their belongings. His carpetbag was beside his feet, his greatcoat on the seat next to him. Boston was only minutes away. He was ready. The battle was about to begin.

Two

"**W**hy can't we just eat upstairs, Aunt Mary?" Rebecca asked. Mary Margaret was attending to her coiffure, checking that the center part was straight and the neatly crimped hair on either side lay snug against her forehead. Tea would be served in fifteen minutes, and she wanted to be ready.

"Grandmother Townsend would like us all to be together on your first day here," Mary Margaret said, speaking to the girl's reflection while she tugged gently on the braids tucked snugly around her nape, making sure the ends were well hidden beneath the coronet of hair swept up and back from her face.

"But Mama always lets us eat upstairs when company comes."

With a painful twinge, Mary Margaret ignored the girl's use of the present tense. "I don't think there will be any company tonight, sweetheart. At most there will be a close family friend or two, and I'm sure they would love to see you."

Rebecca pouted and Mary Margaret felt a fine tension seep into her muscles. The last thing the children needed was to be put on display as symbols of their grandparents' loss. But Mrs. Townsend was oblivious to their needs, and

Mr. Townsend firmly believed that the home was the woman's sphere. Just as he would look askance were his wife to offer him advice on his business, he would never think to interfere in her running of the household.

Thomas looked up from where he was idly rocking on the platform rocker in the corner of Mary Margaret's room.

"How long do we have to stay here?" There was a grim resignation to his tone that barely hinted at the despair Mary Margaret saw in his eyes.

"Not long, I'm sure. Your uncle should arrive any day now."

"And then what will happen?" Thomas asked neutrally, as if he were afraid to put too much hope into the future.

"Will he take us back to our house? Will we get our own rooms back and all our toys and things?" dreamed Rebecca.

"I don't know exactly what will happen. All I know is that your parents intended that your uncle take care of you."

"I bet you he isn't coming." Thomas leaned his weight forward on the rocker until his feet touched the bright carpet.

Mary Margaret twisted on her stool to face him. "Don't give up yet, Thomas Henry. The battle was never won by default." She stood, stretching to her full height of five feet seven inches, then tilted her dressing table mirror up so she could center the knot of her fichu.

Her dress for the evening was of black wool, suitable for mourning. The overskirt fell straight in the front to hug her body, while the back gathered in flounces and intricate folds over her bustle.

Satisfied that she was presentable, she turned around and held out her hands to the children. "Let's go down together and show them what we're made of." She took Rebecca's hand with her left and looked Thomas in the eye. "Are you with me?" she softly challenged him.

"I'm with you," he promised at last, catching her fire, and jumped from the chair, offering her his arm. With a pleased smile, she accepted his invitation and slipped her hand into the crook of his elbow. With Rebecca on her left side and Thomas on her right, she headed for the stairs.

Teatime was a strain, just as Mary Margaret had feared. A few close friends of the family stopped in to convey their condolences, having dropped off calling cards earlier in the day. Most of them stayed only briefly, following custom, but a few of the more intimate friends lingered. Mrs. Townsend held court in the front parlor, ensconced on an armchair beneath her daughter's crape-draped portrait, which hung suspended from the molding near the ceiling on long, visible cords. Mr. Townsend sat more removed, leaving his wife clearly in charge of this domestic scene.

The two grandchildren perched on ornate, upholstered stools that served as backless chairs, one on each side of Mrs. Townsend. They were dwarfed by the portrait of their mother and their grandmother's regal presence.

Mary Margaret watched the tableau from her assigned seat on the settee across the room. Memories of this same room nine years ago added to the poignancy of the moment. How clearly she remembered Reed Townsend's death. Claire's brother had been her first true love, the object of her girlish fantasies. Now Claire was gone, too. Mary Margaret felt the loss deeply. Her eyes filled and she was thankful for the privacy afforded by her isolation at the far end of the room.

Her isolation was augmented by the shadowed lighting. No sunlight dared enter here. At each window, sheer lace curtains, hanging straight with no tiebacks, filtered the daylight outside, subduing its splendor, while the heavy-cut velvet drapes, with their fringed valances, reduced the remaining brightness to a mere glimmer.

In honor of the sad occasion, a few selected gas wall sconces had been lit. The side table between the two pocket doors on the long side of the room was laid with the tea equipage: several plates of thin sandwiches and two platters of cakes, cups and saucers for· tea, and the teapot itself.

The guests' voices were hushed, and some of the women cried softly when they chanced to glance up at the portrait of Claire. Most visited for just a short while. Only Mrs.

Brockton came early and stayed late, but such was her right, being Mrs. Townsend's oldest and dearest friend.

A few of the younger couples sought out Mary Margaret, and with a raised eyebrow or a subtle nod of the head, silently asked after the fate of the children. Just as subtly, she lifted her shoulders and let them drop, not knowing herself what the future held.

After an hour, Rebecca began to fidget on her uncomfortable chair, and Thomas shot several desperate glances at Mary Margaret. She nodded her understanding, rose from her seat, and approached Mrs. Townsend.

Keeping her voice firm but polite, she said, "It's time for the children to retire now. They've had a long day. I'll take them up so you can stay down here with your guests."

It was an order, but conveyed with just the right touch of deference, giving Mrs. Townsend no choice but to agree. She even went so far as to murmur her thanks, as befitted a woman of quality and breeding, though her eyes shot daggers at Mary Margaret.

Mary Margaret knew her impertinence would not be forgotten. Ah, well, she thought as she led the children away from their evening purgatory, no one ever said the lot of a poor relation among her wealthy kin would be easy. And she smiled briefly, refusing to take herself too seriously while she garnered her strength for the coming challenge.

The front hall was deserted when she descended those same stairs a short while later. The exhausted children had tumbled into their beds, falling asleep despite their best efforts not to. Now, the sounds of conversation from the drawing room were muted, indicating that most, if not all, of the evening's callers had already departed.

Mary Margaret stood on the last stair, silently debating whether to reenter the drawing room or make a strategic retreat. She had not yet made her decision when she noticed the butler emerging from his pantry behind the stairs to once again open the front door.

Curiosity kept her in place. All who had expressed an interest in visiting today had done so. Who could be so underbred as to call this late in the day, and without having left a calling card earlier to warn of the visit?

"Uh, excuse me, sir..." The butler began, his uncharacteristic stammer piquing her interest. Her decision made, Mary Margaret stepped down from the stair and headed for the front entry, rather than seeking sanctuary in the drawing room. It was not proper at all, but infinitely more intriguing. She'd never heard Sedgwick at a loss for words before.

"I say, sir," the butler protested, "you can't bring *that* in here."

"It's only temporary. I'll take everything with me when I go. You have my word," soothed a weary, baritone voice. A calfskin-covered trunk tumbled onto the white marble tiles of the foyer. A cloud of dust rose around it, glimmering in the last rays of the dying sun.

Sedgwick coughed pointedly. "Yes, sir," he said, drawing himself up to his considerable height. But while his intimidation tactics worked on the usual guests at the Townsend house, they didn't stop the new visitor for a moment.

A man Mary Margaret had never before seen stepped inside, carrying a large traveling bag made of carpet. From the doorway, Mary Margaret could hear the clatter of hoofbeats as the conveyance that had brought him pulled away.

"Who...uh, whom may I say is calling?" asked Sedgwick, flustered for the second time in as many minutes.

"Mr. Worthington, I presume," drawled Mary Margaret, guessing at once that the visitor was Henry's long-overdue brother, arrived at last to claim the children. Politely inclining her head, she walked toward him. "It's so nice of you to finally come by."

If she'd thought to put him in his place with her less than gracious greeting, she instead found herself taken down a peg or two as she faced his impassive stare. He was tall, she noted. His eyes were blue and shuttered, showing nothing of his state of mind. His hair was hopelessly out of fashion, wind-blown and shaggy, the tips bleached golden so that they reflected red and gold highlights as the sun sent a few last rays through the open doorway.

His shoulders were broad, and standing next to him, Mary Margaret felt unusually petite. The overcoat he wore fit him well, stylishly almost, except that that particular cut was never seen on men of quality in the East.

His boots were dusty. Of fine leather and with a high heel, they were obviously handmade and hand-lasted, but not the typical Jefferson shoes one would expect to find on a native Bostonian.

Unfortunately, he met all her expectations. And if she were disappointed in this hoped-for savior of the children, she at least had the dubious satisfaction of knowing that her worst predictions had been right on target.

"You have the advantage of me, Mrs.—" he said as he handed his hat and coat to the waiting butler.

"It's *Miss* Simpson," she corrected, not giving him an inch. After today's turmoil with the children, she was hardly in a forgiving mood. Where had he been when they'd needed him? "Mary Margaret Simpson," she clarified. When he did not seem to recognize the name, she added, "Claire's cousin. We've been expecting you for several days now."

As Sedgwick shut the door behind him, Mary Margaret felt suddenly closed in. John Worthington was a big man—a man who looked as though he belonged outdoors. Even the high ceilings of the foyer did not dwarf him or take away from his powerful aura. She backed up a pace as unobtrusively as she could. "You don't have a six-shooter or anything else that needs to be put away, do you?" she continued boldly, hoping he could not discern her inner qualms.

"No, *Miss* Simpson, I do not." He answered with the same artificial politeness she had used on him, eyeing the spot on the floor where she had recently stood. He hadn't missed a thing, to her embarrassment.

"Do sit down for a minute," she said quickly, gesturing to the padded bench just inside the front door. She'd heard the underlying menace in his tone but refused to be intimidated. "I'll go and announce you to the Townsends."

She took another step back, then turned slowly to go toward the drawing room door, but couldn't resist a parting shot over her shoulder. "That is why you're here, isn't it, Mr. Worthington? To see the Townsends?"

The abrupt narrowing of his eyes sent a warning that he would not tolerate being toyed with. A sudden charge raced through her. He was unlike any man she had ever met, and the giddy fluttering she felt in her stomach was definitely because of him. She wondered why this particular man should affect her like this.

Certainly, she was angry with him. His delay in arriving in Boston was unconscionable. But that fluttery feeling inside her had very little to do with anger and a lot to do with... she wasn't sure with what, just as she wasn't sure if the feeling was pleasant or not. Well, whatever it was, it was her secret and would remain so. Good breeding demanded it.

Unconsciously, she tipped her head up slightly and straightened her spine, her bearing regal as she swept across the foyer. Only the hand pressed against her bodice gave her away, and then only to herself. No one else was close enough to notice.

Reaching the drawing room doors, she slid them open. Mr. Townsend had retired, leaving Hester and Mrs. Brockton the only occupants of the room.

"The whole situation is preposterous," Hester pronounced, her voice carrying clearly to the doorway. "Giving my grandchildren over to the care of that... that bounder. I can hardly credit it."

Mary Margaret winced at Hester's words. Thank goodness she had thought to leave John Worthington in the front hall. Imagine if he had heard himself being gossiped about like this! Perhaps it would be wiser to simply withdraw and have him meet Mrs. Townsend another day.

She started to pull back and bumped into a large, unyielding wall—one that had not been there scant seconds ago. A callused, masculine hand gripped her upper arm with ruthless strength, compelling her to halt. Shocked, she looked over her shoulder into the coldest blue eyes she had ever seen. They dared her to make a sound, and she knew in that instant that he, too, had heard.

Mary Margaret stood glued to the spot, held in place more by her own palpitating heart than by any threat John Worthington could make. As if sensing her capitulation, he took his hand away from her arm, but made no other move.

"Well, all I can tell you, Sybil, is that I'm more than glad I brought those children here today. Just in time, too," Hester went on. She had moved to the center ottoman, a large circular sofa located in the middle of the room, right under the chandelier. She and her friend sat next to each other, leaning against the central cushions, their backs to the door. They were so involved in their conversation they hadn't noticed the door open. Nor were they aware of how loud their voices had become.

"You are the clever one, Hester," Sybil cackled. "Always were. I'll never understand to my dying day how you let poor, innocent Claire get tangled up with one of their kind."

"It wasn't my idea, as you well know, Sybil. And in any case, I tried to warn her," Hester defended herself. Lowering her voice, she added, "Even after they were married."

Mary Margaret was appalled. She had known the Townsends had not been pleased with Claire's marriage, but she had never dreamed they had gone so far as to confront Claire with their displeasure after she was wed. Mary Margaret shifted her weight slightly, wishing she could simply vanish, or at the very least, make good her escape. Instantly, John Worthington's hand was again on her arm, cautioning her against any precipitous action.

Sybil had also pulled back, her expression of surprise barely masking her greedy interest at this latest tidbit of information. Divorce was becoming more common every day, but not in a family such as the Townsends. It would have been unthinkable!

"Do not put on airs," Hester admonished her friend with no small impatience. "You know as well as I do we would have done whatever was necessary to save her from that family. But nothing would budge her."

"And him?" ventured Sybil, too caught up in the delicious hint of scandal to watch her tongue.

"He was even worse. Once he had her caught, nothing would induce him to let go."

"Nothing?"

"You heard me. William tried everything." Her voice lowered conspiratorially. "Even money. A lot of money—but it wasn't enough for Mr. Worthington." She shook her head emphatically. "Oh, no, not for Henry Clay Worthington. He'd gotten what he wanted, and no decent amount of money would make him let go."

Mary Margaret stood in mortified silence, regret coursing through her. If only there had been some tactful way of avoiding this scene! She dared not make a noise for fear Hester would discover them.

Nor could she budge Mr. Worthington. Though the biting grip on her arm had eased once he'd realized she would not cross him, he had moved less than a single step away, barely giving her space to breathe. He stood so close behind her she could almost imagine she felt the heat of him along her back.

She wondered what the ominously silent man was thinking. Unable to resist finding out, Mary Margaret whipped her head around.

For an instant, John Worthington's expression was unguarded, as if he hadn't expected her to turn and face him. This time his eyes were anything but cold. They burned with an anguish and pain far deeper than any she would have imagined him capable of feeling. Then he blinked, and when his eyes opened again, she saw only blue, like the sky on a cloudless day, clear and empty, all emotion washed away.

Soundlessly, he signaled his wish to depart from the room. Just as quietly, she nodded her agreement. With mixed feelings of relief and growing tension, Mary Margaret closed the parlor doors, leaving Hester and Sybil to continue their conversation in privacy while she faced down the cold, forbidding stranger.

John Worthington strode to the middle of the foyer. He needed space, room to catch his breath and put his thoughts in order. He was vaguely aware of Mary Margaret Simpson standing nervously behind him, but couldn't summon up much sympathy for her. If she was scared of him, so much the better. He would need every advantage he could find to hold his own in this house—that much had become abundantly clear during the short time he had been here.

He paced in a half circle, walking past the bottom of the imposing staircase without stopping to admire either the intricately carved balustrade or the imported panels from Italy lining the opposite wall. Then he swung around to the right, passing by the equally expensive double doors before stopping in front of Miss Simpson.

She stood at the center of the circle he had marked out, her hands clasped tightly together against her dark wool skirt. Her ash-brown hair was caught up in a complicated hairdo, not a strand out of place, and her eyes were demurely cast down to the floor.

He searched his memory for any scrap of information about her, but all he could recall was Henry Clay mentioning what a help she'd been to Claire. He had never formed a clear-cut image of her in his mind, for he'd dismissed Henry's passing references to the woman caring for the children. At the time, she'd been of no interest to him. Now he wished he'd paid more attention.

"Not exactly the reception I expected," he said harshly when it had become obvious she was not going to start the conversation.

"Eavesdroppers never hear well of themselves," she replied. Her hazel eyes flashed sparks of amber and green in the glittering gaslight of the foyer. Even her plain brown hair seemed suddenly to come to life. He realized at once that what he had mistaken for nervousness was really anger—a passionate anger that threw him for a moment. Then, without thinking, he let his anger rise to meet hers.

"Oh? You mean that if I had not been present, you would have defended me?"

"If you had not been present, there would have been no need to defend. I would not have been in the drawing room to overhear a conversation that was none of my business . . . or yours, for that matter."

All of a sudden, she was the prim and proper schoolmarm lecturing one of her recalcitrant students. All traces of passion were gone; he could hardly believe he'd seen them in the first place. All that was left was this slightly starchy, sanctimonious spinster.

"So, you're condoning their discussion," he said tightly.

"Nothing of the sort."

"No?" He could not quite believe her. After all, she was Claire's relative, so it would be natural for her to side with the family.

Miss Simpson bristled visibly at his goading and clenched her jaw. It was all he could do not to smile. At least he'd managed to rattle her—no small accomplishment. For all her primness, she had a fiery nature he could not resist provoking. But she quickly regained her control and, in a tone bordering on contempt, said, "Under the circumstances, defending you might have been difficult, don't you think?"

This time, he bristled. "Under what circumstances?" he demanded. If she wanted to slur his background, he was going to make her say the words out loud, rather than let her hide behind the polite implication she could so easily deny.

"The circumstances of your arrival here," she answered, glaring at him. "It certainly took you long enough."

Worth was finally beginning to understand. Her angry contempt had nothing to do with his scurrilous background and everything to do with the timing of his visit. He now remembered how upset she had been with him when he'd arrived.

"I explained all that in my telegram," he told her, suddenly anxious to appear in a good light. "I had pressing business in Cheyenne. I got here as soon as I could."

"Did you?" Her tone was laced with sarcasm, and he was disappointed that she maintained her frosty demeanor. He tried to assure himself she was just another member of the Townsend family, but the words rang hollowly inside him.

"Whether I did or not is really not any of your concern, is it?" he said defensively.

Her sudden pallor at his comment surprised him. He had meant to put her in her place, nothing more. Despite her irritating attitude, he was forced to admit she intrigued him, and this sign of vulnerability only added to her appeal. He wanted to soften his words, but she gave him no chance.

"Well, the important thing is you're here now," she said briskly, as if nothing untoward had occurred. "I suggest we start again, so to speak, and let me introduce you to the Townsends."

"All right," he agreed, recognizing that they both needed time for their charged emotions to settle. At least he knew where he stood with the Townsends. They held no surprises for him. "Lead on," he offered politely.

"This time, I expect you to show some manners and wait here in the foyer until you've been announced," she stated, stiff and starchy once again.

"At your service, ma'am. I'll just sit over there on the bench until you call me." He gave her his "good little boy" smile, thinking to gently tease her, but she gave no response beyond a brief nod.

The fight had gone out of her after his previous remark, and she had shut him out. His first reaction was one of disappointment, but then his good sense took over. It was all for the best. He had more important issues at hand right now, like dealing with the Townsends and getting to know his niece and nephew. He did not need Miss Mary Margaret Simpson, or anyone else, confusing his already complicated life. Still, he felt a brief stab of regret as she left him alone in the foyer.

Mary Margaret sat in the corner of William Townsend's study, her quiet presence all but unnoticed by Hester, William, and John Worthington as they took each other's measure. Mr. Worthington's cutting question in the foyer echoed once more in her head. "It's really not any of your concern, is it?"

"Yes, it is my concern!" she had wanted to scream at him. "Those children are a large part of my life, my happiness." But just then, the crushing reality of her situation had dawned on her. No one else felt she should have any say in deciding the children's fate. They were more than happy to absolve her of any responsibility other than temporarily caring for the youngsters. She was merely a convenience in their eyes, not a woman with hopes and dreams and feelings of her own.

Meanwhile, they were arguing among themselves about what should be done, though nothing she'd heard so far bore any resemblance to what she thought the children needed.

"And I'm telling you—" John Worthington pointed his finger at William Townsend's face from his side of the oversized desk. Despite his crude manners, he was an imposing man. Masculine energy radiated from him, fueled by his anger. Mary Margaret wondered what it would feel like to have all that passionate intensity turned on her. The thought made her blush as she listened to him. "—the children were left to me. The lawyer said so in his letter. Don't try to deny it."

"Now, now," soothed William Townsend from his padded leather desk chair. "There's no need to be so upset. No one is trying to cheat you out of anything. Why don't you have a seat? Every penny's been accounted for, after all."

"I'm not worried about the money," Mr. Worthington said, not bothering to hide his contempt for the other man's attitude. "My worry is for the children." He flopped down onto the padded wicker armchair. The chair creaked in protest, but Mary Margaret was relieved. Without his distracting presence dominating the very air she breathed, she could pay better attention to the conversation at hand.

"Of course," William agreed. "The children are our main worry, too. That's what this is all about, isn't it?" he asked the group at large.

Mary Margaret kept her silence. Hester was not so discreet. "It most certainly is," she decreed. "That's what I was trying to tell Mr. Worthington earlier."

"Oh, really?" John Worthington sat up in his seat. "I thought you were telling me how wonderful Boston is, with all its 'social advantages.' I'm so glad you cleared things up for me." His tone gave full vent to his disbelief —a disbelief Mary Margaret shared. "Now, let me make something clear to you. I don't need you or anyone else to tell me what is or isn't good for the children." His gaze swept around the cluttered study, encompassing both of the Townsends and then settling on Mary Margaret.

Mary Margaret felt her cheeks redden. How dare he imply she did not know what was right for the children? She could not believe his audacity.

"What makes you think you know what's best for the children? You haven't even met them," she retorted angrily. Somehow, Mr. Worthington brought out the worst in her, and now was no exception. "It's not as if you were available for us to ask your advice or permission."

"You've already made *that* point, Miss Simpson. Have you nothing new to add?" he retaliated.

"Now see here, Worthington," William Townsend protested. "There's no need to attack Mary Margaret. She's right, you know. We did the best we could before you came. How were we to know what you wanted?"

"Don't think you're fooling me. I know the children were brought here only today—and I know why it was done."

Mary Margaret did not understand the import of his innuendo, but Mr. Townsend looked uncomfortable and was tugging nervously at his stiff collar.

Hester, however, was not intimidated in the least. "Of course you know why," she charged. "Everyone knows the children need their family at a time like this, and you were nowhere to be found. My poor Claire has been gone a week now, all because of that . . . that . . ." Mary Margaret's heartbeat quickened as she realized Hester was just a breath away from maligning John Worthington's brother again. She found herself ready to leap to his defense, but her worries were unnecessary. With a steely-eyed look, John Worthington managed to stop Hester. ". . . that trip she had to make with your brother," Hester finished, showing her first sign of uncertainty.

"Just hold on one minute," John Worthington said, each word precisely bitten out. "I am family, too. And don't tell me you didn't know when I was coming. I made sure you would. The station agent guaranteed my message would be delivered before today. Back home we read our telegrams first thing. Of course, big city ways are something I don't know much about."

Mrs. Townsend's face reddened and a vein stood out in her forehead, but neither she nor William contradicted his statement. Suddenly, Mary Margaret understood the Townsends' haste in getting the children moved into their house. They had known Mr. Worthington was scheduled to arrive today, though they had not said a word, either to her or to the children. Her sympathies were suddenly with the irate visitor.

"Well, that's all water under the bridge," Hester said, rising from the side chair near the shuttered window. She went to stand behind her husband, dismissing Mr. Worthington's claims as if they were of no consequence. "The important thing now is to see to the welfare of the children from this point on."

Hester laid her hand on William's shoulder. Mary Margaret found herself unexpectedly allied with John Worthington as they faced the formidable couple across the clutter of papers strewn over the desktop. After what she'd just learned, she was relieved not to be included in their number.

"What are your immediate plans?" Hester demanded, and Mary Margaret waited with curiosity and a tingling anticipation to see how Mr. Worthington would react now.

He simply slouched into his seat and placed one dusty boot over the other on the petit-point footstool near his chair. His insolent pose was calculated to annoy, and Mary Margaret saw it had hit its mark. Hester's mouth was tight with disapproval as she stared pointedly at his misplaced feet and the dust covering the delicate pink roses she herself had embroidered.

"First, I'll get to know the children and let them know me," John Worthington drawled once he'd made himself comfortable. "Then, we'll see."

"And just how do you plan on doing that?" Hester snapped.

"By spending time with them. Tomorrow I'll be seeing Henry Clay's lawyer to learn the full details of Henry's will. Since I intend to be with the children, I can stay here.

Or the three of us can move back to Henry Clay's house. I'm sure we can work it out."

The unspoken threat was clear. If they did not see things his way, he would invoke the power of the law to take the children from them. There was more to this blue-eyed man than she'd imagined, Mary Margaret realized. So far, he had beaten the Townsends on their own turf. She couldn't help but admire him.

William Townsend understood his position, too. "Of course," he agreed heartily. "We expected no less. The children will need a familiar environment to get them over this trying time. And familiar people, as well. Surely you do not disagree?"

John Worthington inclined his head slightly and let the silence do his work for him.

"Yes, well." William paused to clear his throat. "Well," he said again, but no one stepped into the breach to help him.

From her post on the side chair, Mary Margaret could see Hester's white-knuckled grip on William's shoulder, illuminated by the light from the desk lamp. The flexible rubber hose feeding the lamp gas from the chandelier cast a flickering shadow across William's face, but he seemed not to notice. "You probably should stay here," he finally got out, looking to his wife for confirmation.

Hester accepted the inevitable and stepped into her role as mistress of the house. "Mary Margaret, would you see our guest to the blue room?"

"Of course." Turning to look at John Worthington, she stood and motioned to the door. "If you'll follow me."

As he passed in front of her, the scent of bay rum and tobacco filled her nostrils, making her acutely aware of his masculinity. The fluttery feeling she'd first experienced in the foyer returned and her knees went suddenly weak. Not since her girlish responses to Reed had she reacted in quite this way to another person, let alone someone so forceful, so dynamic . . . so male.

She took a deep, quivery breath, seeking an elusive calmness that stayed just out of reach, and preceded John Worthington from the study. Fortunately, he seemed unaware of what she was feeling, and she gave herself credit for being able to maintain her outward comportment regardless of the flurries of excitement bombarding her from within.

In the hallway, John Worthington waited with some impatience while his escort quietly closed the doors. With the exception of her one outburst, she had stayed remarkably neutral during his battle with the Townsends. And in fairness, he had to admit he had goaded her to get that response.

What were her feelings now? he wondered. Did she still condemn him, or had the Townsends' arrogant attitude gained him her grudging support? He heard the rustle of her dress as she approached and shut down his thoughts, waiting for her to make the first move.

He did not have long to wait. As soon as the doors were shut, she murmured a soft, "Well done."

Worth couldn't believe he'd heard her correctly.

Three

"I beg your pardon. What did you say?" Worth asked. He wanted to be certain his ears weren't playing tricks on him.

"I thought you handled them very well."

Her expression showed neither contempt nor admiration, so Worth was not sure just how she meant the remark. Then he noticed the bright gleam in her hazel eyes and the way the corner of her mouth tilted upward before she composed her face.

He grinned at her. "Thank you. I'll assume that was a compliment."

She relented enough to give him a brief smile, cementing their truce.

"Your room is this way," she said, walking to the stairs, then waiting for him to follow.

"I'd like to see the children first." He watched her with narrowed eyes, looking for the small, telltale signals that would let him know if he'd overstepped the bounds of their fragile partnership.

"The children have had a long day and are already asleep." She hesitated, considering. He held his breath. "You will be quiet and not wake them?"

His breath eased out. "I'll do my best."

"All right. Their rooms are near your own. I'll show you the way."

She started up the stairs, her skirts rustling with each step. Worth followed, relief and anticipation energizing him despite his travel fatigue. Nothing had turned out the way he had anticipated today, and he was bone-weary, but the thought of seeing the children was too compelling to deny.

"They'll be sorry to have missed seeing you as soon as you arrived," Mary Margaret was saying. He noticed with a start that he was no longer thinking of her as Miss Simpson—not since she'd smiled at him. "They were so excited about meeting their uncle."

"I'm sorry, too. I went straight to Henry Clay's house from the station. It took me a while to find out what had happened. The house was completely shut down—even the servants were gone."

"Yes, I know. I imagine it was quite a shock."

"It seems it was a shock for all of us," he said, picking up on the remnants of her emotion as he joined her at the top of the stairs. He was learning to read her unspoken cues.

She gave him a startled glance, as if she'd inadvertently revealed too much. "Come along. Just down this hall."

Mary Margaret led him down the wide hallway, and paused before a large oaken door.

"This is Thomas's room, and Rebecca's is to the right." The transom over the door was open, so Mary Margaret kept her voice low. "Please be as quiet as you can. They've had a very long and trying day."

Her expression softened when she mentioned her two charges. Worth felt his heart quicken. Her face, with its high cheekbones and fine lines, was more dramatic than beautiful, but the tenderness in her expression made his breath catch.

"They've been worried to distraction, wondering who would be coming to take care of them and knowing there was the possibility they would be moving to the middle of beyond, far away from their family and friends," she said earnestly, her hand lightly touching his arm.

The placement of her hand told him more than her words. In a less emotional state, he was sure she would never have taken the liberty of touching him. She obviously cared deeply about the two children. Worth suddenly understood the nature of their recent truce. He had become her ally because they shared a common goal—the children's happiness.

"I'll do my best not to disturb them," he promised, but her last words stabbed at his conscience for he did, indeed, hope to take them back with him. What would Mary Margaret think of him then? And when he did take them home, how would he handle the burden of responsibility that being their guardian entailed? He had no answers yet, but at least he could reassure Mary Margaret that he would not wake them.

"Please don't worry." He placed his hand over hers, where it lay so comfortably on his arm. Her skin was soft and delicate, and he left his hand on hers for a second longer than was necessary. Her eyes widened at his touch, and for a moment she was motionless. Then she hastily withdrew her hand from under his. She took a step back, away from the door.

"Aren't you coming in with me?" he whispered, suddenly needing the comfort of an ally. "Just in case they do awaken?"

"If you like," she answered hesitantly, but kept her distance. He nodded once, then pushed the door open slowly and silently entered the room.

He heard Mary Margaret follow behind him and felt his tension ease a little. He glanced around the large bedroom, using the small amount of light filtering in from the hall to distinguish various objects.

"Not exactly what I would have picked for a young lad," he commented in a hushed voice, taking in the formal furnishings cluttered with knickknacks and bric-a-brac. It was hardly appropriate for a boy, let alone one who had recently lost both his parents.

"I had no say in the matter of room arrangements," Mary Margaret quickly replied, her tone defensive.

"I'm sure you didn't. Not in Hester Townsend's home."

His inflection conveyed exactly what he thought of his gracious hostess.

"All of the rooms on this floor are very similar. None are really suitable," Mary Margaret finished softly, and their eyes met in understanding.

At last, he'd run out of excuses. Quietly he walked over to the bed and peered down at the shadowed face of the sleeping boy. Straight brown hair fell over the youth's forehead, and Worth fought the urge to push it back, not wanting to awaken him.

"He looks just like Henry," Worth said, his voice unusually husky. The pain of his loss filled his heart, and his hand trembled as it hovered over the boy's head.

Mary Margaret nodded from her position at the end of the bed but made no comment, giving him time to deal with his sudden onslaught of emotion.

Worth turned from the bed and headed for the hallway. He waited outside the room while Mary Margaret tucked the cover around Thomas.

"If I could see Rebecca now?" he said past the tightness in his throat when Mary Margaret joined him. Seeing Thomas had moved him more than he had anticipated.

"Certainly."

She motioned to the next room. He entered and she followed without being asked.

A small night-light had been left to illuminate the corners, but this time he spared no glances for the room. The tiny child bundled under the covers held his full attention. She seemed to be having a dream of some sort; her movements were restless and fevered. Perspiration-damp curls clung to her brow, and the soft moans she made drew him closer still.

"Is she all right?"

"Yes, it's just a bad dream. She's been having quite a few of them lately."

He reached out to touch the child but stopped, afraid of disturbing her.

"It's all right," Mary Margaret whispered. "You won't wake her."

He laid his hand on Rebecca's head and smoothed back

the tumbled curls. Her restlessness instantly abated, and she quieted into normal sleep.

Mary Margaret smiled at him from across the bed. He couldn't manage a smile back. His emotions were in turmoil, but one thing was clear. He felt a burning need to embrace and protect. He had never experienced such strong feelings before, certainly never for a child. He stood unmoving, looking down at his small niece.

The night-light picked up the faint glints of red in Rebecca's hair and made the smattering of freckles across her nose stand out against the white skin of her face. He could well imagine her with her hair pulled into long braids, running after her brother, her cheeks rosy and her voice high with excitement. He wondered about the color of her eyes. Would they be the blue that dominated in his own family or the tantalizing hazel he had glimpsed in Mary Margaret's?

Again, a feeling of supreme protectiveness surged through him. He remembered the sleeping face of his nephew and now, looking down at the small figure of his niece, he knew no responsibility would be too great when it came to these children. He loved them, not because they were family, but because they were already a part of him.

He gently tucked the flowered quilt around the little girl and smoothed the wrinkles from the pillow under her head. A new peace settled over him. Though his brother's death remained a grievous loss, the connection Worth felt with the children helped ease his pain.

His reluctance to leave the room must have been obvious, for Mary Margaret finally said in a hushed tone, "We'd better go now."

"Yes, that's fine. Thank you for letting me see them." He felt better now, more sure of himself.

His plan would work out. He knew that now. He just needed a little time for the children to get to know him, and for him to know them. But he knew exactly what he would do; all his doubts were finally laid to rest.

That night, the dream came to Mary Margaret again— the one she both longed for and dreaded. Only tonight there was a difference. For the first time, the family took on shape and substance. There were two parents, two children—a boy and a girl.

The dream was born of a yearning so deep no one else could understand, except perhaps another woman like herself: a woman in limbo, belonging to no others, having none to call her own. When she was younger, the dream had held the promise of a bright and rosy future, filled with love and caring. But that future had passed her by with Reed Townsend's death.

In recent years, the dream had come to taunt her, showing her what she could not have, raising her spirits in the night, only to dash them cruelly on morning's rocky shore. She thought she had made peace with her new life, dedicating her energies to her career as a writer and forsaking her girlish plans. But the dreams proved her wrong.

That she was the wife and mother in the dream had always been clear. Only the other details had been left hazy, disappearing into a fog of forgetfulness as she awoke. But this morning she remembered it all. The children resembled Thomas and Rebecca in happier times, their cheeks flushed with excitement, their eyes sparkling with joy.

But the biggest surprise was the husband. He was usually the most nebulous figure of all, but this time there was nothing left to chance. His eyes were as blue as the sky on a crisp fall day; his hair was dark, sun-kissed at the tips, and windblown; his voice was deep, soothing, and exciting, all at the same time, sending a shiver down her spine; and his face was John Worthington's.

She had awakened with a start, her heart pounding and her breath coming in gasps. The vivid dream was still with her in every detail, more like a memory than a figment of her imagination. She shook her head to clear it.

What had come over her? She could not comprehend it. Why, she hardly knew John Worthington! How dare he enter her dreams! But her momentary anger at him was misplaced, and she knew it. He had done nothing more than come for his niece and nephew, as was his right. He had no way of knowing how deeply she'd been affected by the expression on his face as he'd watched them sleep.

The mixture of strength, compassion, wonder, and vulnerability had cut straight to the vacant place in her heart.

John Worthington had dismantled her defenses without even trying. He'd invaded her thoughts, dominated her dreams. She was afraid to even imagine what he might do next.

Gingerly, she left the warm comfort of her bed and dressed for breakfast.

Breakfast at the Townsends' was not a gathering of the family around the kitchen table, as it had been in Claire's home, where everyone had helped himself to some food and chatted over the plans for the day. The Townsends breakfasted in a grander style, seated around the dining room table while the servants silently fetched each desired item from its chafing dish on the huge sideboard.

Still, breakfast was a more relaxed time, when perfect manners and social conversation were not required, and William Townsend could bury his nose in the morning paper without reproof.

Today was no different from any other, the added guests notwithstanding. Mary Margaret poked her head around the doorjamb and breathed a sigh of relief. John Worthington sat with his back to her. She would have time to compose herself in his presence before he turned his remarkable blue gaze in her direction.

Her heartbeat was still erratic, and she felt a curious languor in her limbs, both unwelcome remnants of her vivid dream.

The children were not down yet, although places had been set for them on either side of Hester's. A plaid drugget had been laid over the carpet under their seats to catch crumbs and accidental spills.

Taking a deep, calming breath, Mary Margaret entered the room. William Townsend was too absorbed in his reading to spare her more than a glance, but John Worthington nodded and said, "Good morning."

Her throat felt suddenly dry as she looked into his eyes; their blue was so clear and full of light it mesmerized her. He seemed just as she remembered him from her dream—

his shoulders wide, his jawline arrogant, his bearing richly masculine, even at rest. A deep heat settled at the pit of her stomach, and she had to force her glance away from him.

"Good morning," she murmured, her voice sounding hoarse even to her own ears. Quickly she turned and headed for the sideboard to study her breakfast choices, as if her life depended on it.

She was greatly relieved when William Townsend broke into the expectant silence with his outrage. "Will you listen to this, Worthington! That M. M. Simms is at it again, the scoundrel."

Hearing his words, Mary Margaret knew she could relax her guard. Politics was a man's topic. Ladies were not expected to have any opinions on it—at least, not in this household. And M. M. Simms wrote on political subjects —the more controversial, the better, as Mary Margaret Simpson well knew.

"Sir?" questioned Mr. Worthington. She sensed the instant his gaze left her back: her breathing eased and her heartbeat slowed to a more normal pace.

"This balderdash about the Declaration of Independence," William clarified behind her. "Really, Simms has gone too far this time. Haven't you read his column yet?"

Without waiting for a reply, William began to read, "Nearly a century ago, these colonies did first seek to gain their independence from a lazy and overbearing England. The first shot of that glorious conflict was fired right here, just across the Charles from our own fair city."

Ordinarily, Mary Margaret found it difficult to hear her own words being read and discussed without letting on that she was, in fact, M. M. Simms. But today, William's voice was a welcome distraction. She finished choosing her food as William continued reading.

"Our battle for freedom was won, grueling though it was to fight. But a far more grueling battle rages on. For Abigail Adams's admonishment to 'Remember the Ladies' was all but ignored. To this day, nearly one hundred years later, the Ladies are still fighting.

"Women are still not equal to men, either economically or under the law. They have had to fight to gain access to higher education, to retain control of their property, and to live independent lives. Nowhere is the inequity more striking than in refusing women the right to vote. . . ."

William Townsend stopped and looked up at his listener. "Have you ever heard such nonsense? Doesn't he know what will happen if women get to vote? Why, they will make a farce out of everything! Imagine, petticoats in the legislative chambers. We'd be the laughingstock of the world. Mark my words, a woman's place is in the home, and if she doesn't see that, then there is something wrong with her!"

That Mary Margaret was in the room and seated a mere five feet from him seemed not to have occurred to Mr. Townsend. Moreover, she knew her presence, or that of any other female, would not have stopped him had he given it any thought. But at the moment, she was much more interested in John Worthington's thoughts than William's.

"Actually, women have had the vote in the Wyoming Territory for seven years, and we've seen no dire results," John Worthington answered mildly.

"Perhaps you haven't looked for them," came the unyielding reply. "It is well known that women are less capable than men of making the decisions necessary for public life. They are too moral and pure, too spiritual. They are the guardians of the home; their special role is the rearing of children. They rule the hearth. What more important responsibility could they have?"

"Well, as I said before, we haven't had any problems with women voting or sitting on juries."

"Sitting on juries?" William gave a sharp bark of laughter. "And do they have to stop deliberating so the women can go home to feed their men and children?"

"I believe they manage just fine. It's the men who seem to have the problems."

His tone had a matter-of-fact quality to it that told Mary Margaret his replies were genuine and had nothing to do with her presence at the table. How refreshing it was to find someone who accepted women's rights as a simple fact of life.

Still, she kept her eyelids lowered, watching him covertly through the screen of her lashes lest her eyes reveal secrets she had yet to fully acknowledge herself. Her dream image of him was merging with the reality, hinting at promises beyond her experience. An unfamiliar excitement raced through her veins, and she ducked her head as she felt her cheeks flame.

William Townsend returned his attention to his newspaper, much to John Worthington's relief. Worth had more interesting things to contemplate, like the prim Miss Simpson seated across from him.

She was dressed in dark gray for mourning. He'd noticed every detail when she'd crossed the room to the sideboard before coming to the table: the tight-fitting cuirass basque, trimmed with black silk and showing off her fine waist; the tied-back skirt, stark in its simplicity and gently draping over her bustle in back while falling straight to the floor in front; the black lace choker at her neck setting off her face.

Her cheeks were a rosy pink and her hazel eyes had a vague, distracted look to them that had been absent the night before. He had felt so close to her then, in the children's room. Now she would not deign to meet his gaze.

"I did not expect to see you this morning," he announced to get her attention.

"Oh?" She still would not look at him. Instead, she nodded her head to the servant offering her oatmeal, accepted a cup of coffee, and quietly asked for a serving of scrambled egg. Worth waited until she had no other excuse to avoid him.

"Yes. I thought you might be with the children." His mention of them was deliberate. He wanted to remind her of their closeness yesterday, to see her hazel eyes gaze at him in empathetic understanding.

"I was with them until a few minutes ago. Kathleen is getting them ready to come down for breakfast."

"Kathleen?" Worth asked.

"That Irish girl? What's she up to now?" William Townsend demanded gruffly, raising his head from his paper as he turned the page.

"Kathleen is dressing the children." Worth noticed the way Mary Margaret emphasized the other woman's name.

"Ah, I see. Does Hester know?"

"Aunt Hester set her to the task, Uncle William."

"Then it must be fine, mustn't it?" he remarked absent-mindedly as he settled back to reading the newspaper, which again lay neatly folded by his plate, revealing a new page.

"The children are very excited about meeting you, Mr. Worthington," Mary Margaret said, her eyes finally meshing with his. "I was sent on ahead to make sure you did not leave the house before they made it down to breakfast."

She smiled at him and the somber, formal dining room took on a brighter air. Their truce was still on, and he was inexplicably gratified—far beyond what he should have been had he given it any thought.

"I'm not planning on going anywhere until this afternoon. I'm looking forward to meeting them, too."

He felt the need to tell her he had seen them again this morning, early, before they had awakened. He'd been unable to sleep in the strange bed. Restless and still worked up over his confrontation with the Townsends, he had sneaked down the hall at the very break of day. The children had still been asleep, and he had been able to stand by each bed and drink in his fill of their innocent presence.

If William Townsend had not been here with them now, Worth would have shared it all with Mary Margaret—the overflowing emotions that surged in his chest, his sadness at the children's loss, his deep regret over his brother and sister-in-law's deaths, his sudden love for the children, and his newfound certainty that he could care for them and provide them with all they would need.

As it was, he could only return her smile and hope his eyes relayed the rest.

His eyes were different today, Mary Margaret noticed at once—open and beckoning where before they had been closed and shuttered. He seemed to be reaching out to her, and she had to fight his subtle lure. Already she could feel her cheeks heating again. What if William should glance up, or worse yet, Hester enter the room and catch her with her thoughts so clearly displayed, her wishes so blatantly exposed?

She felt vulnerable, with a giddy breathlessness that attacked her whenever her glance chanced upon Mr. Worthington. She looked away, confused and excited at the same time. Where had she lost herself—the part of her that always knew what to do? She didn't know this woman who lived in the heady reaches of emotion, who longed for the impossible and reached for her dreams.

Anticipation joined forces with a heightened tension when she heard Hester and the children approach. She could see John Worthington had also tensed, as the moment he'd been waiting for so anxiously drew nigh.

"I told you, no running. You must mind your manners if you want your uncle to like you," Hester was saying to the children as they neared the entrance to the dining room.

A quick frown of annoyance crossed John Worthington's brow at Hester's words. Mary Margaret realized he, too, must have recognized that Hester had begun the battle, undermining the children's confidence in his love before they had even met him.

"Yes, ma'am," Thomas's voice answered in the second before the trio rounded the corner into the room.

There, the children stopped and stared. Slowly, without looking as he did it, Thomas reached down and grasped Rebecca's hand. She took a small step backwards and closer to him, using his body as a shield to hide behind.

"Thomas and Rebecca, come forward now. It's time to meet your uncle."

Hester completed the introductions and hustled the children into their seats. Then, without asking their opinions, she ordered up servings for them both.

"Good morning, Thomas. Good morning, Rebecca," Worth said quietly, once the clatter of dishes and tableware had subsided.

"Good morning, Uncle John," they answered politely and in unison. Neither looked directly at him, though he could see Rebecca sneaking a peek when she thought his attention was elsewhere.

"Sit up straight, Rebecca," Hester broke in before Worth

could continue. "You, too, Thomas Henry. We don't want your uncle to think you underbred, do we?" The smile she sent to Worth, ostensibly seeking his approval, contained a trace of smugness, as if she knew she had thwarted his plan to gently reach out to the children and put them at ease.

He refrained from making any comment, refusing to give her a victory, however fleeting. Instead, he smiled at both children and waited until Hester took a bite of food. As soon as her mouth was full, he again addressed them.

"I'm glad to meet you both, though I did meet Thomas once before." He paused for a second, relishing the children's undivided attention. Rebecca actually looked right at him, her eyes bright with wonder and curiosity. Thomas maintained more control, but couldn't quite hide his interest. Even Mary Margaret gave him her full attention, her eyes wide and puzzled.

"Oh, really, Mr. Worthington? How very interesting. When was that?" Hester asked, having quickly swallowed her portion of egg. Her bright cheerfulness fooled no one.

"Long ago, Thomas," Worth answered, acting as though Thomas had asked the question. He fixed his gaze on the boy, all but ignoring Hester. God, he looked so much like Henry Clay! Worth couldn't believe it. He swallowed past the lump in his throat. "You were just a baby, then. I don't think you remember me at all." His voice grew husky, but did not break.

Thomas shook his head.

"It was just before I headed West. I came to visit your mother and father. And there you were, barely able to stand on your own two feet, but eager as all get-out. The first time your ma handed you to me, I nearly dropped you."

Worth smiled at the memory, enjoying the surprised expressions of both children.

"How about me? Did you almost drop me, too?" Rebecca asked, momentarily forgetting her shyness.

"No, I'm afraid not, sweetheart. But I would have, if I'd been there," he reassured her, earning a pleased smile. He saw a sparkling mischievousness in her that had not been evident when she slept, and knew he would do anything to get another of her smiles.

He glanced across the table to see how Mary Margaret was reacting. She, too, was smiling, her gaze drifting from Rebecca to him, as if she approved of what he was trying to do. Even Thomas seemed to relax; his shoulders were no longer so rigid with tension.

"Now, children, you aren't eating your breakfast," Hester said, destroying the companionable silence. "Rebecca, stop playing with your oatmeal, and Thomas Henry, finish up your eggs."

"But I don't like oatmeal," Rebecca complained.

"Nonsense, child. It's good for you. If you'd stop playing with it and eat it, it would be gone in an instant."

"But Mama never makes me eat it," Rebecca stated.

"Well, your mother is not here now. In this house, everyone eats oatmeal."

Tears glistened in Rebecca's green eyes and threatened to run down her cheeks. The child was obviously unused to such unfeeling treatment.

Worth needed all of his self-restraint to keep from shouting at Hester. Fortunately for his self-control, Mary Margaret chose that moment to intervene.

"Except, perhaps, for today, since it is such a special day," she said firmly, then scooped up Rebecca's bowl and Thomas's plate and handed them to the nearest servant. "Today, with the children's Uncle John here, we can make an exception. Don't you agree, Uncle William?"

"What? What?" William Townsend glanced up from his paper in some confusion.

"I beg your pardon," Mary Margaret replied sweetly. "I said, don't you agree?"

Worth watched her with unconcealed admiration. She'd asked the question as if there was no doubt whatsoever that William should agree. And agree he did.

"Certainly, certainly," he said expansively. "Why not?"

"Thank you, Uncle William. Now, what would you like to eat, Rebecca?"

Worth silently applauded Mary Margaret as she reorganized the children's breakfast and orchestrated a pleasant, if inconsequential, conversation. Though she could not suppress all of Hester's admonitions to Rebecca and Thomas, she managed to minimize them.

Nonetheless, Worth felt his nerves were tightly strung by the time the meal was over. All he wanted was some time alone with his niece and nephew. As a stranger in the house, he did not know how to manage it subtly. The last thing he wanted was to upset the children or rekindle Hester's spite.

Mary Margaret came to his rescue once again. "I think Mr. Worthington and I should take Thomas and Rebecca for a walk on the Common," she suggested. "It would give you a chance to catch up on your correspondence, Aunt Hester, and the fresh air will be good for the children."

"What a wonderful idea," Worth declared, his tension suddenly a thing of the past. "I'm sure you agree, Mrs. Townsend." He felt a sudden impulse to hug Mary Margaret there and then.

Caught off guard, Hester fumbled for an answer and found herself swiftly outmaneuvered. Within twenty minutes, the two children were outdoors, skipping along the brick sidewalk leading from Beacon Hill down Joy Street to the Common. An iron fence surrounded the entire Common, and they crossed Beacon Street to enter at one of its several openings.

"Well, children, where do you want to go?" John Worthington asked. Rebecca pulled shyly away from him and clung to Mary Margaret's skirts. Thomas seemed equally loath to voice his opinion, although he did not physically move. "Come on, now, Rebecca," John Worthington cajoled, softening his voice and bending his knee so he was at the girl's eye level. "Surely you have a place you like to visit?"

Rebecca whispered something to Mary Margaret. "She'd like to see the Punch and Judy show. It's up on the Tremont Street mall," Mary Margaret informed him.

"That's fine with me, if Thomas doesn't mind." He looked to the boy, who nodded his agreement. "All right, then, we can go, except for one tiny little problem."

He paused, and Rebecca sneaked a look at him. He

smiled at her, his white teeth flashing in the sunlight. Mary Margaret did not know how the child could resist him. If he'd smiled at her that way, she would have done almost anything he'd asked of her. The now-familiar tingle shot through her at the thought.

Having secured Rebecca's attention, John Worthington continued, "Yep, just one little problem. I might get lost if no one holds my hand. You see, I don't know where to find the Punch and Judy show. Do you think you might be able to help me?"

He held out his hand, still squatting on the ground, oblivious to the curious stares of passersby. For several seconds Rebecca just stared at him, her eyes darting back and forth from his face to his outstretched hand.

Finally, her expression totally serious, she asked, "Do you really not know where the Punch and Judy show is?"

"No, I really don't. Could you show me?" His answer was given just as seriously, and still he did not move.

"I guess I better. You can get lost here if you aren't very careful and listen," she said, obviously repeating words that had been drummed into her many times. "Isn't that right, Aunt Mary?"

The truce faced its most severe test right then, and Mary Margaret felt torn between her selfish desire to keep Rebecca to herself for just a little while longer and the child's need to learn to trust her new guardian. She stared into John Worthington's eyes and read his plea for help. She could not deny it, no matter the cost to herself.

"Yes, that's right, sweetheart. Your Uncle John hasn't—" she paused to clear her throat "—hasn't been in Boston for a long time. I'm afraid he's forgotten his way around. Do you think you could help him?"

"You'll come along, too?" the child asked, a quaver of uncertainty lurking in her voice.

"Of course I will. And so will Thomas. We'll all go together." *For now, at least,* Mary Margaret thought, and blinked her eyes rapidly to clear her vision. Oh, this wasn't at all what she had planned when she'd suggested this outing. She had wanted simply to help Mr. Worthington, not tear out her own heart.

Reassured, Rebecca reached out one hand to grasp Worth's. She clung to Mary Margaret's skirt with the other one until she made contact with him. Fleetingly, she looked over her shoulder at Mary Margaret, a question in her eyes. Worth also glanced up into Mary Margaret's face and saw her give a brief nod.

The child released her hold on Mary Margaret's skirt and came to him. "Come on. It's this way." She tugged him toward the path cutting across the Common.

Worth stood, reveling in the warmth of the tiny hand in his. It was barely as large as his palm, and his fingers easily closed all the way around it. He felt ten feet tall, filled with triumph at conquering the little girl's fear and gaining her trust.

Only the look of raw pain in Mary Margaret's hazel eyes dimmed his pleasure. He knew now what their truce would cost her, and there was little he could do to save her grief.

"Thank you," he silently mouthed as he let the small child lead him away.

After the Punch and Judy show, the four of them strolled over to the deer park. By now, Rebecca was more than happy to take Worth's hand, having spent the better part of an hour sitting on his lap watching the quarreling puppets. Thomas had also warmed toward Worth, asking eager questions about his ranch, and especially his horses.

Only Mary Margaret had grown progressively more silent. She smiled at the children and laughed at their jokes, but Worth could see the bleak shadows that made her hazel eyes look cloudy and dark. He wished he could cheer her, could share his joy in the children with her, but he knew he would just be pouring salt on her wound.

"I'm glad you're here today," he said when they had been sitting for a few minutes, watching the two children pass leaves and bits of grass through the chain-link fence that confined the family of deer. "You could have made things difficult for me, but instead, you made them easier. I appreciate it greatly."

"I really had no choice," she answered, looking anywhere but at him. "I couldn't hurt the children."

He understood her intent. She had not been helping him so much as the children she loved with a fierceness only their mother could have exceeded.

"I know, and I still appreciate it. Not everyone has been so understanding."

"You sound bitter. Surely you did not expect to be greeted with open arms?"

"No, not open arms." He sighed. "There are . . . things you don't know about me—things better left where they belong, buried in the past. No, I certainly did not expect open arms." He, too, looked into the distance, seeing not with his eyes but with his mind.

"Yes, I know what you mean. Often it is better to forget the past and move on."

He looked at her then, confused. Did she know about his past? If so, how much? His family's reputation, infamous as it was, had no doubt survived the deaths of his parents. Had all the old scandals been resurrected at his brother's demise? Or had she secrets of her own that she did not want to face?

"At least the weather's nice," he said, to change the subject, which had threatened to become unduly personal.

"Yes, it is lovely, isn't it? I am sorry to be so . . ."

"There's no need." Impulsively, he covered her clasped hands with his own and imagined he felt her warmth through her gloves. "I understand. You're doing very well."

She looked at him then. Did he really understand? Could he really know what the loss of the children meant to her? The children and Claire had done much to ease the pain she'd always felt at her father's habitual aloofness, given her the love of family she so desperately wanted. Now Claire was gone, and soon the children would be, too.

"I wouldn't want the children to guess . . ."

"I'm sure they don't. You're a truly remarkable woman, Miss Simpson. I'm very glad to have met you."

His words should have cheered her. Sitting so close to him on the bench, hearing the last few birds of the season calling to each other as they gathered together for the trip south, watching the leaves begin to turn on the trees—all of this should have brought her peace.

Instead, she felt edgy and unsure, yearning for something just beyond her grasp. The imminent loss of the children was part of it, but certainly not all. She wanted them to have the love he so freely offered, the warmth that would enrich their lives. She knew too well the cruelty of indifference, having grown up with it herself.

As a child, she'd longed for greater love from her parents. As she'd grown, her wishes had changed. She'd wanted a family of her own—a husband and children. The death of Reed Townsend had put an end to those dreams, or so she had thought. Now she was no longer sure.

The feelings with which she'd awakened this morning taunted her mercilessly. Her love for Reed Townsend had been a girlish love, filled with shy glances and unfulfilled longings, but now she wanted more. She wanted to know a man's touch, to feel his lips on her skin, his hand at her breast.

And not just any man. She wanted this man beside her to look at her as though she mattered in his life, his eyes full of promise, his heart filled with love.

She had never thought she would feel this way, but John Worthington had reawakened her, brought unfamiliar feelings to life—warm, ticklish ones that swirled inside her in spirals of inchoate need. They were a woman's feelings, not a child's. Even now, his gloved hand lying on her own had the power to stir her deeply. She wanted to move closer to him. She wished she could unclasp her hands and turn them to hold his, instead.

She wished. . . .

He had turned his head to watch the children, a smile tugging at his lips. He was being so careful not to hurt her, she knew, yet he could not completely hide his joy at their acceptance of him. His dark hair gleamed in the bright morning sun and his eyes matched the cloudless sky.

His lashes were also dark—surprisingly so for a man with blue eyes. They were thick and lustrous, softening his hard-eyed stare when he was angry, as she well knew from the night before. His cheeks were cleanly sculpted, with high cheekbones, and their faint hollows gave him a lean and predatory look as he squinted against the sun.

He seemed to sense her scrutiny, for he suddenly looked at her, his gaze melding with her own. Caught unaware, she had no time to hide her thoughts. Flustered, she tried to move her hands from under his, to shake his hold on her, both emotional and physical.

She wanted to look away, but he wouldn't let her. His free hand barely grazed her cheek, but it was enough to still all movement.

"Don't," he whispered and his eyes seemed to darken, the pupils growing large as he stared into her eyes. Slowly, his head moved closer to hers. Her breath caught, then held.

"Uncle John! Uncle John! Come and see!" young Rebecca called out as she ran toward them. "Thomas has got a branch of leaves and the deer are all coming to eat at once. Come and look."

The moment shattered into splinters of glass, each one cutting her heart.

Four

*M*ary Margaret carefully pushed the needle in and out of her tapestry. John was sitting on the rocker across the parlor from her, idly glancing through the paper. She felt a certain pleasure in sharing the room with him, more so than she would have imagined a mere week ago. They'd even fallen quite naturally into calling each other by their given names, neither asking the other's permission.

"It's nice to finally have some peace and quiet," John said into the silence.

"Yes, it is. Since your arrival, we seem to be getting many more visitors coming to pay their respects. Tonight we had a considerable crowd."

"I think more of them are coming out of curiosity than real sympathy."

Mary Margaret caught the note of bitterness underlying his cynicism. She placed the next stitch in the intricate leaf design she was embroidering, then said, "You've been handling things very well, considering."

"You mean, considering the way I behaved when we first met?"

"No, of course not," she answered, flustered, and felt

the warmth of a blush creep up her neck. Then she looked up and saw the amusement on his face.

Their eyes met, and for a moment, her breathing stopped. Then, just as quickly, they were both laughing, knowing there was some truth in his remark, despite her denial.

The laughter slowly died, leaving Mary Margaret with a heightened awareness of John. His eyes were intent on hers; his newspaper lay forgotten on his lap. Could he see the yearning in her eyes? Did he know that beneath her proper manners and calm exterior she longed for him to . . . what?

His gaze moved down her cheeks and lingered on her lips. She was tempted to moisten them with her tongue— they felt suddenly dry—but she feared the action would be too revealing. Though there had been no repeat of the events on the park bench, sometimes, like now, she wished there was more between them.

At night, her dream continued to visit her, growing more elaborate each time. She would wake to find her pillow cradled in her arms, her head snuggled against it as if she had been lying in a lover's embrace. The more intense her dreams grew, the tighter the control she placed on her emotions during the day.

"Thomas and Rebecca have grown very fond of you," she said to break the spell he'd cast. "You must be pleased." She quickly took another stitch, using her sewing as an excuse to look away from him. Later, she would have to undo all her mistakes.

"Pleased and relieved. I've grown very fond of them, too."

"I noticed. You manage them so well—almost as if you know what they're thinking. That's a real talent. They feel comfortable with you, like they've known you far longer than just this week."

She was telling him no less than the truth. Thomas and Rebecca had wholeheartedly taken to their uncle. Mary Margaret was the only one who felt lonelier and lonelier as each passing day brought the time of their departure nearer. Soon she would have only her writing to keep her company. She would need something more, perhaps a bigger project on which to focus her energies, to keep her from noticing the empty places in her heart.

"I feel more comfortable with them, too," John said. "I know it sounds odd, but at first I was unsure what to say to them, how to treat them. Now I realize they're just like real people."

His tone was earnest, and Mary Margaret knew he really had been worried. She shouldn't have been so surprised. After all, what opportunities had he had to deal with children as a bachelor?

"They are real people," she corrected with a laugh.

Her laugh was light and silvery, inviting him to join in with her. There was no mocking superiority in her glance, only genuine understanding and empathy. Worth smiled sheepishly, feeling amazingly at ease with her. He couldn't remember so enjoying a woman's undemanding company before, laughing so easily, talking about anything he pleased without worrying about what the other person was thinking of him.

They were almost like an old married couple. Except that if they were, he'd be sitting by her side right now, loosening his tie and collar as they exchanged tidbits of information about their respective day's activities. He'd be reaching over to gently finger the softly curling tendrils of hair along her nape, and then he'd . . .

He rocked forward in his chair. What was he thinking of? He could no longer deny it, at least to himself: thoughts of Mary Margaret had been tantalizing him ever since their near kiss on the Common. Could similar thoughts be haunting her? He thought it possible. Sometimes, when he unexpectedly caught her watching him, her hazel eyes glowed with highlights, like a green fire burning. He smiled to himself and eased the rocker back, enjoying his daydreams.

"Have you given any thought to how you will care for Thomas and Rebecca in Wyoming?" she asked conversationally, a few moments later.

"No, I'm afraid I've been more concerned with getting along with them here in Boston than with what will happen later on," he answered honestly. "Do you have any suggestions?" He was pleased at her interest.

"Well, I worry about their schooling. Thomas, especially, has to be handled carefully. Do you know someone in Cheyenne who could teach them?"

Suddenly, reality struck Worth straight on. He remembered Lucy, waiting for him at home in Wyoming. She had trained to be a teacher and had offered to help him when he brought the children home. Though he'd made no commitment to her, he felt her presence here in this room, cutting short his fantasies about Mary Margaret.

And how realistic were his fantasies, anyway? Where would Mary Margaret fit in his life? Here, she was surrounded by family and friends. Why should she want to leave? He had little to offer a well-bred lady from the East except possibilities. And who could predict the direction those possibilities would take?

"Yes, I do know someone who could care for them . . . and teach them their lessons, too," he answered slowly, reluctant now to pursue the topic she had introduced. "But there's still time to worry about all that, don't you think?"

"Why, yes," she answered, and he saw she looked relieved.

They lapsed into another silence naturally, each consumed by his own thoughts. A faint smile played across Mary Margaret's lips, and Worth was glad she didn't guess the turmoil in his mind.

He knew he had to move slowly right now. His first priority was to take care of the children, to make them feel secure again, as well as loved. Only then could he worry about his own needs.

Still, he was glad he would be staying in Boston for a while longer. He needed the time as much as the children. They had formed a strong bond with him already, but what really made him want to linger was Mary Margaret.

She was far more complex than he had realized when he'd first discovered who she was. He had thought her a poor relative living off her wealthier kin when he had read of her in Henry's letters. Then, when he'd met her, he'd seen her as a prim and proper spinster, taking out her frustrations on him simply because he was a man.

Now he knew better. Her cool exterior hid smoldering embers—embers that had briefly flared to life under his touch and now simmered just out of his reach. The changing green and gold patterns in her eyes drew him like the proverbial moth, and even now, he couldn't keep himself from looking at her. He squinted against the light from the gas fixture that haloed her head from behind. What color were her eyes tonight?

"Aunt Mary! Aunt Mary, are you here?" The parlor door burst open to reveal a frantic Thomas, winded and pale.

Mary Margaret sprang from the settee, her embroidery falling unnoticed to the Persian carpet as she hurried to the boy. "What happened? Why aren't you in bed? Are you ill?"

Her hand automatically went to Thomas's forehead, and he suffered her attention without pulling away. "No, no," he cried, desperation giving a high edge to his voice. "I'm fine, but . . ."

He stopped to take a breath. "I heard something," he whispered. "I didn't mean to, but . . ." He paused and glanced over his shoulder at his uncle.

Mary Margaret understood at once that Thomas had overheard a conversation and had come away panicked. It seemed to be a family trait. "Is this something private?"

She needed to know whether he was afraid of John Worthington or simply embarrassed about his eavesdropping.

"No. He needs to know, too. What should I do?" Thomas was still whispering, and she could feel him trembling in her arms. She looked into John's face and saw only concern for the boy.

"Come sit by me and tell us what you heard." She put her arm around Thomas's shoulders and guided him back to the red settee.

"It's Grandmother Townsend. She's gone to a lawyer, and they're going to take us away from Uncle John."

"What?" Mary Margaret felt a sinking feeling in her

stomach—a cold lump of dread that sent a shiver through her.

"How do you know this, Tom?" John asked, his calm voice soothing, lessening the tension in the room.

"I heard her talking to Grandfather Townsend just now. I didn't listen on purpose, Aunt Mary," he put in apologetically. "They thought I had gone upstairs to bed, but I lost my whistle and had to go find it. It must have fallen out of my pocket. I didn't want to lose it—it's the one my father gave me just before . . ."

His voice trailed off, and Mary Margaret hastened to reassure him. "That's all right, Thomas. Just tell us what you heard."

Now was not the moment to discipline him, especially if he had correctly interpreted what he'd overheard.

"Grandmother said the lawyer, Mr. Hargrove, told her they had a good chance of overturning the will. He says he can get the papers put together within the week and get them to a judge right away."

"How can you be sure she was talking about your father's will?" John asked, coming across the room to join them.

"She said so."

"Can you be more specific? What did she say?" he pressed the boy, putting his hand on Thomas's shoulder.

Thomas looked to Mary Margaret, as if asking for guidance. She gave a quick glance up at John and decided he would be understanding about whatever Thomas had to say.

"Go ahead, Thomas. Tell us what you heard," she encouraged. "Make sure you get things exactly right."

Thomas sighed and stared at the rug. "She said Mr. Hargrove agreed with her that no court in the land would agree to let a man of Uncle John's low character keep custody of Rebecca and me. She called Uncle John all sorts of names—" He stopped and looked at Mary Margaret. She shook her head, telling him he could skip over these details without worrying.

Her gaze settled on John. She had never seen him look so fierce. The combination of anger at the Townsends and compassion for the boy mingling with his own pain wrenched her heart.

"What do you want, Thomas?" Worth asked, his voice suddenly hoarse as he realized the moment of decision was upon them all, like it or not.

"I don't understand, sir." Thomas looked to Mary Margaret and then back at Worth.

"Do you want to stay here? In Boston?" Worth clarified.

"With you?"

"No, not with me. With your grandparents, here in this house."

"I don't know, sir." His voice stayed low as he continued, "I don't think so." He stared again at the carpet.

. "Would you like to come with me to Wyoming?"

Worth held his breath as he waited for the answer. He dared not look at Mary Margaret. He was destroying her world, piece by piece, yet he could not turn back.

"To your ranch?" The boy's voice held a touch of excitement, but Worth would not lie to him.

"Sometimes. You would have to go to school, though. I own a house in Cheyenne. We'd spend a good part of the year there. I also have my law practice to attend to."

He did not miss Mary Margaret's surprise at his last comment. He had inadvertently inflicted another wound by not revealing more of himself to her. "I thought it best to keep some of my cards out of sight once I saw how things were going here. I meant to tell you before, but everything's been so hectic. . . ."

She nodded her understanding. At least, he hoped she understood.

"Well, Thomas," he said, turning his attention back to the boy. "Have you made up your mind?"

"I'm not real fond of school," Thomas said, consideringly. "But . . . could I have my own horse?"

Worth heard Mary Margaret's sharply drawn breath and knew he had won. He let himself sneak a peek at her. She sat rigid, her eyes closed, her face pale. Her hands were knotted together in her lap; her tight grip made her knuckles white. He hated what he was doing to her, but there was no alternative.

"Yes, Tom, you could. But . . ."

Without waiting to hear more, Thomas flung himself into Worth's arms.

Worth enfolded the boy in his embrace as he watched Mary Margaret. She sat very still, then slowly opened her eyes.

"We'll have to move quickly. I imagine you'll want to leave right away," she said quietly, with a good deal more calm than Worth had expected. He had never admired her more than at this moment.

"Yes, I think we'd better. Henry's lawyer can handle the rest of the estate details without me."

"In that case, Thomas, you'd better get to bed. Tomorrow will be a long day. I'll be up in a minute to tuck you in." Mary Margaret stood and held out her arm to Thomas.

He ran across the room to her and hugged her around the waist. "You be good, now, you hear me, and don't tell anyone what we talked about. All right?" she murmured near his ear.

"All right, Aunt Mary. I won't say a word," he promised.

As soon as Thomas had left the room, Mary Margaret turned to Worth. She was still pale, and her eyes glittered with unshed tears. He started to apologize, but she held up her hand, stopping him.

"Don't say anything, please. We both know this is the only way. Fortunately, Aunt Hester and Uncle William are leaving on a trip tomorrow. That will make it easier for you. I'll have Kathleen get their things ready. If you'll excuse me now, I'll see you in the morning." She turned away just as the first tear trailed down her cheek. Worth cursed silently. He had never intended to cause her such pain.

Mary Margaret carefully cleaned the nib of her pen and replaced it on the inkstand. She arranged the pages of her proposal in proper order and placed them inside the leather binder for safekeeping. Tomorrow she would take everything over to Garth Devereaux, her agent and friend. If he was successful in selling her story idea to the paper, she would soon be off on adventures of her own, writing about life along the transcontinental railroad. It would be a major and daring step in her career—exactly what she needed to fend off her feelings of loss.

She had always wanted to travel, to see how other people lived, to experience the freedom of the West. Boston, with its rigid social conventions, had little use or respect for a woman like herself: single and no longer a desirable marriage prospect, no matter how attractive she might be. Here, she lacked the two essentials—a fortune and a good name.

Though she was by no means poor, neither did she have unlimited wealth. And with her parents' deaths, she'd slipped into the uncomfortable category of single female relative, a role she disdained, preferring to make her own way in the world. As to her birth . . . well, it was never spoken of with her father present. Her questions as a child had been hurriedly turned aside, her mother worriedly chewing on her lower lip as she sought to distract her daughter. Her birthdays had been a time of tension, her father walking around tight-lipped and grim, her mother fluttering around him, apology written all over her face. Yet nothing had been said—at least, not to her.

The warmth and love she had craved had come from Reed and Claire. And when Claire's older brother had died, Henry Clay had welcomed Mary Margaret into his household—not as a burden or duty, but as an honored member of the family and his wife's dearest friend. Now Henry Clay and Claire were gone, and soon their children would be out of her life, too.

She had thought she'd have more time with the children, and with John Worthington, but after the conversation Thomas had overheard between the Townsends last night, her whole life was changing again. Before the morning was over, John, Thomas, and Rebecca would be on a train heading for Cheyenne, and she'd be waving good-bye to them from the train depot. So much for her dreams. Perhaps if they had had more time together, new dreams might have been forged.

Mary Margaret felt the sting of tears and fought to control them. She'd been up most of the night, unable to sleep, trying to cope with this latest turn of events. She wanted to be in control when she saw the children again. They needed her full support in this move. Any emotional display on her part could well damage all the hard work John had done in gaining their affection and respect.

Hearing a wagon rattle down the back alley, Mary Margaret peered through the murky light of dawn outside her window to the delivery entrance below. The vegetable man was unloading the day's supplies of fruits and the like to Cook. She checked the time on her lapel watch—half past six. She'd go down to breakfast soon but stay in the kitchen until the Townsends left. Then there would be no chance of accidentally disclosing the plans.

What a stroke of luck, Aunt Hester and Uncle William deciding they could leave on this trip. They were so confident their secret plans regarding the children were well in hand, it never occurred to them to think they'd been discovered. With their absence, Mary Margaret would have time to find new lodgings. She had already sent Garth a note asking him to work on it.

Even though she hadn't been at the Townsends' home long, she had settled in. Any sweet memories she had of John Worthington were associated with this house. The thought of him as just a sweet memory hurt so much. She'd come to feel more for him than she had for any man, and now he was going and taking with him the only family she had ever cared for.

A knock at the door interrupted her sad thoughts, and Mary Margaret pushed them to the side. She still had several hours with the children and she would make the most of them.

"Come in," she called as she pulled her emotions into line.

"Miss, what are you doing up so early—and all dressed and ready for the day, too?" Kathleen asked, closing the door with her free hand. The Irish maid had come to the Townsends from Claire's home; she had been one of the few servants not immediately let go.

"Kathleen, how nice to see you!" Mary Margaret looked

appreciatively at the breakfast tray Kathleen was carrying. "You shouldn't have brought the tea all the way up here— you have so much to do. But I must say, I'm glad you did. I need something to distract me this morning."

"I thought you'd prefer not seeing the master and mistress before they set off on their holiday," Kathleen said, placing the tray on the cleared desk.

"You're probably right. We're lucky the governor invited them out to his country home for a few days. Come, sit down for a moment."

"I was surprised to hear they had accepted," Kathleen commented as she settled in her usual seat on the side of the bed. She took up her own cup of tea, as she always did on the mornings she came to Mary Margaret's quarters.

"So was I," Mary Margaret concurred. "But Aunt Hester has been complaining about their restricted social life lately, and the governor was quite insistent—he claimed he was concerned about their state of mind. I think they are more than happy for the excuse to take a few days away from the 'hustle and bustle of city life,' as Aunt Hester put it." Mary Margaret knew her tone had become quite acid, but she considered Kathleen a friend.

She took a sip of her scalding tea and waited a moment to let its comforting warmth spread through her. "I guess we should look on the bright side. It might have been difficult smuggling the children out with Aunt Hester and Uncle William around. Have the children gotten up?"

"Yes, miss. They've had their wash and are ready for breakfast. I've told them they must be extra quiet this morning, what with all that'll be goin' on. Mr. John said he'd look in on them when it was time ta go downstairs."

They sat quietly, each sipping her tea. Mary Margaret sensed that Kathleen had something on her mind. The maid appeared edgy and nervous, but did not seem ready to talk about whatever was bothering her.

"How is the packing going?" Mary Margaret asked to keep the silence from becoming oppressive.

"It's fair done, miss. Only a few odds and ends from the morning need to be put away. Oh, I also heard Paddy had been called to fetch the carriage, so the master and mistress should be on their way before long."

Mary Margaret would heave a sigh of relief when Aunt Hester and Uncle William were gone. She knew what she was doing was right. The Townsends were not fit to care for the children, as she'd witnessed on more than one occasion. The children needed love; the Townsends offered duty.

Mary Margaret knew from her own experience how a misplaced sense of duty could destroy a child's fragile trust in the goodness of the world and his rightful place in it. Not only did John Worthington have legal custody of her cousins, but he loved them, too. In Mary Margaret's mind, that overrode her dislike of sneaking behind people's backs—even the Townsends'.

"Kathleen, I can't begin to thank you for all you've done," Mary Margaret said, placing her cup gently on its saucer.

"I've done no more than any good Christian woman would have. Seeing those poor little babies here with the mistress was enough to make my blood run cold. It's far and away a better thing for them to go with their uncle. He loves them, that's for sure, and they feel the same way about him, though I fear the final parting between you and them."

Kathleen's words sent a chill down Mary Margaret's spine. To hear her own concerns finally voiced made them even more real. She shuddered and swallowed the lump forming in her throat. The children would soon be gone, and so would John.

A touch on her arm brought Mary Margaret out of her thoughts.

"Miss?" Kathleen stood and moved to the desk. Her voice was tentative as she twisted the cotton of her apron with nervous hands.

"Yes, Kathleen. Is something wrong?"

"You've been so good ta me. If you hadna worked with me on my writing and reading, giving me a reason ta keep going, ta make something of myself..." Kathleen's voice faded and tears gathered in her eyes.

"I enjoy helping you with your studies. You've made me very proud of you."

"And now I feel . . . Oh, miss, Mr. John has asked me if I'd like ta go along ta the Wyoming Territory with the children. You know I've been a-talkin' ta him about the ways out there, and it seems just the place I could make something of my life. He asked me last night. At first I was scared, remembering how hard it was, coming over from Ireland all alone. But this time, I'd be goin' with the children and Mr. John. Do ya think I'm bein' foolish ta want ta go and all?"

Mary Margaret was overwhelmed by Kathleen's speech. She had imagined herself being in the place Kathleen was right now—going West with John, Thomas, and Rebecca —but she knew in the end it could not be.

She felt a twinge of jealousy, but firmly pushed the emotion away. This was Kathleen's chance to move up in the world, to get out of the kitchens and maid's quarters of the spoiled rich and make a new life for herself. And Mary Margaret would have the assurance of knowing Thomas and Rebecca would be well cared for.

Mary Margaret rose, walked over to Kathleen, and put her arm around the younger girl's shoulders. "Why, Kathleen, I think it's a wonderful idea. This would be a real chance for you. And my mind would be at ease, too, knowing you would be watching over Thomas and Rebecca. But you must promise me you'll keep up with your studies."

"I promise, miss. And I'll be ever so watchful of the children."

After giving the young woman a hug, Mary Margaret walked with her to the door. "You have a lot to do before the train leaves—you'd better hurry."

Kathleen nodded her agreement and left the room, taking the tea tray with her. Mary Margaret turned and quickly dabbed at her eyes. She would not cry—not now. She would have plenty of time for that later.

The wind whipped along the platform of the train station, and Mary Margaret fought to hold her skirts in place.

John had taken the children inside the station to look over what the vendors had to offer. They had gotten restless, and he had hoped some new toys might lessen their tension.

Mary Margaret glanced at the bare trees lining the farthest track. Only yesterday the skies had been alive with the clear blue of Indian summer. Today, winter had arrived with a vengeance. The clouds overhead matched her mood —gray and depressed. The children, Kathleen, and John were leaving on the nine-thirty for Kansas City, and she was staying behind.

Mary Margaret pulled her hands inside her cape to warm them and watched Kathleen hurry over from the station house, threading her way through the departing passengers. She carried a hamper of food for the trip. John had told them to pack as much as possible, since the food along the rail line was boring, at best.

"Oh, miss. This is happening so fast."

Too fast, Mary Margaret thought. Within twelve hours' time, everything she held dear was disappearing. She would still have her writing, but would it be enough? Even her friend Kathleen was leaving. She could see the tears forming in the girl's eyes already. Mary Margaret knew she would have to be the strong one, but it was so hard.

"This will be a new adventure for you. You'll see the West and Indians and everything we read about in your study books. You'll have a new position, too—housekeeper. Can you imagine Mrs. Barnes's face when she hears you've gotten a position similar to hers?"

Kathleen laughed, as she was meant to. "She was always telling me I'd make no good of my life, saying I spent too much time with my nose in a book and not enough time with it to the grindstone." Suddenly, Kathleen's smile dimmed. "Where will you be a-goin now that we're leaving?"

"You mustn't worry about me. No matter what you've heard Aunt Hester say, I do have money of my own— more than enough to get by—and a friend is arranging lodgings for me. I'll be starting a new life, just like you and the children." Mary Margaret could hear the false ring beneath her encouraging words. A new life without the children? *Without John?* echoed a small voice in her head, and the pain in her heart quickened. What kind of a new and happy life would that be?

Mary Margaret shook her head, determined to keep her spirits up, at least until the train left the station. "You'll write me letters and let me know how the children are doing? Here, I'll give you the address of my friend. He'll relay all my mail to me, no matter where I am."

"You know I'll write you, miss. I'll keep you up on the news of the children." Kathleen stopped. "There is one thing I'm worried over—those papers you gave me for Thomas, to help him with his schoolwork."

Mary Margaret gave Kathleen's arm a reassuring squeeze. "I'm sure they'll have a good teacher out in Cheyenne. Mr. Worthington would never allow the children's lessons to lapse. Just give the notes to Thomas's teacher, and she should be able to use what I've written out to help him with his reading problem. And don't worry so. Mr. Worthington loves the children very much, and I'm sure he will do everything in his power to help them adjust to their new home."

Mary Margaret's voice was strong and sure. She had no doubt John Worthington would love and care for Thomas and Rebecca. She was also firm in the belief he would do his best for them all. But was all this the best for her? Should she have gone against convention and asked to go with them to Wyoming? Would John have considered her too forward and demanding if she had suggested such a thing? But why should he want her to go? She had nothing to offer. He had Kathleen to care for the children and there were good teachers in Cheyenne. She'd have no place or position in his life. Of course, she'd never know for sure now. Her courage had failed, and she had never asked.

"Aunt Mary, Aunt Mary!" the children yelled in unison as they ran toward her. "Look what Uncle John bought us."

Their arms were full of treasures and their eyes brimmed with pleasure and happiness.

"My, my. Did Uncle John buy everything in the store?"

Mary Margaret asked, bending to take some of the slipping parcels from the little girl's arms.

Rebecca took Mary Margaret's question quite seriously. "No, he only bought one of each. He left lots of things for the other children."

"I'm sure he did." Mary Margaret's eyes met Worth's over Rebecca's shoulder. Even though the sun wasn't shining, his hair gleamed with golden highlights. He looked smart and dashing in his dark-brown traveling coat and trousers. His eyes were gentle with concern as he searched her face.

"I promise—I only bought one of each. Don't reprimand me for spoiling the children."

"I would never..."

"I was teasing, Maggie."

Maggie? He had never called her Maggie before. She found she liked the sound of it on his lips and felt the heat of a blush color her cheeks.

"Her name is Aunt Mary." Rebecca pulled on Worth's traveling coat. "Don't you know her name?"

Worth bent down on one knee in front of the child. "Of course, I know her name. But everyone needs a nickname. Aren't you sometimes called Becky?"

The little girl nodded her head.

"And isn't your brother called Tom?"

Again the child solemnly nodded in the affirmative.

"Well, your aunt should have a nickname, too. And I think Maggie is perfect."

Since Uncle John could do nothing wrong in his niece's eyes, Rebecca immediately agreed. "Yes, we'll call you Aunt Maggie for always."

"For always." The words swirled in Mary Margaret's head. For always would be the few minutes they had left before the train pulled away. Tears formed in her eyes as she looked at her precious children.

"Yes, I like Aunt Maggie, too," Thomas said after some thought. "I'll be Tom. Rebecca will be Becky. Uncle John, what will you be?"

"Out in Wyoming I'm called Worth."

"Then you'll be Uncle Worth, and Aunt Mary can now

be Maggie. But what about Kathleen? Shouldn't she have a nickname, too?"

While the children huddled with Kathleen to decide on her nickname, Worth pulled Mary Margaret to the side.

"I'm sorry if I embarrassed you. I never meant to. The name slipped out and . . ."

Mary Margaret laid her hand on his arm. "You didn't embarrass me. Besides, the children seem quite taken with the idea." She couldn't tell him she was quite taken with it, too.

"I've often thought of you as Maggie in the past days—Maggie with the laughing eyes, Maggie with the glowing hair." Worth was saying more than he had ever intended—more than he should be saying at the side of the train that would be taking him away. But the words kept coming. "You've come to mean . . ."

Worth's words were interrupted by the call of the porter, the signal for all to board the train. Maybe it was for the best. What would be the point of such a speech at this late date? He and the children were going to Wyoming and Maggie was staying here in Boston. There would be no point at all.

Mary Margaret's heart was still aflutter from Worth's impassioned words when the porter's shout made it stop beating. Time for them to leave already?

"Children, give your Aunt Maggie a hug good-bye. We'd best board now," Kathleen said as she ushered the children over to their aunt. She took the remaining parcels from Mary Margaret's unresisting fingers.

Mary Margaret dropped to her knees and gathered both Thomas and Rebecca close. "Promise me you'll be good for Uncle Worth and Kathleen? That you'll study hard? And that you'll write me and tell me all about your wonderful new home and all the marvelous things you'll be doing?"

"We promise," the children replied together, their voices laced with tears.

Easing the children back, Mary Margaret looked into their faces. "I love you both very much, and I always will. Don't ever forget that."

"Board. Board. Last call for the train leaving for..."
The porter's voice faded as he walked down the platform.

"Kathleen, why don't you take the children on the train
and get them settled?" Worth suggested as more and more
people hurried past.

Kathleen nodded. Giving Mary Margaret a quick hug,
she steered the children toward the closest car.

Mary Margaret watched the children until they disappeared inside the train. Frantically, she searched her purse
for a handkerchief, but before she could find it, a clean,
white linen square was pressed into her hand. She swiftly
dabbed at her eyes and glanced around to assure herself no
one had seen her tears.

Gently, Worth grasped her shoulders and turned her to
face him. "I'll take good care of them. Don't worry.
They'll have all the best. I promise."

"I know you will and I know they'll be much better off
with you than with Aunt Hester and Uncle William. I'm
just going to miss them so much. They've been such a big
part of my life." She could feel the tears starting up again,
but there was nothing she could do to stop them.

The tears coursing down Mary Margaret's cheeks were
Worth's undoing. He pulled her to his chest and held her
tightly against him. His hands moved up and down her
back to comfort her. She felt fragile and womanly. A
heightened awareness of her flooded him, engulfing his
senses, and he wanted nothing more than to stay like this
forever.

"Oh, Maggie! What am I going to do about you?" he
whispered raggedly.

Mary Margaret looked up when he spoke and before she
could say a word, Worth's lips closed over hers.

The kiss was all she had ever dreamed of, holding
warmth and longing, passion and surprise. Her lips tasted
him and his flavor was sweet and exciting. When his
tongue gently traced her bottom lip, she gasped, allowing
him entrance. The feel of his tongue against hers sent spiraling waves of desire through her body and she leaned
more heavily into him.

She heard his breath quicken and knew he, too, was

experiencing the same desire. She wanted the moment to go on forever.

A loud and sudden blast of steam from the train's engine pulled both Worth and Mary Margaret from the warm, living fantasy they had created, back to the cold, gray reality of the train station.

"Maggie, I have to leave."

"I know, Worth."

What else could she say? *Wait and I'll go with you.* He hadn't asked. *I'll give up my writing and follow you and the children west.* He knew nothing of her secret career. There was nothing left to say except . . . good-bye.

The tears continued to roll down Mary Margaret's cheeks as the train pulled out of the station.

Five

*M*ary Margaret pushed open the door to Garth Devereaux's office suite and let the brisk fall breeze blow her into the welcoming warmth of his waiting room. Barely twenty-four hours had passed since the departure of John Worthington and the children, but Mary Margaret wasted no time putting her plans into action. She hoped her agent had good news for her.

"Well, now, Miss Simpson, don't you look nice," greeted Garth's clerk, a young man of good family but poor means. The shadow of a crease in his trousers told Mary Margaret his clothes were store-bought, an economy measure much frowned upon in the Townsends' social circle.

"Good morning, Mr. Johnson. I'm afraid I'm a bit early for my appointment with Mr. Devereaux. I hope it's not inconvenient." Mary Margaret rubbed her hands together to warm them. The bone-chilling cold had penetrated her thin leather gloves.

"Not at all, Miss Simpson. I'll just let him know you're here. Please, have a seat by the stove and warm yourself. Can I offer you a cup of tea?"

Mary Margaret declined, having finished her breakfast

only a short while before. The young clerk took his leave to inform Garth she had arrived.

Within minutes, he returned and escorted her into Garth's inner sanctum, closing the door behind her as he left the room. Garth was dressed impeccably, as always, the quintessential Boston businessman. Not a hair was out of place; his shirt and collar were stiffly starched and bleached a startling shade of white; his cravat was knotted to perfection. He stood to greet her.

"Why, Mr. Simms, how refreshingly lovely you look today," Garth said, smiling mischievously down at her from his unusual height.

"You're so gallant, Mr. Devereaux," Mary Margaret said, with a demure curtsy. Then she spoiled the effect by grinning up at him. "So, how is M. M. Simms faring this week?"

"The usual. Most of the letters are from irate gentlemen demanding you be dismissed immediately for your pig-headed gall. But I think you'll be especially pleased with these." He reached into one of the small drawers in his large Chippendale secretary, a family heirloom that had once belonged to his grandfather, and retrieved a stack of envelopes. "Here," he said, handing her the pile.

Mary Margaret sat in one of the two armchairs before the fireplace and slipped off her gloves. The conveniently placed fire screen kept the worst of the heat off her face while allowing her to bask in the fire's warmth.

Curious, she picked up the first envelope in the pile. The handwriting was fine and delicate—a woman's!

Quickly, she scanned the rest of the pile. "All from women?" she asked.

"Yes," Garth confirmed.

"Have you read them?"

"Only a few. Mr. Johnson culled these from the rest of the mail, thinking you might wish to answer them yourself. The more vituperative ones got the usual form reply."

Mary Margaret couldn't resist. "Do you mind?" she asked as she pulled a letter from its envelope.

"No. Go ahead." Garth lowered his lean length into the opposite chair and sat watching her, a smile on his face.

Mary Margaret eagerly read the first few letters, then leaned back and caught the appreciative expression on Garth's face. His brown eyes were warm, his interest frank but not aggressive. He would wait for a signal from her before making a move. Sadly, she realized she would now never give him that signal.

For a moment, the image of blue eyes and dark, sun-kissed hair filled her vision, obliterating the brown and blond of the face before her. Mentally giving herself a shake, Mary Margaret said, "These are wonderful. I'm so glad you showed them to me. You see, it's just as I told you. The ladies are ready for a change. It isn't just a few radical agitators making trouble. That's why I want to do this new series so badly. Have you had any luck arranging my trip?"

With a reluctant expression, Garth stood and walked to the fireplace. "Are you sure about this, Mary Margaret?" he asked, leaning one arm against the mantel and kicking idly at the hearth with one well-shod foot. "This whole plan seems rather sudden to me."

Mary Margaret also stood, refusing to give Garth more of an advantage than his six-foot-some frame already gave him.

"Yes, I'm sure. Times are changing. The West is much more civilized now. Why, from what I've heard, Cheyenne is more cultured than New York City or even Philadelphia." She didn't tell him how she had learned this information, but once again, Worth's face shimmered before her eyes. Feeling herself blush, she turned away from Garth, pretending an interest in the still life hanging on the wall.

"And Chicago may be rough and ready, but it's not without the amenities," she added persuasively. "The railroads are changing the face of this country." She turned once more to face him. "I want to investigate that change, to see firsthand what the future holds."

Garth must have comprehended her determination, for he made no more objections. He merely gave a resigned sigh and said, "I know there's no arguing with you when you've got your mind set on something. Come on over to the desk and I'll show you what I have so far."

At that moment, Mary Margaret appreciated just how good a friend she had in Garth Devereaux. He didn't question her motives or point out her limitations for being a mere female. He simply accepted her word at face value and did what he could to help her.

Pulling a leather folder from a bottom drawer, Garth motioned Mary Margaret to the chair by the desk. "Here's a tentative itinerary I've worked out for you." He handed her a piece of paper containing a list of railroad lines, stopping points, dates, and schedules.

"I've also arranged for you to write a variety of articles. Of course, everyone expects M. M. Simms to concentrate on the political issues. That part was easy to set up. With all the stories filtering back here, the papers are more than eager to hear about the adventurous West."

"And the articles about the status of women?"

"They're harder to sell, you know. The suffrage press will be more than happy to print what you send."

"I know." She sighed, disappointed. "But that's preaching to the converted. I was hoping I could reach some more mainstream publications. All the railroads have flashy advertisements pointed directly at women. I just wish . . ."

"Well, don't give up hope. I've sent a couple of letters around. Some of the magazines are leery of making a commitment without first seeing what you write. They don't want to offend their readers. You just send me everything you have and let me worry about finding a buyer. The expense allowance you have for the M. M. Simms articles should be sufficient for the first leg of the trip. And I've also arranged for you to write some simple travel pieces."

She saw his eyes narrow as he looked at her, as if anticipating her objections. He knew she hated to write tourist articles, but this time she would surprise him.

"Sounds perfect," she said, her excitement building. She'd just skimmed the schedule he'd set up for her and one word had jumped out at her: Cheyenne. Not right away—the winter weather precluded visiting the Wyoming

Territory without a pressing reason—but come spring, she'd get to see the children again. And Kathleen. And John Worthington. Worth.

Mary Margaret descended from the hired carriage and once again hurried up the steps of the Georgian-style house on Beacon Hill. In the few days since she had left the Townsends', the house and yard had acquired a barren look, settling into the austerity of a Boston winter. A few dried-out brown leaves blew in a flurry around her feet as she pulled the bell.

Though common courtesy dictated leaving a calling card this morning before dropping by in the afternoon, Mary Margaret had decided to take her chances and simply appear unannounced. She wasn't looking forward to this meeting with Hester and William Townsend, but it had to be gotten through.

As usual, Sedgwick opened the door.

"Hello, Sedgwick," she said. "I'd like to see Aunt Hester and Uncle William, if they're in."

She knew they were; she'd taken pains to make sure of their presence this afternoon.

"Come in, miss. Let me see if they are still receiving guests," the butler replied stiffly.

Mary Margaret entered the foyer and sat on the very same bench she had indicated to Worth barely three weeks earlier. How she missed him and the children, though they'd only been gone a very few days. She had hoped the pain of loss would ease with time, but so far, not enough time had passed. She wondered if it ever would.

"This way, miss," Sedgwick said, breaking into her thoughts. He indicated the front parlor, slid the door open to let her pass, then closed it behind her.

"Well, are you pleased now?" Hester Townsend demanded by way of greeting. She stood in the middle of the room with her arms crossed in front of her ample bosom.

"Now, now, Hester. None of this is Mary Margaret's fault," William Townsend said from the side chair where he sat, a book lying open on his lap. "I'm sure you've heard of our loss, Mary Margaret. So uncivilized, those Worthingtons." He shook his head, his expression mirroring his dismay.

"Yes, Uncle William. I heard." Mary Margaret remained by the door.

"Of course she heard," Hester said crossly. "She was here, after all. We thought we could trust you to handle things, Mary Margaret. How could you let him get away with it—a worthless bounder like him!" Hester stomped across the room as she spoke, stopping in front of Mary Margaret and glaring up at her face.

"I beg your pardon, Aunt Hester," Mary Margaret answered calmly. "How did I let whom get away with what?"

"Don't play coy with me, young lady. You know very well we never anticipated his stealing away while our backs were turned."

"Really, Aunt Hester," Mary Margaret protested. "Mr. Worthington was hardly stealing away. And taking the children was well within his rights—at least, as I understood Henry Clay's will."

"Hummph," snorted Hester. "Shows how little you know about anything."

It was a sign of Hester's pique over the situation that she let down her company manners to such an extent, though Mary Margaret knew she was not considered real company. In any case, Mary Margaret let the charge pass, deciding this was not the time to blurt out just how much she, in fact, knew.

Hester turned her attention to William. "So, what are we going to do now?" she demanded.

"Do?" asked William, glancing worriedly in Mary Margaret's direction.

"About the children," Hester clarified, impatience giving her voice a harder edge than usual.

Mary Margaret took advantage of Hester's preoccupation to take a seat on the center ottoman, facing both of her relatives. She leaned back unobtrusively, curious to discover if they had more mischief planned.

"There's nothing we can do," William said, regretfully,

his gaze still pointedly on Mary Margaret. "I can't very well go out to Wyoming, now, can I?"

Hester seemed finally to pick up on his unspoken message, for she looked over her shoulder at Mary Margaret and her eyes grew dark with cunning.

She came over to the ottoman and sat close beside Mary Margaret. "So, tell me, Mary Margaret," she murmured, "what do you think his plans are now? Did he say anything before he left?"

Mary Margaret noticed Hester couldn't bring herself to even say Worth's name. "I don't know," she answered honestly.

"It's a terrible shame, what's happened here. After all, the children are family—our closest living relations. They should be with us, here, where they belong. Don't you agree?"

"Mr. Worthington is their family, too, you know." Mary Margaret felt bitter anger rise in her breast on Worth's behalf. Why couldn't they accept him? Didn't they realize their attitude was a good part of the reason Worth had returned to Wyoming?

"Only by marriage," Hester returned. "This is all Henry Clay's fault. If he hadn't married our Claire, none of this would have happened."

"If he hadn't married Claire, there wouldn't have been any children to discuss. In any case, the point is moot. The poor man is dead. Why can't you let him rest in peace?"

"Why, Mary Margaret, don't you take that tone with me! If you had been more astute about what was going on, you could have prevented this entire disaster. Don't you care about those children at all? Why, if it hadn't been for them, Henry Clay would never have taken you into his household. What would you have done, a single woman like yourself? Now it will be up to us to take care of you."

"Not hardly," Mary Margaret bit out. Hester had a way of sullying even the best of motives. Poor Henry Clay— how had he stood the constant barrage of disdain from his mother-in-law? Mary Margaret had to put some distance between herself and Hester before she lost her composure entirely.

She stood and moved away a couple of paces. "Actually, that's what I came to talk about," she announced loudly enough to grab William Townsend's attention from the depths of his book. "I'm leaving Boston for a while."

"What?" Hester exclaimed. "Where are you going?"

"Traveling."

Hester looked both relieved and annoyed. Mary Margaret understood that Hester's relief came from not having to provide for her "poor" relation, while the annoyance stemmed from the lost opportunity to have Mary Margaret at her beck and call.

"Will you be gone long?" William inquired.

"A few months, at least. I'll keep you informed as my plans became clearer. I have a small legacy from my father," Mary Margaret reminded him, having used this fiction before to keep her writing career secret. "I shan't be needing any financial support."

"Oh, yes, how fortunate for you." William smiled vaguely. He, too, seemed relieved, though Mary Margaret found his concerns petty. The Townsends were well known for their family wealth and rarely considered the fortunes of those beneath them. "Will you be leaving soon?" he tacked on.

"Tomorrow, actually. I came to say good-bye, at least for a while."

William shot a satisfied glance at his wife. "Have a good trip," he said, turning again to Mary Margaret.

"Yes, I will. Thank you."

Mary Margaret hastily made her escape. Her thoughts were troubled, and not because the Townsends weren't interested enough in her welfare to inquire about the details of her trip. She couldn't help but notice they seemed overly happy she would be gone.

Were they planning something she was not to know about? Should she warn Worth to be careful? She dismissed her concerns as plain foolishness, deciding she was merely looking for an excuse to contact him.

Seated again in the hired carriage, she felt a wave of intense longing break over her. The sooner she left on this trip, the better. She needed new memories to help mask the old; otherwise, she would be haunted forever by the image of two small faces and a pair of devastating blue eyes.

Worth's gaze moved around the table, stopping first on Becky and then passing on to Tom and Lucy. In the four months since he'd brought the children to Cheyenne, he'd made every effort to get home for lunch and share some extra time with them. He smiled to himself. He had definitely made the right decision in bringing them to Wyoming. He couldn't imagine his life without their cheerful chatter and loving hugs.

"It's true, isn't it, Uncle Worth?" Becky vied for his attention.

"What, darlin'?"

"That rabbits grow to four feet high out on the range. Bobby John Osborne says so. And you can live off 'em for a week, but they're tough and you gotta have a good sit-to-tion."

Bobby John was Becky's latest hero. She had latched on to the hired hand the last time they'd been out at the ranch and considered every word he uttered gospel.

"I think Bobby meant *constitution*. And the jackrabbits do get mighty big out in the wilds."

"Uncle Worth, you know no rabbit ain't gonna get as big as Becky says," Tom piped in.

"Thomas Henry, watch your language," Lucy admonished. "And we do not use the word ain't.

"Worth, you simply must not allow these children to consort with the cowboys out at your ranch. Every time they come home, it takes me days to rid their speech of vulgarities." Lucy sent him an appealing look.

"But, Uncle Worth, you said Bobby John knew every damn thing there was to know about Wyoming, and if he didn't know it, it wasn't worth knowing."

"Rebecca Townsend, you will not use that kind of language at the dinner table." Lucy's face was turning red and her voice rose an octave on the last word. She glared meaningfully at Becky and Tom, then turned her gaze back to Worth, her expression softening. "Worth, I hate to keep bringing this up, but I worry about the children. Surely you don't want to have two little heathens for a niece and nephew?"

Worth could barely hold in his laughter. To hear his own words, repeated verbatim by Becky, struck his funny bone, but he tried to control his mirth. From the outraged expression on Lucy's face, he could tell she was about to bust her bustle. You'd have thought the little girl had scandalized the whole town, not just said the word *damn*. Worth knew he was going to have to say something to Becky about the matter—Lucy obviously expected it.

"Becky, you mustn't use *that* word. You know it isn't the way polite people respond. Sometimes men use cusswords when they don't think, but that doesn't mean it's right. Let's make a deal: I'll try not to say it anymore and you don't either."

"All right, Uncle Worth," Becky said, her confusion evident, despite her willingness to go along with whatever he wanted.

"Talk about jackrabbits and the like shouldn't be mentioned at the dinner table, anyway," Lucy said, resuming her lecture on polite dinner conversation, her voice again at its normal pitch. "Thomas, why don't you tell your Uncle Worth what you did at school this morning."

"It's Tom," Worth heard Tom mutter as he pushed the caster holding the salt and pepper toward the boy. Thomas continued, in a louder voice, "Nothing much happened in school today. Same old stuff," he added, shaking some pepper on the few remaining pieces of chicken left on his plate.

"Yes, it did," Becky said, her cheeks flushed a pretty pink, excitement in her eyes. "Don't you remember? Mr. Cassen told you you'd better mind what was happening or you'd find yourself doing all the same work over again."

"Becky!" Tom bellowed, sending his little sister a resentful stare.

"Are you having trouble in school, Tom?" Worth asked. This was the first he'd heard about any problems with Tom's schoolwork.

"Nothing that I can't handle," Lucy answered for Tom, and then hurried on, "Now, why don't we have some of the

nice cornstarch pudding for dessert that I saw Kathleen
making this morning."

Lucy picked up the bell beside her plate and gave it a
small shake. Soon Kathleen was standing beside her, waiting for instructions.

"We're ready for our dessert now, Kathleen. It's cornstarch pudding with a circle of peach marmalade, isn't it?
We're looking forward to it. Rebecca, sit up straight and
stop wiggling. Proper young ladies always sit quietly."

"Lucy, if there's something about Tom's schoolwork . . ."
Worth began as Kathleen went back to the kitchen to get
the dessert.

"We have everything well in hand, don't we, Thomas?"
Lucy asked the young boy.

"Yes'm," Tom mumbled.

Worth looked into Lucy's light-blue eyes. He found her
acting more and more like Hester Townsend every day. He
knew she was just trying to please him, to show him how
grown-up she was. Still, her attitude bothered him.

"There's no need for you to worry yourself, Worth,"
Lucy said soothingly. "I'll handle the problems that arise
here at the house. I know you have *so* much to worry about
with your law practice and everything out at the ranch."

Ironically, her attempt to please him only irritated him
more. He wanted to know what was happening in his
house. After all, it was his home, and the children were his
main happiness. But such a discussion could not be held in
front of the young ones. He'd have to find a better time to
bring the subject up again.

At times like these, Worth wished Mary Margaret were
here. She'd know exactly how to handle the situation.
Even after four months, thoughts of Maggie swirled in his
mind every day and with regularity every night.

"Ah, here's Kathleen with the dessert." Worth smiled at
the girl as she placed a bowl of pudding on the plate before
him. "The luncheon was excellent, Kathleen. The chicken
and rice melted in our mouths."

"It's a recipe I got from the pastor's housekeeper. She
said 'twas his favorite." The young housekeeper blushed

prettily as she gathered up the dirty dishes from the side-board.

"Well, Reverend Leisch is a lucky man, too, if Mrs. Cassidy cooks as well as you do. Don't you agree, Lucy?" He looked in Lucy's direction, but she kept her eyes trained on the children.

"Yes, of course. Come along, children. Finish your pudding. You mustn't be late for your return to school. Didn't you say you had a client coming at one o'clock, Worth?"

Pulling his watch from his vest pocket, Worth checked the time. Lucy was right—if he didn't hurry, he'd be late for his meeting.

He popped the last scoop of pudding in his mouth and hastily wiped his lips. "I won't be home till six tonight, but you don't have to stay, Lucy. Kathleen and I can manage the children."

"Oh, I don't mind."

"But I do. Your father will have my hide for keeping you from his company. I know he misses you, so run along home by four."

Walking around the table, Worth dropped kisses on the tops of the two children's heads. "And you two have a good afternoon at school. Try not to get into any trouble." Worth gave Tom's shoulder a squeeze as he spoke the last words. He nodded good-bye to Kathleen and Lucy and headed out the front door.

"Thomas, how many times have I told you you mustn't bother your uncle with the trivial problems you have at school," Lucy demanded as soon as Worth was out of earshot.

"But, I didn't. Becky..."

"I will not have your uncle worrying about your schoolwork when all that needs to be done is for you to work harder. If you didn't dally, you'd have no problems. I really don't know what's to become of you."

"Miss? What about those papers I gave you from Miss Mary Margaret? She'd said they'd help Thomas and..."

"I have my own teaching methods, Kathleen," Lucy replied, dismissing her comments. "I expect much better work from you, Thomas, or you'll find yourself copying the first ten pages of the dictionary. Do I make myself clear?"

"Yes'm."

"That should be 'Yes, Miss Lucy.'" She glared at him, waiting for his response.

"Yes, Miss Lucy." Thomas's head was bowed and his chin was tucked into his shirt collar.

"Very well, the two of you run off to school, and I'll see you at three o'clock. Hurry now, so you aren't late. I don't need to hear another bad report today." Lucy placed her napkin on the table and headed to the front parlor. "Kathleen, make sure they're cleaned up before they go."

Kathleen smiled at the two children. "Come on, you two little leprechauns. Let's see ta those faces."

"Kathleen, I'm sorry," Tom said, raising his face for inspection, his voice heavy.

Kathleen wiped away the trace of tears that ran down his face. "There's nothing ta be sorry for. Are ya doin the best ya can?"

"Yes'm," he sniffed.

"Then, there's nothing more we can ask of ya, till we find a way of using Miss Mary Margaret's papers."

"I miss Aunt Maggie," Becky said, her lower lip beginning to tremble.

"And I did much better when Aunt Maggie taught me."

"I know ya did, and we'll find a way. Now, neither one of you worry," she said, helping them on with their coats. "And don't forget to smile. You'll feel better for it," she encouraged.

After seeing that both children were headed back to school, Kathleen ran to her room and found the yellowed and many-times-folded piece of paper she needed.

Grabbing her coat and bonnet, she tucked her purse in the pocket of her dress and headed for the telegraph office, the address of Garth Devereaux clutched in her hand.

Back in his office, Worth tried to keep his mind on his client's problems, but thoughts of Mary Margaret kept distracting him. He would have considered four months to be more than enough time for her image to fade, for the unfulfilled ache inside him to subside or find a different outlet. But such was not the case.

He could remember entire conversations they'd had as if they had occurred yesterday. He could close his eyes and see her face in every detail: from the red highlights in her brown hair to her stubbornly rounded chin, from the sparkling hazel eyes with the hidden fire burning inside to the smile that reached straight into his soul.

Though Lucy tried to fill the emptiness in his life, her youthful eagerness could not compare to his memories of Maggie. He could see the growing strain in Lucy's face as the days passed and he did not respond to her womanly overtures. She did not understand his withdrawal, and he could not explain it to her. Not only was she his best friend's daughter, but now, somehow, his heart was no longer unfettered.

The children also felt Maggie's loss. He knew Lucy was determined to hide the details of their lives from him, thinking she was protecting him from undue bother. But the truth was, he wanted to be bothered. He wanted to be a part of their lives and make them part of his.

But every time he tried to talk to Lucy, her face became pinched and she got that desperate look in her eyes. He couldn't bear to hurt her, but he couldn't let things continue this way. Tonight, after the children were in bed, he would go to Marcus's house and talk to her.

The winter had been relatively mild, which made traveling unusually easy. Mary Margaret reveled in her new freedom, enjoying her various adventures even as she turned them into stories to delight her readers back east. To her great satisfaction, Garth had sold some of her more serious pieces to prestigious magazines, garnering her the audience she sought.

Despite her success, however, something was missing from her life, and while she refused to put a label on it, deep inside she yearned for more. After more than four months en route, she still missed Thomas and Rebecca desperately. Often, she woke in the night to an aching feeling of loneliness. Worse, she still dreamed of a family—a dream she should have put behind her long ago. And at the center of it all stood Worth.

She would think of him at the oddest times. His memory always hovered on the fringes of her consciousness. If she hadn't had her work to keep her busy, the ache inside her would have taken over her life. At least with her travels, she had plenty of distractions and opportunities to meet interesting people, like her new friend, Adeline Cross.

Today, a blustery day in late March, found her seated across from Adeline at a table in the dining room of the recently opened Fred Harvey House. The young actress had become a comfortable traveling companion in the past few days; her acting troupe shared Mary Margaret's itinerary.

"I can't believe this," Adeline exclaimed. "Real linen, well-dressed waiters, dishes, silverware—and in Topeka!"

"You left out the most important thing—delicious food," Mary Margaret said. "I didn't fully believe the stories I'd heard about the greasy offerings along the railroad, but this trip has been eye-opening."

Both women laughed. The railway food they'd consumed certainly deserved its poor reputation.

"Well, Fred Harvey is a real miracle man," Adeline said. "This place is magnificent. I'm glad we're stopping here for a few days. What are your plans?"

"I think I'll make Topeka my base for a few days, too. Traveling is exciting, but I also like to settle in one place for a while and get a better sense of the people and their lives. I got a very interesting interview with the news butch on the train, and he recommended staying here."

"You mean that nice young man who kept us from missing the train yesterday?"

"Yes. Seems he started out selling papers but quickly discovered travelers wanted other items available, as well. He's got a cache of chocolate and fruit hidden all over the train. Does a booming business, if you can believe half of what he says."

"He really was a conscientious lad. Remember that one stop? We barely had fifteen minutes to wolf down our meals before the train left. If it weren't for him, half the passengers would have been left behind when the train pulled out of the station. I don't understand why they can't give the passengers a warning signal a couple of minutes before the train leaves the station."

"That would be too reasonable. I think the conductors enjoy keeping the passengers on edge—adds to the excitement." Again the women laughed, enjoying the camaraderie brought about by a wealth of common experiences.

As they ate, they exchanged stories about their travels. "What will you do in Topeka?" Adeline asked over the meat course, a fillet of beef with mushroom sauce.

"I want to do a story on the recent Mennonite emigration. Almost two thousand of them arrived here a couple of years ago. I thought Topeka would be a good place to begin my investigations. I'm hoping to hire someone to take me out to one of their villages—preferably, someone more fluent in German than I am."

Mary Margaret had shared the details of her writing career with Adeline and had learned much about the actress's profession in return. The other woman was an excellent and supportive listener, and she enjoyed helping Mary Margaret get her stories.

"Gustav may be able to help you there," Adeline now said, referring to an older actor in her troupe. "I believe he came over from the old country about twenty years ago, but I'm sure he still remembers the language. We don't begin rehearsals until Monday, so he should have some free time. Would you like me to ask him about it?"

Mary Margaret was about to agree enthusiastically when a black-coated waiter came up to their table.

"Excuse me, ladies, but is one of you Miss Simpson?" He looked down at a piece of paper in his hand. "Miss Mary Margaret Simpson?"

"Yes. I am," Mary Margaret answered.

"There's an urgent message for you from the telegraph office. They sent their boy over to see if you were here."

Mary Margaret stood abruptly. "Did he bring the telegram? Is he still here?"

"Yes, ma'am. He's waiting in the foyer. If you'll step this way, I'll be happy to escort you."

Mary Margaret glanced questioningly at Adeline, who nodded at her and said, "Go on. I'll take care of things here."

With a murmured, "Thank you," Mary Margaret turned and followed the waiter out of the dining room.

The telegraph office messenger was a scraggly, rough-dressed boy of maybe thirteen. He wore filthy denim pants and looked as if his hair had been neither washed nor combed in at least a month. But the envelope he held in his hand was clean and neat and had her name scratched out on it in a spidery script.

"You Miss Simpson?" he asked.

"Yes."

"The station agent said to give this to you."

Mary Margaret paid the boy and tore open the envelope. She took a moment to catch her breath, then reached in and pulled out the message: "Kathleen wired. Thomas and Rebecca need you. Signed, Garth."

That was it? No details, no other information? She peered into the envelope again. Empty. There was no question in Mary Margaret's mind about what to do next. She would catch the next train to Kansas City, then work her way north to the Union Pacific line and Cheyenne.

"Bad news?" Adeline inquired from behind her.

"I don't know," Mary Margaret answered, turning to face her friend. "Garth didn't send any details. But I know Kathleen wouldn't have sent for me unless there was a problem she couldn't handle."

"Kathleen? That's your friend in Cheyenne, isn't it?"

"Yes. She went with Thomas and Rebecca." Mary Margaret had told Adeline some of her story, though she hadn't dwelt on Worth. Her memories of him were too special, too private to share. She had concentrated instead on the children and Kathleen.

"What can I do to help?" Adeline asked.

Mary Margaret was touched by Adeline's interest and obvious sympathy. She could use the company, she realized, to keep her mind from fabricating frightening reasons for Kathleen to have sent for her. "Help me pack?"

The two women retired to Mary Margaret's chambers.

"I'll miss you," Adeline confessed just before Mary Margaret left for the train station. "I've never had a close woman friend before."

"Come to Cheyenne," Mary Margaret urged impulsively. "Bring your troupe. Cheyenne is full of theaters and variety houses. I'm sure you'll do well there."

"I don't know," Adeline said slowly. "We have to do our run here. Then Gustav has some other commitments lined up."

"Oh, Adeline. Talk to him. I'm sure he'll listen to you. Try to come soon so we can see each other again." Though Mary Margaret had known the actress for only a short time, she recognized a kindred spirit in her. She didn't want to lose contact with her.

"All right. I'll see what I can do," Adeline promised, though her voice lacked total conviction. Mary Margaret hoped Gustav would agree to come to Cheyenne without opposition, for she sensed her friend might not find the strength to fight him.

Once again, Mary Margaret stood on a train platform. Only this time, when the train pulled out of the station, she was on it.

After four months of waiting, of traveling on every type of railcar, of dust-ridden passengers and opulent parlor rooms, of days of endless, stark countryside, and long nights of fevered, impassioned dreams, she was finally headed for her unstated goal, the Wyoming Territory and the city of Cheyenne. Maybe dreams could come true, after all.

Six

*C*heyenne was the brash mix of sophistication and raw wildness Mary Margaret had come to expect of rail towns. As she rode away from the low-slung Union Pacific station in the specially ordered carriage, she saw streets lined with grocery stores and meat markets, livery stables and druggists, shoe stores and men's furnishings. On one side street, there was a sign for a bath parlor proclaiming that baths were a dollar, but ten bath tickets could be purchased for five dollars.

When her driver turned yet another corner, Mary Margaret could see a whole other side to the city. Here the rowdy element of town lived life to the fullest, partaking of drink, women, and cards. There were more concert and gambling saloons with loud, garish signs than she could count. As they slowly drove past one prefabricated saloon, a man in a filthy buckskin shirt and trousers came flying through a window, landing just clear of the carriage wheels.

"You wanna drink, you gotta pay! Don't come back here no more!" shouted a beefy man in a white shirt and dark vest from where he stood framed in the now-gaping opening.

The driver didn't even bother to glance at the bleeding

man in the road, as if the sight was so common it didn't bear noticing. Mary Margaret shuddered and closed her eyes. She'd seen similar scenes often enough since she'd left Boston, but she still wasn't used to them.

Finally, a more residential district came into view. Another block and they reached the boardinghouse where Mary Margaret planned to stay.

"Hello, miss. How can I help you?" A small, gray-haired woman stepped out from the porch. She stood on the top stair and watched Mary Margaret alight from the carriage.

"This is Miller's Boardinghouse, isn't it?" Mary Margaret asked, looking around but not seeing any sign.

"Sure is. You must be Miss Simpson. I'm Sarah Miller. I own this place. Have since my Sam died two years ago. Still miss him." She paused to sigh briefly, almost as if she were talking to herself, then she continued, "Come on up, and I'll show you to your room. I stirred up the stove in there a while ago. Figured you might be chilled. April out here ain't quite the growing season yet. We still gets us some mighty cold days. Snow, even." The garrulous old woman bent her head back and scanned the cloudless sky. "No sign of snow now, but you never can tell. Blows up right quick in these parts, then blows away just as fast."

Sarah Miller lowered her gaze back to her quiet audience and addressed the driver. "Hey, Tex, you bring this here lady's stuff upstairs. I put her in the front room—the one above the parlor. Figured she'd get a better view of the town that way.

"That's what you're here for, ain't it? To see our fair city—the 'Magic City of the Plains,' we call her. Of course, there's some what still calls her a place to raise hell, but not in this part of town. You don't have to worry none here. Come along now."

Her arms akimbo, strands of gray hair blowing in the breeze where they weren't tacked down in a tight bun, Sarah Miller waited until Mary Margaret began climbing up the steps. Then she turned on her heel and led the way inside.

Mary Margaret smiled as she followed Sarah into the

spacious entry foyer. Everything about the house was
grand, from the huge external dimensions to the heavy,
dark furniture lining the walls—furniture that would have
been as much at home on Beacon Hill.

"Like my decoratin'?" Sarah asked, catching the direction of Mary Margaret's gaze. "It's the latest thing from the
East. Came here on the train, just as fast as can be. All
ordered from a catalogue and next thing you know, the
stuff's sittin' in my parlor."

"The sideboard's lovely. Reminds me of home," Mary
Margaret replied, though where her home was now, she
really hadn't the faintest idea. Certainly not at the Townsends. They had been only too glad to see her off on her
tour of the West! Especially after their spiteful descriptions
of John Worthington and what they considered to be his
kidnapping of the children.

"So, what brings you out to these parts?" Sarah asked,
her curious brown eyes appraising Mary Margaret from
head to toe. She looked like an inquisitive sparrow, darting
her head from side to side as she looked up at Mary Margaret.

"Wait, wait, don't say a word. I'm forgetting my manners," she exclaimed before Mary Margaret had a chance
to reply. "Let's get you up to your room, first. Once you're
settled in, we can have a nice long chat. Come along,
now."

She took Mary Margaret up the same stairs the driver of
the carriage had just descended. They traversed a long
hallway, turned a corner, and stopped by a tall, paneled
door.

"Here we are," Sarah announced as she swung open the
door. "Now, wash up and rest for a while, then come on
downstairs and I'll feed you. You look like you could use a
bit of fattening up. I hear tell railroad food ain't fit for man
or beast. Take your time now. There ain't no rush," she
added as she slipped out the door.

Mary Margaret didn't think she'd had the chance to say
more than a half dozen words since she'd met Mrs. Miller.
The woman would make a great story for her newspaper
series. She would have to set aside some time to interview

her and find out how she'd ended up owning this staid boardinghouse.

But first, Mary Margaret had more important things to do. She was finally in Cheyenne. She wanted to see Thomas and Rebecca as soon as possible, to hug them close and share all her varied experiences and theirs, to be part of their lives again.

Even more, she wanted to gaze into Worth's eyes and see if they still held the unspoken promises of their last few seconds together, to see if there might be a place for her out here, after all.

"Leave me alone! I won't do it. I won't!" Thomas screamed as he slammed his slate on the desk. The board split jaggedly down the middle.

"Now look at what you've done! I've told you fourteen times not to slam your slate. Go to your room and don't come out till supper. Your uncle's going to hear about this, mark my words. He won't be pleased to find out you've been sassing me again," Lucy Robertson shouted back, all semblance of poise lost as she faced the fuming, red-faced boy.

Tom stared at her for another moment, undisguised hatred streaming from his eyes. Then he turned abruptly and raced out of the room and up the stairs, leaving Lucy feeling inadequate and furious with herself no less than with the boy.

She followed him out of the dining room, nearly colliding with Kathleen, who stood gazing up the stairs, her lips turned down in a disapproving frown.

"Did you want something?" Lucy challenged Kathleen, her voice still full of anger.

"No, miss," Kathleen answered, lowering her eyes. "I was just about ta attend ta the bedrooms. I'd better get busy."

It's not my fault! Lucy wanted to scream. *The boy is impossible. I try my best, but he just can't learn*. But, of course, she would say nothing of the kind—certainly not to the help. So she simply took a deep breath and said, "Fine. I've some things to do myself."

She waited until Kathleen was halfway up the back stairs before she headed for the front parlor. She wished Worth would get home. He was working too hard, spending too much time at his law office. Why, she hardly saw him anymore!

She wanted to tell him about the party at the Danbys' on Saturday night. The masquerade ball would be the best of the season; she'd been so excited when she'd first received her invitation. She loved to dress up—the more lavishly, the better. And for this occasion she had the most perfect new costume. She had ordered the gown from New York, and it was finally hanging in her closet.

After Worth saw her in her gown, he'd forget all about his silly notion that he was too old for her. She'd always known he was the man for her and nothing he could say would sway her from this essential truth. Her ball dress was French, with a daringly cut décolletage. She hadn't even let her father see it, for fear he would make her send it back. She could hardly wait. Saturday seemed years away instead of only a few days.

If only that wretched boy hadn't been so awful today! Now her mood was spoiled, leaving her feeling out of sorts and vaguely resentful. Things weren't going at all the way she had planned when she had volunteered to help Worth out with the children.

Lucy sighed and tried to decide what to do next. She didn't want to leave in case Worth got home early, but she didn't want to appear to be obviously waiting for him, either. She was still undecided when a knock sounded on the front door.

No one else was nearby, so Lucy went to answer. "May I help you?" she asked, eyeing the visitor suspiciously.

The woman looked back just as warily. "Is this John Worthington's house?" she asked in a proper, Boston accent. Lucy recognized it from her days at the finishing school back east.

"Yes, this is his home," Lucy answered curtly.

"Could I see him, please?"

"He's not at home right now. Who may I say called?" Lucy put on her best company manners. No fine Eastern lady was going to show her up, especially not an Eastern lady who wanted to see Worth.

The woman looked flustered for a minute, as if she had not expected this turn of events. "I'm Mary Margaret Simpson. We . . . that is, Mr. Worthington and I met in Boston. Could you tell me when he will return?"

"I don't rightly know," Lucy answered honestly enough. "He doesn't always tell me exactly when he'll be coming home. You know how men are, don't you? They love their independence."

Lucy knew she was stretching the truth. Worth had no obligation to tell her his plans. But she hadn't outright lied, and she could see the other woman had gotten the message. Worth was spoken for, and Miss Simpson could just go back where she came from.

"I see. I wonder, then, if I might see the children? I cared for them before they moved out to Wyoming, and if they aren't engaged in their studies . . ."

Oh, no, thought Lucy, suddenly panicked. This was the children's vaunted Aunt Maggie, the paragon of virtue who could do no wrong. Lucy peered at her more closely, noting her fine bone structure and tall, elegant carriage. A bright intelligence shone from her hazel eyes, and she had an undefinable air Lucy found intimidating.

Was she the reason Worth had come home so reserved and distracted? Had Worth somehow fallen under her spell, just when Lucy had hoped he would fall under hers?

A chill ran down Lucy's spine. She must not let this woman get close, particularly not today, with Tom so upset and Becky running a slight fever. Lucy would only end up looking bad. She couldn't risk anyone else knowing about today's disaster!

"I'm sorry. I can't let you in. Worth has strict rules about having strangers in the house. Why don't you tell me where you're staying, and I'll be sure he gets the message? Or, you could try again another day. Will you be in town long?"

Again, the woman seemed a little taken aback. "I'm not sure what my plans are yet. I'm staying at Miller's Boardinghouse, up on Seventeenth Street."

"Oh, yes, I know the place. It's not far from here. I'll be sure to tell him you came by."

Lucy flashed her most becoming smile as she shut the door. As soon as it was closed, she leaned back against it and stared at the ceiling, forcing herself to breathe slowly.

"Damn, damn, and damn," she muttered at last, glad no one was around to hear her say the scandalous words.

Mary Margaret walked slowly down the steps toward Ferguson Street. The sun was out, the sky a brilliant mountain blue, but all Mary Margaret could see was the girl's piquant face. Framed by silky blond tresses and set off by bright sapphire eyes glowing like jewels, it was a face no man could resist. Mary Margaret had been so stunned by the girl's presence in Worth's house she hadn't even asked her name.

Who was she? And just what was her relationship to Worth? Had Mary Margaret made a mistake in coming here? Maybe she shouldn't have left her name. Maybe she should have just turned around and raced for the next train out of town. But, of course, she couldn't. Kathleen had said the children needed her, and their needs took precedence over her own foolish insecurities.

By the time Mary Margaret reached the wrought-iron gate by the street, she was very tired, though she had walked barely forty feet. Too many emotions churned inside her—fear, jealousy, anger, longing . . . the list went on and on.

Most of all, she felt hollow inside, as though she had lost something infinitely precious she hadn't even known she possessed—something essential and life-sustaining.

A scrabbling sound behind her caught her attention as she lifted the clasp on the gate. Looking back at the house, she saw a blur of motion sliding down the porch support from an upper balcony.

"Aunt Maggie, Aunt Maggie! Don't go! Wait for me!" a young male voice cried out as the blur took shape and Thomas Worthington dropped to the ground from the porch railing. He got up on the run and sped toward her.

His knees were scraped and his face was grimy. She

thought he might have been crying and had wiped his cheeks with hands that were not quite clean.

"Thomas, my love, is it really you?" Her heart filled with joy and she hugged him, content simply to hold him. Her reticule swung from her wrist as the two of them swayed together.

"Let me look at you," she said after a few seconds had passed. She could have held on to him longer, but she did not want to injure his masculine pride. He was grown now, or so he thought, and would be embarrassed by too much of a show of affection. "You've grown at least two inches since I last saw you," she added with some exaggeration.

"You think so?" he asked, drawing himself up proudly.

"Seems like it to me," she confirmed. He looked so different from the little boy she had sent out west. His hair was longer and fell into his eyes. The shape of his face was changing and losing all traces of its former childish roundness. Her little Thomas was turning into a full-blown Tom.

"So, how are you and how do you like living out here? Has Wyoming proved to be good to you?"

Having received Kathleen's message, Mary Margaret already knew something wasn't going well. The evidence of tears still fresh on Thomas's face added to her concern, but she wanted to hear his opinion.

"I like the ranch, but it's not like home," he admitted reluctantly.

She saw the shimmer of tears start again in his eyes and tactfully diverted her gaze. He was trying so hard to be grown up, yet he was still feeling the loss of his parents and familiar surroundings.

"Have you come to stay? Will you be living here now?" he questioned hopefully.

She raised her eyes to his again, and what she saw made her speak without thinking. "I'll be staying for a while."

As she said the words, she knew them to be true. Clearly Thomas needed her, and maybe Rebecca, too. But would Worth?

"How's your sister?" she asked.

"Becky's fine, most of the time. She's sick now—fever or something, but Kathleen says it's most likely nothing."

The mention of Rebecca's nickname brought back a surge of poignant memories, reminding Mary Margaret vividly of the last time she'd seen Thomas and Rebecca. And Worth.

"Uncle Worth called the doctor," Thomas went on, "and he agreed with Kathleen."

Her heart raced at the sound of his name. It was all she could do to keep track of the conversation. "So, Becky's in bed today?"

"Yeah." Thomas scowled in the direction of the house. "Lucy's probably in with her now, poor Becky."

"Lucy?" Somehow, without being told, she guessed that Lucy was the fair-haired beauty she had met earlier.

"Her last name's Robertson, but we have to call her Miss Lucy." His contemptuous tone told her more than his words about his feelings for Lucy Robertson.

"But you do get along with . . . your Uncle Worth, don't you?"

"Of course!" Thomas looked at her questioningly, surprise written on his face, as if he couldn't fathom why she would even think to ask such a silly question. "Uncle Worth is grand. Only . . ."

She waited, holding her breath, wondering, worrying.

"Well, he's just so busy all the time. And we have to stay with *her*," he said, his tone bordering on insolence. Mary Margaret knew she had to put a stop to his behavior.

"I'm sure your uncle is doing the best he can. And so is Miss Robertson."

Her voice carried a warning, and Thomas picked it up right away.

"I guess so," he answered politely but without conviction. Then he brightened. "But now you're here, and we won't need Miss Lucy anymore. Whoopie!" he crowed, then glanced guiltily over his shoulder at the house. "I'm not supposed to be out here, you know. She doesn't know I left my room. Uncle Worth will tan my hide if he finds out I didn't tell her. He says we have to show her respect. You won't say anything, will you?"

"Not if you go back right away. But, Thomas, you know he's right. You have to be respectful to your elders and you really mustn't leave the house without telling anyone, and definitely not in that way." She nodded her head toward the second-floor balcony set on top of the porch. "It's too dangerous. You could fall and get seriously hurt."

Thomas had the grace to look abashed. "I know," he admitted softly, then went on more cheerfully, "I'll be more careful. What about you? Where are you going? How will we find you? Can you stay with us at Uncle Worth's? Boy, will Becky be mad when she learns that I saw you first and she didn't even get to."

Mary Margaret couldn't help but laugh at his enthusiasm. "That's too many questions for right now. I promise you, I'll be back tomorrow. I'm staying over at Miller's Boardinghouse, so you don't have to worry about finding me.

"Now, you'd better get back in the house before Miss Robertson looks out the front window and sees you for herself. Then, even if I don't say anything about where you got to this afternoon, she'll know."

With a final hug, Thomas scampered off, sneaking around the back so he could enter through the kitchen rather than hazard climbing up the way he had come down.

With Thomas gone, Mary Margaret once again felt the desolate sense of loss come over her. She sighed deeply, then hurried down the street, back to her lonely room. Strange, the cozy bedroom had seemed so welcoming earlier in the day—a haven from the rigors of rail travel. Now it seemed no more than a cold, impersonal cell. She'd built a castle in the sky, and because her dreams were pinioned on clouds, the walls were beginning to tumble.

Worth rushed down Ferguson Street and turned on to Seventeenth. As he neared Mrs. Miller's boardinghouse, he slowed his pace so he could catch his breath. It wouldn't do to appear all breathless and red in the face from running.

He was nervous—nervous and elated. The anticipation

burning in his veins left him feeling things he'd tried hard to suppress since arriving back in Wyoming.

Oh, he'd managed well enough, settling in with Tom and Becky, preparing the ranch house for winter, setting up house in Cheyenne. He'd arranged for Lucy to help the children with their lessons and Kathleen to settle them in at night. He'd caught up on all of his cases and taken on some new ones, as well.

But still, he wasn't happy; his life seemed strangely empty. The children filled his hours with a quiet joy, but it wasn't quite enough. At odd moments, he would catch himself staring into space, and later, he couldn't remember what he had been thinking of. All that lingered was a fleeting image, a shadowy memory: a woman's face, the curve of her jaw, the delicate feel of her skin, the whisper of her breath in the instant before his lips touched hers.

"Can I help you, sonny?" a female voice rasped into the evening air from the darkened porch. Worth could hear a rocker's sliders squeaking rhythmically against the floorboards.

"Are you the owner here?" he called out from where he stood on the walk.

"Yup. I'm Sarah Miller. You looking for a place to rent? I'm mostly full up, but I might have an empty room if you're needin' somewhere to stay."

"Thank you, but I live here in town. I was hoping I could visit with one of your guests."

"Oh? And who might that be? I've got quite a few guests nowadays. Not like the old days, no sirree. I run me a respectable boardinghouse now. None of those cowboys or railroad men shootin' up the place or fallin' down dead drunk in the middle of the hall. 'Tweren't no life for a lady, you know, 'specially once my Sam was gone."

She paused for a moment, then added, "Are you going to stand in the street all night or come up here where I can see you better?"

Worth smiled. "I reckon I can come up for a while," he replied and came through the opening in the white picket fence surrounding the front yard.

Mrs. Miller stayed silent until he'd climbed up onto the

porch with her. "Dinner's just over a few minutes ago, and everyone's just settling in for the evening. Who was it you wanted to see again?"

"I didn't say, but I'd like to speak with Miss Simpson. I heard she arrived today." Worth tipped his hat.

"She sure did, but she's pretty well tuckered out by the long trip. I don't rightly know if she's up to having any visitors tonight. A'course, you're welcome to set a spell. Don't bother me none."

"That's very kind of you, Mrs. Miller, but if you could check with Miss Simpson, I'd be mighty grateful."

In the fading twilight, he could barely see the old woman ensconced in the wooden rocking chair. She stood up slowly, the top of her head barely reaching his shoulder. "You wait right here, now," she admonished. "Don't go away. I'll be right out."

Worth gave his word and sat on the wide porch railing, leaning back against a pillar with his left leg stretched out in front of him. Idly, he tossed his hat in a circle by its brim. The door opened once again, and Worth caught his breath.

She stood in the bright glow of light, her hair a coronet framing her face, her silhouette dark and mysterious, feminine and alluring. He felt his blood heat as it surged through his body. His heart pounded like a drumbeat, thundering in his ears.

"Maggie." Her name escaped his lips in a reverent whisper as he rose from his improvised perch.

She turned her head in his direction. "Oh, John, I'm afraid I didn't see you in the dark. It was nice of you to come over so promptly. I wasn't sure what . . . when you would. . . . How are you?"

Her voice was husky and her words came out fast and jumbled. Had his unplanned kiss in their last, desperate seconds together made her so uncomfortable she couldn't even exchange polite conversation? What else could explain her flustered greeting?

For himself, just heartbeats ago, he'd been ready to grab her in his embrace and swing her around on the porch. Now, he met her final question with a restrained politeness he was far from feeling, realizing she wasn't ready for what he'd had in mind.

"I'm doing well and the children have adjusted much better than could be expected. They certainly will be surprised to see you. They never mentioned that you had plans to travel out this way."

The shock of seeing him after so many months turned Mary Margaret's legs to jelly. She reached out to steady herself against the doorjamb. He was more handsome than she'd remembered, and his voice . . . She had expected him to call, but she'd thought she'd have more time. She wasn't ready to face him yet—not after the shock of seeing Lucy Robertson in his home. Beautiful, sweet . . . young Lucy Robertson.

"The trip was planned rather quickly. Before I knew it, I was on a train. The Union Pacific is very persuasive with their written brochures. The lure of the West and all. Of course, the chance to see the children was also a big draw," she answered, grateful she'd had time to gather her wits about her and reply in a less flustered manner. Though she wanted to call him Worth, she couldn't quite bring herself to say the nickname—not now, after seeing Lucy Robertson in charge of his household. "John, would you care to come in? Mrs. Miller is in the kitchen preparing coffee and cake."

Mary Margaret stepped back and indicated the front parlor room with her right hand. Her hand trembled slightly, and she quickly thrust it behind her before he could see how nervous she was.

"There's no need to go to any trouble. I just wanted to make sure you were settled in. I'm sure Tom and Becky will be thrilled you've come for a visit. Speaking of the children, I'd best get back home before they get worried about where I've gotten off to."

"They're all alone?" she blurted, disconcerted by his refusal. She'd hoped he'd stay and tell her about his life since his visit to Boston. She'd hoped he had come by because he wanted to see her and talk about what had happened between them on the platform before he boarded the train, but obviously she'd been wrong. He seemed anxious to leave even though he'd only just arrived.

"I'd never leave the children alone," he answered with an edge to his voice, as if she had accused him of negligence. She hadn't meant to, but she could see where he might have misinterpreted her concern. "Kathleen is probably giving them their nightly snack right now."

How stupid he must think her. She'd completely forgotten about Kathleen since finding Lucy Robertson at Worth's front door. "I honestly didn't think you'd go off and leave them. I'm sorry if it sounded that way. Have you told them I've come to see them?"

Her voice had gentled, and Worth wondered if she were just as confused and uncertain as he. Why had she really come out West? He was almost certain a gaudy advertisement from a rail line wasn't the real reason for her visit. He'd hoped it was to see him, but her next words made that appear unlikely.

"I really can't wait to see Tom and Becky, if it's all right with you. I stopped by your house today and Miss—" she faltered, then went on resolutely—"Robertson said she would have to check with you first."

There, she'd given him an opening. He could tell her all about Miss Robertson now if he wanted to.

"Certainly it's all right for you to see the children," he returned, his voice strained. "I'd planned on telling them about your visit as soon as Lucy gave me your message, but Kathleen had taken Tom to the church for a meeting and Becky was resting. They'll probably be too excited to sleep when I tell them tonight. I'll talk with Lucy about your visiting in the morning. When might you come by?"

The way he said "talk with Lucy" made her heart drop to her toes; it sounded far too familiar. But hadn't she guessed as much already?

"I don't know when to come by. When would be the best time to see them? I wouldn't want to interfere with . . . anyone's plans." He still hadn't said anything really informative about his relationship with the younger woman. Mary Margaret didn't even know where Lucy Robertson lived. Was she staying with Worth? Mary Margaret's hidden hand clenched into a fist.

"Any time is fine," Worth assured her, and her fist unclenched. "The earlier the better. I don't think Tom and Becky will be able to contain their excitement for longer than an hour after eating their breakfast."

Tom and Becky again. Much as she loved them, she longed to hear a more personal reason from Worth about her coming over. At least he had no qualms about her coming over early.

"I wouldn't want to disturb their studies," she said in one last attempt to worm information from him.

Worth grimaced. "That would hardly be a problem." He sighed, then pinched the bridge of his nose as if his head ached. His cryptic reply revealed little, but Mary Margaret could tell something was bothering him, so she waited in patient silence.

"Sorry," he said after a moment, then confessed, "There have been a few difficulties. Minor ones," he added hurriedly, seeing her distressed expression. "You know, adjustment problems for all of us. It's a different life from what the children were used to. I'm sure everything will work out fine, but it just takes time. Don't you think so?"

She wasn't sure just what he was asking for—reassurance? Assistance? Or something else—something just for the two of them? "Yes, I'm sure you're right. My mother always said, 'Time cures all ills, even when nothing else works.'"

"You'll come by tomorrow, then?"

"Yes, yes, I will. You're sure you won't come in for a few minutes?"

"Thanks, but I better not." His eyes went to Mrs. Miller, who was standing in the doorway. He knew any hope he had of a private conversation was lost for now, and a totally private conversation was what he wanted. "I'll see you tomorrow. We can talk more then." *And I'll find out exactly what happened to change the Maggie I knew in Boston.*

"All right. Till tomorrow, then."

"Good night." His mind added the word *Maggie*, but he

didn't say her name aloud. Too much stood between them
—too many questions and uncertainties, too much time
apart after too little time together. It all came down to one
thing: time. At least she was here now in person, not just in
his imagination. It was more than he'd hoped for, more
than he deserved.

Mary Margaret walked slowly up the stairs and down the
hall to her room. Her thoughts were in a whirl, alternately
optimistic and depressed. Worth had come to see her—had
rushed over, in fact; her spirits soared. He had called her
Maggie, she was almost sure of it, and her insides turned
liquid and warm. How she had dreamed of hearing her
name from his lips in just that tone of voice! A smile
warmed her face and her eyes lost their focus.

She drifted toward the padded daybed and reclined
against the satiny softness . . . remembering. He had looked
so handsome in his western suit, the formal white shirt and
stiff collar setting off his golden skin. He was not quite as
tanned as she remembered, but that was to be expected
after the long winter just past.

His hair was a shade darker, the golden tips trimmed off
by a barber, no doubt. His eyes had blazed blue; the hall
lights had been reflected in them like so many bright-
yellow suns in a clear blue sky.

But as soon as she'd spoken, the mood had been lost.
He'd withdrawn into the shell she remembered all too well
from their first encounter. Had she said or done something,
or had he taken one look and realized she did not belong in
his life?

Had she only imagined the sound of her special nickname on his lips? She could not be sure. All she could
remember was her own voice rattling on and on, never
saying what she really meant.

What did it all mean? She lowered her face into her
hands, caught between elation and despair, confusion and
determination.

At least she would see Tom and Becky. That would be a
start. As before, the children would serve as the link be-

tween Worth and her. Somehow, they would work things out.

Mary Margaret rose from her seat and walked to the large chiffonier across the room. Absentmindedly, she changed into her nightgown and prepared for bed. Tomorrow could not come quickly enough; it might come only too soon.

Seven

Mary Margaret adjusted her mask for the tenth time
in as many minutes. She felt distinctly uncomfortable in her borrowed costume, a low-cut dress
of Grecian design leaving a good portion of her back and
shoulders bare. The copper-colored silk draped low over
her bosom and fell in soft folds from her waist to the floor.
A white rope belt accentuated her slender waist and the
matching slippers on her feet were only a shade too small.

Her costume for this masquerade ball had been fash-
ioned by Sarah Miller from a dress borrowed from another
boarder, an actress who was touring the West, just like
Adeline Cross. In honor of the centennial theme, Sarah had
decided to dress Mary Margaret as the woman holding the
torch for liberty, basing her design on the newspaper stories
of the copper statue being built by the French sculptor
Bartholdi.

Sarah herself had dressed as an elfin Martha Washington
and had long since been lost in the crowd. Mary Margaret's
gaze swept the ballroom of the Danbys' house. Red, white,
and blue bunting hung from every balcony and column
surrounding the central dance floor. Ruby-red prisms hung
from the chandeliers, casting patriotic shadows on the
brightly smiling faces below.

"Quite a spectacle, eh?" commented her escort for the evening. Peter Edward Neville Dunsmore was the younger son of an English duke, sent overseas to keep an eye on the family investments. Lord Peter was also staying at Sarah's boardinghouse. "Keeping an eye on the beeves," he liked to say about his overseeing the family's cattle holdings.

As far as Mary Margaret could tell, he spent most of his time keeping an eye on the ladies.

"I didn't anticipate such a large crowd," Mary Margaret responded conversationally. "Many of the costumes seem to be imported, except for all the George and Martha Washingtons."

"Yes, the Danbys certainly know how to put on quite the good show. All the best people are here tonight. No one would dare miss it. A masquerade ball is such good fun, don't you think? Such inventiveness. Just look at those costumes."

Lord Peter scanned the crowd, and Mary Margaret had the distinct impression he was searching for someone in particular, though he was trying to be subtle about it.

Suddenly he stiffened. "Mrs. Danby always puts out a most elaborately prepared collation. Might I get you something to eat or drink?"

"Why, yes, that would be nice. Where . . . ?"

"Just wait here, my dear lady. I'll be right back," he cut her off smoothly, and before she could say another word he was gone, lost in the press of the ever-growing crowd.

Mary Margaret glanced around and nervously twisted the strap of her small bag. She could feel her palms perspiring inside her kid gloves. Now that she was alone, she felt . . . what? Out of place? No, everyone had been more than kind. On edge? Yes, that was it. Everyone of import would be at the Danbys' centennial masquerade ball, including Worth.

She hadn't seen him since the night he'd visited her at the boardinghouse. When she'd gone to his home on Thursday, only the children and Kathleen had been there; Worth had been called out by a client. The same thing had happened on Friday. But tonight they would surely meet.

A flurry of movement by the large double doors from the

main landing caught her eye, and there he was—a dashing pirate with a fierce black patch on one eye, a flowing white shirt accentuating the breadth of his shoulders, a bright red sash around his lean waist, and black leather britches molding his thighs.

There was no mistaking Worth as he made his grand entrance to enthusiastic applause. Nor was there any doubt as to the identity of the blond-haired damsel in distress hanging on his arm. Lucy Robertson looked stunning in a light rose satin dress ornamented with natural flowers and trimmed in white lace. She was the picture of seductive innocence, at once virginal and sophisticated.

Mary Margaret shivered but couldn't drag her eyes away from the sight.

"You must be the delightful Miss Simpson I've heard so much about." The voice so close to Mary Margaret's ear startled her, and she turned to face a handsome, redheaded man in his late thirties, dressed in the garb of a South American gaucho.

"I'm afraid you have an advantage over me, sir."

"Then, allow me to introduce myself. Marcus Robertson at your service, miss."

Robertson? Could he be any relation to the young woman from whom she'd just dragged her gaze? "Then you must be Lucy's . . ."

"Father," he said, placing a large sombrero back on his head.

"Father?" Mary Margaret could not hide her astonishment. She would never have guessed this man had a daughter the age of the young woman flaunting her décolletage under Worth's nose. She reached up to her own low-cut neckline, mortified by her imprudent thoughts and her equally imprudent garb, and hoped he would attribute her sudden flush to the heat building up in the close ballroom.

"I'm duly flattered by your disbelief."

The twinkle in his eyes behind the black mask belied any such notion. Mary Margaret might not have a great deal of personal experience with men, but she could see this one might well be a rogue—a very dashing, likable rogue.

"If I may have the honor of this dance?" Marcus invited, his elbow bent in invitation.

"But, my escort?" Mary Margaret protested, searching the room for the young man who had brought her.

"You came with young Peter Dunsmore, didn't you? Dressed as an English lord, wasn't he? A real stretch of the imagination for him, I'm sure."

Mary Margaret nodded yes to the first two questions and ignored his final comment, trying not to smile.

"I saw him heading downstairs with a woman dressed as Marie Antoinette. He's a young devil, that one. Handsome, but fickle. You'll do much better with me as your partner."

Mary Margaret had no doubt this would be true. There had been something about Peter Dunsmore she hadn't liked when he was first introduced as a fellow boarder at Sarah's, but he had been so insistent she accompany him to the masquerade ball, she'd reluctantly agreed. Could one abandon one's escort? Would it be a grand faux pas?

Marcus must have seen the indecision on her face because he hurriedly reassured her. "You are a member of Worth's family, and as his best friend, I feel it is my duty to be your partner. I'm sure he'd want me to take care of you, since your escort has been so ungentlemanly as to leave you all on your own."

She. *had* been uncomfortable standing all by herself, and the music soaring around the corners of the room beckoned. She might also chance another glimpse of Worth if she were moving around the floor. Did Worth consider her one of the family? She wasn't sure if that made her feel better or worse.

"Come along, it's only one dance," Marcus coaxed. "Doesn't the music tell you it's time to dance?"

Mary Margaret graciously put her hand in the crook of his arm and smiled. "As you said, since my escort has been so ungentlemanly as to leave me on my own, and the music's been calling to me all evening . . ." Mary Margaret nodded her acquiescence and Marcus led her to the dance floor.

It was only after they'd circled the large room twice that Mary Margaret thought to ask him about his own partner.

"I've found attending these affairs unaccompanied much more interesting, as has been proven tonight."

Mary Margaret looked at him, not sure what he meant.

"I found you, didn't I?"

His statement would have set any woman's heart aflutter. Marcus Robertson was a very gracious and dashing man. It would be best to change the subject, and quickly.

"I saw your daughter here earlier tonight." Mary Margaret was appalled when she heard the words come from her mouth. How could she have changed the subject so awkwardly, and to such a disastrous topic! On the other hand, it was better to know exactly how things stood between Worth and his young friend.

"Yes, Lucy's here somewhere. She convinced Worth they should attend together."

"I see."

"Do you? I don't think so, but you'll have to find out for yourself." His eyes sparkled with secrets and the corner of his mouth turned up as if he had just heard a delicious joke but didn't want to share it.

"You're being most cryptic," Mary Margaret said, giving him a boldly flirtatious smile.

"Yes, I am, aren't I?" he replied smugly.

Before she could question him further, he whirled her around the dance floor, making her so dizzy she could only cling to his arms.

"Why don't we retire to the refreshment tables, Mary Margaret?" he suggested as the band took a well-deserved break. "You will allow me the courtesy of addressing you by your given name, won't you? After all, I'm old enough to be your father."

Mary Margaret laughed, as he had intended. "Unless your youth was more misspent than most, I doubt you could have fathered a child as old as me, but by all means, call me Mary Margaret."

"Thank you for the honor, and you must call me Marcus." He paused and seemed oddly satisfied. "Now, all this dancing has worked up quite a thirst. Why don't we start with some punch?"

Taking her arm, Marcus led her out of the ballroom to the banquet room next door.

On the far wall, a damask-covered table was laden with small cakes and tarts, cookies and tea sandwiches, all arranged around the biggest punch bowl Mary Margaret had ever seen. Across from them, an even larger table was laid out with a bountiful supply of the choicest viands—oysters prepared three different ways, lobster and clam, ham and chicken, black-tail deer and mountain sheep.

"There's so much to choose from," Mary Margaret said, impressed.

"The Danbys do their darnedest to make their party the biggest and best of the year. With the excuse of the centennial, it's even bigger than usual. I understand the whole East Coast is in a state of centennial fever. The reports in the papers tell of large crowds and elaborate parties. Have you attended any of the festivities?"

While Mary Margaret regaled him with tales of what she'd seen, they filled their plates for the midnight supper and found themselves a cozy table for two.

For the most part, Mary Margaret was able to keep her attention centered on Marcus and their light conversation. Only occasionally did her gaze wander around the room, ignoring the colorful decor and the equally lavish costumes, seeking only the painful confirmation of what Marcus had implied: Worth had invited Lucy to the ball.

Worth stood off to one side of the banquet room. He'd sent Lucy to dance with one of the George Washingtons and set out to find Mary Margaret. The unmasking had occurred at the stroke of midnight, but he hadn't needed that to recognize her. Now he had found her, much to his dismay, deep in conversation with his best friend!

She looked wonderful in the shimmering dress she was wearing. Her creamy skin glowed in the warm gaslight, the bare column of her neck gracefully set off by a single strand of pearls. He longed to touch her, to run his fingertips along her smooth shoulder, to gently cup her chin and draw her lips to his.

She laughed at something Marcus said, and Worth shivered despite the warmth of the crowded room. Resentfully, he noticed how well she seemed to be getting along with Marcus—too well.

Worth worked his way around the tables until he was standing above Marcus and Mary Margaret. "Good evening, Mary Margaret, Marcus. You seem to be having a good time."

"Yes, yes, we are," Marcus said jovially. "Perhaps you'd care to join us. There's an extra chair at the next table."

Worth didn't trust Marcus's expression one whit. The man was up to something, but he couldn't put his finger on what. He looked down at Mary Margaret. "You wouldn't mind?"

"Oh, no, of course not." Her cheeks were pink, probably from the heat, and her eyes were shiny.

"I didn't know you would be coming tonight," he said after pulling up the chair.

"Peter Dunsmore was kind enough to bring her," Marcus said. "And kinder still to leave her so I could make her acquaintance." He gave Mary Margaret his most charming smile, and she smiled back.

Worth felt jealousy tear at his gut, though he knew he had no right to the feeling. "Peter Dunsmore? The young fop from England?"

"The very same," Marcus confirmed, then leaned over to confide to Mary Margaret, "Lord Peter, they call him over there—second son of a duke or some such. Hear he had to leave London in a hurry after getting into trouble. Even the considerable family fortune couldn't buy him out of his latest scrape. Fortunately for him, they had a place to send him, though I don't suppose he's much of a cattle manager."

"I hear he's quite the ladies' man," Worth felt compelled to point out. Mary Margaret should know to be careful of the rake.

"Seems to be. Last I saw, he was following a very pretty Marie Antoinette out into the garden. But, as I said earlier, his foolishness is my gain." Marcus gallantly lifted Mary

Margaret's hand from the table and brought it to his lips, a roguish gleam in his eyes.

Mary Margaret blushed prettily and laughed as Marcus released her hand. "You flatter me, Marcus, but you've more than made up for any feelings of rejection I might have felt at Lord Peter's desertion."

Worth clenched his jaw and restrained himself from punching his friend. What had happened to Marcus? He never flirted with women—not since his wife had left him so many years ago. And what about Mary Margaret? He could hardly believe she was the same woman he'd known in Boston—the one whose very correctness had bordered on an overblown prudishness.

"If Lord Peter has deserted you, I would be more than happy to escort you home after the ball," he offered impulsively. He sent a brief challenging glance at Marcus, but Marcus seemed unperturbed.

"What about Lucy? I thought you came with her," Mary Margaret said.

Lucy! Worth had forgotten about her. He cringed inside. What would Marcus think? After all, Lucy was his beloved daughter. But to Worth's surprise, Marcus merely smiled and said, "Don't worry about Lucy. I'll take her home. We've seen so little of each other since she's taken up with your young ones. I've been hoping to catch some time with her."

"Are you certain she—" Mary Margaret started to say.

"Don't you worry," Marcus interrupted, holding up his hand to forestall her concern. "Matter of fact, why don't I go find my best girl and see how she's doing. You two can keep each other entertained, can't you?"

Without awaiting their response, Marcus pushed back his chair and stood.

"Pleased to make your acquaintance, señorita," he said, bowing with a flourish befitting his gaucho costume. "I'm sure we shall be seeing each other again." Then he turned on his heel and took off, much to Worth's relief.

For the first few minutes after Marcus's sudden departure, Mary Margaret didn't know what to say. She sneaked a peek at Worth from beneath lowered lashes. He looked dashing in his pirate garb; the soft material of the full-cut shirt clung lovingly to his broad shoulders and draped over the smooth muscles of his chest.

Mary Margaret's breath caught and she had to look away. She had never been so aware of a man's masculinity before. Striking as he had been in Boston, here in the West he was even more imposing. His earthy ruggedness matched the challenge of this untamed land, and spoke to a hidden wildness inside her.

She sneaked another peek at him, only to find him staring at her. An appreciative intentness in his gaze set her insides quivering.

"Your costume is most becoming," he said, catching her eye.

Mary Margaret self-consciously covered the low-cut neckline of her dress with her palm. "Thank you. Mrs. Miller helped me put it together. I wasn't sure what such an occasion would call for."

"It's not much different from Boston," Worth commented.

"No, it's not. I didn't expect to find Cheyenne so civilized. The city is so cosmopolitan—so many Europeans live here, as well as Americans from the East."

"The cattle boom has enticed many speculators out here. And the Union Pacific can bring them and anything the world has to offer right to our door." Worth's voice lowered. "Even you."

Mary Margaret glanced up at him, hearing an unexpected warmth in his tone. Was he, then, glad she had come?

"Especially me," she said, staring mesmerized into his eyes. They were just as she remembered from their day in the park, warm and open, inviting intimacies and sharing.

"Why do you say that?" Worth asked. He leaned forward, staring at her intently.

"Didn't I tell you? The railroad has made my trip possible. I'm writing a series of articles on life along the rail lines. One of the Boston papers is paying my way."

"Oh, yes. Tom and Becky mentioned you had been traveling for several weeks before coming to Cheyenne."

"Several months, actually," she corrected.

Worth frowned. "Months? Exactly what do you write?"

Mary Margaret wanted to share this part of herself with him. She had held herself back in Boston, preserving her secrets against the time he would leave. She was still trying to decide what to tell him when he said, "I didn't realize women's publications paid so well. What kinds of things do women like to read about?"

His assumption her only readers were women annoyed her. "Some women like to read about everything, just as some men do. Others have more circumscribed tastes," she told him.

"I realize that," he said in a mild tone. "I meant, what sorts of articles are you writing?"

Mary Margaret sat back in her chair and regarded him through narrowed eyes. Should she tell him about her M. M. Simms articles—the ones reporting on social and political issues plaguing the West? Or maybe she should tell him of her M. Saunders articles—wild adventure tales describing the romantic West, filled with stories of cowboys, Indians, dance halls, and saloons?

He probably wouldn't believe her and might even scoff. Only her Mary Simpson stories fit his preconceived views of her work. These stories appeared in young women's magazines and were highly sanitized accounts of her trip, most suitable for the genteel readers the finishing schools turned out.

"I write of what interests me," she said, which was no less than the truth. "Of people and places, of similarities and differences, of the unique and the commonplace, and of what I think about it all."

"How long have you been writing?"

"Forever. I started as a child, I guess." She could remember so well—the misfit girl, too smart for her own good, retreating into her bedroom when the austerity of her home life became too much to bear. "In those days I wrote make-believe stories. I used to read them to my friends."

"And now?"

"As I said, I write about the world around me. It's much more interesting than fiction, don't you think?"

He was staring quizzically at her. "I don't know," he answered with seeming reluctance. "I guess I don't read or write much unless I have to—outside of my law practice, that is."

He was watching her carefully, as if her reaction to his statement carried a significance over and above the mere words.

"Most people are like you," she agreed, leaving the deeper message in his words for another time. "But not me. Writing makes me feel . . ." She didn't know how to phrase it, even though words were a large part of her life.

How could she tell him that when she wrote, she became someone else—not the poor, unattached female no relative wanted to claim. ". . . it makes me feel complete."

Conflicting emotions assailed Worth—relief, on the one hand, since Mary Margaret had accepted that he did not read or write much. Of course, he had not confessed the full extent of his problem, but at least she didn't sound horrified by what she had learned so far.

He also felt a sense of loss, for Mary Margaret sounded wedded to her writing. It was more than a stopgap measure in her life. It was a career that made her complete, to use her own word. Was there room in her life for anything else? More important, was there room in her life for him?

"How do you find your stories?" Worth asked, needing to discover more about this intangible rival.

Unexpectedly, Mary Margaret laughed. "Usually, they find me."

"I don't understand. How do they find you?" Writing had always been somewhat enigmatic to him, and her statement wasn't helping any.

"Well, take today, for example. Sarah and I were out in the back garden and we heard a small cat mewing. Sarah said, 'You don't hear too much of that anymore around here.'

"I asked her why not, and she said, 'One of my friends took 'em all away. He and Sam and I go way back, before Sam died. He used to drive the stage to Deadwood Gulch in the Black Hills.'

"Why'd he take the cats, I wanted to know. And you'll never guess what she said."

Worth shook his head and smiled expectantly, enjoying the sparkle he saw in her eyes, the animation on her face.

"It seems he felt the dance hall girls in Deadwood Gulch were lonely, so he came here to Cheyenne and offered two bits apiece for cats. He loaded all the cats he found up in his wagon, drove them to Deadwood, set up a shop near the saloons, and sold those cats for ten to thirty dollars. Made his fortune in no time flat. Can you believe it?"

Worth laughed. "Sure I can. They've been saying there's gold in those hills for a long time. I guess this fellow found a surefire way to get himself some."

Mary Margaret laughed with him, glad to see that the haunted look had left his eyes. She liked sharing her love of writing with others, making them see the magic in the world around them, and the sadness, too. She couldn't help but feel for the poor girls who bought the cats—girls so lonely they would pay so much for companionship—and from a cat, no less. What were their lives really like, she wondered, but her thoughts were cut short by Worth's surprising comment.

"I like it when you laugh," he said. "Your eyes light up and your mouth curves so becomingly."

The mood was suddenly intimate. Worth slid his hand across the white damask tablecloth until his fingers lay over her own. She'd removed her kid gloves earlier and could feel the calluses on his fingertips caress her softer skin.

"I like it when you laugh, too," she confessed, feeling an unbidden warmth wash over her. "I just haven't been sure . . ."

"Me, either, Maggie," he said, using her nickname for the first time since she'd thought she heard it at the boardinghouse on her first night in Cheyenne. Worth's hand moved completely over hers, his fingers gripping her palm. "Dance with me?" he asked, already pulling her up. "Please," he added as she hesitated, her breath caught in her throat.

He looked so different from before—so intense, so desperate. She couldn't refuse him, though her rational mind protested. They had too many unresolved issues between them, too much still left unsaid. But the only issue her body cared about was Worth. His need had become hers. Something in him reached out to her—his wanting, his yearning, his pain, and his pleasure.

The barriers between them would not be breached in an evening, but they had forged the first links across them.

"I'd like that." She rose and let him sweep her back into the ballroom. She slipped into his arms as the waltz began, and he led her into their own private world. Dizzily she clung to him as they spun together, her hand held in his, her heart beating against his chest.

She lost all track of time and place. Her feet moved of their own accord as she surrendered herself to the music and the magic of his touch. Blurred images teased the edges of her vision; Worth's face dominated the center. His scent surrounded her, dark and mysterious. His pirate shirt gaped low enough that she caught sight of a sprinkling of dark hair on his chest. It was scandalous. More scandalous yet, she wanted to touch him, to see if the hairs would be as soft as they looked, if they'd curl around her finger like the down of a thistle.

She closed her eyes, overwhelmed by sensations. The music stopped but her feet kept moving, faster and faster. Suddenly she felt the rush of cool air. She opened her eyes to the darkness of night. Here, on the outskirts of the city, the sky was a panorama of stars, glittering like diamonds clear across from one horizon to the other.

"Maggie, don't look at me like that," Worth whispered raggedly.

The woman in his arms was all soft curves and satin skin. The scent of flowers drifted in a cloud around her, drawing him closer, then closer still. On the dance floor, it was all he could do to remember they were in a public place. No sooner had the music ended than he'd had to escape, taking her with him out the ballroom doors.

If he'd thought the cool night air would bring him back to his senses, he couldn't have been more wrong. The darkness surrounded them in a cocoon of privacy, the in-

sects chirped with a music of their own, the tinkle of
laughter and the low hum of conversation from the house
provided a muted counterpoint to nature's song.

"Come with me," he entreated, drawing Maggie farther
away from the party, around the side of the massive house.
She let him guide her, her hand trembling in his though her
steps did not falter.

"Where are we going?" she whispered.

"Just a few more steps. There's a stone archway here
that leads to the side porch. See? It's just there."

A yellowish glow from the lights in the parlor faintly
illuminated the circular porch. With their eyes adjusted to
the darkness, they could make out the five stairs leading up
to it.

Quietly they climbed to the porch. A few pieces of
wicker furniture were set around a small table. Worth led
Mary Margaret to the cushioned settee and drew her down
beside him. They had come only a short distance, but
Worth was as out of breath as if he had run a mile uphill.
His heart hammered in his chest and thunder sounded in his
ears.

At his side, he could feel Mary Margaret shiver.

"You're cold. I shouldn't have brought you out here," he
said.

"N-no, I'm fine. Really." She wasn't lying, exactly. Her
shivers came from more than just the chill air. A fine trembling shook her very core, eddying out in ripples of fear
and excitement, desire and expectation.

"Come closer. Let me warm you. I forgot how cold
these spring nights can get, even after a warm, sunny day."

He slipped his arm around her shoulders, and a sudden
heat raced through her. His hand drifted down along her
arm and he hugged her close. She leaned against him, cradled next to his body, her shoulder pressed against his
chest, her knee alongside his, and every point between
screamed out its awareness of the contact with his body.

If it weren't for the sheltering darkness, she would have
had to run, to push him away in feigned outrage and make
good her escape. Hadn't that been drilled into her from the

time she was a child? Men want only one thing and you must never let them have it, not until the marriage bed.

But there had been no marriage bed for her—not yet, maybe never. And whatever Worth wanted, she yearned for it, too. Her head lay on his shoulder. With every breath, she savored the scent of him, masculine and enticing. And the dark made it all so unreal—like a dream come true, yet still a dream.

And in dreams one can do anything, even reach across with a brave hand and gently stroke one fingertip down the profile of a man, from his forehead to his nose to his firm, soft lips, around the curve of his stubborn chin, where the bristly skin felt like sandpaper. She didn't stop there but traced a path down his throat to where his skin smoothed out again and a pulse raced like a runaway train down a steep incline.

"Oh, God, Maggie, what you do to me," he said hoarsely, trapping her hand in place while his chest heaved with the effort of breathing.

The hand on her arm pulled her closer to him, almost onto his lap. She raised her head from his shoulder to look into his face, and his mouth came down on hers, open and hungry, hot and wet. Her lips parted; she wasn't sure whether it was from desire or surprise, but it didn't matter. One taste of him and she was lost.

Nothing had ever been this wonderful. He tasted tangy and sweet, all at the same time. Her hand crept around his neck, reveling in his strength as she ground her mouth against his.

He responded with equal fervor, tilting his head at an angle to gain better access to her treasures. In one motion, he twisted her sideways onto his lap, snuggling her against his chest. She draped her arms around his shoulders and arched her back as he blazed a fiery trail of kisses down her neck.

His mouth burned lower, to the very top of her dress, where the creamy swell of her bosom was just revealed. His tongue rasped along her skin, and for a moment she had the wildest thought—that her dress should disappear entirely, leaving her open to his caresses. One of his arms anchored around her waist while his other hand swept up her rib cage and paused tantalizingly just below the curve of her breast. She almost cried out when he stopped, wanting him to touch her, needing him to.

Then the night air hit her moist skin, chilling her and bringing back a vestige of sanity. She pulled away from him, confused. This was no dream. Her feelings were too real, her senses too alive. The man beneath her was warm and hard, his heartbeat as real as her own, and as fast.

"Worth," she whispered desperately, and felt his hands slip down to her waist. For a moment he simply held her, his body unmoving, not even breathing. She felt the tension in his muscles—it gripped his entire length until he let out the breath he was holding and slowly relaxed.

"Are you all right?" he asked, brushing a stray lock of hair off her forehead.

She nodded, then answered, "Yes," when she realized he couldn't see her well in the dark.

"I wish I could say the same. You pack a pretty powerful punch, but I think I'll survive."

She saw a brief flash of white and decided he must have smiled. "I'm sorry," she whispered, and tried to clamber off him.

"Don't be. There's nothing to be sorry about," he murmured, and held her in place. "Give me just another minute. I don't know when I'll have the pleasure of holding you again with the children around. You feel so good."

"I thought . . ." She swallowed her words, appalled at what she'd been about to say.

"You thought what? That once started a man couldn't stop?" A laugh rumbled in his chest. "Don't worry, it's not true."

"But . . . are you all right?"

"Me? I'm just fine, under the circumstances. Not that I don't want more, mind you, but for right now, I'm more than fine. How about you?"

"I don't know. It's like a dream."

"A good dream, I hope, Maggie mine. Don't fret about what's happened here tonight. It was meant to be. Nothing this good can possibly be wrong, I promise you. And I'm a man of my word, Miss Simpson," he drawled with a western twang.

She could hear the smile in his voice as he teased them back into the real world. She was grateful for his patience and his self-control. She wasn't sure when she would have stopped him, or whether she would have at all.

"I think we better get back now, don't you?" he asked. "Someone's liable to start missing us pretty soon and we don't want to set tongues wagging."

He eased her off his lap and helped her stand. "Come on, sweetheart," he said, and put his arm around her shoulders. "This way."

They went down the stairs and headed back toward the ballroom. The band was on its last break and people were milling around, unwilling to bring the evening to an end, though it was nearly three in the morning.

As Worth and Mary Margaret entered by the rear doors, they could hear a commotion across the room.

Eight

"*W*here is she?" a slurred voice demanded. "Where's Annie? Have you seen her? Don't lie to me now. I know she's here."

A dark-haired man weaved drunkenly through the crowd, accosting a number of people, loudly shouting that he wanted to see Annie right away.

"Uh-oh," Worth muttered. "We've got trouble now. Jesse isn't usually like this, but when he's drunk too much, there's no telling what he might do. Stay back here a minute while I find out what's going on. I don't want you getting hurt."

If anything were needed to remove the last remnants of her dream, the reality of the drunken man more than provided it. Mary Margaret watched with some trepidation as Worth approached him after stopping briefly to question one of his friends.

"What's going on, Jesse?"

"You tell me, why doncha? Why should I always be the last to know, huh?" He spun away, staring at the crowd now gathered in a wide circle around him. They were avidly watching the scene unfold while trying to stay a safe distance away. "You all know where Annie is 'cause you saw her here tonight," he yelled. "Why don't somebody tell me?

"Annie? Where are ya?" he shouted to the ceiling. The people closest to him took a step back.

"Jesse," Worth called to him. "Calm down and I'll help you." Worth took a few steps toward Jesse.

"You know where she is? You been with her? I thought you were my friend, you bastard." Jesse lunged at Worth and tripped over his own feet, falling in a heap. He started to weep. Tears ran down his face.

Mr. and Mrs. Danby broke through the crowd, two burly men in their wake. Worth held up his hand to stop them and kneeled next to Jesse. "I don't know where Annie is, Jesse. I haven't seen her all evening—not to recognize, anyway. Are you sure she came here?"

"Yes," came the muffled reply. "She wore some Frenchified costume—Marie something or other. I ordered it special for her." Jesse lifted his head to look at Worth. He seemed more sober now. "I was supposed to come along, but one of my mares has been sick. I couldn't up and leave her. Next thing I knew Annie was gone."

"She's probably on her way home by now. Come on, let's get you out of here." Worth helped the man to his feet and signaled to the Danbys' men to assist Jesse out of the room. Mrs. Danby gave the band a sign to start playing, and her guests dutifully took up with their partners for the last dance.

Mary Margaret made her way around the dancers and followed behind Worth and Jesse as they headed for the front door. "What's really going on, Jesse?" Worth asked. "Drinking's not like you."

"I don't know. Annie's acting crazy lately. I just can't control her. I don't know what's going on and it's making me crazy, too. I'm sorry I spoiled the party."

"I'll make your apologies to the Danbys. You better go sleep this off before you see Annie."

Jesse went off with the two men, and Worth stood at the door watching them, shaking his head.

"Is he always like that?" Mary Margaret ventured.

"No, Jesse's a good man. Something must be really

sticking in his craw. Maybe he's spread himself too thin. This is cattle country and he's trying to make a go of raising horses. Poor man. Annie's not much use to him, I don't think."

From what she'd seen, Jesse wasn't much use to himself, let alone his wife, but it was not her place to pass judgment on Worth's friends.

"You want to go back to the party?" she asked.

"Not unless you do." Worth looked tired, she noted; his skin was stretched tight over his cheekbones. She could tell he was still worried about Jesse.

"No. This evening's been most interesting, but I think I'm ready to leave." *That's an understatement of significant proportions*, she thought to herself. Interesting didn't begin to describe the evening's events, from her first sight of Lucy on Worth's arm to a kiss that even now made her temperature rise just thinking of it. And then there was the spectacle of Jesse MacIntyre weeping on the ballroom floor. Her readers wouldn't believe half of it, even if she were daring enough to write about it!

Worth got her wrap and they thanked their hosts before leaving.

"What about Peter Dunsmore?" she thought to ask at the last minute. "He won't know I've left."

"Oh, Lord Peter left quite some time ago," Mrs. Danby remarked. "He was with a young lady. I didn't realize—"

"Oh, no, it's fine. We came together from Mrs. Miller's boardinghouse, and I didn't want to cause any confusion."

Worth looked grim again as his carriage was brought around.

"Is something wrong?" Mary Margaret asked once they were underway.

"What's with you and Lord Peter?" The way he emphasized the man's title made Mary Margaret smile. He was so transparent.

"You know as well as I do he's staying at Sarah's."

"You're laughing at me," he accused.

"Not laughing, exactly," Mary Margaret hedged. A heady giddiness filled her to bursting. If she laughed, it would not be at him, but because of him—because of all the wonderful things he made her feel. Endless possibilities danced before her eyes.

"I know just the thing to cure you," he growled in a low tone.

Before she knew what was happening, he slid across the seat and wrapped one arm around her, holding her still while he stole a kiss. Sensing his lack of concentration, the horse slowed, then stopped and nibbled at a few stray blades of grass growing by the roadside.

For a few seconds, Mary Margaret couldn't help but respond. Her lips parted expectantly as she hungered for the taste of him. Her hand threaded through his hair and she moaned softly as his tongue swept through her mouth, learning all her secrets.

The horse shifted his weight, taking a step forward to reach a more succulent clump of grass, and the carriage creaked as it rolled.

Mary Margaret pushed on Worth's shoulder as she came back to her senses. "Worth, please. We're in the middle of the street."

He raised his head and looked around. "Yeah, I guess we are, but at least you're not laughing anymore."

He straightened slowly but didn't slide back to his side of the seat. Gathering the reins in one hand, he once again put his arm around her, then set the horse on a slow walk home.

Mary Margaret put her hand to her lips. They felt swollen and unusually tender, and ached for more. She could still taste Worth on her skin, and she took a deep breath to clear her head. She certainly wasn't laughing, but she wouldn't have changed a second of the last few minutes.

In the dark, her mouth curved in a smile, and she snuggled against Worth's side.

The boardinghouse was quiet the next day. Most of its residents had been to the Danbys' party, and none had come back early.

By the time Mary Margaret made her appearance, it was after eleven and the main parlor was deserted. She wandered to the kitchen, and found her landlady drinking a cup of coffee while the cook cleaned up after the late breakfasters.

"There's still some porridge left, and I can get you some bacon and eggs, miss," the cook offered.

"I don't want to trouble you. Just some tea would be nice," Mary Margaret said. "And I can nibble on one of those rolls on the table."

"Oh, no!" the cook exclaimed. "I've some nice hot ones, just resting here on the stove. Now you set yourself down and let me get you the jam. Made it myself, I did—none of the store-bought stuff for our guests. Ain't that right, Mrs. Miller?"

"You better listen to her, Mary Margaret, or you'll put her in a bad mood for the rest of the day. Mrs. Loomis don't like no one refusing her breakfasts," Sarah said.

Mary Margaret let herself be persuaded. "May I at least join you fine ladies here in the kitchen? I really don't feel like eating alone." Alone, she would worry about her behavior last night with Worth.

"Sure, sure," said Sarah. "We don't mind none. Breakfast's a good time to be in the kitchen—warmest room in the house."

Sarah was right. Though the days were warming up, the nights were still quite chilly and by morning, the warmth of the kitchen made it a welcome gathering place for all the residents.

"So, how was the party last night? You have a good time? You didn't get in till late. I left a couple of lights on for you." As usual, Sarah was talking a mile a minute, never waiting for an answer to a question before asking the next one.

"The party was fine, as you well know," Mary Margaret replied. "You danced more often than I did."

"That's only because I didn't latch on to the most handsome man there," Sarah said slyly.

Did Sarah know about Worth? How was that possible? "You mean Lord Peter?" Mary Margaret asked evasively, buying herself some time. She had never thought the blond Englishman particularly handsome, but he wasn't ugly, either. His face was regular enough—all the right features in all the right places—but it lacked strength and character.

"Of course not," Sarah said with a sniff. "Don't think you're fooling me. You were the envy of all the young women, what with Marcus Robertson and John Worthington both courting you. So, which one did you choose?"

Mary Margaret felt her cheeks grow hot, but at least she now knew Sarah was only fishing for information.

"You're exaggerating," she protested, hiding her cheeks in her icy hands. "No one was courting me. Marcus and Worth consider me family because of my cousins."

"Marcus and Worth, is it, dearie?" Sarah cackled. "Now, don't you get bothered none, you hear? I like seeing young'uns get together. Reminds me of the old days, when me and Sam were young."

Mary Margaret recognized an opening here. She and Sarah had already discussed the prospect of her writing some articles based on Sarah's reminiscences. This seemed the perfect opportunity to pursue the topic and distract Sarah from continuing to probe about Worth. "Were you and Sam in Wyoming then?" she asked.

"No, Sam and I came with the railroad, back in sixty-seven. It was a tent city then, but I tell you, there was a fever to build. Every day we'd wake up and find something new had gone up in the night."

"Did Sam work for the railroad?"

"Yup, he was a foreman for a road gang till we decided to settle here. By then we was getting on in years, so it seemed like a good idea—'specially as Cheyenne was growing so fast. Why, I tell you, no sooner had the tracks been laid than along came the train from Julesburg, carrying everything a body could move."

Mrs. Loomis, who'd been fussing by the stove for the past few moments, came by the table with a plate heaped with eggs, bacon, and rolls. She placed it in front of Mary Margaret, ignoring her protests. "Eat what you want. Leave the rest," she insisted.

"What do you mean by *everything*?" Mary Margaret asked, wanting to get the conversation back to early

Cheyenne. She wished she'd thought to bring down some paper and writing implements.

"I mean every single thing that wasn't attached to the ground so hard it couldn't be picked up. They called it 'Hell on Wheels,' but I don't reckon your readers back east would likely take too well to that name. It was every bad thing you ever heard of. Entire saloons were taken apart— walls, floors, bars, furniture, you name it—put on a railcar and brought over here. Even the girls came along, to work the cribs and . . ." Sarah stopped in midsentence. "Lordy, I hadn't ought to be telling you 'bout such stuff."

"Why not?" Mary Margaret demanded. Mention of the cribs—unsavory places where women got paid for being with men—reminded Mary Margaret she wanted to know more about this side of western life, especially since Sarah had told her the story of her friend selling cats to lonely dance hall girls. Who were these women who followed the tracks? Who hung out at mining towns and consorted with all manner of men who weren't their husbands?

"Now, you listen here, missy. I don't see any call to tell you 'bout that sort of thing. You're a well-bred young lady, and I want you to stay that way." Sarah gave her a steely-eyed glare.

Mary Margaret laughed. "Now, Sarah, I explained it all to you already. I'm writing the truth about the West, not a bunch of fairy tales. If it bothers you to tell me, I'll just have to find someone else."

Mary Margaret made as if to stand. She'd eaten as much as she could of the copious breakfast Mrs. Loomis had placed before her and hoped to goad Sarah into telling her what she wanted to know.

"Set back down and don't give me no sass. I'll tell you what I can recall," Sarah snapped. "This younger generation! I don't know what they're getting to."

Sarah stood and stomped over to the coffeepot to pour herself another cup. "More tea?" she inquired over her shoulder.

Mary Margaret shook her head. Sarah harrumphed and stomped back to her seat.

"Now, where was I?" Sarah began. "Oh, yes, 'Hell on

Wheels.' Well, to get a saloon, all you had to do was order one from Chicago. It'd come all in pieces and you just had to put it together. One time my Sam took me down to see how it was done. You'd never believe it. Three men worked half a day, and before the roof was even in place, the bartender was serving drinks.

"First, they put down the floor. Then they set up the bar and all the fixtures—tables, chairs, even the piano. That way, they didn't have to worry about fitting 'em through the doors. Then they put up the walls and lowered the roof. It was something to behold. They had mirrors and pictures —the kind no lady should ever see—and more Red Eye than you could shake a stick at."

"And what about the girls?"

"Never you mind about them girls," Sarah said crossly. "They ain't no friends for you, you hear?"

A bell sounded above the call box by the kitchen door. Sarah looked at it and saw the flag for the front door was raised.

"Someone's at the door. I have to go get it." She scurried out of the room, leaving Mary Margaret frustrated. One way or another, she intended to find the answers to her questions, and if Sarah didn't want to give them to her, she'd find another way.

"Hi, Aunt Maggie," Tom's cheerful voice interrupted her musings.

"Tom, Becky, what are you two doing here?"

Mary Margaret hugged the two children. Was Worth here, too, she wondered. She wasn't sure she was ready to see him—not after the wanton way she had responded to him last night. Nonetheless, a bubbling excitement percolated through her veins.

"Kathleen brought us," Tom said. "Uncle Worth had to go talk to someone this afternoon."

"Now that Lucy—I mean, Miss Lucy—is back at her ranch, we can go visiting in the afternoon, just like Kathleen. We asked Kathleen to bring us here," Becky said, climbing onto her lap.

Mary Margaret hid her disappointment. "Where is she?" she asked.

"Talking to Mrs. Miller in the front room. We didn't want to wait to see you, so we ran straight back here."

Tom's words warmed her heart and eased her momentary sense of loss. She had been afraid the children wouldn't remember her after so many months—or worse, be angry with her, thinking she'd deserted them. But they were as loving as ever—Becky, especially. The girl liked nothing more than to cuddle in Mary Margaret's embrace and regale her with stories about her new friends. Gone was the cowering, shy child from Boston, replaced by this cheerful, sunny, talkative imp. How proud Claire and Henry would be of the children.

"I'm glad you came," Mary Margaret said, then dropped her voice to a conspiratorial murmur. "I know where the cookies are hidden, so you two sit here and I'll get them."

Kathleen found them happily munching cookies and drinking milk ten minutes later.

"I thought you might like some time alone with the children, miss. Poor Mr. Worth had ta work today, even on a Sunday. One of his friends is having problems. Likely he won't be done for the rest of the day. If you don't mind, I'll leave the children here while I go visiting."

"I'd love to watch them. Have a good time."

It was late afternoon when Worth finally appeared at the boardinghouse. The children were playing on the side porch while Mary Margaret took refuge by the fire in the back parlor, where she could keep an eye on them through the lace-curtained window.

"Hope I'm not too late," Worth said once Mrs. Miller had shown him in.

Mary Margaret stood to greet him. He smiled at her, looking natural and at ease. Only the hint of concern in his eyes gave away his true feelings. Somehow, his uncertainty made it easier for her to cope with her own shyness and insecurities.

"No, of course not," she said in response to his query. "Come have a seat. You look tired. Shall I ring for a drink?"

Worth sank wearily into the overstuffed armchair Mary

Margaret indicated. "It's been a tiresome afternoon," he conceded. "A cup of coffee would be nice."

His eyes were still wary, questioning, but the expression in them had gentled.

Mary Margaret rang for the ranch girl who worked at the boardinghouse as a way of bringing in more family income. Almost immediately, Rose brought in a tray laid out with coffeepot, cream, sugar, and some of the cook's famous pastries, still warm from the oven. The spicy, sweet smell of cinnamon filled the room.

Worth took a careful sip of the burning brew. "Whew, this coffee is strong enough to haul a wagon."

"Sarah made it, since Mrs. Loomis has the afternoon off. She says she learned how to make it from a drover who came through with his cattle up the Texas Trail."

Maggie smiled again, more fully this time, and Worth felt the jolt clear down to his boots. She looked so right here in the parlor with the late-afternoon sun sneaking through the lace curtains to touch her hair with red.

Her dress was a dark color and buttoned down the front, skimming her every curve. The white-linen collar stood high around her neck, framing her face. The bright, grosgrain bow, her only ornament, made her eyes gleam like a cat's, somewhere between green and yellow.

"Would you like something else?" She stood and made to move to the bellpull. Worth couldn't tear his gaze away from her figure. He longed to reach for her. In his mind, he could see himself unbuttoning each and every button and slowly peeling the dress down past . . . "Worth?"

"What? No, no. This is fine. Exactly what I need so I don't fall asleep before the children do." He took another sip of the horrid brew to show her he meant what he said. He wanted something else, all right, but he didn't think his Maggie was quite ready to hear what it was.

"If you're certain," she said doubtfully.

"Yes, I'm fine." He smiled at her as she resumed her place by the window. "What about you?"

She laughed. "No, thanks. I already had my quota. Lately I find tea much more suited to my 'refined Easternish ways.'" Her eyes sparkled as she mimicked Sarah Miller's western twang.

"Yes, I can understand that." He laughed with her and put down the cup.

He looked up and their gazes collided, then held for a silent eternity. Quicksilver feelings they could not even name darted between them. Only a shout from right outside the window broke the spell.

"That sounds like Thomas," Maggie said, averting her face to look through the curtains. Worth felt an instant of regret. For a moment, they had exchanged something unspoken but very real.

"He seems to be enjoying himself," Worth allowed, but his thoughts were elsewhere as he remembered their kiss last night, the feel of her skin beneath his fingers, the softness of her body next to his. Had she felt the magic, too?

She let go of the curtain and it floated back into place. "Tom's really grown since Boston. He seems happier here, and sadder, too. I can't quite put my finger on it."

She met his glance again, but this time her eyes were circumspect, guarding their secrets more carefully than before.

"I know what you mean," Worth agreed. He leaned back in his chair, resting his head against the antimacassar crocheted by one of Mrs. Miller's boarders. He rubbed one hand over his brow and pinched the bridge of his nose, hoping to ease some of his tension. Worrying about Tom always made his head throb. "Tom seems to like it out here well enough, especially when we visit the ranch. But I'd be lying if I said there weren't any problems at all."

"Is there something I can help with?"

Worth opened his eyes and saw the love and concern for Tom written on Mary Margaret's face. Would she still feel the same way if his worst suspicions about the boy were confirmed? He remembered his own boyhood. People hadn't taken kindly to him then, and while he didn't think Mary Margaret would have the same reaction, he couldn't be sure. He decided to take a middle ground.

"I'm not sure, but it's very possible. Kathleen mentioned

once that you had worked with Tom on his studies," he said cautiously, watching her face.

"Oh, yes." She brightened. "I'd love to help him again, if I wouldn't be imposing."

She seemed uncomfortable at the latter thought, though Worth couldn't understand where she ever got the idea she might be unwanted. Hell, if she wanted to impose, he'd be all too happy to take her on.

"Of course you wouldn't be imposing. What ever gave you such an idea?"

She flushed prettily, but only said, "Nothing in particular. I–I just wanted to make sure I wouldn't be stepping in where I wasn't wanted."

She looked expectantly at him, but he had no idea what she was waiting to hear. He leaned forward in his chair, propping his elbows on his knees.

"You're definitely wanted," he said, unsure if he were overstepping some unspoken line, and not caring either. This time he wasn't going to let some overblown sense of propriety keep them apart.

Her eyes widened at his words, then she quickly lowered her lids. *Good*, he thought, *she heard what I said—all that I said*. And he smiled to himself.

"Uncle Worth, you're here," Becky cried out as she came into the house, her cheeks red from the cold, her eyes shining brightly.

She clambered into his lap. "You been visiting with Aunt Maggie?"

"Yes, I have."

Mary Margaret watched as he kissed the child on her cheek.

"I love you, Uncle Worth," Becky said and gave him a hug.

"I love you, too," he murmured back, not in the least embarrassed, though Mary Margaret knew such shows of affection were not common in the West and were even frowned upon in some circles.

The display of tender feeling caused a familiar ache inside Mary Margaret. Her solitary life contrasted poignantly with what she beheld. Despite the fulfillment her writing gave her, she was never more aware than now of the side of life denied her.

What would it be like to be married and have children? To have a husband sitting across from her, with their daughter on one knee? And if that daughter were Becky and the husband . . . She didn't dare complete the thought as her heart beat erratically.

Hard on the heels of her fantasies came the more realistic questions. What would happen to her career? To her independence? She'd lived by her own wits and intelligence for so long, what if she couldn't bend them to another's whims? And even if she could, who would want her?

The ache became a pain in her midsection, threatening to tear her apart.

She was relieved when Thomas came in.

"Hello, Uncle Worth. When did you get here?" The boy was polite but guarded, Mary Margaret noticed—not at all comfortable with himself.

"A while ago," Worth answered, and smiled at his nephew. "I've some good news. Your Aunt Maggie has agreed to spend some time with us while she's in Cheyenne. Says she misses working with you two on your schoolwork and such."

Tom's face lit up. "Really, Aunt Maggie? Will you help me with my schoolwork instead of dum— I mean, instead of Miss Lucy?"

The boy looked warily at Worth to see if he'd picked up on the slip, but if he had, he gave no sign of it. Mary Margaret was puzzled. She'd given Worth every chance she could, short of coming right out and asking, to tell her about Lucy Robertson, but he hadn't. On the other hand, if there were something between Lucy and Worth, surely he wouldn't have acted last night the way he had with her. She would have to content herself with that thought, knowing Worth was an honorable man.

She smiled at Tom. "I'd be more than happy to work with you or do whatever else you might like," she said to him.

Tom turned to his uncle. "Could Aunt Maggie come to

the baseball game with us next week? It would make the day extra special, and we'd all be together, just like in Boston."

"Sure, as long as she has no other obligation." Worth looked at her. "Would you come with us? We'd be honored."

Mary Margaret felt her heart swell beneath her breast. "Oh, yes. I'd love to come."

Nine

"Uncle Worth, hurry, or we'll be too late to get on a team," Thomas urged from the back seat of the carriage.

Mary Margaret turned in her seat to get a better view of both the children and Kathleen. Sitting this way also afforded her a better view of Worth.

Though she'd hoped to see him more in the week gone by, they'd had almost no time together when she'd visited Tom and Rebecca. Most days he'd been at work, wrapped up in the intricacies of a new case. Then, when he had been home, the children had been around or she'd been busy, visiting the offices of Cheyenne's daily papers to arrange for some of her articles to appear. All of this gave them little opportunity to be alone or talk.

"Don't worry, Tom," Worth soothed. "They'll save us a place. I promised Reverend Leisch we'd be there as soon as dinner was over."

Mary Margaret settled more comfortably in the carriage, knowing she couldn't sit and stare at Worth forever, though it was a tantalizing thought. She surveyed the passing countryside and listened to the children arguing good-naturedly in the back. Worth had said the trip to Emory Park out by Lake Mahpalutah would only take a short while, but she was more than happy to have it take longer.

This is what her life would be like if they were a family, except then she could sit closer to Worth. She closed her eyes and breathed in the scent of him, remembering the sandpaper touch of his cheek when he'd kissed her, the taste of his mouth against hers.

She gave a sigh.

"What was that for?" Worth leaned over to whisper in her ear.

She blinked and sat up straighter, startled by Worth's close proximity in the confining front seat of the carriage as much as by her own wayward thoughts.

"Just general contentedness, I suppose. I've had a wonderful luncheon, the children are happy, and we're going on a lovely afternoon outing." *No need to tell him more*, she thought somewhat desperately.

"I have to warn you, these baseball games can become very heated—especially if Fred Straight is the umpire." Worth's smile turned into a grin.

"All right, what does Mr. Straight do?" Mary Margaret asked, choosing to take Worth's bait.

"It isn't what he does—it's what he doesn't do."

"And that is?" She savored his teasing, enjoying the chance to have some private time with him, even if it was in the front seat of his carriage with Kathleen and the children right behind them.

Worth only continued to grin.

"John Worthington, are you going to tell me or not?"

"Fred Straight can't see the broad side of a barn, much less that little bit of leather called a baseball."

Mary Margaret smiled. "If he can't see, why do they allow him to officiate at these things?"

Worth had given her a quick lesson in the rudiments of baseball over the noon meal. She still wasn't sure she understood half of what would be going on, but she had learned the umpire's word was law.

"Tradition, I suppose. He started the first games out here. Then, when he busted his knee in a mining accident, he sort of made himself the official referee."

"Look, there's the park entrance," Tom interrupted.

Mary Margaret thought about reminding Tom of his manners, but decided there would be time enough for that later. Looking over her shoulder, she saw the excitement in all three faces in the backseat.

"It doesn't look like our park in Boston, Aunt Maggie, but that's all right," Becky reassured her. "It has lots of other good things, like a great big lake. Uncle Worth says we can come here all the time, now that it's warmed up."

As they entered the park, all Mary Margaret could see were open areas and trees. There were no fences or sidewalks, no deer or swans. But then, this was Wyoming Territory, and as Mary Margaret had discovered for herself, it had a beauty all its own.

Before Worth could get the horse tied to the tethering rope, Tom and Becky were running across the open field, heading for a group of people gathered under the few trees edging the open area.

"I'll chase after the young ones, Mr. Worth," Kathleen offered, hopping down from the carriage. "You and Miss Maggie take your time."

"Does Kathleen seem particularly excited today?" Mary Margaret asked, noting the pinkness of the young woman's cheeks as she hurried after the children.

"I believe our Kathleen is smitten with the pastor."

"You mean Reverend Leisch?" While Mary Margaret found the young Presbyterian cleric a nice enough fellow, she'd not noticed Kathleen's attachment.

"It seems Colin Leisch did some work for the church in Ireland and lived not far from Kathleen's old home—even attended her church. They've become quite friendly. I know Kathleen hasn't missed worship once since they were introduced."

Grabbing a folded blanket and a basket out of the back of the carriage, Worth took Mary Margaret's arm and helped her across the field. "I thought Lucy might have her eye on Colin, but . . ." Worth shrugged.

Mary Margaret knew exactly who Lucy had her eye on, and it wasn't the young minister of the First Presbyterian Church of Cheyenne, but she kept her thoughts to herself.

As she and Worth drew close to the growing crowd, Mary Margaret saw an older man organizing the young men and boys. She noticed his limp and decided he must be the infamous Mr. Fred Straight.

"I'd better get over with Tom, or I might not get a position on the team. You'll be all right on your own, won't you?" Worth asked as he spread the plaid blanket beneath a tree and handed her the basket. Their hands touched and a tingle of awareness shot up her arm.

The thread of worry in Worth's voice was endearing. "I'll be fine. Besides, Tom might need you for moral support. He's never played this game before. Have a good time. I see Becky over there, under the trees. We can keep each other company."

Rebecca waved to her and Mary Margaret signaled for her to come over. Worth gave her a last smile before trotting over to the other men. Mary Margaret couldn't help but compare him to the others, and a feeling of pride swelled inside her. He was surely the best-looking man there—at least, in her opinion.

He was neither as leathery as the cowboys, whose skin had been toughened by the hot sun in summer and the pitiless blizzard winds of winter, nor as pallid as the British boys, who hung around indoors in rain or shine. There was an athletic strength evident in his rhythmic stride and the way he moved when he hefted a bat over his right shoulder.

For a moment, Mary Margaret lost herself in pure sensation as Worth swung the bat experimentally a couple of times. His broad shoulders revealed their power as the muscles in his back flexed and twisted with every swing. She could see him in her mind's eye, riding the range out at his ranch, roping steer or breaking broncos, or whatever it was they did out there, and felt a fluttering in a very private place.

Then he turned toward her and winked, just as Becky ran up.

"Aunt Maggie, here you are. Will you sing with me just like you used to?"

Flustered, Mary Margaret could only stare at the girl while she gathered her wits about her.

"Please, Aunt Maggie, please," Becky wheedled.

Mary Margaret tried to concentrate on the child, but all she could see were Worth's rippling muscles and the dare in his eyes. Had he guessed her errant thoughts? She shivered, though whether with embarrassment or excitement, she couldn't begin to guess.

"Come sit with me, Becky and tell me what you want to sing first." With conscious effort, Mary Margaret brought her wayward emotions under control.

Fortunately, Becky noticed nothing amiss. As was her custom, she crawled into Mary Margaret's lap and they ran through the songs they'd sung together back in Boston.

As they sang, Mary Margaret pressed her face into Rebecca's sweet-smelling hair. She had missed this feeling of family so much.

Mary Margaret looked down at Becky. They had stopped singing a while ago, giving in to the lazy lethargy brought on by the heat of the day. Becky had fallen asleep, leaving Mary Margaret alone with her thoughts. Gently, she eased the child onto the blanket.

More and more people settled beneath the sparse trees ringing the field. Some she recognized from town, but there were a number of soldiers, probably from nearby Fort Russell, and quite a few cowboys, if you could go by their attire.

She watched the young wranglers unstrap their guns from around their waists and carefully place them near their large western hats and coats. The sight of the guns reminded Mary Margaret that under the polite guise of a leisurely afternoon outing hummed the daily ruthlessness of western society.

The great variety of people was a welcome distraction. Setting her writer's mind to work, Mary Margaret drank up the atmosphere. What a story this would make for the readers back east.

Once the baseball game began, Kathleen joined Mary Margaret on the blanket.

"This is only the second game they've played this year, what with the strange weather they have here," Kathleen told Mary Margaret. "The other was more than a month ago. One of my friends from church took me. 'Twas a fine spring afternoon, just like today. Perfect hitting weather, as Reverend Leisch says."

"This game must be more interesting than I realized, Kathleen. Maybe you can explain some of its finer points," Mary Margaret said, keeping the smile from her face. "You obviously have a great love for it. Or could there be another reason for your sudden interest in it?"

"Oh, Miss Maggie, go on with you." Kathleen blushed prettily, picking up immediately on Mary Margaret's oblique reference to the good reverend.

"No more 'Miss' this and 'Miss' that," Mary Margaret said. "We're in Wyoming now. Besides, I expect you to tell me all about Reverend Leisch." It was nice to have someone with whom to share her womanly confidences once again.

Kathleen told her all about the young minister while they watched the game. As they talked, Mary Margaret found herself paying less attention to what Kathleen was saying and more to the action on the field, and to Worth in particular.

The other team was now at bat, and Worth was pitching the ball. Once again she was struck by his physical presence—the way the white linen of his shirt stretched taut over his shoulders when he threw the ball; the way each muscle and tendon bunched and then relaxed as he moved; the way he wiped his brow and squinted at the catcher, smiling with pleasure when a batter walked off the field, frowning when someone got a hit.

Mary Margaret wanted to touch him, to run her hands over every finely sculpted inch of him, to feel his skin beneath her fingertips, hot and moist and quintessentially male. Her thoughts scandalized her, but she couldn't look away.

"Mr. Worth had better mind his business," Kathleen said, unaware of Mary Margaret's lapse. "Reverend Leisch is a well-turned batter."

Mary Margaret blinked twice to regain her bearings. What was happening to her on this fine spring day? Had the bright sun and warm breeze addled her brain?

"Mr. Worth seems to be holding his own," she managed to say. And he did, too. For at that moment, Reverend Leisch walked back to the sidelines and Worth sent a triumphant grin in her direction, melting her insides into a molten core.

"What just happened?" she asked dizzily.

Fortunately, Kathleen assumed her question was about the game.

"He's been struck out—and he's such a fine hitter, too," Kathleen lamented. "You just watch the next time he's up to bat."

Mary Margaret vaguely remembered having been told about outs and innings earlier on, so she simply nodded and quickly asked Kathleen something else about the reverend. This time, she concentrated all her energy on listening to the answer.

About an hour later, Fred Straight called a break in the game. Mary Margaret and Kathleen set out the lemonade and glasses they'd found in the basket Worth had given her earlier.

Worth, Tom, and Reverend Leisch each accepted a glass readily, quickly quenching their immediate thirst. Mary Margaret felt shy around Worth after her earlier thoughts. She couldn't quite meet his eye and was grateful for the presence of the others.

Then Kathleen and the reverend took their refilled glasses and moved off toward the field, and she was left with just Thomas and Worth.

"Did you see the hit I made, Aunt Maggie?" Tom asked. "It was way out past Reverend Leisch. He had to run to get it. Our team has six points."

"Runs," Worth corrected, tousling Tom's hair. "For someone who's never played before, you did a masterful job. I couldn't be prouder. But you need to rest now. Why don't you sit and talk with Aunt Maggie for a while. You can explain more about the game."

Mary Margaret listened carefully as Tom regaled her with tales about his part in the baseball game. She was happy he was excelling in this sport. His schoolwork had certainly fallen below standard, and she was afraid of the effect the bad grades might have on him. He needed something he did well in, even if it was baseball.

"Well, my friend, are you trouncing the pants off the other team?" Mary Margaret glanced up at Marcus Robertson's words. "Begging your pardon, Mary Margaret. I didn't realize you were sitting here."

Standing beside Marcus was his daughter Lucy. She'd taken her arm from her father's and entwined it with Worth's when he'd begun talking.

"It's nice to see you both again," Mary Margaret said.

"The pleasure is mine," Marcus said, as if she'd been talking to him alone. "You're looking mighty fine this afternoon. Been enjoying the game?"

"Yes, what little I can understand of it."

"Maybe I could be of some help?" Marcus said, a gleam in his eye.

"Tom said he wanted to tell his Aunt Maggie about the game," Worth said curtly. "Besides, he's doing such a great job for our team, we have a definite advantage."

Mary Margaret began to rise and both Worth and Marcus moved to help her. She noticed that Lucy kept a firm grip on Worth's arm.

Worth might think that Lucy and the good reverend would make a couple, but Mary Margaret could read the signs, and she was now more certain than ever that her first impression had been correct. Lucy was in love with Worth. How long could he resist her tender charms?

Mary Margaret took the hand Marcus extended and thanked him politely for his help. She brushed some dried grass from the white lawn material of her afternoon dress and straightened the crisp, starched collar.

"So, Miss Simpson, are you enjoying all the sights we have to offer?" Lucy purred.

"I'm certainly enjoying this baseball game."

"Surely you've had time to see more than this since you've been with us, Miss Simpson," Lucy said.

"Please, call me Mary Margaret," she offered, recognizing Lucy's ploy in emphasizing their age difference. "I haven't seen much of the countryside yet, but Worth has promised me a trip out to his ranch. There are so many things I'm interested in exploring in your beautiful territory."

"Like the Golden Plume?"

To anyone else, Lucy's question might have appeared as just a passing comment, but Mary Margaret suspected a darker motive.

"What's this about the Golden Plume?" Worth asked.

Before Mary Margaret could answer Worth's question, Lucy put on her most innocent expression and said, "Why, Mrs. Forrest mentioned she saw Miss Simpson entering the Golden Plume last Thursday, I believe. Yes, it was Thursday, because that's the day the Ladies' Aid Society meets at the church."

"Maggie, is this true?" Worth stepped forward, disengaging Lucy's hand from his arm, his eyes never leaving Mary Margaret's face.

She nodded. She'd made the visit for a story she planned to do on the loneliness of the women on the frontier. And the women she'd found at the Golden Plume had been informative, once she'd gained their confidence.

"I was working on a story . . ."

Worth's voice cut in, colder than steel, "I think we need to speak about this in private, away from the children. Marcus, Lucy, if you don't mind keeping an eye on Becky, we'll only be gone for a minute."

Without waiting for their assent, Worth grasped Mary Margaret's elbow and led her away.

Mary Margaret could only smile apologetically over her shoulder at Lucy and Marcus. Though Lucy had been pleased that her disclosure of Mary Margaret's excursion had angered Worth, now she looked vexed that he was taking her rival off for a secluded and private chat.

The whole situation with Lucy would have been funny if Worth hadn't been so upset and she wasn't so miffed at his overbearing tone. This was exactly what she had worried about—that Worth would be unable to accept her profession and its demands on her life.

"What in the world ever possessed you to go to that part of town?" Worth's words were as clipped as his pace—he was practically running her along the path to the lake.

"As I was trying to say, before I was so rudely interrupted," she said, shaking off his hand, "it is my responsibility as a journalist to show life in all its aspects—good and bad—and that means speaking with as many different types of people as possible."

By the time she had finished talking, they were at the shore of the beautiful lake, but the tranquility of the scene did nothing to sooth the anger and disappointment she felt seething within her.

"I'm telling you, you will not be allowed in that section of town again." Worth's voice had lost none of its steeliness, and his tone brooked no argument.

"You're telling me? *You're telling me*! Let *me* tell *you*. You have no say in what I think or do. I'm a grown woman and can make these decisions by myself. And anyway, the Golden Plume is only eighty feet away from the First Presbyterian Church, as Lucy was so kind to point out."

Worth was visibly holding on to his temper, but Mary Margaret didn't care. If he'd asked, instead of told, or questioned, instead of demanded, she might not have completely lost her own temper. She turned her back on him and gazed out over the lake.

Worth moved around her so she was facing him again and grabbed her upper arms, refusing to allow her to escape his glare.

"It may be only eighty feet away from the First Presbyterian Church, but those eighty feet might as well be eighty miles. The people on the church side dress like you, talk like you, and most often react exactly the way you would, but on the Plume side, it's another story.

"There, they carry concealed blackjacks and knives. The saloon owners don't hire those burly down-country plug uglies as bodyguards and bouncers for no good reason. They shoot first and ask questions later. And the 'ladies' you so casually befriended tote derringers in their garters."

Mary Margaret was stunned by Worth's outburst. She hadn't realized how personally responsible he would feel for her safety. But his chest was heaving as he took long breaths, and she could feel the anger and tension in his body. The pressure on her arms lessened and then tightened again.

"Damm it, you could have been killed and we'd have known nothing about it. Don't you care about the children? Don't you realize how we all would feel?"

"Of course, I . . ." Worth's lips closed over hers before she could finish. She could taste the anger and the fear in his kiss; she could also feel the longing. His mouth ground against hers, taking her by storm. She forgot all about the beautiful lake and the serene scenery. The voices of the children and ball players faded as she lost herself in the wonder of Worth's embrace. Her own anger was forgotten in the onslaught of emotion surging through her.

At last, she was where she wanted to be, even if she hadn't known it herself until this very moment. Something deep inside her recognized she had been waiting for this all day, all week—all of her life.

Worth's hands spread over her back and her arms lifted to his shoulders as he pulled her closer. Her fingers entwined in the soft hair at his nape. Beneath her palms she could feel the heat of his skin.

She opened her mouth under his, wanting more of him. As their kiss deepened, Worth's tongue sought hers, probing, searching for her every secret. Willingly, she yielded to him. His scent surrounded her, musky from exertion and thoroughly male, making her light-headed with desire.

A fire more intense, more ardent than anything she had ever before experienced, burned within her. When his hand moved to her breast, she moaned with relief. She could feel her nipple tighten almost painfully in response to his touch. A sweet tension throbbed in her midsection as she pressed herself against him

Her hands roamed his back, learning the patterns of his body, the way the muscles flexed and tensed, the planes and valleys. She thrilled as his heart raced beneath her hand, beating in time to her own. And then she lost even that small shred of sanity as Worth deepened the kiss, stealing her very breath away.

This kiss held something the others she'd shared with him did not—a depth of desperation, an edge of hunger too long denied. Worth drew her closer to him until there was no space between them, no telling where one of them started and the other left off. She could feel his every muscle and sinew along her entire length, and knew more of him than she had of any man.

His hardness and strength called to everything soft and feminine inside her. She knew the force of his arousal and felt the depth of her own, like a rising warm sea carrying her off on a magical current.

Was this what made women through the centuries capitulate so easily?

Suddenly, Worth tore his mouth from hers. "God, Maggie, I'm sorry."

Sorry for what, she wanted to ask. For making her feel more than she had ever felt before, for giving her something she had craved all her life but never known?

Slowly she became aware of the sunlight glinting off the surface of the lake, the birds calling in the trees, the children shouting just beyond the small knoll.

She looked up into Worth's eyes and saw the turbulence of a summer storm reflected in them. Neither of them had expected such an explosion of need and desire. But now was not the time, and this was certainly not the place, to explore what was happening between them.

More than that, this afternoon had brought their differences into sharp focus—differences they would have to deal with without the blurring effect of passion if they were to create something lasting.

"There's no need to be sorry, Worth," she murmured. "Just give me a minute to catch my breath."

He nodded and walked away from her, his shoulders rigid, his fists clenched by his side.

A sudden intuition told her he blamed himself for what had happened. "Worth?"

He stopped walking but did not face her. "Yes?"

"Thank you," she whispered into the breeze.

The words floated to him on a breath of spring air, caressing his soul and giving him peace. "I didn't . . ."

He turned again and looked at her. Where he had expected to see regret, he saw instead enchantment. Where he had feared revulsion, he saw instead need. "I was going to say I didn't mean to do that, but you know I would be lying."

"Would you?" she asked, and he glimpsed the hope in her eyes.

"You know I would. I've wanted you all day—that must have been pretty obvious."

She blushed. "Not to me—I wasn't sure."

She dropped her gaze to the grass at her feet, her uncertainty shimmering in a cloud around her.

"Maggie?"

She looked up at him, her eyes luminous. In an instant, he closed the space between them and she was in his arms again, soft and womanly, her body a perfect fit to his own.

"Oh, Maggie, Maggie mine," he murmured, and rained kisses on her lips, her cheeks, her eyelids—every place he could reach with the two of them locked tight in each other's embrace. He felt like shouting or singing or dancing—or all three rolled into one.

Once more his lips closed over hers, and she opened to him like a flower, sharing her nectar, her sweetness. He could hardly bear to pull away a second time, though he knew he must.

Breathing hard, he laid his forehead against hers and willed his heart to stop racing.

"We had better head back before the others start missing us," he said after a time.

"All right," she agreed.

He offered her his arm and she placed her hand in the crook of his elbow. Together they started back, neither looking at the other. Their relationship had shifted ground, and both of them knew it. There was a tension racing between them—a sharing of feeling almost intimidating in its intensity. By unspoken consent they walked in silence, each coming to terms with what had just happened, each planning and dreaming of things to come.

They had almost reached the players on Worth's team when they heard shouting from the crowd. Mary Margaret could barely make out the words. From the distance, she could only tell it was a man yelling.

"What in the world is Jesse MacIntyre doing here?" Worth murmured. "The crazy fool. After the ruckus Saturday last, you'd think he'd have more sense."

Jesse caught sight of Worth and waved his arms.

"I'll only be a minute, Maggie. I need to take care of this." As Jesse approached, Mary Margaret recognized him from the masquerade ball. She also saw he was madder than a hornet. She hurried to find Becky and Tom.

"She's done it. I knew she would," Jesse bellowed.

"Calm down, Jesse, and lower your voice. Do you want all of Cheyenne to know your business?"

"I don't give a damn if the whole territory knows now," Jesse said more quietly. "Annie's left me. She's taken rooms at some fancy boardinghouse. What am I going to do?"

"Jesse, you knew she wouldn't be staying after our last meeting."

Jesse shrugged off Worth's comment. "Now she's got herself a snaked-eyed varmint of a lawyer who's spouting off about women's rights and how Annie owns the farm and not me."

"That's not the question, Jesse. You told me Annie signed the farm over to you when you asked me to represent you. That's what we have to prove," Worth said quietly.

"Damn foolish, if you ask me. A man works hard his whole life and then some female goes off and starts yelling about her rights. I gave her rights and look where it got me. Well, let me tell you, I'll give her her rights. I'll make her wish she'd never..."

Jesse's words were cut off in midsentence as Worth grabbed his arm and turned him away from the crowd. Worth whispered in Jesse's ear and the other man shrugged, but he didn't pull his arm from Worth's grasp as they continued over to where the horses were tethered.

Mary Margaret's thoughts were in a turmoil. So many conflicting emotions tugged at her, she didn't know which way to turn. All she wanted was to get back to Sarah's and have some time to herself—to sort through everything that had happened today, to explore in privacy her startling new discoveries about herself and Worth.

When she neared the blanket, she could feel Lucy's penetrating gaze trained on her. Self-consciously she raised her hand and patted the back of her hair, hoping no stray ends were flying loose.

She had nothing to be ashamed of, but she knew she couldn't trust Lucy's keen eye or acid tongue. The girl had her heart set on Worth and wouldn't take kindly to anyone who thwarted her. Mary Margaret couldn't help but sympathize. In Lucy's place, she would feel much the same way.

"You must have had a good afternoon," Sarah said from the rocking chair on the side porch.

"Oh, and why do you say that?" Mary Margaret replied, climbing the porch steps. She knew the older woman well enough now to catch the hint of gentle teasing in her voice.

"By the high color in those pretty cheeks of yours. I don't reckon our weak Wyoming sun could do that alone. Must be some other reason, I'm thinking. Maybe something to do with the young lawyer who picked you up?"

Mary Margaret ignored the question about Worth and focused on the weather. "I found the sun much warmer today than usual. I probably should have taken a parasol with me. I noticed many of the other ladies had them."

"It's not the sun that's put the roses in your cheeks, missy. But if you don't want to talk about it . . ." Sarah let her sentence trail off. "Supper'll be ready in a few minutes. You'll probably want to freshen up after your long day in the hot Wyoming sun."

Mary Margaret laughed. Sarah was incorrigible. "We all had a lovely time this afternoon, and I believe I will wash up before we eat. I'll see you in a few minutes."

The supper bell sounded just as Mary Margaret was leaving her room and she hurried down the stairs. Sarah liked her boarders to be on time for meals.

Walking to her seat at the table, Mary Margaret glanced around at the other guests. She noticed a new face among the seven already seated for supper. Sarah must have rented the empty room in the back.

The new woman was in her early thirties, with light-brown hair. Her eye color was hard to tell—she'd kept her gaze trained on her dinner plate since Mary Margaret had entered the room.

Nodding her greeting to the Pareet sisters, Mary Margaret bowed her head for the grace, a custom strictly adhered to since the good Reverend Charles Hanson had taken up lodging six years before.

"Well, Mary Margaret, what did you think of the baseball game?" Sarah asked as she passed the fried bread for the soup.

"I quite enjoyed it. I'd never seen the game played before. I take it this is a regular Sunday afternoon pastime here?"

"If it don't snow and Fred Straight's not drunk."

"Now, now, Mrs. Miller, we mustn't malign poor Mr. Straight," Reverend Hanson admonished.

"Just stating the truth, Reverend," Sarah returned. "The Good Lord does want us to speak the truth, doesn't he?" The grace at mealtime seemed to be the only concession Sarah Miller made to the minister, if her tart reply was anything to go by.

"Well, of course he does," Reverend Hanson replied, a bit put out by Sarah's questioning.

"Harrumph!" was Sarah's only response.

"Do you think you'll make a story out of the ball game, Miss Simpson?" Estella Pareet asked. "Won't it be wonderful to have a big paper back east carrying a story about our game?"

Mary Margaret didn't want to disappoint the genteel lady. "We'll have to see what the editors will allow."

"Oh, that would be fine," Estella concurred. "It's such a healthful sport, outside in the warm spring air."

Estella turned to her sister, Mirabelle. "Don't you agree?"

Mirabelle seemed to consider the idea, but no one was surprised when she said, "Yes, I do believe you're right." She always followed her sister's lead.

"I, for one, was greatly impressed by the players." The mellifluous voice carried all over the large dining room, its

mere tone commanding attention. This was Cleary Sombalay. She was with a traveling troupe of actors, and her
company was engaged for two months at the McDaniel's
Variety Theater. She'd decided to get away from the other
players and live a "normal life," though with Cleary
present, nothing stayed normal for long, Mary Margaret
suspected. She was outspoken, funny, outrageous, and
kind beyond ken.

"Particularly that handsome young catcher on the red
team," Cleary continued, glancing over to the younger of
the Pareet sisters. "Be honest, Miss Mirabelle, weren't you
impressed with him, too?" Cleary widened her eyes and
her eyebrows nearly disappeared under the swooping fall
of hair on her brow. "Such form, such size." The brazen
young actress nearly swooned into her soup.

Miss Mirabelle, sixty-five if she was a day, hid her face
behind her napkin, glanced at her sister, and began to titter.

"Really, Miss Sombalay! Is this an appropriate conversation for dinner? Or any time, for that matter?" Reverend
Hanson said, disapproval tinging every word.

"Why, Reverend, I was only commenting on the ball
player's ability and the size of his bat—so large and well-
shaped, you know." Sincere innocence echoed in every
word, but the lascivious gleam in her eye belied her tone.

Mary Margaret lowered her eyes and took a deep breath
to keep from bursting out in laughter.

Frederick Hinsford-Hill had no such scruples. His laughter rang out heartily. "My dear Miss Cleary, what a treat
you would be at one of our soirees in London. Don't you
agree, Peter, old man?"

"Quite, quite, Freddie," Lord Peter replied distractedly
to his countryman.

Mary Margaret hadn't seen Peter Dunsmore since the
night of the masked ball. He'd barely greeted her when
she'd arrived, and had neither apologized for disappearing
without her, nor inquired if she'd gotten safely home. Even
now, his interest seemed to be centered on the newest addition to Sarah's little family.

Sarah must have noticed the direction of Lord Peter's

glance, too, for at that moment she remembered her manners and introduced the newcomer.

"If I could have your attention, I'd like to introduce Mrs. Annie MacIntyre. She just moved in this afternoon."

This was the infamous Annie—the woman Jesse MacIntyre had been ranting about at the ball and again this afternoon?

Mary Margaret studied her more closely. The poor woman seemed afraid of her own shadow. She barely raised her head and never looked anyone in the eye. Mary Margaret found it hard to envision her dressed to the nines as Marie Antoinette, alone and unprotected at the masquerade ball. On the contrary, the woman before her looked as though she'd be afraid to cross the street by herself.

It must have taken great courage for her to leave her home and husband—not that she didn't have good cause. From what Mary Margaret had seen, Jesse MacIntyre appeared to be a mean-spirited, drunken man who used his position in a man's society to take what he wanted. And if what she'd heard today was any indication, he wanted total control over Annie's life and property.

When everyone voiced their greetings, Annie MacIntyre meekly nodded her head. Soon the table conversation returned to the baseball game. Only Annie and Lord Peter refrained from voicing their opinions.

Ten

*O*n Friday afternoon, Mary Margaret sat at the dining room table in Worth's house watching Tom do his homework. He tapped his chalk, swung his foot, and hummed, repeating the same four notes with unvarying regularity. He always seemed happiest when he was engaged in unstructured activities. Having to sit quietly at the dining room table was a real chore for him.

Mary Margaret had studied his behavior during his years in Boston and had come to the conclusion that his problems stemmed from the way he saw things. Somehow, when he looked at a written word, it didn't look the same to him as it did to her. The letters seemed to jump around, always out of his control. But recognizing the problem and solving it were two different issues. Mary Margaret just couldn't figure out why he saw things differently or how to correct his vision.

"Tom, you have to think about the direction of the letters, not what they look like as a whole. Up, down, left, and right," she said patiently.

"Why is this so hard for me, Aunt Maggie? Why do my letters always come out backwards? Even Becky can do this baby stuff. Why can't I?"

"I don't know, sweetheart. Some of us are good at baseball and some of us are good at writing. You're good at baseball. Now me, on the other hand . . ." She let her voice trail off.

"You're real good at writing."

"I do all right with my writing, but that wasn't what I meant. Remember how bad I was at baseball when you talked me into helping you practice? I couldn't even throw the ball. It just sort of fell out of my hand."

"Yeah, almost behind your back." Tom laughed. "I'm pretty good at baseball, aren't I?"

"More than good, I'd say, and so do the other members of the team. I bet you'd be one of the first picked if they had to choose up sides," Mary Margaret said, closing his schoolbook.

She was very pleased he'd found something to excel in. And she hadn't been exaggerating his accomplishments, either. Tom was gaining more confidence every day. He seemed to be handling his schoolwork, too, though he still struggled. What he needed was someone with patience and perseverance, and neither Lucy nor his teacher seemed to have enough of either quality.

Luckily, one of Lucy's friends, newly returned home from the same finishing school, had invited her for a short visit to Laramie. This had given Mary Margaret more time to help the children without having to endure her endless sniping. The young woman had gotten no more pleasant as the week had progressed.

"Aunt Maggie, can I go outside now?" Tom said as he finished his last assignment.

"You've gotten a lot done this afternoon and you certainly deserve a break, but put on a coat. It gets nippy out at this time of day."

Tom quickly ran to the hall rack and pulled down his coat. He was buttoning it when the front door opened and Worth entered.

"Where are you going in such a hurry?" he asked the boy.

"Aunt Maggie says since I did such a good job, I can go out. Me and Billy Preston are gonna play catch."

"Have a good time and don't come in as dirty as a flop-eared hound or Kathleen will want to know the reason why."

Very seriously, Tom asked his uncle, "Do you reckon Kathleen will know what a flop-eared hound is?"

Worth caught the glimmer of mischief in his nephew's eye and swatted at him as the young boy scampered out the door. Shaking his head and still laughing to himself, Worth entered the dining room.

"That boy amazes me. Every day he gets more grown-up."

"I know what you mean. He's no longer the little boy I cradled on my lap when he felt sad or hurt. Sometimes I wish he were little again, his problems small and solved with a kiss on the cheek or a hug. Now that he's almost grown, his problems have grown, too, and there's no longer a quick, easy cure."

"It's his schoolwork, isn't it?" Worth questioned as he came around the table and sat down beside her. Today he was dressed for work in a dark suit with a vest. He looked remarkably handsome, and Mary Margaret longed to reach out and ruffle his hair. But his expression was serious, bordering on grim, so she just nodded and kept her hands clasped on her lap.

"Sometimes I get as frustrated as he does," she confessed. "I just can't find the right key—that small something that will open everything up for him." She looked into Worth's strong, sure face, hoping he would have an answer for her.

Instead she saw frustration and anger, not directed at her, but turned inward. "There is no key—not for Tom."

"What do you mean? There has to be something." She'd wanted an answer from him, but not this one. She wouldn't accept that there was nothing she could do to help Tom.

"I speak from experience." Worth hesitated for an instant, as if making an important decision. Mary Margaret looked at him expectantly.

"Since you've been here, I've gotten more involved in Tom's work," he said, then looked away from her. "I'm afraid I see myself over and over again in the problems he's encountering—teachers always saying if he just worked harder, if he just paid more attention. If, if, if."

Mary Margaret could feel Worth's frustration even now. Did he share Tom's problem? But surely, he'd conquered it. Look at his successful law practice and his ability to run the ranch. How could he have gotten so far without reading?

"I don't understand. You seem fine to me. You do everything you want. I've seen you read . . . and write." She had, she realized, now that she took a moment to think about it, but only for his office, never for pleasure. How had she failed to notice?

"Remember at the ball, when we were talking about your writing? I told you then I don't read or write unless I have to—unless my business necessitates it. It's just too hard. It takes every bit of my concentration just to comprehend the facts. There's no pleasure in it for me."

"But what about your law degree and schooling before that?"

"I didn't say I'm stupid. I can remember perfectly when I'm told the information. I just have trouble reading it. In school, I used every trick in the book to get my fellow students to either read to me or talk about the work. And when I couldn't do that, I used a method I devised for myself to get through."

"You must have worked very hard." She could well imagine from what she'd seen with Tom what a difficult time Worth must have had. A sense of pride welled within her, mingling with an undefined sadness that he'd gone through so much. From what she knew of his background, it couldn't have been easy.

His father had never been the most understanding of men, from what the Townsends had said and the hints Henry Clay had dropped, and Boston society put so much emphasis on accomplishments and culture.

Worth stiffened at the look on Mary Margaret's face. He didn't want her pity or her condescension. He'd left Boston for less. Out here, he'd overcome his shortcomings and made a perfectly respectable life for himself. Could she see past the rigid concepts she been raised with to accept him as the successful man he'd become and not as a failure everybody had disdained?

He had to believe so if their budding relationship were to go anywhere. He couldn't bear to look into her eyes and see contempt.

"Yes, I did work very hard," he replied curtly. He started to get up, needing to distance himself from her, from his painful confession, but she placed her hand on his arm, stilling him.

"I feel sorry for the boy you were," she said, as if reading his thoughts, "but I have only admiration for the man he's become."

He looked at her then, searching her face for signs of deceit or cunning, but saw none.

"I . . . thank you." He placed his hands over hers, and she did not pull away.

"I have a favor to ask of you," she said hesitantly. "A big favor." She tightened the hand on his arm, her fingers kneading muscles through his sleeve.

"What?"

"Will you speak to Tom, tell him what you told me? It would make him feel much better about himself. You know how he looks up to you."

Dammit, didn't she realize he'd revealed his darkest secret, laid himself open in a way he hadn't done in years? Tom looked up to him now, but would he still if he knew the truth? "I don't know if I can."

"You can." Her hazel eyes deepened in color as her voice darkened with intensity. Her grip on his arm remained firm. "You think of yourself as a failure, where I see a success. You think you have something to hide, where I see someone who should shout his triumph to the world. Don't you see? You've made it. You have nothing to be ashamed about, and neither does Tom. Can't you help him?"

"How?" Her words both thrilled and scared him. Maybe she was right. Maybe he hadn't really come to terms with his problem. Certainly he was ashamed of it still, but why? It wasn't anything he could help, and he had certainly done well in spite of it.

"You can teach Tom what you learned on your own—to be proud and persistent and never give up."

"Is that the way you see me?"

"Yes. Will you talk to Tom?"

He sighed. "I'll certainly think about it," he answered noncommittally. He suspected he would do more than just think.

"Good."

It pleased him to have her accept his word so unquestioningly. He felt closer to her now—not just physically, but mentally and emotionally. She knew things about him few people did, and still she hadn't pulled away, hadn't turned her back.

"Tomorrow's Saturday. I'd like you to come out to the ranch," he offered. "Spend a couple of days. You haven't seen it yet, and I know the children want to go. Becky's fairly in love with Bobby John, one of my ranch hands."

Excitement swirled through Mary Margaret. Worth was letting her into another part of his life—an important one. They'd weathered their first crisis, for she had no doubt of the trauma Worth's childhood had left on him, and come out closer than before. "I'd love to come visit, but what about the children? Can they miss school?"

"We'll bring them back Sunday night. Anyway, I have a court date on Monday. What do you say?"

The thought of spending time alone with just Worth was tantalizing, if she dared admit such a thing. Of course, the children would be there too, but. . . . She could barely contain her excitement at the prospect. "When do we leave and what do I need to take along?"

Later that evening, Worth strolled down Ferguson Street toward his office, whistling under his breath. He couldn't wait until tomorrow morning, when he and Maggie would be off to the ranch with the children. As he climbed the wooden steps to his second-floor office, he mentally reviewed the status of his cases. Only Jesse MacIntyre's was pressing, and he'd be meeting Jesse in a few minutes.

Worth unlocked the door and lit the two wall sconces in his outer chamber. A mellow glow filled the room, glazing the scattered furniture with a golden patina. Worth surveyed the leather couches and chairs, the bookcases full of leather-bound volumes, the large hardwood desk, with its handsome brass lamp.

Maggie was right. He had a lot to be proud of, and it all came from his own hard work. True, out here fewer people could read than in Boston, but that didn't take away from his achievements. He'd helped a lot of people, one way or the other—people who could have cared less whether he'd been the best reader in Mr. Lowell's second grade class. All they wanted to know was whether he could do the job today.

And he could. He'd won all his cases, when forced into court, but prided himself on his ability to get conflicting parties to compromise without going that far. He didn't often fail, though he had tonight with Annie MacIntyre.

A knock sounded at the door and Worth let Jesse in.

"Good evening, Worth. Hope I didn't keep you waiting."

At least Jesse was sober tonight, Worth noted. "No, I just got here myself. Come on in and have a seat."

He showed Jesse to a comfortable chair and sat across from him. A small gas fire burned in the hearth, a concession to modern times.

"How did the meeting with Annie go?" Jesse asked, fiddling with his hat. The Stetson was old, showing its years of use on the range, but still in good shape.

"Not well, I'm afraid. She won't drop the charges."

"Will she see me?" Jesse looked forlorn.

"Not willingly."

"I don't understand it, Worth. I did the best I could by her. You know that. Why, when I married her she was slavin' away for her pappy, running after them brats of his while he played slap and tickle with Ruby. I took her away from all that and gave her everythin'. I even took in her sisters when her pappy got hisself killed. What more could a man do?"

"I don't know what went wrong in your marriage, Jesse, but that's not the issue here. Right now, you have to concentrate on finding the paper Annie wrote out giving you the right to dispose of her old family farm. Judge Burley has us on his docket for Monday. Without that note, it's your word against hers."

"Cain't you try talking to her again?"

"I'll try, but you better act as though we're going to court and find that evidence."

"How much trouble are we in if I cain't?"

"I don't know. I have to be honest with you, Jesse. Your drinking and carrying on haven't helped your case one bit. On the other hand, most of the men understand what it's like, caring for property and such. Their wives usually let them handle the business end of things. In most places, their wives wouldn't even have a say-so under the law.

"But here it's different. Since sixty-nine women have retained control of their property even after marriage. That means you can't sell something that belongs to Annie without her approval."

"But I *had* her approval. I told you already. We'd agreed to sell her farm and put the money into land as an investment. Later on, we'd change it back into cash and buy stock for the ranch."

"I'm not the one you have to convince, Jesse. If I didn't believe you, I wouldn't have taken on your case. Remember? I told you all this when you first came to me."

"I know, I know." Jesse wiped one palm against his thigh and then the other, switching his hat between his hands. "I just don' know what to do. Annie's my life. Nothin' else seems to matter without her."

Worth stood and walked to Jesse's side. He put his hand on the man's shoulder. "I know you love her, but right now, she's not in a reasonable frame of mind. What you have to think about is finding that paper, even if you have to take the house apart, piece by piece. You could lose the ranch over this, Jesse. Neither one of us wants to see that happen. Right?"

Jesse nodded his head and stared morosely at the floor. "I reckon so," he allowed after a couple of minutes. "I thank'ee for the time, Worth. I'm much obliged for your services."

"That's what I'm here for," Worth said as Jesse headed for the door. "Oh, and one other thing."

Jesse stopped with one hand on the doorknob. "Yeah?"

"Stay off the bottle. It won't help you or anyone else."

Jesse sighed. "I know that, but sometimes the pain gets to be more than I can bear."

"I understand, Jesse, but drinking's not the way. Do I have your word?"

"Yeah, yeah. I'll pour the likker out soon's I get home."

After Jesse left, Worth straightened his desk and wrote out a few instructions for his assistant before leaving.

As he turned out the lights, he thought once again of his meeting tonight. Poor Jesse. If he lived anywhere else but in Wyoming, he wouldn't even be in this predicament, Worth noted. Then Maggie's words rang faintly in his ears.

"Let *me* tell *you*," she once again insisted. "I'm a grown woman and can make these decisions by myself."

And she could, too, he had to admit. So who was right and who was wrong?

He pondered the issue all the way home, but came to no satisfying conclusion. Before going to bed he decided to check on the children, stopping first in Becky's room. She was sound asleep on her stomach, one leg crooked up by her waist, the other dangling halfway off the bed. Worth righted her and tucked her under the blanket. Before leaving, he dropped a kiss on her forehead.

He tiptoed into Tom's room, hoping not to wake him, either. The boy lay still, his face turned to the wall, but something about his posture made Worth suspect he was not asleep.

"Tom? You awake?" he asked softly.

"A little."

The boy's voice had a ragged edge. Concerned, Worth approached his bed. "Something the matter?"

"N-no."

"You sure? I've got plenty of time if you want to talk."

Tom sniffed audibly. "It's nothing much."

Sensing the boy's need, Worth settled himself on the upholstered chair by Tom's bed. "Your Aunt Maggie says you're doing real well lately. She's very proud of you, you know."

"Huh," Tom snorted. "We all know I'm just too dumb to learn. She doesn't fool me none."

"What makes you think you're so dumb?" Worth asked, assailed by painful memories of his own youth.

"How can you ask? You've seen me try to read." Tom turned over to face Worth, propping his head on a bent elbow. In the light from the hallway, Worth could make out the dried tracks of tears on his cheeks.

"Have you ever seen me try to read?" Worth asked, giving up his pride in the hope he could help the boy.

The boy furrowed his brow, thinking. "I must have. *Everybody* reads."

"But you can't remember a time, can you?"

"Well, no—I guess not," Tom admitted.

Worth sighed. There was no going back now. "The only time I do is when I'm working on a case from the office."

Tom sat up, crossing his ankles on the bed. "How come?" He looked openly curious now, his own worries forgotten in the face of this new puzzle.

"Because I have trouble reading, too."

Worth looked into the boy's face. Tom's serious expression reminded him so much of Henry Clay, it was like seeing a ghost come to life—a twelve-year-old ghost, to be sure, but a likeness of his older brother, nonetheless. He felt a surge of pain and pride.

"Are you telling the truth?" Tom asked suspiciously.

"I wouldn't lie about something like this."

"Then, how come you never told me before?"

Worth looked down at his hands and tried to marshall his thoughts. Children were so guileless. They saw straight through to the core of a problem and didn't dress it up in fancy words.

"I guess it's not something I talk about a lot," he finally confessed.

"Because you're ashamed?"

"Do you think I should be?"

Tom looked at him consideringly, his head tipped to one side. "I can't say. I just want to know if you are."

"I used to be—especially when I was your age. I hated going to school, having the teachers yell and fuss, always comparing me to my older brother—and never in a good way."

"My daddy, you mean?"

"Yes. He was a good student—hardworking, smart. Everything seemed to go his way. That made it even harder for me, trying to live up to him."

"You think he woulda been disappointed in me 'cause I don't read good?"

"No. I know he wouldn't be. He used to help me all the time, like Aunt Maggie does with you. He taught me a lot, showed me I could do things if I tried. We're different from other folk, Tom, not stupid. We see things all twisted around when we try to read, but just tell us something, and we understand it quick enough."

"Why can't we be like other people? I don't want to be different. It isn't fair."

"I know, son. But I learned long ago, you have to accept what you can't change and go on from there. There'll be no stopping you if you set your mind to something. I've seen you handle a lot of hardship, and you've been as brave as anyone could be."

Tom looked away from Worth and blinked his eyes rapidly. "No, I haven't. Not really."

Worth laid his hand on the boy's arm, wanting to give him comfort. "What makes you think so?"

"'Cause I'm all afraid inside," he whispered hoarsely, tears falling once again. "I miss my mama and papa so bad, sometimes all I want to do is cry and cry. But I can't, cause I'll just scare Becky. She needs me to be strong and I know I'm not."

The boy's pain cut Worth like a knife. How had he missed the signs? Tom had shouldered tremendous responsibility without leaning on anyone. It was too big a burden.

Moving to the bed, Worth wrapped his arms around Tom. "I'm so sorry, Tom. I should have realized how you felt. I miss your ma and pa, too. There's a hole in my life that will never be filled, but the sorrow will ease with time."

"You're not ashamed of me, then?"

"No. I'm prouder than before. You've given the matter a lot of thought and handled yourself like a man for Becky's sake. That's what bravery is, Tom. Doing what you have to, even though you're scared and alone."

"Are you ever scared, Uncle Worth?"

"Sure. Everyone is. But don't think you're alone anymore. If you're feeling low, come talk to me. I'll do my best to help out."

"All right."

"Also, if you feel like talking about your parents, Aunt Maggie and I would be happy to listen. We remember them, too, and sometimes talking about them brings their memory back to life, even if it's only for a short while."

"Could you tell me some about my pa when he was my age?"

"Sure. Lie down under the covers and I'll see what I can do."

Worth helped the boy lie down, then sat again in the chair, leaning back and closing his eyes.

"Let's see now. Ah, I know. When Henry Clay was just twelve . . ."

Once started, Worth lost all sense of time. One story followed naturally from another. He could almost imagine Henry Clay by his side, hear his laughter, see his bright smile. All their childhood escapades took on new life. Events he'd thought forgotten were suddenly remembered in full detail.

By the time he'd wound down, Tom was sound asleep, his expression relaxed and at ease. Worth, too, felt comforted. Much had been accomplished tonight, and he still had tomorrow and Maggie to look forward to.

Mary Margaret had half the contents of the chiffonier on her bed and she still hadn't decided what to take with her the next day. What clothes would she need out on a ranch?

She considered her white lawn dress, but quickly hung it back up. Ranches sounded dusty to her and white didn't fit the bill at all. She had just packed her brown skirt when there was a knock at her door.

Mary Margaret opened it to find Annie MacIntyre standing on the other side, a stack of freshly folded linens in her hands.

"Mrs. Miller asked if I'd bring these up to you." The small woman rushed through her words as if she'd memorized them, in fear of saying the wrong thing.

"Thank you, but you didn't have to bring them up. I could have gotten them."

"It was no problem," she mumbled, handing Mary Margaret the stack and turning to leave.

"Please, won't you come in and keep me company? Packing is such a lonesome job, and I seem to be choosing and discarding more than I'm packing away."

Mary Margaret felt sorry for the woman. She'd barely said more than six words since they'd met and her life's story was pitiful, if you could go by any of the gossip winging its way through the boardinghouse.

"Well, if you're sure I'm not intruding," Annie answered meekly.

"You can be a great help to me," Mary Margaret said, walking over to her bed and pointing to the pile of clothes strewn all over it. "As you can see, I haven't the faintest idea what to take with me on my trip out to Mr. Worthington's ranch. Having lived on a ranch, maybe you can tell me what I'll need."

Annie followed her over to the bed and looked at the piles. "I'm sure Mr. Worthington's ranch is much nicer than ours. An educated lady like yourself would know far more about the proper thing to wear than I would."

"I don't think education has anything to do with it. I've known some very educated people who wouldn't know the the back of a cow from the front without some prompting."

Annie gave a small nervous laugh. "Jesse always says you need book smarts, but you have to have some sense to begin with."

Mary Margaret could see the tears forming in the other woman's eyes before Annie quickly turned her back and pulled a handkerchief out of the sleeve of her dress.

Urging her into a chair, Mary Margaret knelt beside her. "It'll be all right, Annie. I'm sure everything will work out." But Mary Margaret wasn't so sure. Even though Wyoming gave women equal rights, Mary Margaret knew most of the men didn't believe in them, and Jesse MacIntyre was one of the ones leading the parade.

"I can't understand why he's doing this. It was my papa's farm. I ought to have some say in what happens. How could he sell it and not even tell me?"

"Hadn't you ever talked about the possibility of selling it?" Mary Margaret asked.

"We'd talked some on it, but the farm was the only thing I had left from my family. My kinfolk wasn't the best there ever was, but they were my blood. All I wanted was something to remember them by." Twisting the handkerchief into an unrecognizable lump, Annie looked to Mary Margaret for guidance.

"What are you going to do?"

"I've found a lawyer who says Jesse had no right to sell my papa's land."

Mary Margaret knew the selling of property was pretty informal out here, from what she could tell. Maybe the details didn't matter unless one of the parties involved contested the sale.

"I'm glad you got yourself a lawyer. That way you'll be getting the best advice. Just follow what he says. Maybe there's some way of undoing the wrong."

The more Mary Margaret thought about Annie's predicament, the more she realized that Annie's story just might be the angle she needed for the article the *Cheyenne Daily Star* wanted. She'd been studying the subject anyway, since the Wyoming Territory was unique in the country for the rights it gave to women, so she already knew a lot about the subject.

The *Daily Star* wanted a different point of view to compete with its arch rival, the *Wyoming Gazette*. Well, now, she would give it to them: a woman's view on owning land, written by a woman writer, no less. She could also get into the repercussions of the county's less-than-organized methods of recording sales.

The first piece would compare the new laws with the real situations encountered by women when it came to their property rights. She could work it up tonight, using Annie's experience to guide her. Then, when she got back from visiting Worth's ranch, she'd do some research into how the county kept its records.

Maybe Worth knew how deeds were handled and could help her. It would give him a different perspective on her work. At least he wouldn't be able to voice any objections about her safety on this story. She looked forward to asking him. Now she could involve him in her life, just as he was involving her in his.

She felt warm and excited as they chatted. Annie left as soon as Mary Margaret's bags were packed, and Mary Margaret sat down at her writing desk. Never had her words flowed so smoothly. She finished off the article in record time and prepared a cover letter so she could take it to the newspaper office first thing in the morning.

Eleven

Saturday dawned bright and clear, a perfect day for a drive out to the countryside. The ride to Worth's ranch took about an hour over prairie land rich with new spring grass and the occasional herd of cattle.

The children could hardly contain their excitement about leaving the city. Neither could Mary Margaret, for that matter. She didn't know what would happen in the time she and Worth had together, but she knew she wanted to explore all the possibilities.

"It won't be long now—only about another ten minutes," Worth commented.

"I wouldn't care if it took longer. I'm enjoying the scenery. There's so much wide-open space here, I feel I can see forever. When you've lived your whole life in one place, seeing something different is so compelling."

She looked over at Worth. Did he ever have the same yearnings she did—the need to see more and different things, to experience all life had to offer? Or was he settled now? She really didn't know a lot about his life before he had come to Cheyenne.

"I remember the first time I stepped foot in Wyoming," Worth said, answering her unvoiced question. "I couldn't stop looking. Just like you, I'd spent most of my life in

Boston. And then, suddenly, here I was in this land of wide plains and high mountains. Oh, I'd seen other places, but none of them affected me the way the Wyoming Territory did. The people were real friendly and accepted you for what you were. I was here no more than a week and I knew I never wanted to leave—at least, not for more than just a visit someplace else."

Worth paused for a moment, his eyes filled with dreams. "There's this spot at the ranch, up on a hill, that looks out over the range. And when you're up there at sundown . . . well, it's one of the most beautiful things you've ever seen. I feel like I never get enough of just looking. Every time we visit the ranch, I try to make it out there."

Mary Margaret saw the wonder in his eyes. "Do you think I'll be able to go there?"

"I don't know, Maggie. It's quite a ride—not exactly the place a woman should be heading out for."

Before Mary Margaret could voice her objections, Tom yelled out from the backseat, "There's the ranch, Aunt Maggie. Isn't she a beauty? Wait till you see my horse. He's the best one on the spread—except for Jake's roan."

Tom was so excited he could hardly stay in his seat.

"Tom, you're bouncing on me," Becky complained from the far corner.

Tom scowled at her and then flipped his hand dismissively. "Oh, you're nothing but a whiny girl. Girls can't do anything, and they don't do nothing but complain."

After Worth's comment, Tom's attitude toward females came as no surprise to Mary Margaret, though she found it disappointing. She was about to remark on it, when Worth stopped the horses and turned to face the backseat.

"Thomas Henry, I don't want to hear talk like that again," he chided the boy. "Becky has a right to voice her objections to your jumping all over her. And I don't ever want you to think that because she's a girl, she doesn't count. Do I make myself clear?"

"Yes, Uncle Worth," a considerably subdued Tom replied.

"All right, then," Worth said, flicking the reins to start the horses on their way again.

"Now, who wants to be the first one to show Aunt Maggie the ranch?" Worth asked as if nothing untoward had happened.

"I do, I do," the children responded enthusiastically.

"I want to show her Bobby John. Can I?" Becky asked.

"Let's get her to the ranch house first," Worth said with a laugh. "Besides, Bobby John may have gone on the roundup."

Mary Margaret remembered Worth mentioning Becky's crush on the ranch hand and couldn't wait to meet him. She hoped he would return while she was still there.

Soon Mary Margaret could see a large frame house and several other buildings clustered together. Some of the smaller cabins were made of logs chinked with chips cut from the corners, then covered over with a light-colored clay. The dark-light pattern gave them a distinctive striped look.

The main house had a sturdy look to it, despite its graceful lines. Mary Margaret could see that a lot of time and effort had gone into planning it. There was even a garden dug around the porch, though not much was growing this early in the season.

"It's lovely, Worth," she said as he jumped down from the carriage.

Before she could alight herself, a tall, slim man came around the corner of the house.

"Bobby John, Bobby John, you didn't go on the roundup," Becky cried out with glee.

"And miss seeing my most favoritest person in the world?" he teased as he swung the little girl down to the ground. "And this must be the beautiful Miss Maggie Becky's always talking about. I can see she didn't stretch the truth one little bit, either," he said, offering his hand to help Mary Margaret descend.

So this was Bobby John. No wonder Becky was smitten. The young man was quite an eyeful.

Worth watched Bobby John help Maggie down. Was he going to have to contend with Bobby John's flirting as well as Marcus's? For some reason, back in Boston, he'd never considered that Maggie might have a beau. But out here she was surrounded by interested and interesting men, none of whom failed to see what an attractive woman she was. For all he knew, there could be someone back in Boston, too. A twist of painful jealousy knifed through him.

"Bobby John, why don't you see to the luggage," Worth snapped more sharply than he had intended.

The young cowboy gave him a strange look. "Sure, boss. Where do you want Miss Maggie's bags?"

"The front bedroom over the parlor will be fine. Becky and Tom, you two better change clothes. Kathleen wasn't too pleased with the way your Sunday clothes came back last time you were out here."

Bobby John and the children went off to do his bidding.

"Bobby John is quite a character," Mary Margaret commented as Worth took her arm and escorted her up the front steps.

"Do you think so?" Worth asked. He'd wondered what Maggie thought of the young hand, but he wasn't sure he really wanted to hear her carry on about him.

"He's certainly charming and handsome . . ." she extolled, glancing sideways at him.

If she was trying to get his goat, she was certainly succeeding. He'd thought he'd have some time out here at the ranch for the two of them to get to know each other. But if Maggie found Bobby John so fascinating, maybe he had misinterpreted her responses.

". . . but awfully young and terribly flirtatious. I can see why Becky is enamored with him."

Worth's relief was enormous. Then he realized she had been putting him on all along. "You were doing that on purpose."

"Doing what?" she asked, her smile all innocence and her eyes wickedly tempting.

"Trying to make me jealous."

"Do I need to?"

"No, I was doing all right on my own without you saying a word."

Maggie laughed, a delicious gurgle of sound. She appeared to be very pleased with his reply, and well she should be. He'd never admitted such a thing to another woman, but this one made him do things he'd never considered before.

Worth drew her arm through his and pulled her to his side, changing direction. "Come this way. Let's go around the back so you can see a bit of the ranch before we go inside."

He liked the feel of her beside him. Her wool traveling coat brushed against his leg as she walked, and her flowery scent surrounded him. He wanted to keep her to himself for a few minutes before once again sharing her company with the others. Slowly, he led her around the side of the house. From here they could see the corrals and the barn. They paused for a moment on the back steps.

"I like your ranch. The wide spaces and the sloping lines of the buildings are . . . I can't describe it."

"You're a writer and you can't describe it?"

"The only words I can think of are too sappy and sentimental for such raw elegance and bold determination."

"That sounds pretty accurate to me," Worth declared. "Raw elegance says so much about this country. It's the way I felt when I first saw it. And without determination, you couldn't last out a summer here, much less a winter blizzard."

She certainly had a way with words, a real talent for describing the things he took for granted. He'd even taken the trouble to read some of her articles and been impressed. But did he have what it took to grant her the freedom she'd insist on to pursue her work? That was the question they had to resolve. So far, he didn't know the answer.

"Why do you have so many different buildings?" she asked.

"Each one has a special purpose. The biggest one, right in front of us, is used for stabling the horses. That one over there—" he waved an arm in the direction of one of the smaller buildings "—is a corn crib. We use one building strictly for repairs and housing equipment. That long, gray one is the bunkhouse and mess hall for the men, and the small white house belongs to my foreman and his wife."

"How many men do you have working for you?" she

asked, obviously impressed with the magnitude of her surroundings.

"About twenty-five when we're on roundup. During the winter months, it usually dwindles down to between ten and fifteen. The men who work these spreads tend to be loners, moving on when the mood strikes them.

"My foreman, Jake, was a loner, too, moving from one ranch to the next, never wanting to take on more responsibility than he had to, until he met up with Charlotte. She changed his ideas about staying in one place. I hear the love of a good person can do that to you."

How would Maggie feel about staying in one place, not experiencing all she'd talked about? Could she find happiness? He watched her face carefully to gauge her reaction to his words.

"So I hear," she replied, but Worth couldn't make out what she was thinking.

Just then the back door opened and out spilled Becky and Tom, followed by Bobby John.

"Want me to take the children out for a riding lesson?" Bobby John offered.

"All right. You can use the back corral. Thanks, Bobby John. I'll be along in a while—as soon as I take Miss Maggie in to meet Charlotte."

"Don't hurry yourself none. I've got plenty of time." Bobby John grinned at his boss, and Worth realized the young man had figured out a lot more than he was letting on. "Come on, young'uns. Let's go saddle up your broncs." With a wink, he set off with the children for the barn.

"I guess you'll be wanting to freshen up," Worth said to Maggie. "Let's go on inside."

Charlotte was standing by the stove when they entered the kitchen. She looked over her shoulder at them.

"I thought you two must have gotten lost." She gave them a sly glance. "I'm Charlotte Brown, by the way. I do the cooking for Worth and the children when they come out to visit."

She held out her hand and Mary Margaret took it. "I'm

pleased to meet you. The children have told me how much they like being here with you."

Charlotte beamed. "I love having them here." She reached up into a cabinet and pulled down a cup. "Why don't I fix you a cup of tea and you can relax after your ride from the city."

"That would be lovely," Mary Margaret said. "And then we could sit down and get acquainted. I want to hear what it's like being a foreman's wife."

Worth decided to give the women some time alone to get to know each other. "If you'll excuse me, I'll just go see about the mare Jake's been attending to. He said he was a little leery of leaving it all to Bobby John."

Worth started out the back door. "I'll be back in time for lunch," he said. "I want to take Maggie for a ride this afternoon."

Mary Margaret smiled and her eyes sparkled with excitement. "That would be wonderful. I can hardly wait."

"Good. I'll see you in a while."

By the time Worth returned, not only were the children in the house, but Marcus Robertson was there, too, sitting in the front room with Mary Margaret.

"Worth, good to see you. We were about to send out a search party." Marcus tweaked one of Becky's braids and she grinned up at him.

"Afternoon, Marcus. What brings you to these parts?"

"I heard you were coming for a visit, and I thought it would be neighborly to drop by. Lucy's still over Laramie way visiting her friend, and it gets mighty lonesome at the homestead."

"We're glad to have you," Worth got out with credible good humor. Glad as he was to see his good friend, he'd been hoping for time with Maggie alone. Nonetheless, his ingrained good manners forced him to add, "Can you stay for dinner?"

"Well, I reckon I could, but I can't stay too long. Thought I'd take the children over to my place, long as you don't mind none. Daisy's had her puppies, and as I recall, I offered Tom first pick of the litter."

Tom let out a whoop and started dancing around the

room. "Can we go, Uncle Worth, can we go?" he pleaded.
"I'm not really hungry, Marcus. I could leave right now, if
you had a mind to."

"Me, too," Becky piped up. "I wanna go, too."

Marcus grinned, shooting a glance at Worth. "Well,
now, I don't know. I've a mighty hungry feeling in my
stomach for some of Miz Charlotte's good ranch cooking.
But I'd be willing to leave soon's everybody cleaned their
plates. What do you say, Worth?"

"I'd hate to impose, Marcus, especially with Lucy
gone."

What made it worse was that he badly wanted to impose,
and he had the feeling Marcus knew it.

"No problem, no problem at all." Marcus's golden-
brown eyes twinkled with enjoyment as he grinned at
Worth. "We'll get along just fine, won't we?" He looked to
the children for confirmation, which they were only too
happy to provide.

"You don't mind if the children leave, do you, Maggie?"
Worth asked.

"Of course not, if it's just for the afternoon. New puppies are hard to pass up, especially if you're getting to keep
one, and we'll have a lot of time to be together before we
head back to Cheyenne."

The children beamed, and Mary Margaret had the satisfaction of knowing her answer had pleased everyone.

"Good, it's settled, then," Marcus said. "I kind of miss
having children around, now that Lucy's grown. Remember how she used to tag around behind us everywhere
we went?" he asked Worth.

"Hard to forget. I remember one time she came over
here to show off her new dress and followed me to the
pigpen. She slipped facedown in the mud just as Bessie
decided to charge. Boy, was that old sow mean! I barely
reached Lucy ahead of her."

Marcus laughed with Worth. "Lucy sure was mad that
day. Wouldn't talk to either of us for near onto a week just
'cause we said she'd be starting a new fashion."

"Well, we could hardly help it. She looked so funny with

all that black mud on her face. How old was she then—
ten? Eleven?"

"Closer to twelve, I think," Marcus said, still chuckling.
"Thought she was ready to be a lady till you and Bessie did
her in."

"Now, Marcus, you know it wasn't my fault. I distinctly
recall telling her to wait outside the fence while I poured
the slops. Who'd have ever thought a 'lady' would try to
walk along the top of a fence in her best dress and fancy
shoes?"

They both laughed again, remembering the incident. For
Mary Margaret, what had started out as a most unwelcome
subject—namely, a discussion of Lucy Robertson—had
turned most enlightening. No matter what the young
woman thought of Worth, Mary Margaret discovered to her
infinite relief, he regarded her with the affectionate toler-
ance of a loving uncle who'd helped raise her.

"I guess we hurt her feelings a bit," Marcus admitted.

"Sounds like you two were rather hard on her that day,"
put in Mary Margaret, suddenly inclined to take the absent
Lucy's side.

"Well, we made up for it, didn't we, Worth?" Marcus
reminded him.

"I'll say," Worth concurred. "We each sneaked into town
to buy her a peace offering, and that wily Mrs. Dana sold
us each one of her most expensive dresses, never telling us
the other had put in an order for nearly the same thing!"

"Yup, old Luce came out ahead on that one. Mrs. Dana
even managed to clean the original dress, so Lucy ended
up with more fancy dresses than any other girl in town."

The hall clock chimed and Marcus pulled his watch out
of his pocket to check the time. He flipped open the hinged
metal lid of the hunting case and peered at the watch face
while the children solemnly looked on.

"Looks like the day's getting away from us," he said to
them. "Why don't we go into the kitchen and see if we
can't get Miz Charlotte to hurry up. What do you say?"

They thought the idea terrific and followed Marcus into
the kitchen. After a delicious meal of roast chicken, pota-

toes, and early peas, Marcus packed the children into his buckboard and waved good-bye.

Mary Margaret stood at Worth's side in front of the house and waved back until the wagon was a speck on the horizon. At last, they were alone—just she and Worth. It was exactly what she had dreamed of the night before, so why did she feel so awkward?

When Worth turned to face her, she couldn't quite meet his gaze. She suddenly felt nervous and unsure.

"Now we can go on our ride and not worry about the young ones getting bored," Worth said with a soft smile.

Mary Margaret let out the breath she hadn't realized she had been holding. She'd forgotten about Worth's offer to take her riding.

"That sounds perfect."

"Good. You go on inside and get your wrap, and I'll have Bobby John get the horse ready."

She smiled at him, feeling suddenly better, sure of herself again. Lighthearted, she went into the house.

Mary Margaret was somewhat disappointed, a short time later, to see Worth pull up in front of the house in a small but sturdy wagon with a protective canopy over the seat. She'd hoped to ride a horse, but she made no complaint when he jumped down and helped her into the wagon.

"I'll be right back," he promised with a smile, and gave her hand a squeeze. Her skin tingled where he touched her and a deep-seated quivering shook her very center.

She tried to settle herself comfortably in the wagon and wait for Worth's return, but she was beset with a hungry impatience to be with him. He returned quickly, carrying a wicker basket that he placed under the seat before climbing in beside her.

"I wish you'd let us ride out here on horses," Mary Margaret remarked as they crossed the open range, though in truth, she was quite happy tucked in by Worth's side in the tiny wagon.

"Have you ever ridden?" he asked, flicking the reins.

"No, but . . ."

"It's not as easy as you think. Tom's been taking lessons

for over a month and he's just getting out of the corral. Do you think you can just take off and fly across the prairie?"

Mary Margaret glanced at Worth. She was intrigued by the image his words evoked. "Could you teach me how to ride? Astride?"

"You don't have the proper clothes for it. And, it isn't something a lady does."

"Ladies don't have control over their own land, either, except here in Wyoming Territory. I figure if they control it, they should be able to ride on it. On a horse. And astride."

She could tell Worth was weakening; the corners of his lips were losing the battle to stay turned down. "If you can find some adequate clothing, I guess I'll consider it," he agreed with some reluctance. "But only if you can find some clothes."

"Don't worry about that. I'll find something. Soon."

"That's what's got me worried."

He grinned in capitulation and reached over with his free hand to tuck a stray lock of hair behind her ear. His fingers brushed against her skin and she turned her face into his palm. His palm was hard and callused, his touch gentle.

He held his hand still for a second, then slowly drew her face up to his and lightly touched his lips to hers. She closed her eyes and saw red sparklers behind her lids. They lit her up inside, charging through her veins to the farthest reaches of her body with their message of excitement.

"Come closer to me," Worth said. "I need you near me."

Sliding across the bench, she shifted closer.

Worth put his arm around her, and she felt surrounded by his presence. Inhaling deeply, she savored his rich, male smell as it mixed with the earthy aroma of the rolling prairie awakening from winter's slumber.

She felt as if she, too, were awakening from a deep sleep, like a fairy-tale princess kissed into a new awareness of herself and her prince, of love and life.

"Is this better?" she whispered in his ear. His only answer was to squeeze her tightly and steal another kiss.

The word *love* drifted through her heart, filling all the empty spaces, echoing back and forth till her mind finally faced the truth. She loved Worth. When she looked back, she thought it had started the very first day they'd met, when she'd watched him reverently touch Tom's face and stroke Becky's hair as they lay asleep.

When she considered how her cowardice had almost made her lose him forever, she realized her foolishness. She should never have let social propriety stand in her way when he had left Boston—not if what she had really wanted was to go with him. And she had—more than anything in the world.

"I feel so lucky to be here, to have found you again," she murmured.

"I wish I'd asked you to come with me when I first left Boston," he said.

"Did you want to?"

He looked down at her, his blue eyes intense. "Of course."

Silence grew between them as they both pondered the thought.

"Would you have come?" he asked.

That was the question. "I wanted to," she confessed. "But we'll never really know, will we? Neither of us took the chance."

"It may have been for the best, Maggie. When I first came here, my whole life was in an uproar. I wasn't sure how things would turn out, with the children or myself. Now, I know what I want—the changes that need to be made, the things I want to keep the same. What counts is where we go from here, not how we got here in the first place."

"I'm not sure we can leave the past behind. Where we came from has made us what we are today."

"I like what you are today, Maggie, however you got here. And if you hadn't come west on your own, I would have found some other way to see you again. I hadn't forgotten you—not for a single day."

"I hadn't forgotten you, either," she said in the second before his lips crushed hers, underlining his declaration in no uncertain terms.

She returned his kiss with unbridled intensity, knowing

one way or another, even had Kathleen not telegraphed her, she would have found her way here to Worth.

And now she knew more. He would have been waiting. A thrill ran through her and she opened her mouth to him, drawing him deeper, closer, wanting the impossible: to make him part of her.

He eased away from her, breathing hard. "Wait. I need a moment. I don't want to—"

"What if I want you to?" she broke in, sensing how tight a rein he was keeping on himself. But she wanted more, from him and herself—an answer to the desire raging through her, an affirmation of the love filling her soul.

"To what?" He regarded her with narrowed eyes, the pupils dark and enlarged and burning with a deep blue flame.

She didn't have the words. "To give in to what's between us," she said slowly. "To follow where it leads."

"I know where it leads," he said harshly. "Do you?"

"I know how I feel. I just don't know what to do. Teach me?"

She felt him draw an unsteady breath. The flame in his eyes leaped higher, and then he dampened it.

"Are you sure?" he asked.

She nodded wordlessly.

He hugged her tightly to him, pressing her head to his shoulder. "Oh, Maggie. I'll show you everything I know. We'll teach each other," he promised.

He turned the horse to the right and up a knoll, keeping one arm wrapped around her. She could hear his heart beat strongly in his chest.

The horse stopped near the crest of the knoll and Worth kissed the top of her head. "Come with me," he said, his voice a velvety rasp. The sound stroked down her spine and made her tingle with anticipation.

"Where?"

"I'll show you."

She nodded, waiting in the wagon while he unharnessed the horse. He grabbed the basket he'd packed earlier and lifted Mary Margaret from her seat with easy strength.

Silently, Worth led her by the hand through the trees and

halfway down the far side of the hill to a tiny, spring-fed meadow, a sheltered oasis hidden in the arid plains of Wyoming—a special, secret place he'd shared with no one else.

He watched Maggie as she absorbed the beauty of his hideaway. The sun glinted off the crown of her head, sending sparks of red flying through it. Her eyes were wide with appreciation, their color deepening to a dark forest green.

"It's lovely," she said, turning slowly in a circle.

"Yes," he answered.

A small copse of balsam poplars stood near the creek where the underground spring emptied itself. Their red blossoms filled the air with a sweet, resinous scent. The meadow itself lay on the slope of the hill, overlooking a dark-blue range of mountains in the far distance.

"Is that where the sun sets?" she asked, reminding him he'd told her of this place on their way here.

"Yes. Right behind the mountains." He didn't want to talk, but she seemed so enchanted, and he wanted to please her.

"I can see why you love it here."

She threw her head back to catch a glimpse of the top of the tallest tree and the fabric of her gown tightened, accentuating the full curve of her breast, enticing him closer and sending his blood coursing to his loins.

He put down the basket, quickly spread the blanket he had brought, and moved to her side. Her scent floated up to him, mixing with the ripe odors of wet earth and blossoming trees. The mixture was fecund, heady. The afternoon sun bathed everything in a golden haze, warming the air until it felt hot and heavy.

His limbs felt hot and heavy, too, gripped by a sensual languor that made his movements slow and dreamlike. He reached out to stroke her hair and her hands followed his, helping him remove the hairpins until her hair flowed in a heavy cascade down her back. He wanted to lose himself in it.

He threaded his fingers through the fragrant, silky mass

and drew her to him. His mouth greeted hers like an old friend, reclaiming conquered territory with nary a battle.

She had removed her wrap soon after they'd started out on the trip, in deference to the growing warmth of the day, and now only the thin wool of her dress and undergarments separated his hands from her skin. Her body was fragile and delicate, but he felt its resilient strength as he bowed her into him.

Her arms circled his neck, and her fingers burrowed into his hair as they kissed, but he wanted more. He wanted to feel her skin against his own, to finally touch and be touched. Desperately, he undid the buttons of his shirt with one hand, unwilling to let go of her for even a second.

When he finished, he slid his hand along her arm, past her slim wrist, until his palm lay along the back of her hand where it cradled his nape. Gently, he urged her hand down, along the side of his neck and onto his chest.

"Touch me," he rasped.

A groan escaped him when he finally felt the heat of her skin against his flesh. He breathed in her answering moan.

"Oh, Maggie, you feel so good," he gasped out as fire storms of need exploded through him.

He stood unmoving as her hand swept tentatively across his chest, savoring her touch. Her nail grazed his nipple and his muscles jerked.

"I'm sorry," she said, and tried to pull away from him, but he trapped her hand with his own, pressing it more tightly to him.

"Don't be," he got out hoarsely. "You didn't hurt me." Her touch made him yearn for more, for a fuller expression of the sensations rising within him. But how could he explain what he felt? Words were not enough.

Carefully, he undid the tiny buttons on the front of her two-piece dress. When the top was completely undone, he pushed aside its edges and brushed gentle kisses along the lacy edge of her low-cut chemise.

Mary Margaret arched her back, unable to comprehend what was happening to her. Never before had she needed so much. Never before had she had so much to give. The line between giving and taking blurred as desire heated her blood.

The gentle breeze caressing her skin brought all her nerve endings to startling life. The gentle touch of Worth's lips brought on an ache like none she had ever experienced —an ache that settled low in the pit of her stomach, then radiated out again through her whole body.

At last she understood. There was no way to describe the yearning engulfing her; she could only yield to its demands. She wanted to get closer to Worth, to remove the last barriers separating them. Eagerly, she pushed the linen shirt from his shoulders and helped him disengage the cuffs from his arms.

He tossed the shirt carelessly aside and stood before her, smooth muscles tapering from broad shoulders to a narrow waist, tan skin burnished to light gold and covered by a mat of darker hair that glinted in the sunlight. She followed the swirl of hair with her hand as it arrowed to a thin line and disappeared into his pants, mesmerized by his texture and shape.

"Not so fast, Maggie mine," he said, his voice deeper and darker than she'd ever heard it. "We have plenty of time."

He stilled her hand and drew her into his embrace, kissing her lightly on the forehead between deep, gasping breaths. When he had regained a measure of control, he held her away from him and began to undo her skirt. She helped him loosen the fastenings, first on her skirt, then on the two petticoats below—one of highly starched cambric with the back flounced to the waist, the second of pale-blue flannel. Here in the country, she'd seen no need to wear more.

Last, she undid her corset, shyly opening the front fastenings when Worth's fingers stumbled over them, until she stood before him nearly naked, wearing only her chemise and pantalettes.

"You're beautiful," he told her before she could even think to be embarrassed or worry about propriety. She could see the truth of his words in his eyes and a warm glow suffused her, making her stand proud before his loving scrutiny.

"So are you," she said timidly, daring to scrutinize him as boldly as he did her.

He laughed. "I'm glad you think so. That's how it should be."

He led her to the blanket, where he quickly shucked his pants and boots and stood before her in just his drawers. The wool clung tightly to his body from waist to ankle, revealing the lean line of his legs, the tight curve of his buttocks, the heavy state of his arousal.

"Come to me, Maggie," he said softly, giving her the choice, the last chance to change her mind before there was no turning back.

He held out his arms. She stepped into them.

Twelve

A hot ache gripped the pit of her stomach as Worth's mouth moved over hers, and his arms closed around her in a tight embrace. Her own arms went to his shoulders, then slid around his neck, pulling him close. A low, animal sound came from deep in his throat —a sound between pleasure and pain. Instinctively, she knew she was responsible for it, and was glad.

Her hands roamed freely over unfettered, tawny skin, kneading his shoulders, stroking his back, absorbing his maleness. When she breathed, Worth's scent filled her lungs, but she didn't want to waste time on breathing. She only wanted to feel, to absorb sensation, to give to him as he gave to her, wave after wave of pleasure and ache, building and building to one fathomless need.

So this was desire—fueled by passion, fed by love. How could she never have known it before? How had she survived with no inkling of its splendor? She felt like a blind person suddenly given sight, overwhelmed by the vibrancy of color and pattern, the swirling images of blue sky and green grass and bright yellow sun.

She felt cherished as Worth's lips gently caressed her own, then nibbled along her jaw, leaving a warm path of sensuous moistness. The spring breeze followed his path, swirling around her ear as he dipped his tongue inside, listening to his whispers as he told her how he felt. And she was shocked to find she felt the same.

His hands roamed lower, heating her skin until she burned. When he cupped her breast and gently stroked its peak with his thumb, her knees gave way. With tantalizing slowness, he lowered her to the blanket and undid the buttons down the front of her chemise.

"You're more perfect than I imagined," he whispered, awed. Her breasts were creamy white, high and firm, with rosy-red peaks. They beckoned like the Sirens of the deep, and he could no more resist than the sailors of old.

She gasped when he took one ruby nipple in his mouth and swirled his tongue around it. When he released her to lift his head, she wound her fingers in his hair and pressed him back.

"Don't stop," she pleaded, and held him to her.

Worth needed no other encouragement; his world was now centered entirely on pleasing Maggie. He suckled first one breast, then the other, and when she arched her back to meet him, he slid the sleeves of her chemise off her shoulders so she lay bare beneath him. His heart raced, roaring in his ears and pumping his blood furiously through his veins to pool at the very core of his being.

Gently he lowered himself onto her, getting her used to the feel of his weight, brushing the tips of her breasts with his chest as he lay in the cradle of her thighs. She gazed at him through slumbrous green eyes, a smile softening her passion-darkened lips.

He moved against her, letting her feel his hardness throb against her thigh. Her eyes opened, wide and questioning.

"Worth?"

"It's all right, Maggie," he crooned. "This is how it's supposed to be. Don't be afraid."

He moved against her again and this time she accepted him, relaxing even as he tensed. He ached for completion, needing desperately to plunge into her, to make them one, but he held himself back, slowing his breathing, taking his time. He wanted everything perfect for her, not just for himself.

He shifted his weight sideways, loosened the satin draw-string of her pantalettes, and slowly eased them down her legs, taking her stockings with them. He spun a web of kisses along her hip and down her thigh as he went, then worked his way back, stopping at her navel to blow a thin stream of air.

She laughed. "That tickles."

He blew on her again, his eyes gleaming wickedly.

She put her hand between his face and her belly, then stroked his cheek. The rasp of his afternoon beard sent erotic tingles through her body. She raised her head and shoulders off the blanket and pulled him to her.

His mouth tasted rich and dark, its heated cavern spicy and intriguing. She explored him avidly, learning from his responses what he liked, then giving him more.

He settled his weight on her again, making a place for himself between her thighs, moving much closer this time, until she felt the hard shaft of his manhood against her most intimate self. She moaned, feeling the pleasure, ris-ing up to meet him as he pressed down.

Only the thin covering of his drawers separated them. Suddenly, even that seemed too much. She glided her hand down his side until she touched the barrier. Hesitantly, she slid her hand over his buttocks, feeling the firmness of his muscles as they contracted, and he groaned, grinding against her.

She withdrew her hand. "Did I hurt—"

"God, no," he whispered hoarsely in her ear, antici-pating her reaction. "I just ache for you—to love you, to be inside you, Maggie mine."

"Help me. I don't know how to please you." She only knew her need had grown, expanding deep inside her so that she ached for him. And with her need, her love had also expanded, until Worth filled her mind and crowded out all else. She wanted only to please him, to love him, to have him love her.

"You know everything there is to know," he said. "You please me more than you can imagine."

He kissed her and guided her hand to his belly, then down. She felt the smoothness of his stomach, the softness of the hair growing there . . . the hardness of his manhood through the wool of his drawers. He moved her hand along his length, holding her to him with gentle strength, showing her what he liked.

Her fingers found the buttons that held the drawers closed and bravely worked them open. And then he was free, hot and throbbing in her hand, buttery smooth yet hard, a study in contrasts unlike anything she had known before.

His own fingers had hardly been idle, smoothing over her skin from shoulder to thigh, sending ripples of pleasure swirling through her. Her body cried for more. As if he heard its plea, his hand slowly decreased its circuit, homing in on the most secret part of her, the center of her femininity.

He stroked her thighs, and she knew it wasn't enough, though she couldn't have told him what more there was. But he didn't need to be told. He knew and he showed her, gently probing with the tip of his finger, finding the bud of her desire and taking her breath away as he stroked.

Her hands clenched on the blanket and she thought she would faint from the pleasure he gave her.

"I think you're ready for me, Maggie mine," he murmured, but he did not cease his stroking. He delved deeper and deeper inside her as she strained against him.

He could feel her readiness. The scent of musk hung in the air, ripe with promise. Her eyes were dark and half-closed, her cheeks flushed red to match her well-kissed lips. Her head was thrown back as she arched into his hand.

"Please," she whispered to him. "Love me," she pleaded.

He kicked off his drawers and flung them away, then took a moment to look at her. She was beautiful, he thought, made for love. His love, he added possessively.

And then he could look no longer. Passion claimed him with fierce intensity; desire overwhelmed him with need. His lips touched hers once, and the fire burned inside him. His glance locked with hers, and he saw the answering flame.

He rolled her under him as he held his weight off her with his elbows. She would have none of it; she pulled him down until he lay upon her like a blanket, warm and heavy.

"Maggie, don't let me hurt you," he whispered, and stroked back the damp tendrils of hair from her forehead.

"You won't," she promised. "I know you."

She raised her mouth to his and the world fell away. She filled his thoughts, memory upon memory, till he knew he would never forget this time, this place—this woman.

"It might hurt at first . . . this first time," he managed to warn her as he held himself back.

He lay between her thighs. She could feel the heat of him, waiting, straining, wanting. His skin was slick and hot, like her own. His muscles trembled in their strength.

"I'm not afraid," she said, and knew it was a lie.

"I am," he confessed, and she knew he told the truth. He was far braver than she. "I want this time to be perfect."

He rocked gently against her, making her throb with longing. Her entire being focused on his motion, rising and falling like the tide against the shore. She echoed his movements, shyly at first, then with wanton abandon as she lost herself in passion and let inhibitions fall away.

She couldn't imagine what more there could be. Then he slipped inside her, pausing only for an instant as he reached her maidenhead, then breaching the barrier quickly and cleanly.

She barely registered the pain as pleasure overcame her. Her eyes filled with tears, her lungs with laughter, her heart with love overflowing. She held Worth to her, not letting him move, her fingers sinking into the firm muscles of his buttocks. She didn't want him to leave her—ever.

"I'm sorry. It had to be," he whispered. "Next time will be different."

She sensed he was apologizing, but for what?

"I don't want it to be different. I want it just as wonderful. Oh, Worth—"

His kiss cut off her words of love, so she tried to show him with her body what she felt. Her tongue dueled with his as she drank him in, absorbing his every essence. His scent wrapped around her, to be inextricably woven into the moment.

His skin was hot and smooth as she ran her hands up his back; she felt every muscle ripple at her touch. She thought she was sated, completely satisfied, brought to the highest heights of human emotion.

Then he moved—slowly at first, until she caught his rhythm. Her eyes widened, and she gasped with pleasure and surprise. He did not let her catch her breath. Faster and faster, he took her with him. Higher and higher they flew. Endless horizons of blue sky and bright light surrounded her. Weightless, she left the earth behind. Soaring, she reached for the clouds and found the heavens.

She cried out with joy and heard his answering shout as his release coincided with her own. They floated back to earth together, slowly spiraling down like the falling blossoms of the poplar trees nearby.

Gradually, she became aware of the birds twittering in the trees, the spring gurgling gently, the warm scents of spring. She felt replete, contented. She wished time would stand still, hold this moment safe in eternity, though she knew it could not be.

Already she was coming back to herself, to an awareness of where she stopped and Worth began. She could separate his scent from her own, knew which arms and legs were hers despite their tangle, heard her heartbeat differ from his.

She buried her face against his neck and closed her eyes, holding tight to the memory of oneness, to the welcome loss of self in a lover's arms.

He kissed her cheek softly, reaching out to her with tenderness rather than passion. She turned her face to him and their eyes met.

"I never imagined it could be like this," she said, and brushed an errant lock of hair from his forehead. Stubbornly, it fell back into place. "I felt I had no boundaries —no me, no you. It was just us—together."

He heard the wonder in her voice and knew it matched his own. "What we had was special, Maggie. I felt it, too."

He leaned his weight on his forearms and timed his breathing to hers. His heart had slowed to a normal pace,

though he still felt his blood running hot. He had told her
no less than the truth. Never before had he reached such an
emotional pitch. For the first time he understood the difference between having sex and making love, and he knew he
would never settle for less again.

A sudden breeze chilled him and he feared Maggie
would get cold. Reluctantly, he rolled off her.

"Don't go," she protested.

"I don't want you taking ill. The weather's changing."
He looked at the sky. Above it was blue, but to the west,
behind the lowering sun, he saw wild, angry clouds. He
gave Maggie a quick kiss, not wanting to alarm her, then
said, "We'd best hurry."

She must have heard something in his tone. "Why?" she
asked anxiously and quickly sat up, holding her chemise to
her breast. She followed his gaze.

"Are those clouds dangerous?"

He shrugged. "I don't know. Let's not take a chance."

She nodded once. "All right."

Worth pulled on his drawers, then bent to help her up.
"Hurry," he couldn't keep from saying as he drew on his
pants.

With a brief, worried glance in his direction, she complied, donning stockings, shoes, and pantalettes, strug-
gling with her corset and petticoats before accepting his
help with her dress.

By the time they were back in the wagon, the blanket
and basket stowed beneath the seat, the sun was partial-
ly obscured by the fast-moving clouds. A cold wind had
picked up, whipping the prairie grass into a green froth.

The horse snorted unhappily and shied when a spiral of
dust blew by.

"What's happening?" Maggie asked as Worth put the
horse into a fast trot home.

"Looks like a storm. They blow up right quick this time
of year. Wyoming's like that. The old-timers say, 'If you
don't like the weather, stick around a few minutes and it'll
change.'"

The sky darkened overhead and a flurry of snowflakes
blew by.

"Snow?" Maggie sounded shocked.

"It's still April. A blizzard's not out of the question," Worth confirmed, pushing the horse to go faster. The animal needed no encouragement. He could sense the storm's rapid approach and had no desire to be caught in it.

"What about the children? How will Marcus get them home?"

"I'm counting on him keeping them until this thing blows over. This late in the year, the snow will melt right off in a day."

"I hope you're right. What if he didn't see the storm coming?"

Worth grinned wickedly. "Unlike us, he probably had nothing better to do than watch the weather. We were a bit . . . preoccupied."

Maggie blushed and looked away. Worth sensed her discomfort. Did she have second thoughts? Regrets? He couldn't bear to have made her unhappy. He put his arm around her and drew her close. "Are you sorry?"

"Oh, no." She leaned toward him and gave him a quick kiss. "I guess I'm just not used to talking like this. Are you sorry?" She looked at him from beneath her thick lashes. They shielded her eyes just when he wanted to see them clearly.

"It was everything I ever dreamed of, Maggie mine."

"I'm glad." She squeezed his arm and sat snuggled by his side as they raced back to the ranch house.

Thick, wet flakes of snow fell from the sky, clinging to the ground and obscuring Worth's vision. Though skittish, the horse knew his way home, and Worth relied on the animal's instincts more than he would have liked to. Already, his visibility was down to only a few feet. He could just make out the horse's ears, but not his nose.

At the house he let Maggie off, then fought his way to the barn. A dark shadow emerged as he drew near, and he recognized Bobby John's voice.

"Afternoon, boss. Need some help with the horse?"

"Appreciate it. What's happening with the roundup?" This was the first year Worth hadn't been riding the range in the spring, collecting cattle for branding. Between the children and the demands of his practice, he'd been forced to leave this most important part of running the ranch to Jake.

"The boys brought in a few newborns with their dams, but I'm hoping this'll blow over quick. The rest of the herd is making do in the wild. Jake's kept most of the cowboys out with him, to keep an eye out for trouble."

"They shouldn't have too much trouble," Worth said, "unless some fool cow decides to give birth tonight."

"Not much anyone can do about that, boss. Ya cain't see your hand on the end of your arm out there now."

"Any word from Marcus?" Worth asked.

"Yeah. He sent Mitchell over to say he would keep the children overnight. Mitchell's bunking with me till this blows over."

They finished rubbing down the horse together and Bobby John offered to take care of the wagon and tack.

"Fine. I'll see you in the morning, then," Worth said before leaving Bobby John to his work.

Bobby John gave Worth a lazy salute.

Outside, the wind was blowing fiercely, swirling the snow into knee-deep drifts and cutting with bitter cold through Worth's jacket. He raised his collar and hunched his shoulders as he ran across the open space separating the barn and the front corral.

He couldn't see much, and was glad to bump into the corral fence. At least he knew where he was now. Stories of people dying just a few feet from their houses in blizzards like this raced through his mind, but he shook them off. Placing one hand along the fence to guide him, he pushed on toward the house.

The snow was so thick, Mary Margaret could see nothing through the window. Where was Worth? Shouldn't he have been back by now? She paced the room, noting the fire blazing comfortably in the fireplace. The savory aroma of stew simmering on the stove filled the air. Everything was in place except for Worth. Was he all right?

Maybe she shouldn't have let Charlotte Brown go home. At the time, it had seemed the prudent thing to do. Charlotte had told her Becky and Tom were safe at Marcus's.

She had her own family to think of, and Mary Margaret hadn't wanted her to be trapped at the ranch house as the snow worsened.

But now she was alone, in the middle of a blizzard that had come out of nowhere, racing across the plains with nary an obstacle to stop its course other than this house itself. The wind whistled past the windows, singing a dirge. A chill ran down Mary Margaret's spine.

She wasn't superstitious, but this had been no ordinary day. She had come face-to-face with her dreams and found the reality much more fulfilling than her fantasies. Still, she wouldn't be human if she didn't harbor a passing doubt.

Hester Townsend would call her a fallen woman if she learned what had happened today. Mary Margaret tried to think of herself in those terms, but failed. She hadn't fallen at all—she had taken flight. Hugging herself, she closed her eyes and once again saw blue sky and green grass, felt the warmth of the earth beneath her back, the greater heat of Worth above her.

Her flesh still experienced the heightened sensitivity Worth had brought to life; her nerve endings tingled with awareness. When her tongue passed over her lips, she still tasted him, sweet and tangy; his scent rose from her skin to mingle with her own.

The sense of oneness returned, and with it, a deeper longing for Worth. She had thought herself self-sufficient and now knew she had merely been marking time. She had planned her life in detail and now knew it to be someone else's. Hers would go another way. The thought no longer scared her.

Just as the weather had changed, sweeping suddenly across the plains, so had her life, moving from bleakness to promise. Now she needed to be with Worth again, to see if he felt the same.

She returned to the window and pulled back the curtain. Narrowing her eyes, she thought she saw a shadow, a darkened shape with no definable outline, save that it moved—Worth.

She ran to the door and flung it open. "Worth!" she

called, and the wind tore her breath away. She cupped her hands around her mouth and screamed again. "Worth! This way."

The shadow seemed to falter, then regain its purpose. The wind howled in anger, but to no avail. Covered with snow, ice clinging to his brow, she watched him fight his way up the steps and through the kitchen door. Mary Margaret slammed it shut behind him, locking out the cold.

"My God. You should have stayed in the barn. You could have gotten lost out there," she said, helping him to a chair before grabbing a towel from the hook behind the door. Gently she dried his face and hair while he sat, shivering in his jacket, by the stove.

"I wanted to be with you," he rasped hoarsely and rubbed his hands together. They were red and raw, and when she touched them, felt colder than ice.

"You're freezing. Let me get you some tea."

She dipped the ladle into the large pot of hot water at the back of the stove and poured the boiling water into the pot she'd prepared earlier. "It will be ready in a minute."

"Th-thanks," he managed through chattering teeth.

"Will you be all right alone? I want to get you a blanket. You have to take off your clothes. They're going to soak through once the snow melts."

He nodded and smiled wanly. She hurried to the stairs, taking them two at a time. In her bedroom, she swept the feather quilt from atop her bed and tucked the crocheted afghan under her arm. On her way back to the kitchen, she detoured through the main room and picked up the bottle of whiskey, carrying it unceremoniously by the neck.

Worth had shrugged out of his jacket, but his fingers were too stiff and clumsy to deal with his clothes.

"The tea's ready," she said as she piled the blankets on the large kitchen table. She crossed the room to the stove, poured out a mug, and liberally laced it with sugar. As a final touch, she filled the mug to the brim with the whiskey, then held it out to Worth.

"Smells potent," he said with a grin and took a tentative sip. "Whew, this'll put hair on my chest."

"You already have enough," she answered archly, remembering the silky feel of it as she'd run her hand through the curls and down. . . .

He grabbed her wrist and pulled her onto his lap. "Then, maybe I should give you a sip. I don't remember seeing too much on you."

He nuzzled his face between her breasts. She laughed and hugged him carefully, wary of spilling the hot brew on them both. The sensuous web of the afternoon once again spun around her, then a shiver shook him, reminding her he was still in his wet clothes.

She hopped off his lap. "You'd better get out of those things."

He held his hands tightly around the mug, warming them. "Just give me a minute, Maggie mine, so my fingers can limber up enough to undo the buttons."

"No need," she said briskly. "I can handle them."

He saw the hesitation behind her brave front, the hint of uncertainty she hid behind her primness. In Boston, she'd put him off at first with this very same disguise. Now he'd learned to see through it.

"I'd like that," he said to her and reached out a hand to bring her to him. He felt her slight resistance and looked up quickly to catch her true emotion—confusion, touched with fear, overcome by something nameless. Or perhaps he was afraid, himself, to put a name to it. "Come here," he whispered and tugged on her wrist.

She let him draw her right up to his side. "I couldn't stay in the barn, Maggie. I wanted to be with you—here, now. It was worth the risk."

Her eyes darkened. "Not if you'd come to some harm," she answered fiercely, surprising them both with her vehemence.

"But I didn't, Maggie mine. I'm fine."

"You're cold and wet," she scolded, "and I'm going to do something about it. Drink your tea."

He took a quick sip of tea, then tried to help her as she fought with his wet clothes. She batted his hand away.

The whiskey doubled the warmth of the hot drink and his weary muscles relaxed. His mind became comfortably blurry, and he dared steal a kiss as she bent over him. Maggie blushed and glared at him.

He laughed, then gasped, as her fingertips trailed across his bare skin, peeling away the cold dampness, replacing it with burning heat.

He had no more need of spirits or stove. Wrapping his arms around Maggie, he pulled her into the cradle of his thighs and rested his head on her shoulder. He could hear her heartbeat accelerate and he smiled, content at last.

Mary Margaret came awake slowly. The first thing she noticed was the silence. The wind had died down and the world was unnaturally quiet. The second thing she noticed was that she was alone in the bed. While that shouldn't have surprised her, it being the usual course of her life, she had never been alone in this bed before.

She sat up, stretching muscles she had never used so strenuously before, and smiled. She liked the pleasant ache permeating her body. The gratifying soreness reminded her of the love she and Worth had shared—a love that had taken nearly the whole night to express.

She assumed Worth had gone out to check on the livestock, and she was glad to have this time alone. Their awakening could have been so awkward—at least, on her part. She was unsure of the proper etiquette in such a situation, and she was positive Miss Emily Thornwell didn't have any pertinent recommendations in her *Lady's Guide to Perfect Gentility*.

Mary Margaret decided she would dress and go downstairs.

She shivered in the chill pervading the kitchen. The stove must have gone out sometime during the night. Neither she nor Worth had given a thought to it when they'd gone upstairs to bed.

She looked around and found the wood and kindling laid out in a bin beside the stove. All she had to do was get the fire started, and she could have breakfast fixed in no time at all. Though she had never lit this type of stove before, she figured it couldn't be too hard. Besides, she had this undeniable urge to make everything perfect for Worth.

She located the matches on the top shelf of the pantry and pushed some small chips of wood and bark into the black cast-iron stove. She'd already inspected the pantry and decided to make oatmeal, coddled eggs, and soda biscuits.

Carefully striking the match, she lowered the burning tip to the kindling and waited. Nothing happened. Then the match sputtered out.

She pulled another match from the box and tried again, with the same result. Ten minutes later, half the matches were gone, she had black soot all over her hands and dress, and still no fire burned in the stove. Her dreams of a cozy breakfast for two were shattered when she heard Worth stomping the snow off his feet on the back porch.

She was so frustrated, she wanted to cry as she knelt in front of the black monster. She had so wanted to do something special for Worth, and now, because of her inadequacies, it wouldn't be. She was sure Lucy Robertson would have been able to handle this trivial task. After all, she'd been brought up in this part of the country. She was exactly what Worth needed in his life—not a citified easterner who couldn't even light a stove.

"Maggie, what are you doing down here? I thought I'd find you still tucked up in bed," Worth said as he shucked off his heavy coat and rubbed his hands together. "By the way, the snow's beginning to melt already."

Mary Margaret could hear the smile in his voice, but she couldn't respond in kind. All she could think of was the disaster she'd made. How long would it be before Worth realized she couldn't give him what he needed? She kept her head down and felt tears gather in her eyes.

"What in the world is the matter, Maggie mine?"

Worth hurried to her side. Noticing the slight shaking of her shoulders, he gently grasped her upper arms, pulled her to her feet, and turned her to face him. Her hair fell in long strands over his hands and he tenderly brushed it back.

His fingertip caught one of the tears clinging to her lashes before it fell to her cheek. "What's happened, sweetheart?"

"I can't light the fire," she whispered, keeping her chin tucked into her chest. She resembled a young child.

"A fire isn't something to shed tears over," he murmured softly. His thumbs massaged her upper arms, trying to soothe the tension from her body. What he really wanted to do was run his hands through her silken brown tresses and wrap them around her naked body, but she needed something else from him.

"I wanted to have breakfast ready for you when you came in, and I just couldn't light the stove," she finally confessed.

"I have trouble lighting this old stove myself, Maggie. Only Charlotte seems to have much luck with it. You shouldn't take on so." Worth pulled her more fully into his arms, but her tears did not stop. Nothing he said seemed to help.

"Maybe the kindling is damp," he tried, hoping to ease her dismay.

She shook her head. "I should have been able to get it started," she said, her voice muffled against his shirtfront.

"Maybe you didn't use enough kerosene."

"Kerosene?" she questioned through her tears. "I didn't know you had to start it with kerosene."

Worth was perplexed by Maggie's unusual behavior. The Maggie he'd come to know would never have let something so trivial weigh her down. He'd never seen her like this before—so vulnerable, so unsure of herself. A protectiveness he'd felt for no one else sprang to life inside him.

"You couldn't be expected to know."

"I wanted to have everything perfect for you."

Suddenly, he understood. Gently, he led her over to a chair by the kitchen table and pulled her down onto his lap.

"Maggie, I didn't expect you to have the fire lit and breakfast done when I came back—not because I didn't think you could do it, but because I was hoping you would still be in bed, so I could come in and kiss you awake." He ran his finger up and down the curve of her cheek, marveling at its softness. "I like kisses in the morning. How about you?"

"I've never been kissed in the morning," she confessed

softly, her tears subsiding, her words interspersed with only an occasional sniff.

"Why don't we try it and see how you like it?" he prompted.

His mouth ravished hers, and his hands traced the long, slim lines of her back. He could tell she hadn't put on her corset, for he felt the softness of her curves beneath his fingers. He explored those curves and reveled in her immediate response.

Raising his head, he looked into her dreamy eyes. "I think you take very well to kisses in the morning."

Worth watched the color rise in her cheeks and her eyes grow more luminous. She tried to hide her face in his shoulder, but he wouldn't allow it. He bent his head and nuzzled her ear, then whispered, "As a matter fact, I think you should be kissed thoroughly every morning. Of course, I'm the only person eligible for the job."

After last night, he wouldn't allow anyone near her—much less close enough to kiss her.

"You're the only one I'd want to do it," she replied softly, then gasped as he plunged his tongue into her ear, seeking one of the pleasure points he had recently discovered.

His body hardened as Maggie squirmed on his lap, and he shifted to ease the pressure. His hands continued to explore her through the pale blue material of her day dress. The tiny buttons running down the front were too much of a temptation; he began slowly unbuttoning the top few.

His breath became labored, and he was just about to suggest they move upstairs, when he heard footsteps on the outside porch.

"It appears we have company," he said, his voice taut with suppressed longing. "We'd better make ourselves presentable, though I'd much rather take you back upstairs."

Mary Margaret could see the heat in his blue eyes and knew the truth of his statement. If she were honest, she would have chosen the same option, but instead, she gathered her flying hair with both hands and tried to smooth it into some kind of order. Now she wished she had tied it back earlier, but she'd been too excited at the prospect of cooking Worth's breakfast.

Rebuttoning her dress, she realized how silly she must have seemed to Worth, sitting there crying in front of the stove. And now, looking back, it seemed silly to her, too. But then. . . .

Looking in Worth's direction, she saw his profile as he stared out the window. She wondered what he was thinking, but knew she wouldn't ask, even if there had been time. She was still too unsure of their relationship to chance it.

The back door opened and Charlotte entered the large kitchen.

"Are you two trying to get that there stove started? Look at your pretty dress, all covered with soot," she fussed. Then, in a whisper to Mary Margaret, she said, "Worth never did have the knack for lighting this black monstrosity, and now he's gotten you all dirty as well."

Mary Margaret was about to admit it was she who had had no luck with the stove, when Worth intervened.

"I'll never get the knack for lighting it, Charlotte. And I think you like having me at your mercy when I'm out here at the ranch." Worth smiled teasingly at the older woman.

"It does give me a feeling of superiority, that's for sure," she laughingly agreed. "Mary Margaret, you'd better go upstairs and get cleaned up. Marcus will be bringing the children home soon since the snow's almost gone. I'll have your breakfast on the table when you're ready."

"Charlotte's right. You go on upstairs, Maggie," Worth prompted. "I'll stay down here and find out Charlotte's secret to lighting this stove."

Worth sent Mary Margaret a knowing look. It seemed to say, I wish I were coming upstairs with you, but if I did, we might not come down till lunch. Her cheeks reddened and she had to fight her overwhelming need to be near him. She hurried up the hall.

By the time they finished breakfast, Mary Margaret could hear the children's voices raised in excitement over the sound of horse hooves pounding on the front drive. She went out front with Worth to greet them.

"Uncle Worth! Aunt Maggie! Did you see the snow? Wait till you see my puppy—he's the best," Tom shouted as he jumped from the seat of the buggy.

"He's my puppy, too. Uncle Marcus says so," Becky insisted as she held her arms out to Worth to be helped down.

"We didn't have heavy coats or anything. Uncle Marcus let us wear Lucy's clothes," she continued, hugging her uncle's neck. "Could I wear your clothes, Aunt Maggie, if I didn't have my own?"

"Any time," Mary Margaret answered, smiling at the little girl's earnestness. Claire would have been so proud of the way Becky was adjusting to the changes in her life. She felt a pang of sadness at the memory of her dear friend; the loss still weighed heavily on her heart. There were so many things she longed to share with Claire and now never would.

"When can we bring the puppy home, Uncle Marcus?" Tom asked.

Marcus had finished tying the horse to the waist-high hitching post and walked over to stand by Worth. "I'd say in about four weeks. You want to make sure he's good and strong."

"He's the biggest and the strongest already," Tom informed Worth and Maggie. "That's why I'm calling him Thor, after one of those Greek gods we're studying at school. He's the best dog you've ever seen." Before anyone could comment, he was off and running.

"I hope the children weren't any problem," Mary Margaret said to Marcus as they watched Tom speed toward the barn.

"None at all. I really enjoyed having them. It's been a long time since I had any little ones around. I miss the joy a child's presence can bring."

"Uncle Marcus made us a sled out of feed bags real early this morning and we got to slide down the hill in front of his house before the snow melted. Can we do that again?" Becky asked, slipping her hand into Marcus's larger one.

"Sure thing, sweetheart. Next time it snows, just ask Uncle Worth to drive you out."

"Thanks, friend." Worth grinned at Marcus. "I'll remember this the next time you need a favor. Can you stay for coffee?"

"Nope, need to get back to the ranch. My men need help with the stock. After this thaw, the cattle'll be stranded in mud up to their bellies and bellowing their fool heads off 'cause they can't work themselves out. You heading back to the city today?"

"Yep, right after lunch. I'd like to stay longer, but I have some pressing cases. One of them comes up for a hearing tomorrow."

After Marcus left, Mary Margaret helped Charlotte prepare one of her favorite chicken recipes for lunch. The dish was a big success, and though she still felt uncomfortable with the way she had acted this morning, not being able to light the stove no longer bothered her.

"This is the best chicken I've ever tasted. You have a real flair with that stove," Worth commented, grinning at her from across the table.

Mary Margaret smiled back, savoring their private joke.

Thirteen

*M*ary Margaret had barely opened her bags to begin unpacking when there was a knock on her door. She was sure it was Sarah, coming up to inquire about her trip to the ranch. She smiled to herself; Sarah wouldn't hear about *everything* that had happened.

"Come in," she called as she continued folding her clothes and placing them in the bureau.

"Oh, Miss Simpson, the town is just aflutter," Estella Pareet twittered as she entered the room, her sister two steps behind her. "And to have you living right here, under the same roof as us. It's simply too grand.

"I told you, Mirabelle, how exciting it would be to have a writer in our midst," Estella continued, turning to her sister and then immediately back to Mary Margaret. "Didn't I tell you so, Miss Simpson, the night after the first baseball game?" She didn't wait for an answer. "Everyone knows the editorial you wrote was about Mrs. MacIntyre, and with her living here, too. . . . Well, I'm just too excited."

Mirabelle went over to the corner and sat on the very edge of the platform rocker. "But I have heard that some of the men are very upset," she put in, all in a dither. "I can't imagine what will happen if they decide to take matters into their own hands."

"Now, Mirabelle, why would you even think of such a thing? You'll have Miss Simpson all upset with your foolishness."

Mary Margaret looked from one sister to the other, trying to understand what they were talking about. She finally figured out that the *Daily Star* must have printed her article right away after all. When she had left it with them, they had said they would print it "when space allowed." She'd found them quite discouraging. So finding out they'd printed it almost immediately was a pleasant surprise. Mary Margaret didn't know quite what to say. Fortunately, with the two Pareet sisters in the room, she didn't have to worry.

"Now, Miss Simpson, don't pay Mirabelle no never mind," Estella said, patting Mary Margaret on the arm. "I don't think it's as bad as she says. Why, only yesterday . . ."

Before Miss Estella could go off on another of her lengthy discourses, Mary Margaret interrupted, giving Estella's hand a soft squeeze in apology. "Do you ladies have a copy of the paper? Since I've been out of town, I haven't even had a chance to see it."

"Why, of course, dear. Mirabelle, run to our room and fetch a copy of the paper so Miss Simpson can see it," Estella ordered her younger sister.

Mirabelle jumped from her chair and ran to do her sister's bidding.

"I can't believe the paper printed it so soon. They seemed hardly interested when I dropped it off. What did you think of it?" Mary Margaret was prompted to ask. Never before had she been able to get such an immediate and personal reaction to her work from a reader.

"Well, I liked it fine, so don't you be upset by what other people might say," Estella cautioned. "Some people are just so stiff-necked, you know. They just can't seem to change with the times, but I've always prided myself on staying current with all that's going on around me."

"And did you think my piece was current with the times?"

Before Estella could answer, Mirabelle was back, waving the newspaper under Mary Margaret's nose.

"See, your article's on the front page. It was the first thing everyone saw when they opened their papers."

Mary Margaret stared at the headline with pride. There it was, her own byline, with her real name, on an article that wasn't the usual "women's literature," but represented her serious thoughts.

"Would you ladies mind if I took some time to read this and rest before dinner?" she asked the Pareet sisters. She needed a little time alone to take everything in.

"Why, of course not, Miss Simpson. I told you, Mirabelle. We shouldn't ought to be bothering her as soon as she got back. You rest now, dear. We'll see you at dinner. Come along, Sister."

As soon as the two old ladies had left the room, Mary Margaret took the newspaper over to her impromptu desk and lit the gas lamp. She spread out the paper and began to read.

"In the history of this great territory, one name will long be remembered—that of Mrs. Esther Morris. For it was she who first proposed that women here be endowed with the rights so taken for granted by men: to vote and serve on a jury, to get equal pay for teaching, and to acquire and hold on to property in their own name, even after marriage.

"Though some on the legislature claimed to have voted for the measure as 'a good joke,' the women of this nation see nothing humorous about achieving equal station with men. And, indeed, in this great territory, women's suffrage has been a force in favor of law and order that has neither disrupted the home nor brought on the vast array of domestic calamities once foretold.

"But now a more subtle attack is occurring on the rights women have come to hold dear. For while the laws themselves have not been changed, neither have they been fully enforced. Public sentiment, and by this I mean male public sentiment, has been founded on the belief that husband and wife are one person, and that person is the man.

"Even here, in the enlightened city of Cheyenne . . ."

The editorial had been printed just as she'd written it, the reference to Annie MacIntyre's case suitably ambiguous while making her point: laws were not enough if they weren't enforced, and the courts were duty-bound to enforce them, regardless of the swell of popular opinion.

A deep satisfaction welled within Mary Margaret when she finished reading. Her eyes drifted back to the top of the page where her name, Mary Margaret Simpson, was printed for all of Cheyenne to see, including Worth. She hoped reading this article would make him understand and appreciate the importance of her writing.

She wished he could be here now, so she could hear his thoughts on her article. Their relationship had deepened immeasurably in the past few days, and his opinion was important to her. More than that, she wanted to share her sense of accomplishment with him on having finally achieved a cherished goal.

She sighed. Here she had just spent the entire weekend with Worth. Surely she could not begrudge him some time alone with the children, especially since she had been the one to insist on going back to the boardinghouse to do some work.

Well, now that she was here, she had better get busy. Spurred on by the success of her first article, Mary Margaret began writing her second, stopping only for a short supper break. Ideas flowed as her work claimed her full attention.

She was startled a half hour later when Sarah called up the stairs saying she had a visitor in the front parlor. She quickly wiped the nub of her pen clean and closed her inkwell, her heart racing all the while.

Who but Worth would come visiting this late in the day without leaving word first? She looked in the mirror. Her hair was an absolute mess. She didn't want to take the time for a complete toilette, not with Worth only a few feet away. Instead, she hastily brushed the stray wisps off her forehead and neck, securing them in place with combs, and hoped he wouldn't notice the patchwork job she'd done.

When she reached the first floor, she could hear his

voice, along with Sarah's, coming from the front room. Her heart skipped a beat and a nervous anticipation filled her stomach.

She took a deep breath and entered the parlor. "Good evening, Worth, Sarah."

Worth looked so male and powerful in the formal sitting room. Once again he was dressed in his city clothes, his hair neatly groomed and his face cleanly shaven. Even from this distance, she imagined she could smell his fresh-washed, masculine scent. She couldn't keep from staring at him, and knew she had a silly smile on her face. How had he known she wanted nothing more than to see him again tonight?

"Well, I'll leave you two young people to your own company," Sarah said into the silence. "I kin see you don't need no old woman like me in the way."

Sarah had barely shut the pocket doors behind her before Worth was out of his chair and sweeping Mary Margaret into his arms. His mouth closed over hers, and Mary Margaret felt she was home again, exactly where she was supposed to be. In less than a heartbeat, Worth totally obliterated all her senses to anything other than him. He held her tight in his arms, crushing her to his chest, bringing vividly to life her memories of the previous night and the passion they had shared.

"I couldn't wait until tomorrow to see you," he whispered in her ear, his breath warm and delicious against her lobe.

"I wanted to see you just as much," she whispered back shyly. Their coming together at the ranch seemed like a moment out of time, while here all the trappings of their regular lives surrounded them. She was having a difficult time piecing the two together.

"Would you like to sit down?" she asked, falling back on politeness to smooth the way.

"I'd tell you what I'd really like, but I'm afraid this is neither the time nor the place."

Her cheeks, already flushed from his kiss, reddened even further as her mind toyed with the brazen images he'd evoked. She felt like a young girl with her first beau, all giddy laughs and lighthearted pastimes. Yet she knew there was much more to her feelings. What she felt for Worth was no young girl's adoration, but the full passion of a woman grown.

Unconsciously, her hand rose and caressed his cheek, relishing the slight roughness of his beard under her fingertips. What a wonderful freeness she felt in being able to touch him so.

She had only started to explore his face when his hand came up and captured hers. Turning it palm up, he brought it to his lips and gently kissed the very center, his tongue trancing its delicate lines. Then he closed her fingers into a fist, sealing in the magic.

"As much as I'm enjoying this, we must stop," he said, his voice deep and dark. "If anyone were to walk in here now, I wouldn't want you to be embarrassed. My sweet Maggie, I lose all control when I'm with you."

Worth lowered himself to the sofa and patted the seat beside him. It was all he could do not to grab Maggie in his arms again. Whenever he was around her, he lost all perspective on what was proper and what wasn't. But this place held no promise of privacy, and he would not subject Maggie to cruel gossip or idle speculation, no matter how great his need.

"Will you sit and talk with me a moment, Miss Simpson?" he asked in a very correct and impersonal voice. He could tell from Maggie's knowing glance that she saw the twinkle in his eye, for she replied accordingly.

"Of course, Mr. Worthington. It would be my pleasure. As a matter of fact, I find I have something of import to discuss with you," she intoned in her most proper Boston accent. But when she looked directly at him, she could not keep up the facade. She began to laugh.

"Oh, Maggie mine. To hear your sweet laugh," Worth sighed. "Do you really have something you want to talk about?" He'd be happy just to sit here and look at her for the rest of the evening.

She smelled faintly of flowers and her hair was not quite as tidy as usual. Somehow, that made her more endearing. Now, when he looked at her, the prim and proper spinster from the East no longer came to his mind. Instead he saw a vital, passionate woman with fire in her eye and a fierce intelligence.

"Have you seen the *Daily Star* since you've gotten home?" she asked.

"I saw it on the table in the hall, but what with getting the children settled, and interpreting their more than colorful stories of the snowstorm to Kathleen, I didn't have time to read it."

His mention of the snowstorm sent another wave of color into her cheeks. Was she remembering all the same things he was? A flash of excitement rippled through him.

He slid his hand behind her on the couch and settled her in the crook of his arm, her head cradled on his shoulder.

"What's so important about the *Daily Star*?" he asked.

"My article ran in it today—on the front page. I was hoping to hear your opinion of it."

He could tell she felt more than the usual pride in her work and wanted to share her achievement. He was glad she was letting him into this part of her life.

Since his confession, he'd been worried she might try to hide her writing or close him out of this side of her life. She wouldn't have been the first. But she was just as open and natural with him as she would have been with anyone.

"Did you bring a copy down with you?" he asked.

She shook her head.

"Well, if I had written a front-page article, I'd carry it on my person all the time. It's quite an accomplishment, you know."

She looked up at him. "Do you really think so?"

Happiness radiated from her face.

"Of course. Am I going to get to read it or not?" he demanded, needing to distract himself. "Do you have a copy handy?"

"Upstairs. I could go get it."

Reluctantly, he loosened his hold. "I'll wait here," he said, knowing he could use the time to assert better control over his wayward feelings.

"All right." She seemed reluctant to part, too, and Worth felt his body quicken with need. "I'll be right back."

He nodded and watched her leave the room, her hips swaying gently with every step, her walk a study in feminine sensuousness though she did not seem to know it.

Their weekend together had brought them to a new and deeper understanding, borne of their physical intimacy and the strong emotional bonds they had forged. Where before he had seen only obstacles to their coming together, now compromise seemed within reach. Once the few details were worked out, they could weave their lives together into one satisfying cloth.

He'd already planned the next fifty years by the time she returned. Smiling, he took the proffered paper.

"You'll take into consideration that it'll take me a while to get through this."

"That's all right. I'm in no hurry." She smiled back at him, her eyes gleaming brightly, her cheeks faintly flushed, reminding him of the way she'd looked in the heat of passion.

"Sit beside me?" he asked, needing to touch her.

"I thought you'd never ask," she said as she cuddled by his side. "If you like, I'd be glad to read it out loud."

"The author quoting her own work. Why, I'll be the envy of all Cheyenne." He knew, then, he had given her his trust—a more profound trust than he had ever shared with anyone. Even Marcus wasn't privy to the secrets Maggie knew about him, but instead of feeling vulnerable, he felt stronger for it.

He grinned and put his arm around Maggie's shoulders, letting her scent surround him and reveling in the feel of her softness. "I'm all yours."

She shot him a quick look, then started to read. "In the history of this great territory, one name will long be remembered—that of Mrs. Esther Morris. . . ."

Worth relaxed as he listened. He'd met Mrs. Morris once, shortly after she'd been appointed the first woman justice of the peace in South Pass City. That was just before he'd come to Cheyenne, in sixty-nine. He'd been impressed by the woman and her grasp of the world.

The sound of Maggie's voice was soothing to his ears, its cadences mesmerizing. He almost lost his bearings, content to let the words flow over him without opposition. Then, suddenly, his muscles tightened at what he was hearing.

"Even here, in the enlightened city of Cheyenne," Maggie was saying, "we see continuing evidence of man doing his best to subjugate woman, using sneers and insults to keep her from her rights.

"But a woman has a duty to herself and her kind. She must enhance her own independence, and in so doing, set a standard for all womankind. No longer can we let the oneness of marriage deny the dignity of woman, for in so doing, a wife becomes but a slave to her husband."

Worth sat up straight, increasingly disturbed by what he was hearing. He watched as Mary Margaret read, her voice filled with conviction, oblivious to his growing dismay.

"The law is a great and wondrous thing. It gets its life not from books and paper, but from living people. It is not enough to write that a woman has rights, to proclaim with great virtue that the law has made it so. Not when women are denied those rights every day, and no one steps in to rectify matters.

"The time has come for women to stand up for themselves—to demand right be done by them, and the letter of the law fully enforced. No longer can a man say, 'Thus it was always done, and thus it will always be'—not if the courts take their rightful stand and hold up the laws of this land.

"And so they must. For the cause of justice is not served by bowing down to popular opinion, no matter how loud its collective voice. Justice is served by honoring the word of the law in protecting the weak from the strong, the downtrodden from the tyranny of their oppressors. And the courts are at the vanguard of this battle. We look to them to stand fast."

She put down the paper and looked at him expectantly. He didn't know what to say. He couldn't believe she'd write something like this—not when she knew he was representing Jesse MacIntyre. Wasn't a woman supposed to stand by her man, at least in public? Had she no idea of what she had done to him, going up against him so publicly?

"What about the effect this will have on the case?" he said very quietly, knowing this damaging publicity was bound to bring unwanted attention to Jesse's battle with his wife.

"What case?" she asked, looking baffled. Her face lost some of its radiance as she took in his displeasure.

Ordinarily, he wouldn't have wanted to hurt her, not in the smallest way, but right now, his own hurt was so great, he couldn't think.

"Jesse MacIntyre's case. Don't you think you should have at least consulted me before you wrote this article?" He tried to keep his voice level, but he could hear the strain in it. And so could she, if her reaction was anything to go by.

She slid subtly back on the settee, until they were no longer touching. Her hands were primly folded on her lap, her back ramrod straight.

"As a matter of fact," she said coolly, in her best Miss Simpson tone, "I was going to ask you about land deeds and the like for my second piece; however, I had no reason to believe you'd want to see this article before it was published."

Worth found he couldn't sit still any longer. Just when he'd thought they'd resolved all their differences, their relationship was blowing up in his face, and her career was right in the middle of things. How had he been so stupid and naive?

He crossed to the other side of the narrow room, stopped by the fireplace, and turned to face Maggie. "What about the fact that I'm representing Jesse MacIntyre? Did you ever consider the consequences of your article on me?"

"You're representing Annie's husband? Legally?"

Worth could see the astonishment on her face. "Why do you think I've been spending so much time with him?"

"I thought he was just a friend you were helping out."

"He's more than that. He's my client, and it's my duty to see he gets as fair and unbiased a hearing as can possibly be had."

Worth kicked at the log already laid out in the grate, frustration and anger warring in him. "I suppose you've taken Annie to your bosom and told her everything was going to be all right."

With every word, Worth could feel Maggie withdrawing from him. He hadn't meant to sound so harshly accusing, but his emotions were in a turmoil. Where he once had felt trust, he now felt betrayal, as if Maggie's attack on Jesse, indirect though it was, was a personal attack on him.

"What was I supposed to tell her?" Maggie defended. "That her husband can do anything he likes with her property and she has no say in the matter?"

Worth tried to remember that Maggie hadn't known about his involvement in the case, but he couldn't hide the truth.

"Annie MacIntyre signed that property over to Jesse so he could sell it and finance *their* horse farm." His voice hardened, and he could feel the muscles in his neck and face tightening.

"That's not what Annie says. She claims she didn't sign anything. Jesse just took what he wanted without so much as a by-your-leave."

They stared at each other across the room, so close and yet so far. A chasm yawned between them as neither gave ground. Maggie looked away from him, biting her lip, and when she again faced him, he saw her pain. But he had pain of his own, and a sure conviction that his client spoke the truth.

Worth felt trapped in a web not of his own making as the tenuous bonds between him and Maggie stretched and threatened to snap. Was there nothing they could give each other? No way to cross the gulf between them?

"I honestly didn't know you were representing Jesse," she offered, as if she'd heard his silent question. Her eyes pleaded with him to understand.

Worth dragged his hand over his face. He was suddenly very tired. "I believe you, Maggie, but remember, there are always two sides to every story." His heart was heavy, each beat marking his passage into sorrow. "It's very hard to tell the good from the bad sometimes—who's in the right and who's in the wrong—especially in a case like this."

He gave her a long look. Her expression was grave and sad, but she didn't say anything. If she had known Jesse was his client, would she have done things differently? He was afraid to ask.

Worth took his watch from his pocket and looked at the time—almost eight. "Come walk me to the door. I need to get back to the children. Kathleen has a meeting of the Ladies' Aid Society at the church, and Becky and Tom like me home for their bedtime ritual. I like to be there if I can."

Maggie came to him, quiet and subdued. He remembered the way she had come flying into the room with her article—so happy, so expectant. He could only imagine her hurt, but thought it must match his own. Would they be able to get past this, he wondered, then set his resolve. He wasn't ready to give up yet—not by a long shot.

"We'll work this out, Maggie mine," he said, kissing her gently. "Somehow, we'll work it all out."

Mary Margaret heard the clock in the front parlor chime twelve times and knew she would not sleep easily tonight. Too much had happened in the last few hours. Had it been only so short a time since she and Worth had been in each other's arms, learning the mysteries of passion and desire?

She was restless and confused. Her body ached for Worth's touch. She longed to once again experience those mindless moments of passion she'd encountered in his arms. Even more, she missed their closeness—the blending of their thoughts and feelings, the sharing of excitement or quiet that came when two people were in tune with each other.

After their confrontation over the editorial, she'd been afraid to make the first move—afraid to be rejected, as she had been by her father when she'd done something of which he'd disapproved. Worth's rejection would have been a thousand times more painful.

Though Mirabelle had said some of the men were upset, Mary Margaret had never even considered that Worth might be one of them. He was more rational and under-standing—or so she had thought.

She'd been so relieved at his parting words. They left her with a sliver of hope that somehow, indeed, things would work out.

She turned over on her back and stared at the ceiling. The moon cast white shadows over the bed, and she remembered seeing the same images last night on the ceiling in Worth's room at the ranch.

The clock struck the quarter hour. There was barely a sound within the boardinghouse. Everyone must be asleep except for her.

And then she heard a noise—the slight creak of a floor-board, a muffled footfall, the telltale whoosh of fabric brushing the floor. Who would be walking the halls at this hour of the night?

She stayed perfectly still, not breathing, listening in-tently as the quiet footsteps passed her door and faded away. Then a door opened and closed in a distant part of the house. She waited, but the footsteps did not return. What was going on?

Maybe because of what was happening between herself and Worth or because of her fertile writer's mind, Mary Margaret suddenly had images of the different sets of boarders pairing off and sneaking into one another's rooms in the dead of night. The thought was ludicrous, but it did take her mind off her own problems. Now, who would she pair with whom?

She twisted back to her side and stared toward her door, as if she could see who might be walking down the hall.

A totally outrageous combination would be Cleary, the flamboyant actress, and the pious reverend, Charles Hanson. She could see the reverend in his nightshirt and cap, with his skinny, birdlike legs, tiptoeing down the hall, for-ever looking over his shoulder, and the voluptuous Cleary opening her arms wide to greet him as he came to her door.

Mary Margaret pulled the covers up over her mouth to stifle her laughter.

Equally unlikely would be Estella Pareet and Lord Peter, though the reason for such a liaison was readily apparent.

Estella had a great deal of money and poor Peter had none —very good reasons, at least from Peter's point of view.

Perhaps she was being a little hard on Peter. He might be a truly wonderful and caring person.

Then, on the other hand, maybe she should pair Sarah with Peter. This was a much more suitable solution. Sarah also had money, but she would keep young Peter in line.

Mary Margaret was just getting to Freddie Hinsford-Hill when she heard someone outside on the front walk—a rather noisy someone.

It was unusual for anyone to be out so late in this section of town. Over by the Golden Plume, people wandered around until the early hours of the morning, but here in the residential section, nearly everyone was tucked up safe and sound in their own beds by ten o'clock.

Mary Margaret could hear voices now, a low murmur of sound. Swinging her legs over the side of the bed, she straightened her nightgown and crept over to the window. She cautiously pulled the lace curtain aside and peeked around the edge.

On the sidewalk in front of the boardinghouse were fifteen men or so, milling about and talking in low tones. From what she could see, they were neither well dressed nor completely sober.

Behind her she heard a soft knock, and her door slowly opened. Sarah poked her head around the frame.

"Can you see what's going on out there? My room's off the back and I can't see a thing."

"It looks like a group of men, and they've all stopped in front of the house."

"Why would they be doing that, I wonder?" Sarah moved in beside Mary Margaret and looked down on the street below. "This doesn't look none too good to me."

As Sarah finished speaking, one of the men stepped forward, leaned over the fence, and called out: "Annie? Annie? I know you're in there. I want to talk to you."

"That there's Jesse MacIntyre. What's the dang fool think he's doing here at this time of night?" Sarah asked, settling herself into a more comfortable position on the window seat.

"Annie? Come on home with me. You know you belong with me out at the farm."

"Yeah, why are you doing this to your man?" one of the men from the group yelled out.

"It looks like Jesse's brought some help with him," Mary Margaret remarked.

"And it's the kind of help we don't need. I recognize some of those boys, and ain't none of them known for their Sunday manners. Most of them have nothing to do except wear their boot soles out on a brass rail. The lot of them probably been down at the Silver Capital Saloon for the last four hours, pouring likker down their throats faster than a deacon takin' up collection."

"What do you think they want?" Mary Margaret was more intrigued than frightened. She wondered what Annie MacIntyre was making of all this, if she even heard it from her small room in the back.

"I don't know, but I reckon we'll have some real goings on, if 'n someone don't go out there and settle 'em down."

Sarah drew her shawl more tightly around her thin shoulders and tried to smooth down her wispy gray hair, which was going in ten different directions.

"Annie, can you hear me? I'm talkin' to you." Jesse's voice had lost its pleading tone and was strident and demanding. "Come out here and talk to me now."

"I'm going to see if Mrs. MacIntyre's up. Mebbe she can talk some sense into her fool husband."

Sarah hurried out the door and Mary Margaret followed her to Annie's room. Sarah knocked boldly.

"Mrs. MacIntyre, you up in there?"

Mary Margaret heard a rustling of bedclothes and then Annie appeared at the door.

"Yes, Mrs. Miller?"

"Your damn fool husband's got a bunch of his wild, drunk friends out in my front yard, and he's wanting to talk with you."

Mary Margaret saw the horror on Annie's face and could well understand her fear. Jesse MacIntyre drunk was not a pleasant experience.

"I can't talk to him. He don't listen to a word I say.

Besides, he knows we're going to court tomorrow. My lawyer said I didn't have to see him."

"I can understand your not wanting to be with him, Annie, but you're probably the only one who can talk sense to him when he's in this frame of mind," Mary Margaret prompted.

"I can't. I just can't," Annie said, and burst into tears.

"Now, now, girl, no need to take on so." Sarah patted the woman's shoulder. "Miss Simpson and I can handle it. You just go on back to your room and don't fret none."

Mary Margaret looked at Sarah as she pulled the door closed. She could hear the men's voices much clearer now; they were getting more agitated. Someone was going to have to acknowledge their presence soon.

"What are we going to do? Those men don't sound like they're going to listen to reason."

"You're a writer, ain't ya? You know how to put words together real good. I know you'll think of something. And I'll be right beside you. Don't worry none."

Sarah might be confident, but Mary Margaret wasn't nearly as sure. She'd never dealt with a mob before, and from the ugly sounds coming from outside the house, that was what the men were fast becoming.

"Let me stop and get my dressing gown. I need to put my hair up before I go out."

"I'll meet you downstairs in the parlor."

Mary Margaret could hear the men much more clearly from inside her room. They were definitely getting louder and more abusive. Something hit the side of the house, and Mary Margaret knew there wasn't much time left to calm the situation. She quickly pulled on her dressing gown and buttoned it to the throat. She wrapped her long hair around her fist, made a knot, and hastily pinned it to the back of her head.

By the time she made it down to the parlor, most of the other residents had heard the commotion and had come to investigate.

"I'm not sure anyone should go out there," Reverend Hanson was saying as she entered the room.

"And what do you propose we do, then? Sit and wait till

they break all the windows in my house?" Sarah demanded.

"I did hear something hit the house," Mirabelle offered, looking toward the front windows from her position on the horsehair sofa.

"Too right," Freddie added. "I think the reverend and I should go out and face the horde. After all, he has an orator's tongue, I'm sure."

The good reverend blanched at Freddie's words. He probably didn't have a lot of experience in settling down unruly crowds, Mary Margaret thought.

"You men would only get them more excited," Sarah decided, shrugging off Freddie's proposal. Reverend Hanson looked relieved, until he heard Sarah's next words. "Besides, the reverend's too old for such shenanigans."

He started to pull himself up, but at that instant, the men's voices rose in volume. He seemed to think better of his protest, for he sat down quietly and shrank into his chair. He was out of the limelight now and planned to stay that way.

"Someone fetch me an oil lamp. Mary Margaret, we'll go out and see if we can't calm 'em down a bit."

Estella came rushing back into the room with an oil lamp in one hand and a small derringer in the other.

"Maybe you should take this with you, too," she said, offering the gun to Mary Margaret.

"Don't be a dang fool, Estella. Mary Margaret don't know how to use one of those. And we don't want more trouble than we can handle."

"But, it isn't loaded. I'd never keep a loaded gun in my room," Estella explained. "I just thought . . ."

"Thank you, Estella, but Sarah's right. I don't know how to use a gun and it might only get the men more excited. Why don't you put it back in your room?"

"Miss Sombolay, you got that lamp lit?"

"Right here, Mrs. Miller," Cleary said, handing the lamp to Sarah. "You two be real careful. Nothing's worse than an audience that don't like your act."

Sarah and Mary Margaret walked into the hall and opened the front door. The men were tramping around in the front yard. They'd come inside the gate and were ready to mount the steps and enter the house.

"Jesse MacIntyre, just what do you think you're doing?" Sarah scolded, holding the lamp up to illuminate the porch.

"I come to get my wife," he said, his speech less clear than it had been ten minutes before. Mary Margaret noticed an uncorked flask sticking out of his pocket.

"Your wife's sleeping, like any sensible person would be this time of night. Go home and come back in the morning."

"I'm not going home till I see my wife."

"Mr. MacIntyre, it's far too late for Annie to come down. Why don't you go home and get a good night's rest. You can come back tomorrow," Mary Margaret tried to reason with him.

"Who do you think you are to tell Jesse what he can and can't do? Who are you, anyway?" a voice called out.

"Why, she's that fancy writin' lady," someone yelled.

"The one who wrote that crap about women in the *Daily Star* today?" a voice from the back of the crowd asked.

"Yeah, she's the one. I recognize her from the baseball game."

"This here is between a man and his wife, and you don't have no call to interfere, lady," another voice called out.

"If this is between Jesse and his wife, what are all of you doing here?" Mary Margaret returned.

She could feel the sudden surge of hostility from the crowd. They didn't like being crossed.

"We men have to stick together. We don't need no uppity outsider comin' here to tell us what to do. Go back where you came from if you want to stir up trouble."

"I'm not the one stirring up trouble. I merely stated the facts. The laws stand on the books. Getting drunk and harassing your neighbors isn't going to resolve anything."

In the heat of the moment, Mary Margaret had forgotten to whom she was talking. She saw a man in the front of the crowd pull his arm back as if to throw something, and knew she had said the wrong thing. Instead of calming them down, she had merely inflamed the men more.

"I'd drop whatever it is you have in your hand, Thorny

Hamilton," a voice boomed from the back—one that expected immediate action and brooked no argument.

"Thank heavens. Someone must have went to get the sheriff," Sarah whispered to Mary Margaret.

"Now, what are all you good gentlemen doing out here at Mrs. Miller's? Aren't you usually down at the Silver Capital this time of night?"

The crowd parted as the sheriff walked forward, and well it should. The man stood over six feet tall, with a barrel chest and a resonant voice. The two guns he wore spoke for themselves.

"All we want is for Mrs. MacIntyre to come on out and talk to Jesse," a voice dared venture from the back.

"Is that all you want, now? And what does Mrs. MacIntyre want?" The sheriff directed his question to Sarah.

"She just wants to be left alone—just like we all do, Sheriff, so's we can get some sleep."

"I think that answers your question, boys. Jesse, you come back when you're sober and know what you're saying. And come back without your friends. You get my meaning?"

Jesse nodded, but Mary Margaret doubted he was sober enough to remember what the sheriff said.

"Deputy, take Jesse down to the jail. I reckon he'll have to be charged with disturbing the peace. Now, the rest of you move along, unless you want to spend the night with Jesse. You'll have every house on the street awake with your caterwauling. Get on home."

When the men began to disperse, Mary Margaret caught sight of Worth standing out by the gate, his gaze trained on her. She stayed on the porch, unable to move, her eyes locked with his.

How she wanted to run to his arms and have him hold her tight. Couldn't he see the longing in her face? Couldn't he sense the loneliness in her heart?

"Sheriff, we was mighty glad to see you," Sarah said as the man mounted the steps.

For an instant, when he passed in front of her, the sheriff blocked Mary Margaret's view of Worth. She greeted him briefly with a nod of her head, then looked back to the gate. Worth was gone. A fierce pain stabbed her, and she closed her eyes against it.

"Good thing that young English lad came to fetch me," the sheriff said. "Didn't appear you were making too much headway with the rascals. And it seemed that you," he nodded his head at Mary Margaret, "was only riling them up more, miss."

"I'm afraid you're right, Sheriff. They didn't seem too interested in the truth."

"Not when they're drunk and mad. The only thing they understand then are these." He patted the guns on each side of his hips.

By this time, most of the men had wandered off in groups of two or three, muttering among themselves and glaring back over their shoulders. Mary Margaret hadn't seen where Jesse had gotten to.

"You don't think Mr. MacIntyre will come back again, do you?" Mary Margaret asked.

"Not tonight. He'll be in jail till morning. His lawyer can worry about the disturbing the peace charge then."

That's probably where Worth went, Mary Margaret concluded, *to look after his client at the jail*. Somehow, the thought brought small consolation, for it only pointed out how deep the differences were between them.

"Thanks again for your help, Sheriff," Sarah said, hugging her arms against the night chill.

"My pleasure, ma'am," he said, tipping his hat. "You ladies get inside now and don't worry none. I'll have one of my deputies keep an eye out."

Mary Margaret followed Sarah back into the house, wondering what Worth was thinking and how they would ever put their differences behind them with the whole town involved in the MacIntyres' problems.

Worth had done all he could for Jesse. By the time he'd gotten to the jail, Jesse had passed out in his cell. He'd made arrangements to return in the morning and get Jesse cleaned up in time for court. He'd have to remember to bring some fresh clothes with him so Jesse would look presentable before the judge.

Jesse sure isn't helping his cause any, Worth thought with a sigh. Innocence was rarely an adequate defense, Worth had learned over the years. It quickly became irrelevant in the face of people's impressions. "Facts" could be twisted and turned to suit any version of the truth a lawyer cared to present. And right now, Annie's lawyer would have the upper hand, thanks to Jesse's stupidity.

Worth came out on Pioneer Street and decided to take the long way home down Seventeenth Street. He needed some time to think. And this way, he'd pass by Sarah Miller's place. If the lights were still burning, he could stop in and talk with Maggie, though he didn't know what he could say.

The differences between them loomed larger than ever. Gone was the anonymity of a small trial between a disgruntled wife and her desperate husband. Instead, he was faced with a public battle that had taken on larger proportions.

He hadn't wanted this battle, though he would not have turned away from it. Even now, he knew he would not shirk his duty to his client. But why did it have to be at such personal cost to himself? Why had the lines been drawn with him on one side and Maggie on the other?

He couldn't let her think he opposed the law. On the contrary, he'd sworn to uphold it—a vow he did not make easily, especially in light of his family's unsavory history. Both he and Henry Clay had had to live their father's reputation down. Surely Maggie would understand his commitment to his principles. An innocent man could not be punished while Worth just stood by.

He had to explain it to Maggie so she would understand. Otherwise, they couldn't recapture those precious moments they'd spent out on the range or feel the same connection with each other. It wasn't only the pure physical release, but the coming together of two souls, the magic felt only by two people who truly belonged together, that he longed for.

They'd found that magic until the article in the *Daily Star* had torn them apart. He knew he was mostly to blame, but the article had thrown him, left him unable to separate his Maggie from Mary Margaret Simpson, the writer.

The irony was, he didn't disagree with her ideas—he just didn't think they applied to Jesse. Words had never been his strong point—or feelings, either. But all that had changed when Maggie entered his life. He only hoped he could find a way to make it clear to her.

Quickening his steps, he rounded the corner onto Seventeenth and looked down the block. The boardinghouse was shrouded in darkness; not a single light burned. Disappointed, Worth stopped near the gate and stared at the building. After a minute, he turned and walked slowly home.

Fourteen

*M*ary Margaret woke up tired after a fitful night of uneasy dreams haunted by Worth's face. First, she'd seen him as he had looked standing in the parlor of the boardinghouse, detached but determined. Then his expresssion changed to the one she had seen as he stood at the back of the dispersing crowd. It held a strange tenderness, but also a trace of desperation. She was afraid to look any deeper—afraid she'd see rejection and mistrust.

She had hoped he might stop by the boardinghouse on his way home from the jail, but the hoped-for knock never sounded at the front door.

It was times like these when she missed Claire the most. They had shared their problems, talking them out until they'd figured out what to do. How she longed for that closeness, that caring intimacy that had taken years to develop and mere minutes to snuff out.

This morning she felt restless and out of sorts. Her new editorial for the paper was finished. Freddie Hinsford-Hill had turned out to be a surprisingly valuable source of information when it came to land deeds. She had gotten all the details she needed from him.

She decided a cup of tea might provide the calming effect she needed. She was heading for the kitchen when there was a knock at the front door.

Not seeing Sarah or the maid, Mary Margaret answered the impatient ringing. She was surprised to find Kathleen and Reverend Leisch waiting on the porch.

"Oh, Mary Margaret, I'm so glad you're in. We have important news," Kathleen said breathlessly.

Mary Margaret noticed that the reverend kept his hand possessively on Kathleen's arm. She bit back a smile.

"Come in, won't you? Kathleen, you sound out of breath. Is everything all right? Maybe we should step into the front parlor," she said, gesturing to the door on her right. "We'll have more privacy there."

Just as Mary Margaret opened the parlor doors, the maid came scurrying out of the kitchen. Mary Margaret requested tea and closed the doors.

Kathleen barely had her coat off before she started talking. "I was just going over ta McGruder's Mercantile ta pick up some ribbon for Becky's hair, when I noticed all this commotion over at the jail. What with it being so early in the morning and all, I couldn't imagine what was happening, so I went ta take a look. There, marching on the sidewalk, were about twenty women, some of them carrying big signs. It was a sight ta behold, I can tell ya. I met Colin at McGruder's and we came right over."

Kathleen blushed prettily as she called the minister by his first name. Colin smiled and gave her hand a reassuring pat.

"Who were the ladies? Why were they there?" Mary Margaret asked, unsure why Kathleen had felt so compelled to bring her this news. Did she think there might be a story here for one of her articles?

"They're the ladies who have taken up Annie MacIntyre's cause. And it's all because of your writing in the paper. They're walking back and forth, chanting lines from your editorial and talking about women's rights."

"Lines from my editorial?"

"Aye! I asked one of the ladies—someone I know from church—and she said your article was what set them all ta thinking."

Reverend Leisch leaned forward and added, "Actually, a number of the ladies of the church came to me early this morning and asked my opinion of their plan. It seems Susan Anthony's sent one of her confederates, a Mrs. Sanders, here to Cheyenne to address the local suffrage committee. After reading your editorial, Mrs. Sanders pointed out how much to the point Mrs. MacIntyre's case is in showing the problems they see occurring."

Mary Margaret was disturbed by Colin's news. A good journalist always hoped what she wrote would spark the interest and minds of her readers, but she hadn't counted on anything like this happening.

First, there had been the midnight visit from Jesse and his cronies, and now, the ladies were taking on the mantle of battle. She'd intended to make people pause and think, not take to the streets. Maybe she shouldn't have sent in her second editorial. What would Mrs. Sanders make of that?

She wondered what an uninvolved person might say about the events of the past few days—especially a man. "And what did you tell the ladies who came to visit, Colin?"

"I said I certainly thought they should stand up for their beliefs. After all, if *they* didn't fight for their rights, who would? And Annie MacIntyre's case appears to be a good starting point."

Mary Margaret nodded. He was right. If you didn't fight for what you believed in, there was no reason to believe. She had always stood up for her rights, and it had made her a better person. If it weren't for Worth's involvement on the other side, she probably wouldn't be having her doubts now. But the fact remained that Worth was involved, and beyond that, the situation was becoming much more volatile than she'd anticipated. Under these circumstances, would she be able to continue with this particular crusade?

"They also asked if I thought they could give Mrs. Sanders your address, since she wanted most fervently to speak with you," Reverend Leisch continued. "I told them they could. I hope I did the right thing."

"Of course," Mary Margaret agreed, but a shiver ran

down her spine and she felt a strange sense of foreboding. "As a matter of fact, I'd like to speak with her and find out more about what she's doing."

She could always use the information in some other way if the local paper didn't want it. The larger papers back east would certainly be interested in what was happening in Cheyenne, even if she had to write about it under her M. M. Simms pen name.

"I can't imagine what poor Mr. Worth thought," Kathleen tacked on.

"You saw Worth?" Mary Margaret's heart stopped beating for a moment, then started again with a large bump. Worth hadn't been pleased about her editorial; she could just imagine his reaction to the marchers. She was afraid he'd place the blame firmly on her shoulders now that she'd become such a public figure. "Where was he?" she asked, dreading the answer.

"He was trying to get through the line of ladies and into the courthouse. He has a hearing for Jesse MacIntyre's trial this morning."

So he already knew about the marchers. That meant his biggest concern had come true: his client had been squarely placed at the center of a large public controversy. And she'd had a major role in putting him there, though she'd never intended to create this kind of furor.

"I kin tell ya, Mr. Worth dinna look none too happy."

"I can well imagine." Mary Margaret felt her heart sink, but what could she do? The Pareet sisters had taken her second article to the paper when they'd gone on their morning constitutional an hour earlier. And after what Colin Leisch had said, she couldn't see backing down from her principles simply to avoid trouble.

"Miss Simpson? Are you in there?" Estella Pareet's voice called through the heavy wood of the parlor door. Before she could reply, Estella had opened the door and entered, followed closely by Mirabelle.

"You'll never guess what we saw happening down at the courthouse after we delivered your article to the paper." Her voice was high and piercing, and her face was bright red from excitement. She hadn't even bothered to take off her light day coat and bonnet.

"You mean about the ladies marching?" Mary Margaret asked.

"You know already?" Disappointment clouded the older woman's face. She had wanted to be the one to tell Mary Margaret the news. Mary Margaret felt a small pang of guilt for cutting Estella off, but she'd answered automatically, her mind occupied by thoughts of Worth.

"Yes. Kathleen was just telling me."

"Well, Mirabelle just wanted you to know." Estella gave her sister a chastising look. "I think we'll stroll back down that way and see what else might be happening."

With a brief good-bye, the Pareets left. Kathleen stood to leave, too. "I have to go fix lunch for the children. They'll be home from school any moment and I haven't even thought about what to give them."

"Don't fret. I'll help," Colin said, also rising. "Take care, Miss Simpson, and don't take on a burden of responsibility that isn't yours. You spoke out when speaking was needed. Don't be ashamed of that."

Although Mary Margaret was heartened by the reverend's support, she couldn't completely absolve herself of complicity in the current situation. She had entered into it so innocently, to help Annie as part of her interest in women's rights. Now, not only were Annie's rights in jeopardy, but so was her relationship with Worth.

The strain would only become greater when everyone in town took sides over the marchers. This wasn't the kind of event people could ignore, and she and Worth were more caught up in it than most, their opposing sides pulling farther and farther apart. What would Worth say to her now, she wondered. Would he talk to her at all?

Mary Margaret heard the doorbell ring again, but this time decided to let someone else get it. The morning wasn't half over and already she felt drained. Her emotions were being pulled in too many directions. She leaned her head against the back of the rocking chair and closed her eyes.

A tentative knock sounded at the parlor door, and Rosie, the maid, stuck her head inside.

"Miss Simpson? A Mr. Melton from the *Daily Star* is here to see you. Are you accepting visitors?"

"Show him in, Rosie."

Mary Margaret sat up in her chair and smoothed the sides of her hair. Maybe Mr. Melton had decided not to run her editorial. She couldn't decide if she was disappointed or relieved.

"My dear Miss Simpson, I'm so glad I caught you," Mr. Melton said when he entered the parlor. "You must excuse me for barging in like this, but I just had to come and tell you how much I like your newest piece. It's exactly what the paper needs."

Mr. Melton heaved his considerable weight into Sarah's ornamental side chair and leaned toward Mary Margaret. The chair creaked ominously but held.

"I'm not sure it's wise to print this new article just now, Mr. Melton," Mary Margaret stated, surprising herself as much as Mr. Melton. Was she being prudent, not wanting to throw oil on a burning fire, or was she yielding to her own selfish desires where Worth was concerned?

"My dear lady, with Mrs. Sanders in our city, the timing couldn't be better. This territory was founded on the rights of all its people. We can't sit back and watch while they're being taken away from some. This case could be the test for the strength of the law."

Mr. Melton had a calculating gleam in his eye. Mary Margaret knew this controversy would sell extra papers, especially if it stayed so heated. Nonetheless, what he said was true. If Jesse MacIntyre should win, a wife's rights would be forever forsaken.

Mary Margaret knew where her intellect lay, but her heart felt otherwise, for if Annie won, Worth would have to lose. And if Worth lost, in some way so would she. She could see no way out, except for withdrawing from the field of battle.

"I want you to write a few articles on Mrs. Sanders and her leader, Susan B. Anthony," Mr. Melton went on. "Tell our readers all about their movement and what's happening back east in relation to here. This is an opportunity not to be missed. Think of all the good you could do."

"You're certainly very persuasive, Mr. Melton, and what you say is true. I'll give you my decision this afternoon, if that's all right."

The idea of writing factual articles on women's rights appealed to Mary Margaret. She believed fully in her cause, and if it weren't for Worth, she would jump at this chance. But right now she needed time to think, to assess the conflicting emotions battling inside her. She stood to indicate the interview was over.

Mr. Melton followed her lead, but turned at the door to add, "There is one more thing you might be interested in."

"Yes?"

"I've had a telegram from a newspaper in New York. They want to run your articles, too—under your byline, if you wish. They were quite eager for me to get back to them so they would know whether they needed to send one of their own people here. I promised I would telegraph back within the hour."

She didn't know if the eastern papers really expected an answer so fast, but she knew Mr. Melton well enough to understand both the bait and the threat. She'd worked a long time for the chance to be published under her own name in a major paper, to be taken seriously by the journalistic profession. Finally, the opportunity was in her grasp. She knew she couldn't walk away.

At her invitation, Mr. Melton rearranged himself on Sarah's best chair. They discussed in detail her future articles, and she gave him Garth Devereaux's address so he could finalize the arrangement.

Once Mr. Melton left, Mary Margaret went up to her room and grabbed her notebook. She'd walk over to the courthouse, to see for herself what was happening, and talk with Mrs. Sanders.

She might also get a chance to speak with Worth. She hoped she could explain her position to him, and he could find it within himself to accept her career decisions as she accepted his. But her stomach was tied in a knot of dread, and the chasm between them loomed wider than ever.

Worth left the courtroom after he'd made sure Jesse took the back way out. He instructed Jesse to go home and stay there until he had to appear again in court at the end of the week. One thing Worth didn't need was Jesse MacIntyre confronting the group of women outside and having a verbal slinging match. After last night's disastrous confrontation with Maggie and Sarah, his client didn't need any more bad press.

He hoped Jesse could find the paper Annie had signed; without it, their case was in real trouble. As it was, between the furor raised by Maggie's editorial and that caused by Jesse's own quick temper, Worth knew justice would be hard to come by in Cheyenne. His best hope was a speedy trial, before things got completely out of hand.

Fortunately, the judge had concurred and set the hearing for Thursday morning, just three days away. By the week's end, Jesse would have his answer. But unless Jesse found that signed paper, Worth was afraid he knew what the outcome would be.

The whole case was bothering him. It just didn't feel right, and not only because of the excessive publicity, either. Worth had developed an instinct about these things over the years, and right now, his instinct was telling him something was very wrong. The problem was, he couldn't figure out what.

"Worth, old man, you seem to have your hands full."

Worth was surprised to hear Marcus's voice and to see him dressed for a day on the range, rather than in his town clothes. Marcus hadn't mentioned coming into the city today when he had returned the children yesterday.

"What are you doing here?" Worth asked.

"Telegraph office sent out a man. Seems Lucy's decided to come home early. I came into town to meet her, but I sure didn't expect all this excitement. I was just passing by the courthouse, minding my own business, when I saw all these fine, upstanding ladies marching out front. Someone mentioned you were trapped inside here. Thought you might need a helping hand."

Marcus's eyes twinkled merrily. Worth was glad someone was getting a kick out of this mess. He sure wasn't.

"I had a minor problem getting in this morning, but I managed."

"I sure don't envy you, kid, going up against the city's finest. You really think old Jesse's innocent?"

"You know I do, but even if he isn't, he deserves a fair trial, not this . . . this circus." That was what annoyed Worth the most—not the ladies' right to speak out, nor their support of a law he happened to believe in, but the blatant disregard for justice, for holding a man innocent until he was proven guilty. And this trial by newspaper, coupled with the marching in the streets, could only have a deleterious effect on the search for the truth. How was justice served here?

"Where'd you hide Jesse?" Marcus asked, looking around the empty hallway. "I didn't see him when I came in."

"I sent him out the back way, hoping he could avoid the ladies."

"I can well imagine Jesse's reaction to them. You were smart not to let them meet."

"You should have seen him last night. He and a bunch of his barroom buddies decided to go over to Sarah Miller's boardinghouse and talk to Annie personally."

"He didn't do any damage, did he?"

"Only to his case, I'm sorry to say. But Maggie and Sarah got caught in the middle when they tried to protect Annie. They were lucky no one was hurt. That kind of crowd can get ugly at the drop of a hat."

"Seems like Mary Margaret's editorial really stirred things up."

"It sure did," Worth commented thoughtfully, wondering how this latest development would affect his and Maggie's relationship.

"She's quite a woman, that Mary Margaret," Marcus said with an amused but appreciative gleam in his eye.

"Maggie is more than some woman, she's my woman." Worth hadn't planned on being so blunt, but the words popped from his mouth. His feelings of primitive possessiveness surprised him, but couldn't be denied. He wasn't sure how to deal with them.

Worth felt torn by guilt, confused about his loyalties and hers. All he knew for sure was how strong his feelings for Maggie had become, and with that knowledge came the certainty he couldn't let her go.

Marcus gave Worth a strange look, but before he could speak, the sheriff rounded the corner and waved at both of them, trying to attract their attention.

"Well, my friend, your Miss Simpson certainly stirred up a hornet's nest around here," the sheriff said by way of greeting to Worth.

"The deputies have their hands full out front, do they?" Marcus asked with a grin.

Worth was glad Marcus handled the sheriff. The man's statement had thrown him. Did the whole town know about him and Maggie? Maybe his guilt wasn't all in his mind. Others might see it in just the same light. Did the very existence of a relationship with Maggie destroy his credibility as Jesse's lawyer? He hadn't considered that before.

"My deputies are hard pressed when it comes to corralling upstanding, churchgoing ladies," the sheriff joked with Marcus.

"Too much for your men, are they, Sheriff?" Marcus never missed a chance to rile someone if he thought he could have some fun.

"My men can handle anything thrown their way," the sheriff said mildly, defending his men without rising to Marcus's bait. "It's not the ladies I'm worried about. It's the men standing around catcalling who could cause the real problems."

"You think there might be more trouble?" Worth asked, putting aside his conflicting thoughts at this latest development.

"In a wild city like Cheyenne, you can never be too careful. I'm always wary. Wasn't so long ago that we were the edge of the frontier."

Worth could see that under the sheriff's bluff manner was a lot of misgiving about what was going on. Men with nothing better to do than sit around drinking and fighting all day were always ready for a good battle, regardless of the cause. The fact that Jesse's case fueled their own feelings of injustice didn't help calm things down either.

He wondered how far each side would go. Though he hadn't mentioned it to anyone, he was certain someone had been snooping in his office. Nothing had been taken, but his files had been disturbed, leading him to conclude that someone had been looking for papers connected to Jesse's case. Everything else he was handling was run-of-the-mill.

Maybe that explained his suspicions about this case. If he could figure out what they were looking for, he might just get a handle on this entire affair.

He took one last look out the window before venturing through the crowd again. Something familiar caught his eye. He looked, then looked again. Sure enough, there she was. With a muffled curse Worth rushed out, leaving his companions staring at him in open-mouthed surprise.

Mary Margaret stood off to the side by McGruder's Mercantile and watched the marchers down the street. She wanted to take a few minutes to observe the crowd before being swept into the thick of it.

There were people of every description wandering in the vicinity of the courthouse—young mothers with small children in tow, old men who had disrupted their morning checker game in front of McGruder's to mosey over and be the first in on the latest gossip, soldiers in sparkling full-dress uniforms mixing with ranch hands in dusty clothes and sweat-stained hats. Once the word had spread, everyone had come to get a closer look.

Stepping from her hiding place, Mary Margaret decided she'd lingered long enough. Now she needed to talk with the milling people and get their opinions on what was happening.

One older man had remained seated on the porch of McGruder's and Mary Margaret started with him.

"Good morning. Why aren't you out there with everyone else?" she asked, gesturing with her hand.

"Don't see no need," the old man replied, and spat a stream of tobacco juice into the bucket at his feet. "I'll hear all about it when I get home this afternoon."

"How's that?" she asked.

"My wife's out there marchin'. Come lunchtime, I'll get an earful over roast pork and creamed taters."

"Do you mind that she's marching?"

"Nope. She's always done what she wanted and never asked my permission. No reason for her to start now."

"Do you believe in what she's marching for?"

He looked up at Mary Margaret, his eyes a watery blue. "Can't hardly say yea or nay. As long as she believes in it, that's what's important." As he finished speaking, his eyes moved back to the crowd, his attention again centered on the courthouse and the line of women walking out front.

Mary Margaret considered what the old man had said as she stepped off the raised sidewalk and headed for the courthouse. He was right. What mattered was how one felt about what one was doing, not what anyone else thought.

Could she follow that philosophy if it meant losing Worth? Could she charge forth without considering anyone else's feelings, including her own? Loving someone the way she did Worth made her more aware of her own power to hurt and influence, but what should she do about it? Where did her rights end and his begin?

Until now, she'd never asked herself these questions. She'd never had to. Now she needed the answers desperately, but they were not easy to find.

She walked into the crowd, seeking out people to interview. All of a sudden, someone grabbed her arm from behind and pulled her toward the back of the building. The pressure was insistent and allowed no sway.

She tried to resist, twisting her arm in an attempt to free herself. Visions of last night's disturbance streaked through her mind. The faces of the dissatisfied men flashed before her eyes, closing in on her. She felt a scream rising in her throat.

"I'm not trying to abduct you—I just want to talk."

The sound of Worth's voice instantly calmed her, though tingles of a different excitement now pulsed through her. She must have been more upset by what had happened last night than she'd realized to have panicked so badly. With her heart beating rapidly, she allowed Worth to guide her to the back door of the courthouse.

She caught only a glimpse of his face from the corner of her eye as they forced their way through the crowd. His hand was warm on her arm where he held her so the crowd wouldn't separate them. Her heart accelerated again, but this time it was from Worth's proximity. Just being near him caused her body to react in alarming yet pleasant ways.

They made it into the building. Worth led her to one of the offices on the ground floor and closed the door securely behind them.

Images of him sweeping her into his arms and kissing her with passion and desire flooded her mind. For the moment, she forgot the crisis that separated them and longed only for the comfort of his embrace, the healing intimacy of his touch.

But he did not touch her. Instead, he paced the narrow room and ran one hand agitatedly through his hair.

"What were you doing out there?" he demanded roughly, dispelling her sensual daydream.

"I'm covering the ladies' march for the *Star*, if you must know," she replied stiffly, straightening the bottom hem of her double-pointed shirtwaist.

His impulsive action, she now realized, had nothing to do with his feelings for her, and everything to do with getting her away from the crowd outside and the job she was doing. To think that scant minutes ago she'd been worrying about how Worth would be affected by her activities! His concern was certainly not reciprocal.

"Are you going to write another editorial for that damn paper?" he asked, walking to the window and looking out. She could barely make out the marchers from where she was, but knew he could see them quite well.

"No, this will be a feature piece on what's happening at the march."

"Have you ever considered that Melton might be using you to get extra publicity for his paper?"

"What if he is? He's also giving me an opportunity to advance my career."

"Advance *your* career? He's taking advantage of who and what you are to advance himself and his paper."

"Are you implying he's only using me because I'm a woman? That if I weren't, he wouldn't have printed my editorials?"

"Maggie, his paper's been selling like hotcakes ever since this case began, and you know it. It doesn't hurt in the least that you are female. Probably makes the ladies buy up the *Star* in droves."

"I see. And the quality of my writing and my ideas has nothing to do with it? Is that what you're saying?" She was angry—angry and hurt.

"No, I'm not saying all of that," he insisted, turning to face her.

"But you are saying some of it," she concluded from his remark. "Back in Boston you . . ."

Mary Margaret didn't finish her sentence. She'd been about to say that back in Boston he hadn't thought M. M. Simms so incompetent, but she didn't want to confide this last bit of information to him—especially now, when they were at such odds.

"Back in Boston what?" He took a step closer to her, his expression no longer angry.

"It's not important," she said with a defeated sigh.

"Dammit, Maggie, what's happening to us?" Worth asked, raking his hand through his already disheveled hair. His voice revealed both his exasperation and his pain; his eyes were shadowed. "Saturday seems so long ago now."

Was it only two days since she'd lain in his arms and thought everything so perfect? Now nothing was perfect—not even her longed-for dream of being published in New York.

"Is it really that long ago?"

She reached out tentatively to touch him, laying her hand gently on his arm. Their eyes met and held, communicating on a level their words could not match.

"Oh, Maggie mine," Worth whispered hoarsely and drew her into his embrace. "Why are we fighting when there are other things we do so much better?"

When his lips touched hers, she wondered the same thing. Wasn't this all that was important? Wasn't this what they were meant for?

His tongue gently probed her lips, seeking entrance. She could not deny him. Her mouth opened under his and she forgot the shabbiness of the small room, the women marching outside, and even the court case that had started everything.

Once again his scent permeated her skin, his taste filled her with exquisite longing, his firm lips had her hungering for more. All that mattered was Worth, and she reveled in the feel of him, pressed close to her again.

Just when she thought there would be no going back, something struck the window from outside and the trance was broken.

"What was that?" Worth asked, his voice husky. He slowly lifted his lips from hers as if he, too, felt wrenched from a dream.

They hurried over to the window and looked out. The sheriff was standing on the sidewalk with his back to the women, addressing the crowd.

"I think I'd better go back outside," Mary Margaret said, torn between her need to be with Worth and settle their problems, and her instinct that something of consequence was happening and she should be there to cover it.

"But, what about us?" Worth asked, barring her exit from the room.

"This has nothing to do with us," she said, her voice pleading with him for understanding. "This is my job—something I feel I must do, just as you must defend Jesse. Is that so wrong?"

He didn't answer; he just stood there unmoving, his eyes filled with sadness and anger.

"You don't want me to cover this story, do you?" She met his gaze unflinchingly. He looked away first. "Please, let's at least be honest with each other."

"Maggie, I feel more for you than I have for any other

woman in my life, and it's because of that that I don't want you to cover this story. I'm afraid it will tear us apart when we've only begun. I couldn't stand that."

Tears gathered in her eyes. "I have to cover this story. It's important to me."

She had discovered that today, in all her soul-searching. Maybe someday she would be content to take on the traditional role of woman as wife and mother, to move out of the man's sphere of politics and commerce and into domestic life. But she wasn't ready yet, and maybe she would never be. Important ideas were at stake here—ideas that would affect generations of women. She couldn't just walk away.

And if Worth couldn't accept her as she was, how long would their relationship last? How long until her resentment against her role turned into resentment against him for keeping her in it? How long until he tired of her insistence on forging her own life, not following the path marked for most women even though it did not fit her?

There was no expression on his face when he said, "I guess you do. I can't keep you from doing what you must." His voice was low, yet she could hear the pain behind each word he uttered. He stepped back and let her leave the room.

Though it hadn't been voiced, she knew a decision had been made. They would go their separate ways. Whether it would be for a lifetime or till the end of the trial, she did not know.

Mary Margaret stepped out of the courthouse and back into the sun, fighting hard against the tears she refused to let fall. She asked someone to point out Mrs. Sanders, the woman suffrage leader. She was off to the side, talking to one of the women from Kathleen's church. Mary Margaret decided to interview her on the spot. Maybe she could forget her pain if she immersed herself in her work. It was worth a try.

"Mrs. Sanders, could I have a few moments of your time? My name is Mary Margaret Simpson and I'm—"

Mrs. Sanders didn't allow her to finish. "I can't tell you how pleased I am to meet you. Your editorials are a boon to our movement. I must say I am most impressed, and I know Miss Anthony will be also. I've sent her copies, by the way, so I expect you'll be hearing from her soon."

Mary Margaret took a quick breath in utter astonishment. Miss Anthony was well-known for being totally dedicated to the cause of women—particularly with securing their right to vote. To be brought to her attention was an honor, indeed.

Gathering her wits, Mary Margaret said, "You're very kind to say so, Mrs. Sanders. I've only written the things I've felt."

"Exactly as I thought. You're just the kind of woman we need in our movement—someone far-thinking who can articulate the aims of our venture."

"Right now I'm doing an article for the *Daily Star* and would greatly appreciate it if you'd give me an interview."

"Of course, I'd be pleased to. Would this afternoon be satisfactory? Say, two o'clock? I'm staying at the Empire Hotel. Do you know it?"

Mary Margaret nodded. "I'll see you at two."

A sudden commotion by the side of the building distracted Mary Margaret as she and Mrs. Sanders parted.

Worth was coming out of the building and the noisy crowd surged around him. Were they attacking him? Would he be hurt? She pushed her way through to the front of the group and saw, to her relief, that people only wanted to question him.

A small man in a black suit with a notebook and pencil stood next to Worth.

"Bevins from the *Gazette*, Mr. Worthington. Can I ask you a few questions?" Without waiting for Worth's consent, he began. "What effect will these ladies have on your case?"

"They shouldn't have any effect."

Mary Margaret moved in closer so she could catch every word.

"Come on, Mr. Worthington, you know as well as I do that this kind of publicity influences cases," the reporter pressed. "What about the editorials in the papers that claim you're taking away the rights of women in this territory? Can you comment on them?"

Mary Margaret held her breath. What would Worth say?

"First, I don't believe any editorial has specifically mentioned our case. Second, editorials have been run on both sides of the issue. That should be proof that this enlightened city is fair-minded and just. It would be inappropriate for me to make any other comment at this time."

Mary Margaret flushed. Worth was using her own words in a subtle attack on her editorial. She looked up and their eyes met, but his expression remained closed, as if he barely recognized her. He looked away. Her heart plummeted, but she forced herself to stay put. She was here as a reporter; she mustn't forget her priorities.

"What about Jesse?" the man from the *Gazette* asked.

"I believe my client to be innocent of the charges leveled against him. If I didn't, I wouldn't have taken his case."

"Therefore, you believe that Annie MacIntyre is lying?" Mary Margaret found the courage to ask. This was one of the hardest things she had ever had to do in her life.

Worth's gaze collided with hers, and Mary Margaret heard her name echo quietly through the crowd.

"That's right!" someone in the back asserted. "If Jesse's innocent, then Annie must be lying."

"What it means," Worth said, never taking his eyes from Mary Margaret, "is that on Thursday morning in court, we will all have our answers."

Her heart leaped. Did he mean that on a more personal level as well? Could all of their differences be solved so easily?

Then she heard Worth's name being called from the back of the crowd. He pulled his gaze from her and looked to the right. Mary Margaret turned her head to see what had captured his attention. Standing off to the side was Lucy Robertson, her hand raised in greeting.

"Now, ladies and gentlemen, if you will excuse me, I have to see a young lady home."

Fifteen

"*T*AKE *CHARGE WHILE YOU STILL CAN!*"
screamed the headline at the top of the
Cheyenne Gazette's front page the next day.
Beneath it, in smaller type: "MEN, CONTROL YOUR WIVES
BEFORE THEY CONTROL YOU."

The article below was a call to arms written by the conservative editor of the *Cheyenne Gazette* himself. He decried the "outside influences disrupting our fair city" and laid the blame for Sunday night's ruckus at Sarah Miller's boardinghouse directly on the poisonous influence of women who refused to accept their God-given place. The men were but victims, trapped by the conniving guiles of the worst of the fairer sex.

He went on to chide the husbands for allowing their wives to roam freely in the streets, disrupting traffic and interfering with the judicial process by marching in front of the courthouse. What would happen to the natural order of the world if women were permitted to upset things in this scandalous way?

Mary Margaret gritted her teeth until her jaws ached, but she couldn't stop reading the inflammatory prose. The editor of the *Gazette* was a dangerous, irresponsible manipulator, inciting his followers to turn back the clock by whatever means came to hand.

"Why, Miss Simpson, there you are. I told Mirabelle we would find you here, now, didn't I, Sister?" Estella Pareet fluttered into the front parlor, trailing yards of striped India silk trimmed with cardinal-red bows and cream-colored lace, all done up in flounces down the back of the skirt.

Mirabelle followed in a more simple housedress of plain black wool with only a hint of lace outlining the neckline and cuffs. If it weren't for her short, plump figure, she would have looked quite elegant.

Mary Margaret moved her chair back from the table near the window, glad of the interruption, especially when she saw what Mirabelle was carrying.

"Here it is, Miss Simpson," Mirabelle said, holding up another newspaper. "Today's *Daily Star*. It just arrived this very minute. We thought you would want to see it right away."

"Of course she does, Mirabelle. Don't dawdle so. Give her the paper, if you please." Estella swept grandly to the ottoman near Mary Margaret's seat, her skirts rustling richly. She sat and leaned forward eagerly. "What does it say? Is your article there?"

Mary Margaret took the paper from Mirabelle. Her hands were icy and she felt a cold dread in the pit of her stomach. What mischief had Mr. Melton concocted to keep pace with his fiercest competitor?

"DOES MIGHT MAKE RIGHT?" bellowed the *Daily Star*'s chief headline, set in type large enough to rival anything the *Cheyenne Gazette* might have to offer. "RIOTING MEN THREATEN INNOCENT LADIES, CHASE THEM FROM THEIR BEDS," the lower headline titillatingly declared.

She laid the newspaper on top of its arch rival and quickly read the story.

This article was no better than its foe. It regaled its readers with tawdry details of a drunken orgy in Mrs. Miller's front yard and followed up with colorful stories about the scene at the courthouse.

"I don't see my latest article," she said with disappointment, after leafing through the rest of the paper. It seemed the *Star*'s editor had decided to put aside logic and reasoned argument in favor of the same bombastic tactics as the *Gazette*.

"Why, that's terrible, dear," Estella said, frowning. "How could they do this to us? We were all looking forward to reading you again. Why, I think Sister and I will have to give Mr. Melton a talking to. Don't you agree, Mirabelle?"

"Well, I don't rightly—"

"That's all right, dear," Estella cut in over her sister's protests. "I'll take care of it. Come along now. We'd better leave Miss Simpson to her work." She stood and went to the door, leaving Mirabelle to follow in her wake. "You will let us know as soon as your article appears, won't you, Miss Simpson? We do so love to read you."

"It's nice of you to say so, Miss Pareet. I'll be sure to keep you informed."

Despite her confident words, Mary Margaret felt growing concerns about what was happening in Cheyenne and about her role in it. The last thing she had intended was to stir up such an emotional and dangerous response to the issue of women's rights.

She wished she had someone to talk to about the whole situation. Worth's face came before her mind's eye, but she knew she couldn't go to him. He'd made his position perfectly clear the day before.

Watching him walk off with Lucy Robertson had been the final blow; it had reawakened all Mary Margaret's insecurities about the younger woman. Telling herself she knew Worth was not romantically interested in Lucy did not assuage her pain. Right now, Lucy Robertson was everything Mary Margaret was not: supportive of Worth's position, out of the public eye, longing for a happy domestic life—preferably, in Worth's house, innocent, and virginal.

The last thought pierced Mary Margaret's heart and left her breathless. With Worth taking himself out of her life, Mary Margaret's view of her actions was much more somber than in the first flush of euphoria after making love. Suddenly, she realized Worth had never made a commitment to her—at least, not verbally. She'd simply assumed he felt the same way she did.

What if he didn't—or worse, having taken what he wanted, had tired of her? He'd never said he loved her, not even in the wildest throes of passion. What did that mean?

She knew so little of men and their ways—just the stories a "good" girl was told. Only Claire had ever mentioned passion and tried to explain to her its joy. But Claire was gone now. Mary Margaret felt tears of loss and despair well in her eyes.

Everything was so complicated. What she had thought would make her happy was only bringing her sorrow. She'd always kept her personal life separate from her professional one, but suddenly they were so finely intertwined, she could no longer tell where one ended and the other began.

If only Garth were here. He would know what she should do. She had written him about Mr. Melton's offer to send her articles to an eastern newspaper so Garth could negotiate the details for her. But right now, she wanted nothing more than her agent's good advice, his unfailing instinct for knowing the right step at any moment. Even more, she longed for his uncomplicated friendship.

Mary Margaret sighed as she stared out the window. The sun was shining brightly, and the young cottonwood Mrs. Miller had had planted the year before was finally in full leaf. Trees were rare on the windswept plains, and this stalwart, albeit small, specimen reminded Mary Margaret poignantly of how far she was from everything familiar.

After a few minutes, she pulled herself together with new determination and decided her best course of action was to get back to work. She turned her chair into the desk and pulled out her notes from the interview with Mrs. Sanders the previous afternoon. Working steadily, she finished a first draft by supper time.

Wednesday morning proved good weather was really here to stay. After polishing her article on Mrs. Sanders in the morning, Mary Margaret felt the need for some exercise to clear the cobwebs from her mind. She would not fall into the trap of feeling sorry for herself again.

Stepping into the sunshine, she took a deep breath. The flowers in Mrs. Miller's garden were blooming and looked decidedly cheerful. Taking her cue from them, she set off with a smile for the milliner's shop—the best source in town for the latest news of the day.

Less than a block from her goal, Mary Margaret passed Johnson's Gun and Hardware Store. A half dozen men were lounging against the wall, swapping tall tales.

One of them recognized her and said, "Well, well. If it isn't the little lady what's stirrin' up all the trouble 'round here."

He shifted his body off the wall, sauntered across the wooden sidewalk, and planted himself directly in front of her.

The man smelled bad, as if he hadn't had a bath in more than a month. He looked worse. He was dressed in filthy denim jeans that had once been blue but were now a nondescript, dingy color. His shirt was of cheap cloth, grimy from wear, and his leather vest was deeply stained.

A wad of tobacco distorted one cheek and a three-day growth of beard added to his menacing appearance. He spat casually into the street before speaking.

"What's your problem, little lady? Ain't you got no man to keep you satisfied? That why you stirrin' up the townsfolk here?"

He leered down at her, his hands on his hips, while his buddies guffawed.

"That's tellin' her, Red," a confederate yelled out.

"Hey, lady, mebbe you want ol' Red to give you some, eh?" shouted another.

"Step aside and let me pass," Mary Margaret said, thankful her voice was steadier than she felt. She drew herself up to her full height and glared at the man, ignoring the rapid beating of her heart and the queasy feeling in her stomach.

Red didn't budge, but a nasty smile curled his lip. "Don't go puttin' on no airs with me, lady. I heard tell about the trouble you been causin'. Ain't a man in town wouldn't mind seein' you put in your place, and I'm the one to do it. Ain't that right, boys?"

Aroused by the potential for violence, Red's cronies circled in like vultures on the scent of death. Mary Margaret took a step back and swallowed dryly. Would anyone step forward to help her if she screamed? Or was Red right in his assessment of the people in town?

She glanced around quickly, hoping to catch someone's eye. All she saw were the grizzled faces of Red's friends. The raw odor of whiskey permeated the air, mixing with the stench of unwashed bodies. Her fast breaths left her lungs starving for air.

"Now, boys, what are you all doing up in this part of town? Haven't you anything better to do than hang around Johnson's?"

Mary Margaret spun around at the sound of Worth's voice. How had he gotten here? How had he known she was in trouble?

"We ain't botherin' nobody, Mr. Worthington. Just makin' a point to the lady, here." Red nodded his head toward Mary Margaret. His friends slunk back toward the storefront, leaving Red to handle matters. "We want you to know we're behind you two hundred percent. Ain't no cause for the ladies to get all riled up like this when Jesse's done no wrong."

"I appreciate your concern, boys, but this is a matter for the courts now. Let the lady by. We don't want any trouble; it won't help either side."

Mary Margaret looked over her shoulder and saw Red shrug coolly.

"We'll be goin' now, if you want," he said. "No harm done. Don't forget what I said, ma'am. Offer's open any time. You just let ol' Red know."

He winked at her as though they shared a dirty secret, then strutted down the planked sidewalk in the opposite direction, his buddies falling into step behind him.

Mary Margaret shivered. She never wanted to see Red or his likes again. She looked back at Worth. He stood stiffly in place, watching Red and his gang depart.

She wished he'd acknowledge her presence. More than that, she wished he'd take her into his arms and tell her this was all a bad dream. She missed him more than she could have imagined. It was knowing he wouldn't be coming by that made everything so painful; knowing he wouldn't take her in his arms or want her to shower him with the kisses they both craved.

"Be careful, Maggie. There's more like him out there. The papers are stirring them up. Watch yourself," he said.

She knew he included her when he referred to "the papers." She felt a stab of anger, followed quickly by guilt, then sadness. His tone may have been detached, but his eyes conveyed a different message: "I miss you. I want you."

"Don't worry. I'll take care," she said softly, wanting to reach out and touch him, even for an instant, but knowing she wouldn't.

"Good." He stayed for another few seconds, looking at her as if engraving her image in his memory. Then he turned and disappeared up an outside staircase. Belatedly, she noticed the brass plaque on the wall by the stairs. "John Adams Worthington, Esq., Attorney at Law," it read.

So this was where his offices were. No wonder he had come by at just the right moment. She realized for the first time she'd never been to see them, and the thought hurt. There was so much about Worth she hungered to know, so much she wanted to tell him, and now they couldn't even talk on a crowded sidewalk in the middle of town.

Would they ever be able to put this episode behind them, or would it destroy their chance for happiness and leave them diminished in some essential way?

Mary Margaret ran her fingers over the raised letters on the plaque, needing the contact with something belonging to Worth. It made her feel closer to him, took the edge off her loneliness.

"How was your walk?" Sarah asked when Mary Margaret returned to the boardinghouse.

"Eventful, I'm afraid—too eventful." She briefly summarized her encounter with Red, adding, "I can't help but feel responsible for stirring up some of this trouble."

"Nonsense," Sarah declared. "Them good-for-nothing

men were just waiting for an excuse to let loose. 'Tweren't nothing you done. And, anyway, unless you're working both ends against the middle and writing them editorials in the *Gazette*, too, I'd say you can lay the blame squarely where it belongs—on the *Gazette*'s doorstep."

She plunked a cup of tea in front of Mary Margaret. "Here, drink this. You'll feel better for it."

"How's Mrs. MacIntyre doing?"

"Right enough, seems to me. Spends most of her time locked up in her room. I don't know quite what to make of her."

"You should have heard what was being said at the milliner's today. Some of the ladies have very strong feelings about this case, and Mrs. Sanders took full advantage of it."

The women were ready for a fight. The tension in the store had been no less palpable than on the street with Red. The town was like dry tinder, waiting for a spark to set off a conflagration and the newspaper editors were busy lighting matches, hoping to touch off an explosion that would increase their sales.

"How's your Mr. Worth doin'?" Sarah asked in her usual blunt manner.

"What do you mean?" Mary Margaret countered defensively.

"Ain't seen him 'round much lately."

"I guess he hasn't been here much," she agreed, hiding her pain.

"Cause of this case?" Sarah's bright brown eyes regarded Mary Margaret piercingly.

Mary Margaret didn't know what to say. The case was certainly a big factor, but there were other conflicts as well, her career being chief among them.

"Now, I don't mean to pry none," Sarah went on after a moment, "but let me give you some good advice. Life's too short to waste on silly misunderstandings. Look at me now, sitting here in my fancy house, eating all this fancy food, with all this fancy furniture. Who would have thought it of old Sarah Miller, eh?

"But let me tell you something, dearie. It all ain't worth

a hill of beans without my Sam here. Mark my words, don't let this business get between you and what you really want." Sarah stood and smoothed down the front of her skirt. "Best I be going now and minding my own business, but don't you forget what I said. Give it some thought."

Mary Margaret wished things were as simple and direct as Sarah made out. She hated this estrangement from Worth, yet she knew their differences were real and profound. How could they possibly come to an agreement on anything when they weren't even on speaking terms?

That night, Mary Margaret felt alone and cold in her solitary bed. She curled up in a tight ball and lay staring into the dark, dreading the onset of her dreams, and even more, the start of the trial the next morning. The first day of testimony was sure to excite the townsfolk. At this point, any excuse for a showdown would be welcome.

The excuse came sooner than Mary Margaret predicted, and from an unexpected source. The sound of bells clanging and vehicles racing down the street brought her awake from an uneasy sleep.

She opened her window, stuck her head out to get a better view, and smelled smoke. Fire—the dreaded scourge of cities. Entire blocks could disappear overnight. She still remembered the devastation, both physical and economic, when several blocks of Boston's business district had been consumed just four years ago.

Craning her neck, she could see a reddish glow in the sky right near where the milliner's shop stood. Had someone set it aflame, angry because the women of the town used it as their unofficial headquarters?

As she had a few nights ago, Sarah knocked on Mary Margaret's door and let herself in. "What's it this time?" she asked.

"Fire. Downtown, it looks like."

Mary Margaret leaned out the window as far as she dared. "I can't quite make out what's burning."

She brought her head back into the room and sat back on her heels on the window seat.

"Think it's got something to do with what's been goin' on in town?" Sarah looked at her worriedly.

A cold chill ran down Mary Margaret's spine—a chill that had nothing to do with the night air pouring in through the open sash.

"I hope not," she said, but even as she spoke the words, both women knew she was wrong. The coincidence of the timing was too great. Their eyes met in silent understanding.

"What should we do?" Sarah asked.

"Nothing, I guess. We'd best leave this to the men to fight." Mary Margaret shivered and wrapped her arms around her chest. "But I don't think I can get back to sleep."

"Why don't we go to the kitchen and get a warm drink," Sarah suggested. "Mebbe I kin get one of the menfolk to take a run downtown and report back to us."

"I'll get my robe on and join you in a second."

Sarah left and Mary Margaret closed her window. The sounds of bells and men's shouts became muted. The smell of smoke still permeated the air, making her throat ache. Or maybe her throat ached from the tears she felt pressing behind her eyelids.

Blinking rapidly, Mary Margaret threw on her robe and made her way to the kitchen.

Annie MacIntyre was sitting next to Sarah, looking white and frightened. "What's going on, Miss Simpson?" she asked nervously, glancing at the door.

"Just a fire in town, from the sounds of it," Mary Margaret said soothingly.

"Do you know where?" Annie asked.

"No, not yet." Turning to Sarah, Mary Margaret said, "Did you find anyone to go downtown?"

"Yeah. Took a bit of doing, though. Seems the menfolk sleep sounder than we womenfolk. Had to knock on three doors 'fore I got an answer. 'Course, the reverend always was a sound sleeper, 'specially if trouble was on the horizon." Sarah cackled. "Reckon he's none too sure he wants to git involved in this here mess."

Mary Margaret went to the stove to pour herself a cup of hot chocolate from the pot Sarah had made. The milk was almost boiling over, so Mary Margaret shifted the pot to a cooler spot and opened the stove's heavy, wrought-iron door to adjust the fire. "Who'd you finally get?" she asked as she bent to her work.

"Freddie Hinsford-Hill. Couldn't wake up Lord Peter to save his life. Freddie should be back any minute."

Annie looked even paler than before, if that was possible.

"Would you like something a little stronger than hot chocolate?" Mary Margaret asked, trying unsuccessfully to wipe the greasy soot from her fingers.

"I've got some cooking sherry around here someplace," Sarah put in, rising to her feet. After rummaging in one of the cabinets for a couple of minutes, she held up a bottle. "Good stuff, this. Care for some, too, Mary Margaret?"

In the intimacy of the night, formality seemed out of place. "Just a sip, Sarah," Mary Margaret replied.

Sarah poured the sherry into three small crystal glasses and passed them around.

The liquor warmed Mary Margaret's insides, leaving her more optimistic. Maybe things weren't as bleak as they appeared. She walked to the rear window and looked out. The clanging bells had quieted down, and while the smell of smoke still hung in the air, the sky no longer glowed red over the downtown.

"Looks like the fire must be out," she said. "At least, it doesn't seem to have spread. I wonder what's keeping Freddie?"

A sharp knocking sound at the front door caught her attention. "Could that be him?"

"Who else?" Sarah asked rhetorically, and started to rise.

"I'll get it," Mary Margaret decided. The older woman looked tired, despite her spritely demeanor. "You keep Annie company. I'll let you know what Freddie has to say."

She went to the front of the house, lighting her way with a small oil lamp. She could still hear a lot of activity and men's shouts in the street, most likely from everyone heading home after the fire.

The pounding at the door resumed. *What has gotten into Freddie?* Mary Margaret wondered. He wasn't usually so impatient. She hurried to the door, threw back the bolt, and turned the knob.

The door flew back, nearly crushing her.

"Whatever took you so long?" Freddie cried, panting hard, as though he'd been running. "Quick. Lock the door. Hurry! They're coming. They'll be here any minute."

"Who's coming? Where?"

Freddie didn't bother answering. He slammed the door shut and bolted it. Then he leaned back against it and bent over, clutching his side as he tried to catch his breath.

In the flickering light of the lamp, Mary Margaret could see that his face was flushed. Trickles of sweat ran down his cheeks and into his shirt collar.

Suddenly, she heard shouts in the front yard.

"Oh, good Lord, they're here," Freddie groaned and seemed to shrink into himself. His eyes showed white around the irises.

Mary Margaret didn't know what to think, though his fear was contagious. Already her heart was pounding in her chest. Dousing her lamp, she whispered, "Who's here?"

But he didn't need to answer. The mob in the yard was very vocal.

"Come out, bitch. Come face us like a man, if'n that's what you want to be so bad," yelled one voice.

"You tell 'er, Red," yelled another.

Mary Margaret peeked through a crack in the curtain covering the side window by the door. She could make out several lanterns and some brightly lit torches. The crowd was all male and much larger than the group the other night.

"Why have they come here?" she asked of Freddie. "What happened in town?"

"There was a fire in one of the buildings. Apparently started upstairs, in a lawyer's office."

"Whose office?" she demanded, but already she knew. Worth's office was just down the block from the milliner's shop, the exact area in which she'd seen the fire earlier.

"Mr. Worthington's, miss. That chap MacIntyre's lawyer."

"Was anyone hurt?" *Please, God*, she thought, *let him*

be all right. She closed her eyes on the prayer and clasped the lamp so tightly her fingers hurt.

"It appeared to be empty. And Mr. Worthington confirmed it when he arrived." Now that Freddie was safe behind a locked door, he'd regained some of his composure.

Mary Margaret felt the air trapped in her lungs escape with a whoosh. Worth was safe.

Her relief was short-lived.

"You comin' out or do we have to come in and get you?" a male voice called, closer than before.

Several sets of footsteps pounded up the front stairs. The mob was closing in.

"Go get Mrs. Miller—quick," she ordered Freddie. "She's in the kitchen. Hurry."

Glad to be relieved of any further responsibility, Freddie raced down the hallway to the back of the house.

Just then, a rock sailed through the parlor window, to cheers from right outside on the porch.

Mary Margaret stepped back from the door. "What do you want?" she yelled through it.

"Who's that talkin'?" a voice she recognized as Red's demanded.

"Go away. We don't want any trouble," she shouted back.

"Too late now. You shoulda thought of that afore you started it," Red called out. "You had no call to set fire to Mr. Worthington's place. We're not going to stand for it."

"That her?" another voice yelled.

"Hey, she's in there. Come on, boys. What are we waiting for?" called another. The call was echoed from one side of the mob to the other.

An elbow came through the side window where Mary Margaret had been standing just moments ago, and a man screamed with pain as the crowd surged forward.

Just before Sarah reached the front hall, the door burst open, tumbling a half dozen men onto the floor.

Another dozen filled the open doorway, squeezed in by the crowd while trying to avoid tripping over their fallen cohorts.

The man she knew as Red was the first to recover. "Well, now, Miss Simpson. We meet again," he said, towering over her. "Told you I'd be back to give ya what ya wanted. Too bad ya didn't just ask for it nicely." He reached out to grab Mary Margaret.

"Stand back, you scum," Sarah Miller cried. She held an old Winchester at the ready. The gun weighed nearly as much as she did.

"Says who, you old bat?" Quicker than the blink of an eye, Red twisted the rifle out of Sarah's hands and sent her flying.

She landed in the corner, and hit her head against the wall. She lay stunned, not moving.

Mary Margaret gasped and tried to go help her, but Red threw down the rifle and grabbed her arm, ripping her robe at the shoulder.

"Not so fast, lady. We've got some unfinished business," he whispered for her ears alone.

Her legs buckled at his menacing threat. If possible, he smelled worse than this morning. His breath was a fetid mixture of too much alcohol and tobacco, combined with too little hygiene. Mary Margaret turned her head away, but he would have none of it.

With one hand, he twisted her arm up around her back, and with the other, he forced her face to his. "Look at me when I'm talking to ya," he roared.

Mary Margaret thought she would faint. A sharp, shooting pain ripped across her back and his fingers dug deeply into her cheeks. She would have bruises by morning—if she lived.

The crowd at the door pressed inward, and through her haze of pain, she could hear the men's shouts.

"Hey. What's going on?"

"Move out of the way."

"Keep your elbows to yourself."

"Stay back. There's no more room."

"You stay back. I wanna see what's happenin'."

"Shut up, all of you," Red yelled at the crowd. "Now move back so's we can see what we have here."

Tightening his grip on Mary Margaret's arm, he pressed

her forward. The men crowding the entry fell back, opening a narrow path that immediately closed as Mary Margaret and Red passed through.

"Hey, Red, how you know she's the one?" a youngish man called out. He seemed more sober than the rest, a voice of reason in a world gone mad. Mary Margaret looked at him with pleading eyes. He was her only hope.

The crowd shouted him down and Red glared at him.

"Don't worry. She's the one. I seen her stirring up the women, telling them they have rights and not to listen to their husbands no more," put in another man. "Why, even my wife went to one of them meetings. Hasn't been the same since. Thinks she can tell me what to do."

"Mine, too. Tells me I've been drinking too much. I had to whack her a good one," yelled a voice from the middle of the mob.

Red smiled smugly, looking at Mary Margaret's hands. "I've got the evidence we need right here, Purvis, if'n you don't want to take the word of yore friends. Git one of them torches up here," Red ordered.

The nearest torch was passed, hand over hand, to the front of the crowd. "See," Red shouted triumphantly. "Take a good look at 'er." He gripped Mary Margaret's hands and held them out to the crowd. "What'd I tell ya?"

"He's right. She musta started the fire. Look at the soot. Her hands is all black."

Mary Margaret started to protest. "It's from the stove—"

"Shut up," Red said shaking her roughly. "We ain't asked your opinion."

"Hey, Purvis, what d'ya say now?" someone asked.

The youngish man shrugged. "I just wanted to be sure, that's all. I have no call to make trouble for innocent women."

"This here's no innocent, believe me. She's doin' the devil's work and I'm gonna stop her."

Mary Margaret's knees went weak as her last hope disappeared. After her previous experience, she knew better than to try to argue with a rowdy crowd of drunken men. Talk didn't help—in fact, it could hurt. Her only chance was to try to escape at an opportune time.

"Whatcha gonna do now, Red?"

Red grinned, showing discolored teeth that gleamed evilly in the glow of the torchlight. "Wouldn't you like to know," he answered, leering. "This here 'lady' owes me a thing or two and I'm here to collect. After that, we can give her to the sheriff or anyone else."

The crowd cheered Red on, catcalling and whistling their appreciation.

"Go to it, Red."

"Show her how a real man acts."

Mary Margaret tried to wrest her hands free of Red's merciless grip. In response, he squeezed her wrists more tightly and twisted her arms, immobilizing her.

"Don't try it again, if you know what's good fer ya," he growled. He turned to the crowd. "Let's get going afore the sheriff comes. We don't want no trouble with him."

He headed for the porch steps, pulling Mary Margaret along behind him. She stumbled on the first step and lost her footing, lurching to the side. Her forehead grazed the porch support but Red kept on going, dragging her down the stairs and onto the walk.

She lost a slipper, scraped her knee, and tore a gash into her robe in the process. She tried desperately to get back on her feet, but Red was moving too fast.

The weight of the small derringer concealed in her robe pocket reminded her she did have some defense. Sarah had gotten it for her after the episode the other evening, and even taught her to use it. If only Red would let her go, she would get it out and shoot him.

She had never known such a mix of dark emotions before, never thought of herself as capable of killing another person. But if Red gave her half a chance, she knew she could do it—without blinking.

As he reached the fence surrounding Sarah's yard, Red slowed. Suddenly, two shots rang out over the heads of the crowd. For an instant, Mary Margaret thought she'd been killed. Then her heart came back to life, pounding like a steam engine, and she knew she was still alive, though for how much longer, she didn't know.

"I think you men have gone a little too far this time," the

sheriff's voice boomed out, and the knot of men parted to let him through.

"Worth, you go take care of Miss Simpson now, while my deputies get rid of Red, here," the sheriff threw over his shoulder as he grabbed the drunken cowboy by the arm.

Worth stepped forward, and for the first time, Mary Margaret saw his eyes alight with fury. She was afraid he would take matters into his own hands where Red was concerned, but then he looked at her, and the furious light dimmed. A much deeper emotion flared to life—one she couldn't quite define. In one motion, he lifted her into his arms and carried her past the milling group of men toward the street.

Worth looked down into the face so close to his, fear and anger knotted within him. When he had first seen her being dragged down the porch steps by Red, he had lunged forward, only to be thwarted by the sheriff, who had fired off two shots. Now, even though Maggie was in his arms, fear and anger still raced through him. What would he do if he lost her?

"Everything will be fine, Maggie mine. I'm taking you home with me."

"Sarah?" she questioned.

"The Pareet sisters are caring for her. She'll be fine. It's you I'm concerned with. I want to make sure you're all right."

"But, the children? I don't want them upset," she protested, though her arms clung more tightly to his neck and she made no attempt to get free.

"They're fine. I sent them out to the ranch with Kathleen early this afternoon. Reverend Leisch escorted them there for me." He admired her unselfish concern for Becky and Tom and hugged her close.

"I'm glad they're safe. Things here are so remarkably different from what I anticipated. I never meant for this to happen." Her voice faded away, a sorrowful whisper.

"I know, Maggie. It's not anything you did. I only wish I'd sent you out there with them. I haven't liked the feel of things for a couple of days now." From the day his office had been broken into, in fact. "I should have done more to keep you safe," he said, his voice thick and unsteady.

"None of this was your fault, Worth." Her voice was thready and her head drooped against his shoulder as he strode the remaining block to his house. He sensed she was near the end of her strength.

Worth took Maggie directly to his room on the second floor and laid her gently on his bed. The graze on her forehead was darkening, and by tomorrow she'd have a fair-sized bruise. Already he could see faint shadows on her cheeks where Red had held her too tightly.

Worth cursed under his breath. "I wish I could have gotten my hands on that bastard."

His anger swelled anew, but he clenched his jaw against it. He had more important things to consider first. With extreme care, he brushed Maggie's hair back from her face and began undressing her, wanting only to rid her of the ripped and dirtied clothes.

She didn't say a word as he removed her dressing gown and the one remaining slipper. Her passivity worried him; he knew it came from shock.

He flung her tattered garments into a dark corner where she wouldn't have to see them, then covered her with a large towel so she wouldn't be chilled and poured warm water from the pitcher into the basin.

Dampening a cloth, he tenderly wiped her face clean, careful not to use too much pressure on the wound near her hairline, then washed away the dirt and soot on her hands and dried them with a second towel.

He helped her into one of Kathleen's nightgowns. It was made of simple flannelette, but was warm and soft to the touch. With infinite care, he smoothed the tangles from her hair and began braiding the silken brown strands.

The simple task soothed him, gave him a feeling of control again. He needed that now, after his helplessness when Red was manhandling her. If only he'd arrived a few minutes earlier! He shut the thought out. There was nothing he could do to change the past, as he'd long since learned.

When he finished her hair, her eyes were closed. He sat quietly, watching her. How he loved this woman. She was everything he had ever wanted. It wasn't until this moment that he had allowed himself to think in those terms—of love and commitment, of permanence.

He'd known he desired her—his body told him that every time she was near. He'd known he liked being with her and talking with her, but he'd desired other women and enjoyed talking to them, too. What he felt for Maggie transcended any of those things. It was something he couldn't explain, but he knew it to be true, to the bottom of his soul.

He unfolded a quilt from the end of the bed and covered her, reluctant to go, but knowing she needed to rest. He bent over, gently kissed her forehead, and turned toward the door.

"Don't leave me." Her voice was tentative and wavery.

"You should get some sleep. You've had a very disturbing night," he said, sitting down again by the side of the bed.

"I need you to stay," she whispered. "I need you by my side tonight."

"All right. I'll stay." Relief poured through him. He hadn't wanted to leave her, but had felt uncertain of her needs. He'd all but spurned her two days ago, and now, for the life of him, he could hardly remember what had seemed so earth-shattering then.

Tonight he'd come close to losing her forever. The thought overwhelmed him, making their differences seem petty and insignificant. All he wanted was to stay by her side from now on, if she would have him.

"You relax and go to sleep. I'll sit right here beside you."

"*No!*" Even though her reply was soft, it reverberated around the room. "I need you to hold me. Don't you want to?"

"I want to hold you more than anything else in this world, but you need your rest." He knew if he got near her, he would want much more than just to hold her. He had to keep his distance, for her sake more than his own.

"Please."

Her one soft word was his downfall. He could not deny

her. No matter the cost to himself, he would give her what she wanted—no more, no less.

With sure, quick movements, he removed his clothes and slipped into bed beside her. Placing his arm around her, he eased her to his side.

She laid her head in the hollow of his shoulder and wrapped her arm around his waist, nestling against him. He noticed a slight tremor in her body, then heard her quiet whimper.

"Maggie, Maggie. It's all right now. You're safe," he murmured.

Instead of calming her, his words seemed to unleash her emotions. The slight tremor became violent shudders, and the whimper turned to ragged sobs. All he could do was hold her and murmur reassurances.

Eventually her sobs lessened and her shaking stilled. Her voice was muffled against his shoulder when she began to talk. "Oh, Worth. I was so frightened. I thought I was going to die. That Red person said he would do all manner of horrible things . . ."

In a voice much calmer than he felt, Worth reassured Maggie. "The sheriff has Red in custody. He can't hurt you ever again."

His last words were a promise. He'd make certain Red Barton was never again a threat to Maggie or anyone else, no matter what it took.

For a long time, neither spoke. He soothingly rubbed her back, and felt her body gradually relax. He lightly ran his hand from her shoulder to her hip and back.

With his cheek pressed against the top of her head, he whispered, "Maggie, no matter what happens, we can't allow others to make us doubt our own feelings. By week's end the trial will be over and we'll begin planning our lives together. I love you, Maggie mine."

Sixteen

A butterfly-soft kiss woke Mary Margaret. For a moment she was disoriented, then memory came flooding back.

"Worth!" She reached her arms around his neck and deepened the kiss. He responded at once, nudging open her lips so his tongue could forage for hers.

"You're dressed," she said when he gave her a chance to breathe, not sure if she felt relieved or disappointed.

"The trial starts today. Did you forget?" He sat on the edge of the bed and gently brushed a few stray wisps of hair off her forehead. "I thought you might want to take it easy this morning, but I didn't want to leave without saying good-bye."

"It's still early. Do you have to go so soon?" Her voice sounded wistful even to her own ears, but she couldn't help herself. She'd come so close to losing forever the chance for them to be together, she didn't want anything to keep them apart now.

"I have to go to the office. The fire didn't do too much damage; it was mostly smoke. The furniture is in pretty bad shape, but my books and papers were spared. I have to get someone to clean things up and arrange to meet my client somewhere else." He looked away as he spoke, and

Mary Margaret noticed he'd avoided mentioning Jesse Mac-
Intyre's name. Was he as afraid as she of breaking their
fragile truce?

"When I saw the fire and heard where it was . . ." her
voice trailed off. Her heart lurched when she thought of the
fear she'd felt for Worth's safety. "I wish you could stay,
but I know you need to meet with Jesse. I don't want to
interfere with your work, Worth, even though I think
Jesse's wrong." There. She'd brought it out in the open.
How would he react? So much hinged on his response.

He brought his gaze back to meet hers. His eyes looked
bluer than she'd even remembered, and the desperate hope
in their depths reflected her own feelings.

"Thank you, Maggie. I know this case stands between
us, but it won't last forever—just a couple of days. I'm
not asking you to back me completely on this, but I hope I
have your respect for doing what I think is right."

Mary Margaret sat up in the bed and laid her hand on
his. "Oh, Worth. You've always had my respect. I just find
it . . . more difficult to believe in Jesse. I can't help but
think he's out for himself. And I can't just stand by and let
him get away with that. The precedent would be shattering
to all women, not just to Annie."

"Only if Jesse's lying and gets away with it. Not if he's
telling the truth."

This time, Mary Margaret looked away. "You're right.
Only if Jesse's lying." She chewed on her lower lip, then
decided she couldn't hold back anything. "It's just that I
believe he is, Worth. I'm sorry."

"And I believe he isn't. So where does that leave us?"

"Agreeing to disagree?"

"All right. I'll try to live with that—on one condition."

Her heart skipped a beat. "Yes?"

"Let's not shut each other out over this. There's no reason our public lives have to destroy our private ones, is
there?"

"None at all." Her heart beat double-time and a wide
smile broke out on her face. She'd won. No, *they'd* won,
both of them—together.

She flung herself into his arms, and their lips met. Their

kiss was greedy as they tried to make up for lost time. Slowly it gentled, turning tender and sweet, full of promise. When Worth finally pulled away, they were both breathless, yet sated. Something important had been decided: they were taking a chance on each other and nothing was going to get between them again.

The courtroom was packed with spectators by the time Mary Margaret arrived. She wore the clothes Sarah had sent over, at Worth's request. The thought brought high color to her cheeks, though she knew no one else was in on her secret. She stood on her toes, looking for an empty seat, but didn't see one. Then she spotted Sarah and the older woman waved, gesturing she had one saved.

Mary Margaret eased her way between the rows, spotting several people she knew. The Pareet sisters were sitting in one of the front rows, and behind them were Reverend Hanson and Freddie Hinsford-Hill. Marcus must have stayed in town overnight, for he was seated near the middle of the room with Lucy.

Wedging herself past protruding knees, Mary Margaret finally made it to the empty chair next to Sarah. They were at the end of a row, well in the back. Mary Margaret had a good view of the front of the room without being overly conspicuous herself.

It appeared she wasn't the only one who hoped not to be seen, for standing in the back corner was Peter Dunsmore. He was almost hidden by the crowd pushing past to get in.

"Are you all right?" Sarah asked as soon as Mary Margaret sat down.

"Except for a slight bump on my head, I'm fine," she reassured the older woman. "I'm more worried about you. Worth swept me away so quickly I didn't know what was happening. He said the Pareet sisters were looking after you."

"It'd take more than what happened last night to get me down. A'course, the fall didn't help my rheumatiz any, but I'm none the worse for wear."

"I'm glad to hear that. You look just fine."

"Thankee girl. You look pretty fine yourself." Sarah

looked her up and down, her brown eyes taking on a mischievous glint. She grinned up at Mary Margaret, then said, "We was all mighty worried about you, you know, what with Mr. Worth just taking you off. We thought you must be bad hurt, for sure, he being in such a hurry."

Mary Margaret felt her cheeks redden again at Sarah's knowing look.

"Now, don't go paying me no mind," Sarah added, chuckling. "I enjoy seeing young'uns get together. Told you so the other day, didn't I? If'n I were thirty years younger, I'd be giving you a run for your money. He's the kind of man that makes a woman forget everything else but him. Wouldn't matter to me none whether people thought t'were right or wrong so long as I felt 'bout him the way you do about Mr. Worth."

Sarah patted Mary Margaret's hand, and Mary Margaret smiled at her.

"Thank you, Sarah. I appreciate your kindness."

The older woman cleared her throat gruffly and pulled her hand back. She looked around the courtroom and changed the subject. "Annie and her lawyer got here 'bout ten minutes ago. His name's Green—Daniel Green. Heard he's good. Mr. Worth and Jesse haven't showed up yet. Reckon they'll be here soon, though."

Annie MacIntyre and her lawyer were seated at the front left table. Annie's head was bent, and she stared fixedly at her lap as Mr. Green spoke quietly to her.

Mary Margaret's heart went out to her. She looked so lost and alone. She no longer had her family home or her husband. Mary Margaret and Worth might have their difficulties, but at least they had the children and each other. Poor Annie had nothing.

"There's Mr. Worth now," Sarah said, punching Mary Margaret in the ribs with her elbow and cackling. "See, he's just coming in with Jesse."

Worth looked more handsome than ever as he entered the courtroom. Mary Margaret's heart beat an extra tattoo at the sight of him. The smooth fit of his suit over his broad shoulders emphasized his manly physique. She remembered well the feel of those strong, lithe muscles, the rough silkiness of the hair on his chest, the steely strength of his arms as he held himself above her.

The heat of her thoughts in this public place embarrassed her, and she glanced around to see if Sarah had noticed, but her gaze was trained on Annie's bent head.

"I don't think that poor girl has looked up once since she got here," Sarah said. "Wonder where she got that there dress. Makes her look helpless as a newborn calf without its mama. I s'pose the jury's gonna feel sorry for her, seeing her dressed that away."

Mary Margaret had to agree. The garment had definitely seen better days. The once-navy-blue material had been laundered to a rusty hue, neither blue nor brown, and the poor cut made Annie look dowdy and forlorn.

"I just hope her lawyer knows what he's doing," Mary Margaret said. She didn't care for these manipulative games, though she understood the reasons for them. Annie's lawyer wanted to make sure she got a sympathetic hearing.

"Now, don't you worry none. Judge Burley runs a fair court. Annie'll get her say. He'll make sure of that. Take a look at old Jesse, all ragged out in his fancy doodads. Why, you'd hardly recognize him in the street, all gussied up that way."

Sarah was right. Jesse was gussied up. He, too, had changed his appearance for his day in court. He was wearing an obviously new suit and a fresh, crisp shirt. His face was cleanly shaven and his hair neatly combed. Instead of trying for sympathy, Worth's client was aiming for respectability and had dressed the part of an established member of the community.

Worth and Jesse conferred at their table, Jesse occasionally glancing in his wife's direction.

The jury filed in, taking their seats over by Annie's side of the courtroom. Then the bailiff called for all to rise as Judge Burley came in, and the hearing began.

Both sides gave opening arguments. Mary Margaret thought the men did admirable jobs outlining their respective cases and explaining why their client was in the right.

Everything was proceeding in a mannerly fashion until

Annie's lawyer called Jesse to the stand. Worth crossed his fingers. Jesse could make or break this case with one misstep.

Jesse strode to the witness box, casting his wife a baleful stare.

"Mr. MacIntyre," Mr. Green began. "You say your wife signed a document giving you permission to sell her inheritance?"

"I do."

"And where is the paper now?"

"I can't find it."

"You can't find it?" the lawyer drawled, his tone on the edge of mockery.

Jesse bristled visibly, but held on to his temper. "No, sir," he said.

"Isn't it true you never had your wife sign any papers, and you, thinking only about yourself, sold her rightful property without permission?"

"Your honor—" Worth started to protest, but Jesse cut him off.

"No! It ain't true. I had her permission. I told you. I don't know why she's telling these stories, when . . ."

"Your Honor," Daniel Green interrupted, "I ask you to remind the witness to answer the questions, nothing more."

The judge banged his gavel. "Mr. MacIntyre, just answer the questions."

"And isn't it also true," the lawyer continued, "you were aware that your wife wanted to keep her parents' property, because it was all she had left to remember them by?"

"She didn't want that property. Her parents treated their kids like dogs. Not a one of 'em . . ."

"Your Honor, I didn't ask the witness for a description of his wife's family."

Again the judge banged his gavel. "I remind you, again Mr. MacIntyre. Confine your answers to the questions."

"I'm trying to answer them, Judge. He just keeps interrupting me with Annie's lies."

"Your Honor!" protested Mr. Green.

"Mr. MacIntyre, do you understand what I am saying?" the judge asked, starting to get angry.

"Please, Your Honor," Worth put in. "My client is extremely upset by this entire action. He intends the court no disrespect. I'm sure he'll comply with your request." Worth shot Jesse a warning glare. If Jesse didn't hold on to his composure, he could lose everything. Worth had given him precise instructions on that point only this morning.

"Sorry, Judge. I didn't mean to cross you," Jesse said, hanging his head.

The judge nodded his acceptance of Jesse's apology. "Continue your questioning, Mr. Green," he said.

"Are you aware, Mr. MacIntyre, of the laws of this territory regarding real property owned by women?"

"Yes, sir. I am."

"Why don't you enlighten us all, in that case."

"The owner has sole right to dispose of the property, be he man or woman," Jesse recited, clearly prepared for this line of questioning.

"Even if the woman is married. Is that not so?"

"Yes, sir, but I had—"

"And what do you think of the law?"

Jesse looked surprised. "What do you mean?" he asked cautiously.

"Do you approve of this law or don't you?"

"Your Honor," Worth objected, "Mr. MacIntyre is not in a position to approve or disapprove of the law."

The last thing Worth needed to deal with was Jesse's opinion of this law. He'd heard it often enough to know how damaging it would be.

"I think his attitude toward the law is at the heart of this case, your Honor," Annie's lawyer countered.

"I'm afraid I have to agree with Mr. Green. The witness will please answer the question."

"I don't like it, if that's what you mean."

"Why not?" Green probed.

"Makes no sense to me. A man works hard for his family, gives 'em all he has. It's only right he should make the decisions about how to care for them. That's how it's done everywhere else I know about."

"And is that how you wish it were done here, too?"

"Yes, sir. It's how it should be. It's nature's law. Even the editor of the *Gazette* said so."

Some of the men in the crowd whistled and cheered their approval. The judge banged his gavel to quiet them.

"But the editor of the *Gazette* isn't on trial, is he?" Annie's lawyer spoke out over the noise. "You are. And I submit that because you disapproved of the law, you decided to ignore it, especially when Mrs. MacIntyre refused you permission to sell her property."

"That's not what happened," Jesse protested.

"Are you telling me she didn't disapprove?"

"No, she did. At first."

A murmur rose up in the court and Worth cursed under his breath. Jesse had never told him this part of the story. Damn it to hell, when would clients learn to tell their lawyers everything!

The judge glared at the onlookers. "I will clear this courtroom if I don't have order. Quiet! All of you."

The crowd settled down again.

"So, Mrs. MacIntyre did disapprove of the sale, but you went ahead with it anyway."

"After I got—"

"I don't recall asking you a question, Mr. MacIntyre," Green said, cutting Jesse off. His tactics were all too clear to Worth. He would goad Jesse until his temper exploded. Then, no one would believe a word he said.

And, unfortunately, the tactic was working. Jesse's complexion had turned ruddy over the last exchange, and his hands clenched the railing in front of the witness stand.

"By the way, what did you do with Mrs. MacIntyre's money?" the lawyer asked.

"I invested it," Jesse answered, his voice rough.

"Did you, now? In what, if I may ask?"

Jesse cleared his throat. His knuckles turned white as he squeezed the railing even tighter than before. "In land."

"Oh? Where?" The lawyer's eyes gleamed like those of a lion going in for the kill.

"California."

"So, if you had to, you could sell this land, just as you did your wife's, and get her money back, couldn't you?"

Jesse mumbled his answer.

"I'm sorry, Mr. MacIntyre, but I don't think the jury heard your response," Green said. His smug expression annoyed even Worth, and he wasn't sitting a mere three feet from the man.

"No."

"No, what?"

"No, I can't sell the land," Jesse shouted and started to stand. Then he remembered himself and sat back down.

"Why not?"

"Because. I just can't."

Green leaned in toward the witness stand, his face just inches from Jesse's. "Come, come, now, Mr. MacIntyre. You can tell the court. Or would you rather I told them?"

Worth rose from his seat to object to the other man's baiting tactics, but the judge forestalled him by saying, "Mr. Green, if you please. Give the witness room to breathe\"

"Certainly, Your Honor. I just want the court to know what happened to the money Mr. MacIntyre made from the sale of his wife's property."

"Mr. MacIntyre, if you would answer the question, the court would be much obliged."

Jesse looked at the judge, then at Worth. Worth nodded his head, signaling Jesse to tell the truth. "I got swindled."

"I'm afraid I didn't hear you, Mr. MacIntyre. Could you speak a little louder," Mr. Green goaded.

"I was swindled," Jesse shouted. "Is that what you want to hear? Well, you got it. There ain't no land—just a useless piece of paper."

"So, you can't pay your wife back unless you sell your own property, can you?"

"I ain't never selling my property, and don't you forget it!" Jesse jumped to his feet, sending the witness chair clattering to the floor behind him.

"No? You seemed to find it easy enough to sell your wife's," Mr. Green shouted back.

"Is that what this is all about? Has she decided to sell my land? I'll never let her get away with it. Do you hear me? Never! Don't even think it, you bitch."

Jesse rounded the guardrail and headed toward Annie, who cowered in her seat. The crowd took sides, yelling, whistling, and catcalling as they enjoyed the show. The judge banged his gavel, but no one cared.

Worth managed to get in front of Jesse and block his way. "For God's sake, Jesse, stop it. What the hell do you think you're doing? This is exactly what I warned you about," he whispered in Jesse's ear as he restrained him.

The light of sanity slowly returned to Jesse's eyes and he lowered his fists. "I'm sorry, Worth," he mumbled, and rubbed one hand over his face. "I lost my temper. I'm sorry. It won't happen again."

Worth got Jesse back in the witness chair and the commotion eventually died down.

Annie's lawyer stood to the side, smiling his triumph.

"Do you have any more questions for this witness, Mr. Green?" the judge inquired.

"Only one. I'd say you were pretty lucky, Mr. MacIntyre, that your wife can't sell your property out from under you the way you did hers. Wouldn't you agree?"

"Your Honor, I object," Worth cut in.

"No further questions," Green quickly added, turning to walk back to his seat.

"Mr. Worthington," the judge said, gesturing at the witness to indicate Worth should proceed.

Mary Margaret watched Worth walk to the witness stand. He had his work cut out for him. Jesse had done nothing but damage his side. He had fallen right into the trap set by the other lawyer, especially when he'd gone after Annie. Mary Margaret didn't see how Worth could salvage this case.

"Mr. MacIntyre, did you have your wife sign a document giving you permission to sell her property?" Worth asked, his voice calm, his manner unruffled, as if none of the commotion had occurred earlier.

"Damn right, I did," Jesse answered, glaring at the other lawyer, who now sat by Annie's side.

"And when was that?"

"September of last year."

"How do you remember so exactly?"

"We decided the night of Annie's birthday. As a matter of fact, she signed the paper right then."

"Did anyone else see this paper?"

"Sure—the man at the land assessor's office."

A loud muttering rippled through the courtroom and Sarah leaned over to Mary Margaret. "I never heard tell of nobody else seeing that there paper. If'n Jesse can find the man, he might have a case, after all."

"No further questions, Your Honor," Worth said, taking his seat behind the long table.

So that was Worth's strategy. He didn't need to make the jurors like Jesse; he only needed to place doubts in their minds, make them question what really happened. Mary Margaret could see by looking at their faces that Worth's tactic had gained back some ground. The jurors hadn't liked Jesse's outburst one bit, but at least they seemed willing to listen to the other side now.

The judge pulled out his watch and checked the time, then called a recess for the midday meal. Mary Margaret stood to stretch and Sarah rose more slowly beside her.

"You feeling all right?" Mary Margaret asked.

"Yep. I'm just a bit tuckered out, is all," Sarah said, rubbing her shoulder and arm. "I think I'll go on home and rest this afternoon. You can tell me what happens when you get back. You will be coming to my place, won't you?"

Mary Margaret wished she could say no, she'd be staying over at Worth's, but she knew it wasn't possible.

"I'll be home as soon as the trial lets out. I think I'll find somewhere close by to eat."

Saying good-bye to Sarah, she walked out the side door and looked around, undecided about where to go. The sheriff must have moved the protesters to the opposite side of the courthouse, for the front and this side were empty, except for a woman standing about ten feet away. When she turned around, Mary Margaret recognized Lucy Robertson.

Mary Margaret knew the time had come to make the first overture to the younger woman. With Worth and Marcus being such good friends, she would be thrown into Lucy's

company often. She crossed the sidewalk to Lucy's side
and said, "Hello, Lucy. Are you waiting for someone?"

"No. My father had to go see the mayor about something, and I was just going to find someplace to eat."

"How about joining me, then? I hate eating alone."

"But, don't you do that quite often?"

Mary Margaret stiffened at the cut. "I have, on occasion.
Sometimes I find my own company considerably more
pleasant than that of others. If you'll excuse me."

Mary Margaret turned to leave. *So much for making the
first gesture*, she thought. The young lady could keep her
barbs to herself.

"Please, Mary Margaret, I'm sorry," Lucy pleaded from
behind her. Mary Margaret stopped and looked over her
shoulder. "I didn't mean it the way it sounded," the girl
confessed. "I only meant with your traveling so much, you
must have had to eat alone a lot."

"You're right, I have. That's why when I get the chance,
I always try to find company." Mary Margaret thought of
the two weeks she'd spent traveling with Adeline Cross
and the many meals they had shared together. She missed
the company of a woman friend—someone to confide in
and share reminiscences with.

"I'd like to share lunch with you, if you can forgive
me," Lucy said, looking chastened.

Mary Margaret gave her a questioning look.

"Please, don't be polite. You know as well as I do that I
behaved abominably when we first met."

Mary Margaret was surprised by Lucy's candor, but
didn't know quite what to say.

"I thought I was in love with Worth," Lucy explained,
"and I was afraid you'd steal him away. But now I realize I
never loved him at all." She said this with such earnestness
Mary Margaret had to hide a smile.

"And what made you realize this?" Mary Margaret
asked, seeing for herself how young and charming the
"grown-up" Miss Robertson really was.

"Because now I'm really in love." Lucy's face took on a
dreamy expression as she clasped her hands in front of her
heart.

"I see." Mary Margaret coughed delicately. "Who's the lucky man?"

"My friend April's older brother. April introduced us. She saw right away that Worth's *much* too old for me. I have more in common with her brother. He's been in Philadelphia studying architecture until recently. He arrived home while I was visiting April, and he's absolutely wonderful. We like the same things, and we even know some of the same people. He's so smart and sophisticated. Besides," she said with great seriousness, "I'm not sure I really want to stay in Wyoming all my life, and April says her brother has all sorts of plans."

"He sounds like quite a young man."

"Oh, he is. And he's asked me to come back to Laramie for their Fourth of July celebration. I haven't talked to Daddy yet, but I'm hoping he'll let me go. What do you think?"

Lucy had taken Mary Margaret's arm and was leading her down the street as she spoke.

"Well, I certainly can't speak for your father, but it does sound as if April's brother has a good head on his shoulders. As long as you're well-chaperoned, Marcus probably won't mind."

In fact, Mary Margaret was sure Marcus would let his daughter do whatever she wished. Now that they were no longer rivals, Mary Margaret could see the endearing side to Lucy's personality and understood Worth's fondness for her.

They ate at a small restaurant not far from the courthouse and were back in the courtroom a little before two.

It was late afternoon before Annie's lawyer finished calling witnesses for their side. One after the other, they attested to her integrity and portrayed Jesse as a greedy scoundrel. The most damaging witness to Jesse's case was the land assessor, who denied Jesse's claim that he'd seen Annie's signature on any paper. The assessor said he'd thought Jesse alone had the right to sell the old farm or he never would have handled the transaction.

Because of the lateness of the hour, Judge Burley adjourned court until morning, saying Worth would begin first thing. Worth protested, asking the court's indulgence for another hour—just time enough to cross-examine the witness, but the judge was adamant.

Mary Margaret understood Worth's frustration. The jury would have the entire night to ponder the land agent's testimony. Though Worth had attacked the various witnesses' credibility and knowledge of Jesse all afternoon, the land agent had gotten away unscathed.

By morning, the jury would be set against Jesse and that much harder to sway. Despite Worth's brilliant defense, things didn't look good for him—he just didn't have enough to work with.

Mary Margaret slipped quietly out of the courthouse. She was in no mood to linger with Annie's supporters, who were already celebrating the victory within their grasp. Annie's win meant Worth's loss, and she couldn't find joy in that.

The clock struck one o'clock in the morning, and Mary Margaret turned over onto her side. She'd heard it strike every quarter hour since eleven, when she'd turned out the light. She longed for sleep to speed the dragging hours until she could be with Worth again.

After tomorrow, they could get on with their lives, fulfilling the promises of last night. But first, they had to survive the next day, with all its painful consequences. For tomorrow, someone would win and someone would lose, and Mary Margaret very much feared she knew which way things would turn out.

Could they accept the outcome of this trial and not allow it to interfere with their lives? What had seemed so possible in morning's light now loomed as insurmountable in the dark of night.

Mary Margaret's gaze traveled to the lace curtains at the window. Everything was so quiet. There were no voices tonight to distract her from her thoughts. She shuddered, remembering the violence of the night before. She had never been more frightened in her life. In the instant when she thought she might die, her one regret had been that she hadn't told Worth she loved him.

She turned her pillow and pressed her face against the cool material, remembering how she had cradled her cheek against Worth's muscular chest. He had held her in his arms all night long, and she had awakened in the same position in the early morning.

Would she ever sleep that way again; with Worth's heartbeat steady beneath her ear, his skin warm and pliant against her hands, his arms holding all her fears at bay as he gently cradled her, his legs so tangled with hers she could not distinguish his from her own?

An ache grew low in her abdomen, and this time she knew what it was. A moan escaped her throat and she sat up, cursing her vivid imagination. Tonight it was giving her no rest.

She got out of bed and slipped on her dressing gown, then went to the window and stared at the moon. She considered going to the kitchen and making a cup of tea. It couldn't hurt, and if Sarah were to be believed, it might even help her get to sleep.

Quietly, she opened her door and crept down the hall. Just as she was about to round the corner to the stairs, she heard muffled voices coming from the back room— Annie's room. Who could she be talking with this late at night, she wondered. And then she recognized the other voice.

She listened for a few minutes, unwilling to believe her ears, but knowing she heard the truth. What should she do now? The thought had hardly been born when she knew the answer: Worth had to be told.

Mary Margaret hurried to the courthouse, opened one of the back doors to the courtroom, and slipped inside. The noise level in the crowded room was greater than on the previous day, as everyone had an opinion of how the defense should proceed.

Once again, Annie MacIntyre sat demurely by her lawyer's side, except today, her meekness did not fool Mary Margaret. She caught the shrewd, assessing glances Annie cast at the crowd and the jury box from beneath her lowered lashes.

The woman was far more clever than Mary Margaret had given her credit for being—so clever, in fact, that she would probably win her case, even though she shouldn't. Mary Margaret wondered what Worth could possibly do to shake her story, especially at this late date. There was no time left to develop an elaborate strategy. She only hoped that her morning discussion with him had been of some help.

She sat forward, her hands clasped tightly in her lap, as Worth came in with Jesse. The judge soon followed.

"Mr. Worthington, I believe you were about to cross-examine a witness. Are you ready to proceed?" Judge Burley asked.

"Yes, sir."

The judge reminded the land agent he was still under oath and Worth began.

"Mr. Fleming, I believe you have been a land agent for some time, is that not true?"

"Yes, sir."

"And are you still holding that position?"

"No, sir."

"Why not?"

"I quit."

"Oh? I hadn't realized that. Why did you quit?"

The land agent scowled and shifted in his seat. Mary Margaret held her breath. Was it really going to be this easy? She crossed her fingers.

"Got a better offer," the land agent said.

"I see. Now, let me ask you this. During your time at the land office, did you have occasion to do business with other people from Cheyenne?"

"Certainly." The land agent relaxed, and Mary Margaret bit her lip. Why was Worth letting him off the hook? He knew the man was lying.

"I don't see the relevance of this line of questioning, Your Honor," Annie's lawyer protested.

"I'm merely trying to ascertain the nature of Mr. Fleming's work, to establish if it is reasonable to assume he would remember any particular transaction, such as the one he made with my client."

"Continue, Mr. Worthington," the judge said.

"So, Mr. Fleming, do you recognize any of the people in this room, other than my client?"

"Well . . . yes, of course." Once again the land agent shifted in his seat.

"Who, for instance?"

"Your honor—"

"I'll decide when to stop him, Mr. Green," the judge said.

The land agent scanned the crowd. Mary Margaret noticed that he blinked sharply when his gaze skidded past one face in the crowd—the face belonging to the voice she'd heard last night in Annie's room. Her heartbeat quickened.

"There are a lot of people here, sir. It's hard to remember all of them. I think I recognize a couple, though."

"I'm not interested in everyone you ever dealt with. How about a recent client? Someone you saw in the last week or so—say, just before you quit your job?"

The land agent took a handkerchief from his coat pocket and passed it over his forehead. He swallowed nervously and his Adam's apple jumped. His eyes darted toward the back of the room, then quickly slithered away, as if he knew he shouldn't be looking in that direction.

"Uh, n-no, sir. I'm afraid I don't see anyone like that."

"I remind you, you are under oath," Worth admonished him.

Mr. Green stood up again and protested. "Mr. Worthington is badgering this witness, Your Honor, and I hardly see why. Who cares who he saw in the past week?"

"I'm afraid Mr. Green is right this time," the judge agreed. "Unless you care to explain to the court the purpose of your questions."

Worth decided he didn't want to tip his hand yet. "My apologies, Your Honor. I'm finished with this witness, for the moment."

"If I may, Your Honor?" Mr. Green said.

The judge nodded.

Mr. Green walked to the witness stand. "Just for the

record, you do remember your transaction with Mr. Mac-
Intyre, don't you?"

"Yes, yes. I told you already." The land agent wiped his
brow again. Though the room was cool, he was perspiring
freely. Worth could see drops of sweat collecting on his
upper lip. The jury saw it, too, and Worth could tell from
their expressions they suspected he was lying.

"How come you remember it so well?" Mr. Green
asked, clearly trying to salvage this witness's testimony.

"H-he seemed nervous, tense. He wanted to rush
through the paperwork. I remember he yelled at me, said I
was dawdling. Some people are like that, especially if
they're registering a deed for a gold mine. That's what
surprised me so much. All he was selling was this small
farm in the back of beyond. Didn't seem to me he had no
call to be so impatient. Stuck in my mind, that's all."

"Thank you, Mr. Fleming. You may step down."

"If I could ask just one more question, Your Honor,
since my esteemed colleague brought this issue into the
open?" Worth said.

"All right, but make it quick. No more wild goose
chases, if you please."

"Mr. Fleming, when my client came to see you, was he
alone?"

"Uh, what?" The land agent paled. "I, uh, I . . ."

"It's a simple enough question. Did my client come to
your office alone or with someone else?"

The land agent looked around desperately, his gaze settling on the back of the room, then jumping wildly to Mr.
Green, and finally settling back on Worth.

"I think, that is, I'm sure he came . . . with someone."

The land agent's final words came out with a croak, and
once again he checked around the room, as if trying to
determine if he had given the right answer.

"Someone in this room?" Worth pounced.

"N-no. Someone else."

"What can you tell us about this someone else? Was he
tall? Short? Fat? Thin?"

"I–I guess he was tall, but not too tall. I don't remember
exactly. I just remember your client 'cause he was the ner-

vous one." The handkerchief was a sodden mass in the land agent's hand, but Worth knew if he hadn't cracked yet he probably wouldn't.

"Thank you, Mr. Fleming. That will be all."

The land agent left the witness chair and scurried down the center aisle, looking neither to the right nor left as he rushed out the rear door.

Worth walked over to the judge's bench and lowered his voice to say, "Your Honor, I would like the court's indulgence to call two unscheduled witnesses."

The judge frowned, then called Annie's lawyer over. "Mr. Green, do you have any objections to Mr. Worthington's request?"

"Who're you planning on calling?"

"Cleary Sombalay, the actress living at Sarah Miller's boardinghouse, and Peter Dunsmore, the young English lord," Worth said in a hushed voice. He didn't want Peter forewarned.

Green looked genuinely surprised. "Why them?"

So Jesse wasn't the only client keeping secrets from his lawyer. Worth was relieved. He knew Daniel Green to be a good lawyer and had enjoyed crossing swords with him before. He'd have hated to think his colleague was in on this scam.

"They have evidence pertinent to this case."

"Then, why weren't they on your list of witnesses?"

"I only learned some vital information this morning."

"I guess it's all right, Your Honor, as long as Mr. Worthington makes his point quickly."

"I concur, Mr. Green," the judge said. "You may call your witnesses, Mr. Worthington, but don't take too long. I want this case to the jury by noontime. My schedule's backing up."

"I understand, Your Honor, but I would appreciate it if the sheriff would post a guard at the doors. I wouldn't want anyone to disappear before they got a chance to testify."

The judge looked consideringly at Worth, then complied with his request, issuing the order through his bailiff. When everything was in place, the bailiff called out Cleary Sombalay's name.

ʿ Annie clutched at her attorney's arm and whispered something in his ear, but Worth couldn't hear the words over the susurration rippling through the crowd at this unexpected turn of events.

Cleary sauntered to the witness stand, clearly enjoying her role. She had dressed just as Worth had suggested at his early morning visit to the boardinghouse, dignified and restrained. She was his ace in the hole—the way to get at the truth without having to browbeat Annie and risk alienating the jury.

"Miss Sombalay, do you recognize the name New State Sales?"

"I sure do."

"Your honor," Daniel Green rose to speak. "I thought Mr. Worthington was to get straight to the point. What does New State Sales have to do with this case?"

"Your Honor, if I may," Worth responded. "New State Sales is the name of the company that bilked Jesse MacIntyre out of all the money he and Mrs. MacIntyre received for selling her property. I will show a direct link between New State Sales and the bringing of charges against my client."

"Continue, for the moment, Mr. Worthington," the judge ruled.

"And could you tell the court how you found out about this enterprise?"

"Why, I'd be pleased to," she said, smiling at the people gathered in the courtroom. Cleary was at her best in front of a large group, and the sedate dress he'd asked her to wear was the perfect foil for her outlandish temperament.

"As you know, I'm an actress. And though jobs aren't always steady, when I do work, I make a considerable wage. Like all women who have to look after their own best interests, I've learned to handle and invest my own money. As much as I'd like to believe it, I'm not always going to be in such great demand. You can only play the sweet young thing for so long." She sat up a little straighter and gave the courtroom an exaggerated wink. Several of the spectators chuckled at her playful manner.

The judge frowned, and Cleary hastily added, "As I said, I'm always looking for a good investment."

"And you considered New State Sales a good investment?"

"For all of about five minutes. I've learned to spot a phony deal a mile away. Looked a little too shady for my tastes, but the man pitching it was another story." She rolled her eyes and her hand fluttered. Everyone in the courtroom understood her implication.

When the laughter died down, she continued, "While cautious, I'm also not one to let an opportunity pass me by, and let me tell you, this man was some opportunity, if you know what I mean."

The courtroom certainly did. Ribald comments peppered the air, and Annie MacIntyre turned white.

"And just how well did you get to know this person?"

"Why, Mr. Worthington, you know a lady would never reveal such things about herself or her friendships. Suffice it to say, he put a whole new meaning to the term British-American relations." Cleary fluttered her eyelids significantly.

"That's a lie," Annie MacIntyre cried out, standing and shaking off her attorney's restraining hand. "I don't believe you."

"Sugar, I might occasionally exaggerate," Cleary drawled from the stand, "but in this case, it's the absolute truth."

"I don't believe you," Annie almost screamed, her eyes wild. "Peter, you tell them." She turned to face the crowd of onlookers, frantically searching for Dunsmore. "Peter, tell them it isn't true. You love me. I know you do."

She spotted her quarry trying to edge out the rear door and ran to him, ignoring her lawyer's pleas for her to calm down.

"Tell them, Peter. Tell them we're going to California, just like you said, as soon as Jesse pays the money."

"Shut up!" Peter roared, and tried to fend off her clutching arms. "I don't know what you're talking about—either of you."

"But, Peter, you promised to take me away from here. You promised."

"Bailiff, arrest that man," Judge Burley said.

The bailiff and two deputies closed in on Peter Dunsmore, blocking his escape as Annie collapsed at his feet, weeping uncontrollably.

Seventeen

*M*ary Margaret sat in Sarah's chair on the front porch and rocked slowly back and forth. Her head spun from the surprises of the past twenty-four hours. Who could have anticipated the day's events?

The sun hovered low in the sky, drawing out the last few moments of dusk. A noise by the stairs made Mary Margaret turn her head. Worth stood on the top step, a masculine silhouette outlined against an endless orange sky. In Stetson and boots, he looked quintessentially western, despite his dark suit and starched collar.

"I never got a chance to thank you for your help," he said.

Mary Margaret wished she could see his eyes. "There's no need. I did what had to be done." She looked down at her hands, half ashamed when she remembered her terrible thoughts about Jesse MacIntyre.

"I'm sorry things turned out like this."

His voice, though soft, carried in the evening stillness. She heard concern, confusion, and an uncharacteristic hesitation.

"Why?" She was unaware she'd said the word out loud until he answered, mistaking her question for something else. "Because I know how you felt about Annie, and now she's in jail."

The formality of his tone worried her, but she didn't know what had caused this sudden distance between them. The trial was over now.

"It wasn't Annie, so much. It was the idea that a man could ride roughshod over his wife's legitimate objections without being stopped that concerned me."

"And now?"

She wished he would sit, instead of towering over her so remotely. "Now . . . I keep remembering what you said the other night, about Jesse only being a problem if he was lying." She sighed, and a startling thought occurred to her. "Are you angry that I didn't believe him?"

"Whatever gave you that idea?" He sounded genuinely surprised. The tightness in Mary Margaret's chest eased.

"I don't know. You seem so . . . distant."

"I do?" He laughed, sounding relieved. "Here, give me your hand." Tossing his hat onto the wicker settee, he pulled Mary Margaret out of the rocker. Before she knew what had happened, Worth was sitting in the rocker and she was on his lap. "How's that? Better?"

"Much better," she murmured, pressing her face against the side of his neck and breathing deeply of his scent. His arms went around her waist, snuggling her closer to him, and she could feel the rapid beat of his heart against her chest. Her own heart fluttered in response.

"So, what made you think I would be angry? You saved my skin today—my client's, too. I don't think Annie or 'Lord' Peter would have cracked on the witness stand."

"You're right about that. They sounded so smug and sure of themselves last night when I overheard them. They seemed to know all your plans and just how to get around you. It was uncanny."

Her remembered anger at the pair made her tense. Worth caressed her back soothingly until she relaxed against him once more. Then he said, "They had a right to feel self-satisfied. They knew exactly what I was going to do. Apparently Peter had been sneaking into my office regularly to go through my files. In fact, he was the one who started the fire. He'd set a lantern on the floor so he could see what he was doing without lighting up the windows suspiciously. The other night, he accidentally knocked it over in his haste to escape when he heard a noise on the stairs."

"What a shady character! Who would have guessed it? He seemed nice enough. I wonder how many others he's swindled, how many lives he's destroyed." He'd almost destroyed hers, as well, pitting her against Worth and dividing the town into two hostile camps.

"Quite a few, I imagine, what with his well-practiced British charm. The sheriff is going to send an announcement to all the newspapers and see how many people come forward."

"How'd you ever figure out Cleary was one of his victims?"

"I didn't, until she told me. After I left this morning, I turned the problem over and over in my mind. I figured his scheme ran so smoothly, he had to have tried it out before. And the boardinghouse was a reasonable place to start looking for victims. Finding Cleary was just a stroke of luck. Kind of like finding you, only not quite as wonderful."

His lips brushed hers, and a jolt of desire seared through her. She forgot they were out on the porch, in full view of everyone, and returned his kiss, needing the physical bonding.

Heat rippled through her. She pressed against him and his hand moved between them to cup her breast. She sighed her pleasure and he deepened their kiss, opening his mouth more fully to envelop hers, plunging his tongue into every secret recess until her passion burned hotly through her veins.

Sanity returned to Worth first. "We have to stop, Maggie mine," he said, in a husky voice. "Anyone could come by, and we need to talk."

They definitely needed to talk. They had something special together, and the time had come to put a name to it. He wanted her in his life—now, forever.

"Marry me, Maggie." The words popped out of his mouth unexpectedly, but they felt right.

"What?"

He placed his hands on her shoulders and turned her to face him. He saw wonder and fear, love and uncertainty.

"Marry me," he said again.

She trembled in his arms. "Are you sure? What about my writing?"

"It's part of you, Maggie—just like being a lawyer is part of me. It defines who I am and gives me great satisfaction. I imagine you feel the same about what you do. I could never ask you to give it up; I understand that. I know I should have waited to ask you, taken you someplace fancy, given you moonlight and flowers, champagne and romance. But I don't want to wait, Maggie. I want you with me, now and always. There'll be plenty of time for those other things once we're married, I promise you. I just need to know you're mine now. We've been through too much to waste another second."

Her eyes filled with tears and his heart felt hollow with fear. Was she going to turn him down? He tried to prepare himself for the blow, but knew there was no way he could prevent the searing pain.

A tear stole down one cheek, and she laughed as she wiped it away. He heard the breath catch in her throat.

"Oh, Worth, I thought you'd never ask."

She wrapped her arms around his neck, and once again her lips touched his. The hollow feeling inside him disappeared, replaced by a burgeoning fullness, a feeling of completion. Her mouth tasted sweet and hot, welcoming, and he wanted to lose himself inside her.

The front door opened, but he was barely aware of it. Maggie filled his senses—her womanly scent, her silken skin, the feminine sounds of pleasure from her throat. He wanted this kiss to never end.

But end it did—and suddenly, at the sound of Sarah's raspy voice. "Well, now," she said. "Fancy seeing the two of you here."

And in such a compromising position, her tone implied.

"It's not what it seems," he said stiffly.

"No? That's too bad, then. I'd hoped you two'd come to your senses now that the damn-fool trial is over."

"What do you mean?" Worth asked, surprised by Sarah's response.

"Well, any dang fool can see the two of you're made for each other. The only question is, when are you going to do something about it?"

Worth relaxed as he realized Sarah approved of the match. "I've already done something about it, as a matter of fact."

Sarah planted her fists on her hips and glared at him through narrowed eyes. "I know that," she bit out. "But it's not what I meant."

"Sarah, really," Maggie admonished with a gentle smile. "Worth will be embarrassed if you carry on about that. He meant we're getting married." She leaned over and placed a kiss on the corner of Worth's mouth. It took all his control not to capture her lips and deepen the kiss.

"Whooee! You don't say. When?"

"As soon as possible," Worth said, knowing he'd get married that very night if Maggie would allow it. "I'll talk to Reverend Leisch about it first thing in the morning. With a little luck, we can be married before the week is out."

"Over my dead body," Sarah protested, a fiercely protective look in her eye. "You ain't depriving Mary Margaret of a proper wedding. No, sir. What will that little girl of yours think? She'll need a new dress to be part of the wedding, and we'll have to get Mary Margaret a gown, and..."

She went on making plans, then called the rest of the boarders down to hear the news. The Pareet sisters agreed with her. The wedding would be the event of the season and couldn't possibly be rushed.

"Isn't that right?" Estella demanded of Mirabelle who, for once, seemed more than happy to agree.

"Oh, yes, Miss Simpson. Estella's right, you know. We'll all have to make plans. Why, this is the first time one of our own boarders has gotten married here in Cheyenne. It's really too wonderful for words."

Sarah broke out her best whiskey and the boarders partied till dawn, glad to have an excuse to forget the sordid little story played out under their roof by Annie and Lord Peter.

Mary Margaret closed the last book and began tidying the dining room table. She had just finished helping Tom with his homework and had decided to set the table for dinner. She heard footsteps on the porch and her heart began to race. Even after two weeks, she still got excited when Worth came home to dinner.

She smoothed her hair and went out into the hall to greet Worth. He held out his arms and she rushed into them, enjoying the mixture of contentment and excitement she experienced when he was near.

"It's nice to have you home."

"It's nice to be home, especially if I can expect to be greeted like this every day. I'm glad you're here."

"I was helping Tom with some of his schoolwork. I really think he's making good progress."

"I'm glad," Worth said, but he sounded distracted. "There's something I need to talk to you about."

Mary Margaret felt a chill go down her spine. He sounded so grave.

"I got a telegram today."

"From whom?"

"William Townsend."

Worth stiffened when he said the name, and Mary Margaret knew he still felt the pain of their betrayal.

"What does it say?" she asked softly, but inside she was ready to do battle. How dare they hurt Worth again?

"Here, I'll let you read it," Worth said, dropping his arms from around her and pulling a folded piece of paper out of his pocket.

Mary Margaret took the telegram with mixed feelings. She didn't trust the Townsends, especially after her last meeting with them, and would have preferred never having to deal with them again, but she knew that wasn't possible. They were the children's grandparents, after all—the only ones they had.

Her eyes skimmed the two short sentences. "HESTER VERY ILL. WISHES TO SEE CHILDREN."

"What do you think?" she said, raising her eyes to meet his. She didn't want to push her prejudices off on him. After his last encounter with the Townsends, he probably had enough of his own.

"I don't know. You think she's really ill?"

"I hate to say this, but I'm not sure. If she is, it would be cruel not to let her see the children."

"I know. I've thought about it all afternoon, and I've come to a decision. I hope you agree."

Mary Margaret's heart warmed. She loved the way he made her such an integral part of his life, including her in the important decision-making, as well as in the more domestic spheres.

"What are you going to do?"

"I'll wire Boston and see if I can confirm Hester's condition. If she's really ill, I think they should go back and see her. The children shouldn't be kept from their grandparents, no matter how I feel about them."

"I agree with you, Worth. They're the only link they have with their mother. Claire would have wanted them to be close."

She stretched up and gave him a kiss, proud of him for putting aside his bitterness.

"Are the children coming home for dinner?" he whispered against her lips.

"Not today, no. They're going to Reverend Leisch's with Kathleen. They have lots of secret plans since we told them we were marrying."

"You mean it's just the two of us here?"

He tightened his embrace, and Mary Margaret felt a thrill of anticipation scurry through her. "Just the two of us," she confirmed, her voice low and seductive.

"Perfect."

He swept her up in his arms and carried her off to his room, the telegram from the Townsends temporarily forgotten.

All too soon, however, the news from Boston was confirmed, raising a new issue: how to get the children back east.

"They can't go alone," Worth said, late one evening in

the front parlor of the boardinghouse. "And I can't take the
time to go with them—not until this trial is over." Worth
was defending a man accused of murdering a soldier from
Fort Laramie. The trial had already been postponed twice.
"The judge will skin me alive if I ask for another delay.
He's afraid of vigilantes enforcing their own brand of justice—with a rope. I hope Hester Townsend can wait a
while longer."

"Would you like me to take them back for the visit? I
could leave right away."

"I didn't want to ask. I know it's an imposition, but . . ."

"Doing something for you and the children will never be
an imposition. Besides, I can write on the train, and maybe
even come up with some new ideas for articles. Garth tells
me the papers are clamoring for more."

For a moment, shadows clouded Worth's features. Mary
Margaret was sure he was about to object, but he said
nothing. She had thought they'd resolved the issue of her
writing. They'd discussed her career several times and
been in agreement that she would continue her work from a
base in Cheyenne. Did Worth now have second thoughts?

"Is something the matter?" she prompted. Better to get
the problem out in the open now, before they were married,
than face a lifetime of regrets and incompatibility.

Worth hesitated for a moment longer, then blurted, "Just
how close are you and this Garth?"

A rush of warmth filled Mary Margaret. Worth was jealous. What an interesting concept, and his jealousy was
roused by someone he'd never even met.

Slipping her arms around him, she hugged him tight and
looked up into his face. "I'm duly flattered, you know."

He tried to look as if he didn't understand what she was
talking about. "What do you mean?"

"That you're jealous of Garth."

"Jealous? I'm not jealous," he stated emphatically.

She continued to stare at him, and he had the grace to
look away.

"Well, maybe a little jealous. You know all about my
life, but I'm still learning about yours. I just wondered how
close the two of you are."

"He's my very good friend. He's seen me through some rough times, but I've never felt more than friendship for him. You're the only one I want—the only one I love." She'd finally told him, her heart dancing madly in her chest. "Does that satisfy you?"

"Tell me again, Maggie mine," He said, pulling her more tightly into his arms.

"I love you, John Adams Worthington. You and no one else."

The sun was shining, the sky clear and blue, as Mary Margaret waited for the train to take her east. How different she felt from that bleak morning in Boston when she'd watched everything she held dear sweep out of her life. Today, her life was her own, full and rich and deeply satisfying.

The children were excited about going home to Boston for a visit, and Mary Margaret looked forward to seeing Garth again. She only wished Worth could come along. They hadn't even parted yet, and already she missed him almost more than she could bear.

"Aunt Maggie, we got the tickets," Becky shouted cheerfully as she came running up to Mary Margaret. "Can I sit by the window?"

"For part of the way," she told the little girl. "You and Tom will take turns." Tom made a face at Becky, but she was too excited to react.

"I can't hardly remember what Grandmother and Grandfather Townsend look like. Do you?"

Mary Margaret glanced at Worth. She wondered how he felt about the children's enthusiasm over this trip. "Yes, I remember, but I've known them longer than you have."

"As soon as you see them, you'll recognize them," Worth reassured Becky, his voice kind, showing no hint of the bitterness he must feel toward the Townsends. "And don't forget to feed the deer in the park for me, since I can't come along."

"Oh, I will, Uncle Worth, and I'll watch the Punch and Judy show for you, too. You will take us to the Punch and Judy show, won't you, Aunt Maggie?" The little girl turned her attention from her uncle to her aunt.

"If you like." Mary Margaret smiled down at the small child. "Maybe we could take some of your friends along, too."

Tom and Becky immediately began to argue about whom to ask.

Worth took the opportunity to pull Mary Margaret aside.

"I'm going to miss you," he whispered, his fingers caressing the inside of her elbow and sending tingles of pleasure through her. "Write me and let me know how things are going?"

"You know I will." Her voice cracked as his words brought into clearer focus the time they would be apart. She bit her lip to keep from saying what was in her heart. She didn't want to leave him, not for an instant.

"I've had Kathleen prepare a hamper of food for the trip and . . . Dammit, Maggie. How will I bear it here without you and the children?" Worth said harshly, pulling her into his arms.

"I know. I hate to leave, but we'll be back before you know it." She could hear the false cheer in her voice. For the children's sake, they had to preserve their facade of equanimity. "By then, Sarah and Kathleen should have all the wedding plans put together. I hear even Lucy's been called in for advice. All we'll have to do is show up smiling."

"I'll hold you to that," he said, his voice husky as his hand framed her jaw and turned her face up to his. He kissed her with a longing and intensity she had never experienced before.

Her lips parted under his and she tasted the smoky flavor of his mouth, a sure sign of his turmoil over this trip. He never smoked without provocation. His tongue met hers, seeking reassurance. She gave him all that and more, to tide him over until her return—to tide herself over.

She wrapped her arms around him and tried to imprint the feel of his body in her mind, to remember his heat, his hard planes and angles, his loving strength.

"Uncle Worth, you have to stop kissing Aunt Maggie now. The train's coming," Becky yelled to be heard over the approaching engine's roar. Her voice attracted the interest of the other waiting passengers.

Mary Margaret felt her cheeks redden under the watchful stares of the strangers, and she hid her face in Worth's shoulder.

Gently, Worth eased her away. "I don't care who sees us, Maggie. Do you?"

"No," she whispered, straightening her spine. She'd withstood worse scrutiny than this before in Cheyenne, and if Worth didn't care, neither did she.

Slowly, they walked back over to Becky and Tom. Worth gathered up the luggage and lifted it aboard the train. While the conductor carried the bags to the passenger compartments, Worth gave each of the children a hug.

"Tom, you watch out for Becky and Maggie while you're on the trip."

Mary Margaret could see Tom's chest expand with pride at being asked to perform such an important duty.

"I will, Uncle Worth. You take care of my horse for me and tell him I'll be back soon. Tell Uncle Marcus we'll pick up the puppy as soon as we're back."

The mention of the puppy brought a flood of memories to Mary Margaret. She looked into Worth's eyes. The now-familiar blue flame burned heatedly in their depths. He, too, was remembering their first time together.

The conductor bustled by, shouting at the last stragglers to board. The children jumped onto the train and Mary Margaret turned to say good-bye.

Worth kissed her one last time and handed her up the stairs to the conductor, who waited impatiently.

Before she knew it, the train was pulling out of the station and Worth was running alongside, waving. Then the train gathered speed and left him behind.

Mary Margaret kept waving back, even when she knew he could no longer see her. Three weeks had never seemed so long.

* * *

Garth met them at the station in Boston as she had asked in her telegram. It seemed an eternity since she had seen him, so much had happened in her life.

She'd barely gotten the children onto the platform before she was enveloped in a huge hug.

"It's good to see you, Mary Margaret. How was the trip?" he asked as he released her to shake hands with Tom and tweak Becky on the nose.

"Uneventful, long, boring, dirty. Pick any of the above," she said, her voice weary.

"Aren't you the woman who told me how exciting it would be to travel by train out west, to allow the ambience of railway travel to seep into your soul?" Garth asked as he took the luggage from the porter.

"I'm sure I never said any such thing." She laughed. "Only someone with the soul of a poet would say something like that, and my soul is not the least poetic, particularly after four days on the train. What I need is a long, leisurely bath. Would you mind if we stopped at your house before we went to the Townsends'? I really would like some time to pull myself together before I face them. And could we stop at the telegraph office? I must let Worth know we've arrived safely."

"Why don't you stay for luncheon, too? I'm sure Mrs. Farris would love to see the children. When I told her you were coming back for a visit, she insisted you stop by and see her."

Mary Margaret had often chatted with Garth's housekeeper when she'd gone to his home with a new manuscript. Mrs. Farris had taken a liking to the two youngsters and made special treats for them when they came along.

"As long as it isn't too much of an imposition," Mary Margaret said, stepping up into the front seat of the carriage. The children climbed in back as Garth stowed the luggage on the rack behind.

"You know Mrs. Farris would love to see you, and she hasn't seen the children since Claire and Henry's passing."

Mary Margaret watched the scenery, surprised that everything seemed so familiar. Her life had changed so drastically, she thought everything else would have, too.

When she had left, her writing had been of the utmost importance to her, but now, it took second place to her feelings for Worth and the children.

Garth stopped at the telegraph office so Mary Margaret could send a message to Worth. Just this small bit of contact with him warmed her inside.

When they reached Garth's home, he settled the children in the kitchen while Mrs. Farris escorted Mary Margaret to a guest room. After a leisurely toilette, Mary Margaret joined the others for a rousing lunch, with the children telling stories about life in Cheyenne and Uncle Worth, in particular.

"John Worthington certainly seems to have captured the children's hearts," Garth commented as Mrs. Farris readied the children for the trip over to the Townsends'.

"Yes, he's been very good *for* them and *to* them."

"It would seem from what the children say that he's captured your heart, too."

"We're going to be married at the end of June."

"Then congratulations are in order, I believe."

She searched his face for signs of anger or dismay, but saw only goodwill in his open gaze. "Thank you, Garth."

"Does this mean your writing career is over?"

"Of course not. I plan to continue, but there is a problem. I haven't told Worth I write as M. M. Simms."

"Why not?"

"You read the articles I wrote for the New York paper?" Garth nodded in the affirmative. "Well, the man in that case was represented by Worth."

"Oh," Garth said thoughtfully. "I see your point. I take it Worth wasn't too thrilled with your championing the woman's cause?"

"Mainly because he thought his client was innocent, which he was proved to be. The strain between us over the articles eased once the case ended, but Worth can sometimes be . . . quite traditional. He has a fairly restricted view of what my writing entails, and the M. M. Simms articles aren't on that list."

"And the reason you haven't told him?" he prompted.

She didn't even like to admit it to herself, much less

Garth, but she was afraid Worth would change his mind if
he knew. "I'm afraid he'll feel differently about me then."

"But, you're getting married. He loves you."

There was the crux of the matter. She wasn't sure he did
love her. Oh, he wanted her, with a fierce, consuming passion. Some might call it lust. And he fit her into his life, in
all its nooks and crannies. Some would call that practical.
He'd adapted to her needs, giving and taking to create a
seamless whole. He made her feel special—womanly and
feminine. What more could she ask?

She knew it shouldn't matter, but she needed the words.
Words were central in her life, and without them, a nig-
gling doubt ate at her soul like a corrosive acid.

"I know. I'm being foolish. Don't pay any attention to
me. It's been a long trip and I'm tired. Ask me the same
thing tomorrow and I'll give you a different answer," she
said, but her laugh was hollow.

"Are we going to see Grandmother and Grandfather
now?" Tom questioned, coming out into the hallway.

"Whenever you're ready," Mary Margaret replied, but
she was less enthusiastic than she sounded.

They reached the Townsends' long before she was ready.
"Don't forget that Grandmother's ill," she reminded the
children before ringing the bell.

"We won't," both children promised.

"I'll be extra quiet," Becky whispered.

Tom didn't comment. Mary Margaret knew he still held
some resentment toward the older couple over their behavior right after his parents' deaths, so she didn't press him.

Sedgwick, the butler, answered the door, and it was as if
they'd never been away.

"Good afternoon, Miss Simpson. I hope your trip was
pleasant," he intoned in a completely impersonal tone.

"As might be expected, Sedgwick. I see nothing here
has changed," Mary Margaret replied, referring as much to
his tone as to the general atmosphere of the large foyer.
Everything looked exactly the same.

After taking their wraps, he indicated the front parlor.
"Madame is awaiting you. If you and the children will
follow me?"

Mary Margaret didn't know what to expect upon entering the room. The telegram had gone into no detail about Hester's condition, but Mary Margaret had assumed her to be quite indisposed. She was rather surprised to find Hester downstairs, half sitting and half lying on a chaise lounge, the only new addition to the room.

"Well, children, aren't you going to come and give your grandmother a kiss?" Hester questioned.

Mary Margaret noted her voice was neither weak nor thready.

Shyly, Tom and Becky inched forward and placed small, quick kisses on the older woman's parchmentlike cheek, then backed away.

"Is that any greeting after not seeing your grandmother for almost nine months?" Hester grumbled. Then, in an undertone, she murmured, "especially since I didn't get a proper good-bye when you left."

"The children are tired from their trip, Aunt Hester. You must excuse them," Mary Margaret said, ignoring the woman's unpleasantness. Then, in a brisker tone, "You're looking quite well. We were given the impression you were confined to bed."

"Today I insisted upon being up to greet you," Hester explained, but did not meet Mary Margaret's gaze. "This has been a very hard winter for me." On the last word, she pulled a handkerchief from the sleeve of her dressing gown and coughed daintily into it. "But just seeing these lovely children has been exactly the medicine I need."

"I'm glad to hear that. I'm sure you'll be well in no time," Mary Margaret said politely. Though she wished the woman no ill, Mary Margaret found Hester quite a bit healthier than she'd expected. "What is the nature of your illness?" she couldn't keep from inquiring.

"Really, Mary Margaret, not in front of the children." Picking up the bell on the stand beside her chair, she gave it a quick flip, and within seconds Sedgwick was at her side.

"See Mary Margaret and the children to their rooms, Sedgwick. And have cook serve dinner at seven.

"I hope you'll all be comfortable. I've given the children

their old rooms. I know they must have missed them. I've had your luggage placed in the blue room, Mary Margaret. I hope it's to your liking."

Much different from the last time I was here, Mary Margaret thought. Then she had stayed on the fringes of the servants' quarters—not quite servant, not quite family, either. Hester and William's opinion of her must have changed in the last six months.

"We're all quite pleased with your triumph in the literary world," Hester added. "You must tell me all about it. But later, I think. This has been such a strain. I do believe I must rest until the dinner hour." Hester delicately dabbed her brow with her handkerchief. "I'll see you then, shall I?"

She obviously expected no reply, for her eyes were already closing.

"So, I'm to have the blue room now that I'm a literary triumph," Mary Margaret murmured.

"I beg your pardon, miss?" Sedgwick politely responded

"Nothing, Sedgwick. Just talking to myself. We literary triumphs do that, you know."

"Of course, Miss Simpson. Whatever you say," he said, leading them up the grand stairway, never blinking an eye.

"I'm glad you could come with me," Garth said as he drove Mary Margaret home after their dinner engagement.

She and Garth knew many of the same people. He'd been a good friend of Claire and Henry Clay's, and his parents were part of the same social circle as the Townsends.

"I enjoyed the evening, Garth. The Whitcombs are delightful people. Besides, I needed an evening out."

"I can imagine." He lifted one perfect brow for emphasis. "I admire your fortitude. Two weeks of Mrs. Townsend's unremitting company would be more than I could bear. I hear her health's improved considerably since your return."

"Yes, she seems to have made a miraculous recovery." Mary Margaret struggled with her unease. Something wasn't right. "She and Uncle William are attending a ball tonight in honor of the governor. That's why I want to get home early. I didn't like the idea of leaving the children alone with the new maid. I hope I didn't inconvenience you."

"Not in the least, my dear, though I believe the other guests were quite disappointed to be deprived of your presence. You make Cheyenne sound considerably more exciting than staid Boston."

Mary Margaret smiled at Garth, acknowledging his compliment, but her mind was still on the Townsends.

"I wonder if Aunt Hester will be home early, too. She really shouldn't overdo."

"Perhaps she wasn't quite as sick as you thought."

"Or were led to believe," Mary Margaret said, giving voice to her misgivings. "Do you think this is some sort of trick?"

"What do you mean?"

"I don't know. That's what's so terrible. I keep having these unpleasant suspicions, but I really have no reason for them."

Garth sent her an inquiring look.

"Like this evening, for instance," she explained. "They seemed so insistent I go with you. I really didn't want to leave the children, since Hester and William were also going out, but . . . I don't know. I guess this all seems ridiculous to you. It certainly does to me." She sighed.

"You're just overwrought. Between missing Worth and being at the Townsends' beck and call, you're losing your sense of perspective. What could Hester and William possibly do to you?"

"Not me—the children. They hated it when Worth got custody. They were all set to challenge him in court when he left. You remember—I told you most of it."

Garth frowned. "Who was their lawyer then?"

"A man named Hargrove. Why?"

"Maybe your suspicions aren't as outlandish as you think," Garth said, consideringly. "I hear William has been spending quite a bit of time with Hargrove of late, though no one seems to know why."

A chill ran down Mary Margaret's spine and her hands felt icy. She was glad to see the Townsends' house just down the block. She needed to hold the children in her arms.

Leaving Garth to wait in the parlor, Mary Margaret made her way up the elaborate, winding stairway to check on the children.

Easing the door to Becky's room open, she peeked inside. Her bed was as neat as it had been when she'd left for the evening. What was going on?

Running next door to Tom's room, she found the same thing. Her heart pounded and thunder roared in her ears.

"Oh, my God. Garth, Garth, they're gone. The children are gone."

Eighteen

*M*ary Margaret paced to the end of the railroad platform and back again. She looked down the length of the track but saw nothing. Why did the train have to be late today, of all days? She paced again, worrying the inside of her lip with her teeth. Guilt and desperation ate at her.

She still did not know where the children were. Hester and William refused to speak to her and had sent her packing the morning after her dinner with Garth. They considered her a traitor to the family.

Not even the happy news from Cheyenne that Kathleen and Colin Leisch were getting married had lifted her spirits. All she could think about were Tom and Becky.

Her stomach tightened painfully and she clasped her hands tightly at her waist. She would not let panic overtake her now. Worth needed her to be strong, not another burden.

On her next trip down the platform, the engine chugged into the station, blowing off excess steam. Mary Margaret eagerly scanned the faces of those departing the train and spotted Worth exiting two cars down. With no thought to the propriety of her actions, she called to him and ran in his direction.

Worth looked up at the sound of his name and saw Maggie. He'd missed her more than he'd thought possible. Had it only been three weeks? It seemed a lifetime.

He opened his arms and caught her up in his embrace, savoring the feel of her pressed to him, the reality of holding her again.

"Oh, Worth, I'm so sorry," she whispered. "These have been the longest three days of my life."

"There's nothing for you to be sorry for, Maggie mine." He raised her chin and looked into her eyes. They were brimming with tears. He felt her anguish more deeply than his own.

"I should have realized what was happening. I should have guessed what they were up to," she cried. "Instead, I let them take the children without so much as a fight. How could I have been so blind?"

Worth gave her a gentle shake. "It wasn't your fault. If anything, I blame myself. I should have been here. I knew there was a risk, but I took a foolish chance. So you see, we can each go on blaming ourselves forever, but it won't do any good and it won't get the children back."

"You're right, but I can't help feeling responsible."

Worth ran his hands up and down her arms, hoping to comfort her. He knew she would have no peace until they had the children again. That had to be their first priority.

"Come on. Let's go to your hotel, and then we can go see Henry Clay's lawyer. He's been taking care of things for me here since he handled my brother's will. I telegraphed him as soon as I got your message. Hopefully, he's contacted Townsend and has some answers for us."

He walked her toward the exit, where a hired carriage waited. On the ride downtown, she told him of their visit in Boston.

"When we first arrived, I thought Hester looked considerably healthier than her telegram had implied, but I never dreamed the whole thing was a hoax. I assumed she had been feeling poorly and was missing the children. Now I feel like such a fool, and the children are paying for my stupidity."

Once again, tears swam in her eyes. Worth didn't know what to do.

"Now, Maggie, don't be so hard on yourself. After all, the Townsends are Tom and Becky's grandparents. You had no reason to suspect they had anything but the best interests of their grandchildren in mind."

"I still don't know what they have in mind. They've paid so little attention to the children since we've come, except for when their friends visit. I'm not sure what they want other than a couple of mannequins to trot out on display when company comes.

"All I can think about is that they're with strangers. Suppose Becky has a bad dream? Who's going to comfort her in the night? Who's going to help Tom with his schoolwork?"

As she spoke, her tears overflowed and ran down her cheeks. She wiped them away with one hand, but still they kept coming.

"Don't do this to yourself, Maggie. The children are fine," Worth said, taking his handkerchief and catching the drops. "Would the Townsends let anything happen to their only grandchildren?"

Worth hoped he sounded more convincing than he felt. He shared many of Maggie's concerns, but he wasn't going to add to her feelings of guilt. When Worth knew the children were safe, William Townsend would have a lot to answer for.

"Come along now and dry your tears. We'll have the children back before you know it."

Worth glanced out the window overlooking Beacon Street. His lawyer had a prestigious office, but he didn't have a hell of a lot of answers. The Townsends' lawyer had been curt when they had met. All he would say was that the Townsends wanted custody of their grandchildren. But why? They paid the children scant attention at the best of times, and at this point in their lives, they hardly needed such a burden of responsibility, especially when Worth was more than happy to take it on. And, more important, the children were happy with him.

Worth forced his attention back to his lawyer's words. "John, if you were married, you'd stand a much better chance with the children. It's the smartest strategy by far. Fight their fire with your own," Horace Quigley was saying.

Worth glanced over at Maggie. She looked confused. No doubt she was wondering why he just didn't tell the lawyer they'd already decided to marry and had set a date. But he was afraid to say it—afraid the lawyer would say something stupid like "It's about time. I've been telling you that since the first time you came to me. It would make everything far less complicated legally and easier from a moral perspective, as well."

Would Maggie understand he wasn't marrying her for the wrong reasons? That to consider a lifetime without her had become unbearable for no other reason than his feelings for her?

Before Worth could gather his thoughts, Maggie said, "Worth—that is, John and I—have already made plans, but the wedding's arranged for Cheyenne in June."

"Since you've already made the decision, marry now." The lawyer sat forward in his chair to emphasize his point. "I believe presenting a united front is the best legal strategy. Being married, of good moral character, solvent, and able to provide the children with a good home will go a long way with a judge."

Maggie looked questioningly at Worth, letting him know with her eyes that the decision was his. He nodded his head, knowing what he'd just agreed to and hoping the lawyer wouldn't make any careless remarks.

"Can you arrange a special license?" Maggie asked the lawyer.

"We want to have the ceremony as soon as possible," Worth added. He smiled over at Maggie, took her hand in his, and squeezed it reassuringly. She had to know this was what he wanted, too. Even if she didn't, he would make her see it. Nothing in his life was as important as her happiness, and he would make sure she understood that.

Though he would have planned things differently for

Maggie's sake, just the thought of her as his wife filled him with joy. Now, if only the children were with them.

A knock sounded outside her rooms, and Mary Margaret opened the door, expecting to see Worth. Today was their wedding day, and he'd said he would pick her up a little after three to take her to the judge's office.

But instead of Worth, she saw Hester Townsend standing there, a determined expression on her face.

Without waiting for an invitation, Hester marched into the small sitting room of Mary Margaret's hotel suite. "I know you're not expecting me, but this couldn't wait. I have to talk with you right away."

"What have you done with the children?" Mary Margaret demanded.

"The children are fine," Hester said, eyeing the dress Mary Margaret was wearing with great disapproval, "but it would appear the same can't be said of you."

The dress had been packed in Cheyenne on the off chance she might need something special. At the time, she hadn't realized how special it would be. It was a pale blue silk with delicate pink flowers embroidered down the front of the bodice and along the edge of the skirt. Lace insets softened the neckline and cuffs. The underskirt was of pink-and-blue-striped faille, trimmed on the bottom with a bias flounce. The dress was feminine and delicate, and until this very moment, Mary Margaret had found it a most enchanting wedding dress.

"What do you mean?" Mary Margaret asked defensively, her tone less than hospitable. This was her wedding day, and she didn't want Hester Townsend to ruin it.

"It seems the rumors are true, after all. I'm disappointed. Whatever possessed you to agree to marry John Worthington? Have you no family loyalty at all?"

"If you won't tell me where the children are, we have nothing more to say to each other. I think it's time for you to leave, Aunt Hester."

"I will not leave until you answer me, young lady. Surely you owe me a bit more consideration than you've shown so far. Why, Claire would be in tears to see you treat her mother so poorly."

Mary Margaret clenched her jaw tightly to hold in the torrent of anger Hester's words had provoked. When she was certain of her control, she said, "I hardly think it's any of your business, but I'm marrying for one reason only. I love him."

"Love!" Hester snorted. A very unpleasant sound. "This marriage has nothing to do with love. He's using you shamelessly, can't you see that? You're here and convenient. You get along well with the children and know how to handle them. You fit into his plans perfectly. Don't tell me you think he loves you!"

"You're mistaken, Aunt Hester. We already made plans to get married in Cheyenne, before we came east," Mary Margaret retorted.

"He's been planning this wedding since November. I happen to know that his lawyer was pushing him to marry even before he left Boston the first time, and you're a fool to think otherwise."

"I don't believe you."

"No?" Hester pulled a folded piece of paper out of her reticule and handed it to Mary Margaret. "Then, read this. Maybe it will convince you."

Mary Margaret looked at the paper in her hand. It was a letter—more accurately, a copy of a letter—from Horace Quigley to Worth, dated back in April, before Worth had proposed.

Mary Margaret skimmed over the greeting to the middle of the page. Her eyes blurred as she read the lawyer's words:

"I cannot emphasize to you enough the importance of stabilizing your home situation to forestall future attempts at wresting custody of the children from you. As a lawyer yourself, you must know that as long as you are a single man, your hold on the children will be tenuous, at best, especially as one of the children is female. No judge, if put on the spot, will allow a young girl to be raised by you in the absence of a wife. Heed my words, John, before you lose that which is most precious to you."

"Now you see I speak the truth," Hester stated as Mary Margaret looked up from the page. "When he saw you in Cheyenne, Worthington must have thought you were the answer to his prayers."

"How did you get this?" Mary Margaret demanded, refusing to give Hester the satisfaction of seeing she'd hit a nerve.

"The son of one of my friends worked in the lawyer's office. When they heard what Worthington had done to us, they naturally took our side and arranged for us to receive this."

"You mean, they had their son steal it."

"Don't you take that tone with me. What that scoundrel is doing to us is far, far worse than anything we've done. And look what he's doing to you. It's despicable, and you had better wake up and see the truth before your eyes."

"Let me tell you, Aunt Hester. No matter what you may think of John Worthington, he's a highly respected lawyer, a landowner, and a good man. He could have had any woman he wanted...*any* woman. Do I make myself clear? I feel honored he's asked me to marry him, and nothing you can say or do will change that.

"I believe our conversation is concluded, don't you?"

"Time will tell, Mary Margaret. Time will tell." Hester Townsend took back the letter and left, allowing the door to slam behind her.

Alone in her room, Mary Margaret felt a veil of despondency settle over her. The letter confirmed her worst fears —the ones that rose to haunt her in the bleak moments of the night, when she sat sleepless by the window and wondered whether she was making a mistake.

She knew Worth felt something for her. She sensed it in his touch, his gentleness, his tender caring. But maybe that was all he felt—tender caring. Why did such lovely words sound so inadequate? Why did they pain her to her very soul?

She stood up quickly, ashamed of herself. She was no blushing bride, barely out of her teens. She was a woman grown. She made her decisions and stuck by them, aware of the consequences, balancing the losses and the gains.

Worth was a man she knew she could respect—a man who had treated her fairly, made no promises he could not keep. The children needed the kind of home she and Worth could provide. Asking for more was unrealistic. She was living real life, not some dreamy romantic tale from a woman's magazine.

When the second knock sounded on her door ten minutes later, Mary Margaret was glad Worth hadn't come any sooner. She'd needed the time to regain her composure, and she was relieved he hadn't had to confront Aunt Hester.

"Maggie, you look lovely," Worth said when she opened the door. "Your dress is beautiful."

"Thank you," she said, reconciled to forgetting her dream of the perfect wedding with a white satin bridal dress. There was no time for such nonsense. "You look nice, too."

In fact, he looked more than nice. He'd had his hair trimmed and wore a new suit. His boots were polished to a high sheen and his hat was newly blocked. No dream groom could compete with this reality. And soon he would be hers. The thought had become bittersweet.

"Thank you, dear lady," he said gallantly, taking her hands in his and holding them wide. "But I fear all eyes will be on you when we walk down the street. I've always liked you in blue, and this dress is especially fine."

Mary Margaret felt herself blush at his compliment, but Hester's words continued to ring in her ears. She wanted to tell him about Hester's visit, but was afraid. The letter had been damning. She didn't want to face up to its truth.

She forced herself to smile, to put aside her doubts. She wasn't the first bride to be taken by a sudden attack of nerves, or the first to forge a marriage with a man who did not love her.

"I'm very pleased we're getting married, though Kathleen and Lucy are bound to be disappointed. We've cheated them out of a big wedding," Worth said, escorting her down to the lobby. "Are you certain you don't mind getting married in the judge's chambers?"

She looked into his eyes and saw genuine concern. "No,

I'm sure it will be fine. Anything that will help get the children back," she said as he helped her into the carriage at the front of the hotel.

"Are you nervous about this?" he asked as he held her hand, gently chafing it.

She knew her palms were cold, and the warmth of his large hand did little to change them. She didn't know what to say. She didn't want Worth to see her doubts. Whether or not he loved her, despite all Hester had implied, he was too honorable a man to go through with the ceremony unless he felt she entered into it wholeheartedly.

She bit back a painful laugh at her inadvertent pun. She hadn't been whole of heart since she'd first met Worth.

"Should I be nervous?" she countered coyly, needing to get the conversation off its serious track.

"I've heard most brides are." He smiled, and a rush of desire blossomed inside her. How she loved him! Right then she promised herself she'd be the wife he needed. Maybe his love would come later. There was always that hope.

The ceremony was over so quickly. One moment she and Worth were separate; the next, bound together forever, all because of a few words spoken by someone she didn't know, which had taken less than ten minutes to say.

There had been a delay in the judge's court schedule and the ceremony hadn't begun until well after five. Now they were walking quietly back to the hotel in the shadows of early evening, neither of them wanting to be the first to break the silence, both suddenly shy of the other.

When Worth opened the door to her hotel suite, Mary Margaret gasped. Flowers and lit candles filled the room. A heady floral scent wafted through the open door, beckoning her inside.

In the middle of the room stood a table with a damask cloth, laden with covered dishes. For an instant, Mary Margaret thought they had come to the wrong room, but a quick look at Worth's face revealed he knew exactly where they were.

He smiled and brushed her cheek with the backs of his

fingers. "I hope you don't mind," he said. "I had the desk clerk do a few things while we were gone. I wanted today to be special."

Mary Margaret mutely shook her head and allowed her gaze to wander around the room. She was overwhelmed by Worth's gesture. He might not love her as she loved him, but he must care something for her to go to all this trouble. The hollow feeling she'd carried around since Hester's untimely visit eased a fraction.

"I don't know what to say. How did you ever get all this done?" she asked.

"I made arrangements with the hotel and had a messenger let them know we were on our way. I hoped this might make up for some of the things you're missing because of our hurry. We don't have time for a honeymoon now with the court case on us like this."

His gesture was so romantic, but his mention of the court case reminded her again of Hester's words. Had he married her expressly to get control of the children? How would she ever know? The hollow feeling returned in full force.

"Everything is beautiful, Worth," she managed, looking up at him and trying to smile.

"I know it doesn't make up for a church wedding, but we can do it all again when we get back to Cheyenne with the children, if you like."

He looked away as he spoke. He seemed as uncomfortable as she. Why? Was he finally facing up to the reality of a marriage based on need, rather than love? Was he already regretting their precipitate action?

There was no need for them to have a church wedding back in Cheyenne. In fact, she'd prefer if they didn't. To her, a marriage in church signified a loving unit blessed by God. This sham they were playing out shouldn't be blessed in such a way, but she'd argue the point after they got the children back.

Worth moved suddenly to the table laid out with their dinner.

"Mrs. Worthington, can I pour you some champagne?" he said, holding aloft a bottle of the imported wine.

"Yes, please," she answered. Maybe it would warm her insides, take away the deep-seated chill in her heart.

Slowly, she peeled off her white kid gloves and placed them, along with her small purse, on the corner of her desk. Mrs. Worthington. It all seemed so unreal—the quick decision, the judge's dim chambers, the hastily signed documents.

She was Worth's wife now, for better or worse. She wanted to make this marriage work, and she sensed Worth did, too. Maybe her love alone would be enough—her love and his desire. It wasn't perfect, but it was more than many people had.

Simply deciding to make the marriage work was not enough. Mary Margaret knew she had to put all her energies into this new life. Worth and the children were the family she'd never had as a child. She would make sure they knew they were loved and wanted, and someday, who knew? Stranger things had happened.

She heard a cork pop, then the gurgling flow of sparkling wine. Worth held out a filled crystal glass for her. The pale yellow liquid reflected the shimmering glow of the lighted candles. She reached for the glass and her fingers grazed his. Heat radiated through her, melting her inner chill.

"To our life together," Worth toasted, lightly touching his glass to hers.

She looked into his eyes and saw warmth and caring. She was afraid to look deeper, for fear that was all she would see. "To us," she agreed and sipped her wine.

"You're beautiful tonight, Maggie," Worth whispered. He took the half-empty glass from her hands and placed it back on the table. His eyes devoured her. His gaze was like a warm caress as it touched her eyes, her mouth, the pulse point at the base of her neck.

He traced along her cheek with the tip of one finger, slowly, sensually, outlining her face, delineating her profile, skimming her lips.

She quivered beneath his touch, trembling with newly awakened desire.

"Are you hungry?" he asked, pulling her toward him.

"Only for you," she whispered from her heart.

"Me, too," he whispered back, and his mouth closed over hers.

Her fears and doubts vanished as Worth filled her world. This was the man she remembered, his lips firm, cajoling, familiar; his touch gentle yet seeking; his scent uniquely his, masculine and alluring; his taste headier than the finest champagne. Willingly, she gave herself up to his embrace. All that mattered was their being together, wanting each other, needing each other.

The rest would come with time.

"I love you, Maggie mine. I love you so much."

The whispered words cascaded through her at the moment of climax. She hung suspended in midair, joined to Worth by the most magical of bonds. Already she felt the feeling of oneness, captured so briefly, dissipating.

She tried desperately to hold on to the feeling, to prolong its duration by a few fleeting seconds, but to no avail. Slowly, she sank back into reality, her limbs wrapped around Worth, her breathing matched to his.

Once again, she heard his words, "I love you, Maggie mine," but this time, they were an empty echo inside her head.

Mary Margaret closed her eyes and felt the tears slide down the sides of her face into her hair. She dared not wipe them away, afraid Worth would notice her movement and ask their source.

He'd finally said the words she longed to hear from his lips, but she couldn't make herself believe them. She wished he had never spoken.

Worth brushed his lips along the side of Maggie's neck and she murmured his name. She was finally his, all his. He'd never felt so happy in his life.

He smiled down at her as she slept. The coverlet barely covered her rounded breasts. He could see her rosy nipples pushing against the fabric and he felt his body harden in response.

How he loved her. Hearing her mutter his name in her

sleep helped lessen the doubts he'd experienced this morning upon waking.

Last night had not been the wedding night he had planned. There had been no friends to toast the marriage, no party to celebrate their union. And though their lovemaking had been wonderful and fulfilling, he'd sensed Maggie was holding something of herself back. He'd finally told her he loved her, but she hadn't confirmed her love of him or responded in any way to his declaration.

Maggie rolled over in her sleep, onto her side. He gathered her long, brown hair in his hand and pulled it over her bare shoulder so his lips could touch the vulnerable part of her nape.

He heard her gasp as his tongue moved from her nape down her spine. Slowly, she rolled onto her back, his lips and tongue moving as she turned. His mouth found her distended nipple bare of the coverlet and began to gently suck.

Her hands came up to press his head more tightly against her and her body undulated with the rhythm of his lips. The brush of her hips against his manhood sent his pulse racing.

Leaving the one nipple, he started to move to the other, but Maggie wouldn't allow it. Guiding his head up to hers, her lips greedily drank from his.

"I could grow used to waking up like this," he said when she released him to catch her breath.

"Me, too," she responded throatily, but there was something reticent in her response that he hadn't noticed before.

Hoping to ease her discomfort, he changed the subject. "I didn't want to wake you, but the hearing with the Townsends has been arranged for this morning at ten."

Maggie's eyes immediately clouded over at the mention of the private hearing, and she turned away from him.

"I wish we didn't have to go through all this. It wasn't what I had planned," he said, wishing he could shield her from the scrutiny their hurried wedding would undergo as the Townsends sought to discredit him.

"I understand that. I wish things could have been different, too."

She smiled at him, but Worth had the disquieting feeling they hadn't been talking about the same thing at all. Was she sorry to be married to him? Had he pushed her into something she didn't want? He couldn't face the thought —not when he loved her more than life itself. Somehow, some way, he'd make her happy, too.

Before she could roll away, he kissed her soundly on the lips, branding her as his.

"Everything's going to work out, Maggie mine," he murmured in her ear. "I promise."

He only hoped he could keep that promise. His happiness depended on it.

Since the hearing was private, it was being held in the judge's chambers. Mary Margaret looked around the drab room. On one wall stood a bookcase crammed with books, and on the wall next to it hung a diploma. The desk was bare, except for a small pile of papers stacked in the middle. Around the desk were six wooden, straight-backed chairs.

"The judge may be a few minutes late," Horace Quigley said, gesturing for them each to take a seat.

Mary Margaret glanced over at Worth. He placed his hand over hers and gave it a squeeze.

"How long do you think this will take, Horace?" Worth asked.

"No more than two sessions, I should imagine. You're the specified guardian of the children, registered by legal document—Henry Clay's will. That should be a big plus in your favor."

Worth was just about to speak when the door opened and Hester Townsend walked in, followed by William.

Hester barely glanced at Worth and merely nodded her head at Mary Margaret. With great care, she selected the wooden chair farthest from Worth and beckoned her husband to sit beside her.

Mary Margaret could see Worth's tension in the stiff way he held his body. She imagined all the things he wished to say to the older couple and admired his restraint. She reached over and took his hand, wanting to give him the same sense of security he'd given her. His hand closed over hers.

"How charming."

Mary Margaret heard Hester's sarcastic taunt and so apparently had Worth, for his hand tightened over hers, though he said nothing.

Horace Quigley was the first to break the silence that followed. "Will Mr. Hargrove be along presently?"

"Our lawyer has been detained, but should be here soon," William replied, keeping his eyes on Horace. He never once glanced at Mary Margaret or Worth.

At that moment the door opened and two men entered the room. William rose and greeted his lawyer, while the other gentleman, the judge, took a seat behind the desk.

The judge picked up one of the papers from the stacked pile and held it under the gaslight positioned over his desk.

Clearing his throat, he began, "We're here this morning to decide the custody of Thomas Henry Worthington and Rebecca Townsend Worthington. Is that correct?"

Both lawyers nodded.

The judge searched the papers before him and finally said, "At this time, Mr. Worthington of Cheyenne, Wyoming Territory, has guardianship of the aforementioned children, but the Townsends feel their grandchildren would be better off with them and are suing for custody. Is that correct?"

Again both lawyers nodded, but Horace spoke. "Your Honor, I wish to make it known that the children are no longer in Mr. Worthington's physical custody. They have been abducted by Mr. and Mrs. Townsend."

"Your Honor," Hargrove objected, his tone implying his disapproval of Horace's action.

"I will take that fact under consideration, Mr. Quigley," the judge said, glancing back at the papers in his hands.

"But, Your Honor, if you please, the children . . ."

"I said I would take the matter under consideration," the judge rebuked, looking over the top of his reading glasses.

Mary Margaret could see the frustration written on Horace's face. His first strategy had been to get the children back with Worth and out of the Townsends' clutches, but the judge had effectively prevented this.

"Now, Mr. Hargrove. Suppose you tell me why your clients feel it is in the best interests of the children for them to be awarded custody."

"Mr. and Mrs. Townsend are the maternal grandparents of Thomas and Rebecca. They have never felt Mr. Worthington capable or qualified for guardianship of the children. At the time Henry Clay Worthington's will was read, there was some question as to whether Mr. Worthington would even be found. He'd left the city of Boston ten years before to seek his fortune out west, I believe."

"Your Honor, Mr. Hargrove is implying that moving west, in and of itself, is unsavory," Horace objected. "Moreover, the whereabouts of my client were a matter of record. He is an upstanding and responsible citizen of Cheyenne,"

"Mr. Quigley, I'm capable of discerning fact from innuendo. Your client will have a chance to present his side in a short while. This is not a formal court proceeding. I will allow each side some leniency. Proceed, Mr. Hargrove."

"Thank you, Your Honor. As I was saying, it is easy to understand Mr. Worthington's desire to move away from this part of the country. His father's reputation merited it, I'm sure. This matter of reputation, I might add, is also of concern to my clients.

"Everyone in this city knows that the elder Mr. Worthington was a shameless businessman. His one and only goal in life was to increase his fortune, however he could. And we all know how he did it. Most people would agree that selling guns to the Confederacy during the last war was an act of treason."

Mary Margaret couldn't believe that the Townsends were making such a big issue of that old story. She'd heard the details from Henry Clay often enough—the shame he felt growing up with his father's scandalous reputation hanging over him, the difficulty of establishing his own sterling reputation and gaining acceptance among his wife's social class. But that was all so long ago.

Why did the judge allow it? What difference did it

make, in any case? Worth was not his father. He was his own man, honorable and proud. Why humiliate him like this? Her anger at the Townsends mushroomed, and she had to bite her tongue to keep from disrupting the proceedings.

Hargrove went on to list all the advantages and opportunities the Townsends could give the children, both financial and social.

"My clients," Hargrove continued, "feel they are the most competent and viable guardians of the children, as is shown by the list I've just presented.

"Mr. Worthington, on the other hand, has only recently married." Hargrove sent Worth and Mary Margaret a speculative glance.

"Mere convenience," Hester said to William in a voice loud enough for all to hear. Mary Margaret felt Worth stiffen at the remark.

"Until now, he has had sole responsibility for the boy and a very young girl," Hargrove continued. "Both of my clients were extremely anxious over their safety—especially that of young Rebecca."

Mary Margaret was incensed by what the Townsends were implying. She could tell that Horace wanted to speak to Hargrove's accusations, but because of the judge's warning, he was holding himself in check. Tension radiated from both the men sitting beside her.

The outer door suddenly opened. A young man walked over and whispered in the judge's ear.

"I'm afraid you will have to excuse me," the judge said, rising from his seat. "Something has come up that requires my attention. We'll resume tomorrow at one."

The judge walked to the door, but stopped before exiting to look back over his shoulder at William Townsend. "William, I'll see you at the club tonight. Eightish?"

"Right, Clinton. Wouldn't want to miss this match. Should be interesting." William waved good-bye as the judge went out the door.

Mary Margaret was shocked by the familiarity between the judge and William Townsend. It put a whole new perspective on this private hearing. Maybe she'd better talk with Garth and see if he knew what was going on. He had a vast array of contacts throughout the city and probably knew several people from the judge's club. Even if he didn't know anything personally, he would be able to obtain the answers to her questions quickly and discreetly.

Nineteen

Worth glared at his lawyer. "This . . . this filth is the reason you called me here?"

"John, be reasonable. You are going to lose those children otherwise. I guarantee it. We couldn't have had a less fortunate choice of judge and you know it. Now, what do I have to say to get through to you?"

"Nothing. I will not let you do this to Maggie under any circumstances. Is that clear?"

"You're tying my hands behind my back," the lawyer said. "I thought you wanted those children back. Why do you think I hired that detective, anyway?"

"I do want them back, but Maggie's happiness means something to me, too."

"And don't you think her happiness hinges on having the children back? Isn't that why you got married, after all?"

Worth leaped out of his chair and slammed his fist on the desk. "What the hell is that supposed to mean, Quigley? If you think I married Maggie for any other reason than my love for her, you're sadly mistaken. What kind of man do you take me for?"

"All right, all right. For goodness' sake, John, why do you think I invited you here alone? I wanted to clear all this with you first. Now, settle back in your seat, and let's see if we can plot ourselves another strategy. I'm only trying to do the best for you. Keep that in mind, will you?"

"As long as you keep in mind my feelings. I don't want Maggie hurt for *any* reason. Is that clear?"

"Understood," said the lawyer, but he didn't meet Worth's eyes.

Mary Margaret stepped into the restaurant and waited by the entrance for her eyes to adjust to the gloomy interior. She didn't understand Horace Quigley's demand for subterfuge, but she was more than willing to meet with him if it would improve Worth's chances of getting back the children.

"May I help you, madame?" asked the maître d' in a crisp French accent.

"Yes, please. I'm here to meet with Mr. Quigley. He said he had reserved a table."

"*Mais oui.* Follow me, please."

The maître d' led her to a private room in the back of the restaurant. A table was set for high tea with small, crustless sandwiches, a platter of fruit, small cakes, and a silver tea service.

A sofa and two armchairs sat across the room, on either side of a low table. Horace Quigley stood up from one of the armchairs as she entered.

"Mrs. Worthington, thank you so much for coming by," he said. Mary Margaret felt a thrill go through her as he called her by her new name. Mrs. Worthington—who would have dreamed it! "Please, help yourself," he added, indicating the table.

"I'm really not very hungry, Mr. Quigley. I'd appreciate your telling me the purpose of this meeting. I must admit I was rather puzzled when I received your message."

"At least let me pour you a cup of tea. Tea is most soothing in times of stress, don't you think? Have a seat on the sofa and I'll join you in a second."

Mary Margaret nodded and crossed the room to sit. Quigley followed suit, placing a cup of tea before her and resuming his place in the armchair nearby.

She looked at him expectantly. He stared back, a frown

creasing his brow, his hands pressed together, as if in prayer.

"I'm not sure how to begin, Mrs. Worthington. I've some painful news—"

"About the children?" Her heart paused in her chest, then raced wildly.

"No, no, nothing like that," Quigley amended hastily. "No, this is something more . . . personal."

"Worth?"

"You, I'm afraid."

"Me? Then, why the secrecy? Why did you expressly tell me not to bring Worth?"

Horace Quigley turned red. "I'm afraid John would have my head on a pike if he knew I was even mentioning this to you."

"I don't understand."

"I know, and I'm very sorry to be doing this, but if you wouldn't mind, could I ask you a question before I explain things?"

She nodded her head, more puzzled than before.

"How important is it to you to get the children back?"

"What do you mean? It's terribly important. Why, I don't know what Worth would do if he lost them now."

"I'm not asking about your husband, Mrs. Worthington. I'm asking about you. How important is having custody of them to you? How big a price are you willing to pay?"

Price? What was he talking about? Why hadn't he wanted Worth here? Fear took an icy grip on her insides.

"I'm afraid I don't understand. What's going on?" she asked, her voice not quite steady.

"My apologies, Mrs. Worthington. I didn't mean to frighten you. Perhaps a sip of tea?"

She obeyed him mechanically. He'd made it too sweet, but the tartness of the lemon revived her.

"You were saying?" she prompted, glad her voice sounded normal again.

"There's no way to break this to you other than to just say it. I've come across some information that will do serious damage to the Townsends' claim. The only catch is, it may also do serious damage to you.

"I mentioned it to John and he forbade me to use it. He said he didn't want me telling anyone what I'd learned— not even if it meant losing the children."

Mary Margaret couldn't believe her ears. Losing the children? Nothing must stop them from getting the children back. No matter what Quigley had learned, it couldn't be worse than never having Tom and Becky with them again.

"Nothing must stop us from getting the children," she told him.

"I was hoping you'd say that, Mrs. Worthington. If there were any other way, I'd have tried it. I hope you believe me."

"I do. You're a good friend, Mr. Quigley. I'll make sure Worth understands that before this is over. Now, tell me what you learned."

The big Georgian mansion seemed austere and forbidding as Mary Margaret returned once again to see the Townsends. Ever since her unpleasant visit from Hester on the day of her wedding, Mary Margaret had not spoken a word to either of them, except in the judge's chambers.

Sedgwick opened the door and looked at her, frowning. "I don't believe you are expected," he said, his tone clearly implying she wasn't wanted, either.

"No, I'm not. I need to see Unc...that is, Mr. Town..." She stopped, unable to continue, suddenly feeling queasy. What should she call William Townsend now? How should she think of him? Of herself?

"Are you all right, Mrs. Worthington?" Sedgwick asked worriedly. He stepped to her side and gripped her elbow. "You'd better come in. You look faint."

He helped her into the foyer and eased her onto the padded bench by the door. "May I get you a glass of water?" he offered.

"No, thank you, Sedgwick. I'll be fine in a moment. I had some rather startling news today, I'm afraid, and I haven't quite come to grips with it yet."

"Concerning the Townsends?"

"Yes. That's why I have to see them. It's terribly important."

He looked at her searchingly while he considered her request. Undoubtedly he'd been given orders to keep her and Worth out of the house, but he'd known her since she was a child. Surely he had some family feeling toward her, too.

"I'll announce you right away, miss," he said at last and left her in the foyer while he went back to William's office.

In a few minutes he returned. "They'll see you now," he announced.

With a mixture of trepidation and determination, Mary Margaret made her way down the hall.

"To what do we owe this surprise, Mary Margaret?" William asked from behind his massive desk, after indicating she should take a seat.

"I came to see you about some . . . disturbing information that was just brought to my attention."

"Oh? Concerning that scoundrel you married?" William's eyes took on a calculating gleam.

"No, as a matter of fact. Concerning a different scoundrel altogether." She gave him a piercing look. He dropped his gaze first.

"Sedgwick said we have company, dear." Hester's voice preceded her into William's office. "Oh, it's you." Her voice iced over. "What do you want?"

Mary Margaret stood. "I came to see your husband, Aunt Hester. It's private."

"Nonsense, Mary Margaret. William and I have no secrets from each other."

"None?" Mary Margaret asked softly. Had Hester known the truth all these years? Was that why she'd always been so distant?

"What is this, Mary Margaret? Are you threatening us?" Hester demanded.

"I don't think of it quite that way, but yes, I imagine that is why I'm here." Mary Margaret turned her gaze back to William.

"You'd better tell us what is going on," he said, his voice hoarse.

"I think you know. Is it true?" She couldn't quite bring herself to ask the questions. After all, how did you ask a man you'd known your whole life if he was really your father?

"Is what true?" Hester put in angrily. "What are you talking about?"

"Worth's lawyer has some information—"

"So, that's who's behind this—your scapegrace husband. Has he no shame or decency? Will he stoop to the very gutter to get his way?"

A furious anger raced through Mary Margaret at Hester's attack. She advanced on the woman. "Worth has no need for shame. If anything, he tried to suppress this information. His lawyer brought it to me because he feared your conniving plots."

Hester took an involuntary step away from Mary Margaret. "Stay back," she ordered.

"Don't worry, Aunt Hester. I'm not going to hurt you— not that you don't deserve it." She wheeled around and faced William, her anger giving her an emotional strength she otherwise would have lacked. "Is the story true?" she demanded. "Did you and my mother have an affair?"

"It was long ago, Mary Margaret," William croaked. "Too long ago to matter now."

Mary Margaret felt her knees give way. Her anger was suddenly inadequate to deal with the enormity of William's confession. Secretly, she had hoped it wasn't true, but his admission changed all that. She groped her way to the chair she'd used earlier and collapsed onto it.

"Too long ago to matter?" she whispered, more to herself than to either of the Townsends. Her entire life had suddenly changed, and no one seemed to realize it, or care. Bits and pieces of her childhood fell into place with chilling precision—her father's distant disapproval, her mother's anxiousness to please at the expense of her daughter's happiness, the unpleasant undercurrents on her birthdays.

"How could you have let this go on so long?" she finally asked, looking up at William.

He shrugged. "What would you have me do? You were well taken care of. I had my family to consider, my position in the community."

His casual dismissal of her took away Mary Margaret's breath. "And you? What about you?" she asked, turning to Hester.

Hester had moved to William's side. She glared at Mary Margaret, her face mottled red, her jaw clenched.

"Don't be so foolish, Mary Margaret," she snapped. "You're a woman of the world now. What good would it have done to upset things?"

Worth heard Hester's words as he silently entered the room, Sedgwick by his side. The three people inside were so intent on their conversation, they hadn't heard his arrival. Thank goodness Horace Quigley had thought better of sending Maggie here alone and had contacted Worth.

"And now?" he heard Maggie ask.

"Now?" Hester repeated.

"Will you drop this hateful case against Worth and return the children to him?"

"Whatever for? The children belong with us. You've let your emotions blind you to the man's true nature. Why, his family wasn't fit to live among decent folk. You heard it yourself at the hearings."

"Not like our family, you mean? Your sense of what is decent amazes me, Aunt Hester." She gave a choked laugh, but Worth heard only pain and loss in the sound.

"Don't," he said, and three pairs of startled eyes turned in his direction. "Don't do this to yourself, Maggie. They aren't worth it."

"Worth! What are you doing here?" Maggie exclaimed.

"Indeed," William said. "Who ever invited you in?"

"I'm afraid I invited myself. I didn't want Maggie to face you alone." Resentment burned in him for Hester and William's casual dismissal of Maggie, for the pain they had caused her and their lack of remorse. "Let's go, Maggie. There's no need for you to put yourself through this."

"There's every need, Worth." Her hazel eyes implored him to let her do things her way. She looked both strong and fragile—fiercely determined, yet soft and womanly. He couldn't stand to see her hurt, but even less could he oppose her. Tensely he nodded, giving in to the plea in her gaze.

"I want to know your intentions so I can make my own plans," she said, turning her attention back to the Townsends.

As Hester had done with William, Worth moved to stand behind Maggie and placed his hand on her shoulder, making clear his unswerving commitment to whatever she decided. The Townsends seemed to recognize the meaning behind his gesture, for William assumed a conciliatory expression.

"I'm sure we can work something out," he said with a forced, albeit placating smile.

"Only after you return the children to Worth," Maggie countered.

"Why should we?" Hester put in. "We're obviously winning our case. In another day, the judge will rule in our favor."

"In another day, not only the judge, but all of Boston will know the truth of your wonderful reputation."

Worth felt Maggie's tension beneath his palm and gently squeezed her shoulder. She put her hand over his and he laced their fingers together.

"Don't be ridiculous, Mary Margaret," William scoffed. "If you ruin my reputation, you will also destroy your own. Who in Boston would receive a bastard child into their house? Who would give credence to your claim? Your bluff doesn't carry any weight."

"I'm not bluffing. My reputation isn't the question here. The children and their well-being are what count. If your reputation is important to you, you'll heed my words."

William ignored her and began gathering together his papers.

"I should also add, I know what's really behind your custody fight. Garth Devereaux has given me some very interesting information, especially about the panic of seventy-three."

"What is she talking about, William?" Hester demanded.

"Nothing, dear. She's bluffing. I told you that already." He glared at Mary Margaret, daring her to contradict him.

"I'm not bluffing. Since the market crash, your financial

situation has deteriorated significantly. Do you know how much of your holdings were lost, Hester?"

"Is that true, William?"

"It doesn't matter," he told his wife. "The children's estate will more than make up for our losses. Besides, what can she do? Hargrove has completely discredited Worthington and his hasty marriage."

"Will you drop this case?" she asked desperately. If only Hester and William would take the gracious way out.

Neither of the Townsends answered.

"You leave me no choice, then," Mary Margaret said. Too many illusions had been destroyed today. She hadn't wanted to add to the destruction, but what could she do? "By morning, fifteen newspapers will be carrying the story of your financial downfall."

"You write very nice, chatty articles, my dear, but I hardly think you have that much clout," William commented in a patronizing tone.

"But I'm sure M. M. Simms does. Didn't you ever wonder what the initials stood for? Check with Garth if you don't believe me." William paled. "I'm sure your friends would be much more interested in hearing of your losses than the circumstances of my parentage. Which do you think would have the greater impact? I suggest you give what I've said a great deal of thought."

Mary Margaret slipped her arm into Worth's. She was shaking inside and glad to have him near, to feel secure in his love. She looked into his face and signaled her readiness to leave.

"You were magnificent, Maggie mine," he whispered softly, "though I wouldn't have put you through this for all the money in the world."

He turned her toward the door.

"Where are you going?" Hester sputtered. "We aren't through here." William stood silently beside his wife.

Mary Margaret gazed at the man she now knew to be her father. It was strange. She felt nothing toward him—neither love nor contempt—only an emptiness and sense of loss. "Yes, I'm afraid we are," she said with sad finality.

Worth escorted her out, past a solemn-faced Sedgwick, and into the fresh air.

"So, you're M. M. Simms, too, eh?" Worth said lightly.

"I'm afraid so," she replied.

"I should have guessed. M. M. Simms always made a lot of sense to me—even the first time I read 'him.' 'Remember the ladies,' I think you wrote."

"That was actually a quote from Abigail Adams," she clarified.

"Well, no matter. I know one lady I'll always remember." He turned her to face him, then slipped his arms around her waist.

A sense of homecoming filled her as their mouths came together—of having survived a terrible battle and won the only prize worth having, the love and respect of this man. She would cherish it the rest of her life.

"Come on. Let's go back to our rooms," he murmured softly, his eyes filled with promise.

He took her arm, ready to hand her into his carriage, when the discreet clearing of a throat made them both turn around in surprise.

"Pardon me, Mr. Worthington, but if you and Mrs. Worthington have a moment?"

Sedgwick stood behind them, his complexion unusually ruddy, though his blank expression gave nothing away.

Worth nodded, his curiosity piqued.

"I couldn't help overhearing a large part of today's conversation. My apologies, madame." Sedgwick gave Maggie a stiff bow, and his complexion turned an even deeper shade of red. "I'm afraid I find myself in a position of mixed loyalties," he said to Worth.

Worth instantly understood the import of Sedgwick's words. Cautiously, not wanting to put him off, he said, "I would think justice and a sense of fair play might sometimes outweigh a misplaced sense of loyalty—especially where the lives and happiness of the very young are concerned."

"Yes. I thought as much myself. Though to tell the truth, I was not certain until today which way justice would best be served."

"I can see where you might have had some doubts," Worth concurred. He could feel Maggie's hand trembling in his as she followed the conversation, but he didn't dare break eye contact with Sedgwick—not while the man still teetered on the brink of changing sides.

"Yes, it was difficult to decide what to do. However . . ." Sedgwick paused, and Worth felt Maggie's grip tighten on his hand. His own breath caught in his throat.

"I believe you will find this address to be of utmost interest, Mr. Worthington." He handed Worth a folded piece of paper. "My apologies if any of my actions have served to cause you undue pain. I fear I was not fully apprised of all the factors involved in the situation before today."

"Thank you, Sedgwick," Worth said. He placed the paper carefully in his pocket and shook the man's hand. "We won't forget this. If there is ever any way we can repay you, don't hesitate to ask."

"I appreciate the offer." Sedgwick bowed his head at Worth. "Again, my apologies, Mrs. Worthington," he said and turned on his heel, slipping back into the house without another word.

Mary Margaret walked back to the suite she and Worth shared. She'd just finished tucking Becky and Tom in for the night in the room next door. Thank goodness for Sedgwick's change of heart! She felt forever indebted to the man.

Becky had stretched out her good nights, embellishing her stay at the country home of Hester's friend with a narrative of intrigue and adventure. Tom, on the other hand, had been quieter than normal and had even allowed her a good-night kiss, an unusual occurrence for the rapidly maturing boy. The ordeal of their time away from each other had affected them all.

Worth was sitting near the gaslight, waiting. He looked up as she entered and smiled. This was so like her dreams, she wanted to pinch herself to be sure it was really happening.

"Come and sit by me," he said, patting the cushion of the sofa.

Mary Margaret sank down on the seat beside him, and his arm closed around her as she leaned against him.

"Thank you for the lovely dinner," she said. "Becky will be talking about it for the next two weeks. I never realized she was so attuned to the social graces."

Worth chuckled his agreement. "She certainly was the little lady. The way she acted tonight, it was hard to picture her sledding down a snow-covered slope on a flour sack."

Mary Margaret nodded her agreement.

"Did you have any trouble getting them tucked in? I thought Becky'd never stop talking when I went in to kiss her good night."

"I'm sure I got the whole story all over again when I went in." She chuckled, then sobered. "Tom seemed too quiet, though. I'll be glad when we get back to Cheyenne and can put all of this behind us."

Her voice broke on the last words and she felt unwanted tears gather behind her eyes. She buried her face against Worth's chest.

"Maggie? Are you all right?" Worth asked.

She merely shrugged her shoulders, not wanting to talk about William Townsend and her relationship to him. She only wished she could forget about it forever.

"I'm not going to let you get away with this, you know. I'm your husband, and even if I weren't, I'd still want to know what was bothering you. I'm in love with you."

"Do you love me? Really? Knowing what you now know?"

"How can such an intelligent lady be so silly at times?" he asked gently, dropping a quick kiss on the top of her head. "If you're referring to the fact that William Townsend is your father, what do you think?"

"It's not just that he is my father. It's the whole sorry mess. I hardly know who I am, what I am. The whole thing is just incredible."

"I know who you are, Maggie mine. And so do you, if you think about it. You're the same person you were yesterday and the day before. William lost all claim to you the day he walked away from your mother, more fool he. I'll not make that mistake. I love you, and that's the end of it."

Worth pulled her against him until she was snug in his embrace. She cuddled into him, absorbing his warmth, taking strength and encouragement from his closeness.

"I wish it were that simple," she said with a sigh. "But you know yourself how important one's parentage can be. Look how your father affected your life."

Worth cupped her chin and turned her face up to his. Looking intently into her gaze, he said, "I didn't leave Boston because of my father, no matter what the Townsends implied. I left because I couldn't face my own shortcomings. My father might not have been the best in the world, but he did what he thought was best for his family. If we'd lived in Virginia, instead of Massachusetts, he'd have been a hero.

"No," he mused, "I was the one with the problems, and it took ten years and you to help me face them. It wasn't because of my father that I didn't come back to Boston, but because of myself. I had to learn I wasn't only my father's son. I was also myself—a person in my own right. And ultimately, what I did with my life was more significant than anything else in determining who I am."

He kissed her gently. "I learned a lot from my experience, though. Enough to know you're the only one who can decide what's right for you. Just know that I love you, no matter what."

Mary Margaret could see from the earnestness of his expression that he meant every word he said. But, could she be as strong as Worth? Could she stand on her own two feet and leave her questionable past behind? Then a thought struck her.

"Claire was my sister," she whispered, surprise and wonder in her voice. "I always dreamed of having a family—a sister or a brother. And here I had one all along."

The tears she'd held back so long now trailed down her cheeks. If she had only known when Claire was alive, they could have. . . . But would their lives have been any different? They'd been like sisters anyway. They hadn't needed to know the truth; they had had enough love between them to bridge all barriers. Surely that was what counted most, when all was said and done.

The tightness in her throat eased, and she felt a sense of peace come over her. Worth was right. What she had made of herself counted far more than any accident of birth. The tears falling from her eyes were cleansing now, washing away the bitterness of the day.

Worth took out his handkerchief and wiped her cheeks. "Everything will be all right, Maggie," he murmured. "Just give yourself some time."

His tone revealed his worry, and Mary Margaret reached up a hand to touch his cheek. "I don't need more time." She smiled up at him through her tears. "I've just realized Tom and Becky are *my* niece and nephew, as well as yours. Isn't it wonderful? We really are a family."

"We would have been a family no matter what, Maggie. This only adds the final touch."

"You're right, Worth. That's part of why I love you. You bring balance to my life. You show me the other point of view."

Worth laughed. "Is that a nice way of saying we disagree on most things?"

"Not the important ones." She reached her hand around to his nape and gently tugged, bringing his face down to hers.

He kissed her lightly and playfully rubbed her nose with his.

"Oh, Maggie, you make my life very special. Promise me you'll never change."

"Only in good ways," she murmured against his lips. "I love you so much."

She heard his breath catch, and then her lips were crushed by the sudden deepening of his kiss. Everything in her responded to him, openly, freely, with no holding back, no need to protect herself. She had learned today just how much he loved her—enough to risk his own happiness to save her from scandal. Never again would she doubt him.

"I love you, too," he whispered, undoing her shirtwaist.

"I know. That's what makes everything so perfect."

GET
LOVESTRUCK!

AND GET STRIKING ROMANCES FROM POPULAR LIBRARY'S BELOVED AUTHORS

Watch for these exciting romances in the months to come:

September 1989
STAR STRUCK by Ann Miller
HIDDEN FIRE by Phyllis Herrmann

October 1989
FAITH AND HONOR by Robin Maderich
SHADOW DANCE by Susan Andersen

November 1989
THE GOLDEN DOVE by Jo Ann Wendt
DESTINY'S KISS by Blaine Anderson

December 1989
SAVAGE TIDES by Mary Mayer Holmes
SWEPT AWAY by Julie Tetel

January 1990
TO LOVE A STRANGER by Marjorie Shoebridge
DREAM SONG by Sandra Lee Smith

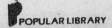